THE CHILDREN OF LIGHT

RUPERT LEGGE is the grandson of best-selling novelist Barbara Cartland. Born in 1951, he was educated at Eton and Oxford where he read chemistry and spent a year researching the philosophy of science. He was called to the Bar in 1975 and practised as a barrister before joining a city firm where he worked as a maritime lawyer. He has travelled extensively in the East and has made a special study of the persuasion techniques used by contemporary cults. He now lives with his wife, Victoria, near Bath.

RUPERT LEGGE

The Children of Light

FONTANA/Collins

First published in Great Britain by Fontana Paperbacks 1986
8 Grafton Street, London W1X 3LA

Made and printed in Great Britain by
William Collins Sons & Co. Ltd, Glasgow

British Library Cataloguing in Publication Data

Legge, Rupert
    Children of Light.
    I. Title
    823'.914[F]   PR6062.E419/

    ISBN 0-00-617257-1

Acknowledgements
Extract from 'High Time' by Jerry Garcia and Robert Hunter.
Copyright © 1970 Ice Nine Publishing Co. Full rights reserved.
Used by permission.
Extract from 'Here Comes the Sun' by George Harrison
© Harrisongs Ltd., reproduced by kind permission of
Harrisongs Ltd.

For Victoria

PROLOGUE

Meenambakkam Airport, Madras

The jet pivoted on an unseen axis and sank through the heat haze tail first. It headed straight for the three men in the middle of the runway. None of them moved.

The black man in the centre removed his dark glasses and polished them quickly, absently, on his red-and-white shirt. He wore a shark's-tooth necklace and a thick gold chain on his wrist. He looked up as the plane landed with a screech, and taxied towards them. The whites of his eyes were dirty. He replaced the glasses and his lips twitched in an impatient little smile.

He was tall and fit. Only his hair betrayed mixed blood. It was pitch black and curly, but the curls were large and shiny. Both the men who flanked him were white. They wore identical grey suits and identical grave expressions. Sweat trickled down their temples but they stood as grim and unmoving as mourners by a catafalque.

The plane halted, its long nose high above the black man's head. The engines still made the air pummel at their ears. The asphalt hummed. The pilot in the cockpit whistled silently, removed his hat and headphones and wiped his brow with his sleeve.

The black man moved forward. One of his companions signalled. Two attendants rolled the gangway into position. He sprang up the steps. The dark-clad men turned outwards like well-drilled sentries. They remained on the runway — on guard.

The black man knew his way. He turned right as he entered and ducked through a low doorway into the main passenger compartment. Fortuny gold-threaded curtains hung over the portholes. Country chintz and engravings covered the walls. Four men, all in suits of charcoal worsted, sat side by side on the needlework banquettes.

9

Each clutched a black leather briefcase with a combination lock.

'Hi,' said the black man. 'Welcome to Madras.'

'Guthro,' the bald man's jowls spread as he nodded. No one made a move to stand. No one extended a hand.

'How long are you staying?'

'We leave for Singapore at 08.10 tomorrow. That gives us just twenty-one hours,' the man rumbled. 'I hope that everything's organized.'

'Sure, sure.' The black man frowned quickly, then smiled. 'Sure. The tour of the ashram shouldn't take more than an hour all told. Then there are the arrangements for the mass marriage ceremony to discuss . . .'

'I'm sure you've everything worked out,' the bald man sighed. His thick fingers drummed on his attaché case. 'Now, while we have a moment, is there anything you want to tell us? Somehow you don't seem to be making much progress out here . . .'

'Is that my fault?' Guthro flapped his hands. 'I've got a hundred and thirty disciples in Madras and about the same in Pokhara. If we're going to see any serious expansion, we're gonna need recruits.'

'They don't seem to be having any trouble in the West,' snapped a small man with slicked-back dark hair.

'That's the point, man!' Guthro shouted. All four men hushed him. The bald man pointed towards the tail section. 'Sorry,' Guthro whispered. 'He asleep?'

'Meditating. You must go through in a minute though,' said the bald man.

'Yeah, well.' Guthro sat on the banquette facing them. He spoke softly. 'You see, that's the whole point! I mean, India is not rich. You can't become disillusioned with affluence if you've never known it. They just don't want to know out here!'

'This is meant to be the land of the spirit,' said the dark man. 'And you are telling us you can't make new recruits?

We got to get production up, Guthro. That furniture you produce is going well. We can't get enough of it, and the mark-up on the clothes made here is the best in the world. We need more.'

'So send me more recruits!' Guthro shrugged despairingly. 'You say yourself you're getting thousands in Europe and the States. You want increased production, send me a few hundred more souls and I'll increase production.'

The little dark man whistled through his teeth. The bald man raised a hand. 'Hold it, Charomski,' he growled. 'If they're not biting here, we're going to have to bring them in.'

'Yeah. OK.' Charomski sighed. 'I still can't see why this guy can't save us a lot of airfares by getting out on to the streets over here. Still, OK. What say we send you — let's see, you got fifty two months ago — what say we send you two-fifty English-speaking recruits now and two-fifty more if you double production by the time of the convention in Madison Square Garden. That sound about right?' He looked from side to side. The three men nodded and mumbled assent.

'Right,' said the bald man. He raised his arm and studied his gold Rolex. 'We'll see to that, Guthro. You'd better go and see him now. It's time we were moving.'

'Yeah.' Guthro stood. 'Yeah, OK.' He gritted his teeth and walked down the compartment. As he passed carved Coromandel screen at the end, he managed to mumble, 'Thanks.'

There was no one in the dining area. Guthro strode, tight-lipped, past the large, low table of Chinese lacquer, inlaid with bronze. Two half-eaten waffles swam in syrup on a porcelain plate. He kicked aside a discarded linen napkin and pulled back silk brocade hangings.

'Father?' he called quietly. 'Father?'

There was no answer. Next came a small bedroom in a lighter style; a circular bed with pale-blue satin covers, gilt-framed oval mirrors on the watered-silk white walls. Guthro flicked his fingers and walked straight on. He looked neither right nor left.

He stopped at the white door, removed his sunglasses and shoved them into the breast pocket of his shirt. He tugged at the broad belt at his hips, then leaned forward and tapped lightly on the door. A little croak from within was just audible above the deep growling of the engines.

Guthro pushed the door open, fell to his knees, then lay flat, arms outstretched on the carpet. 'Divine Father,' he gasped, 'your Children . . . your Children await you.'

Covent Garden, London
'That's the way to do it!' shrilled Punch. 'That's the way to do it!'

The blonde girl turned her head. She did not check her pace, but she smiled and blinked a couple of times as she passed. She carried a battered portfolio under her left arm, a Dance Centre carrier bag in her right hand. The smile vanished as though wiped away. The corners of her full lips now turned downwards. It was early evening. The sky was buffed pewter, the streets and piazza iron.

She walked past the café, then stopped and changed her mind. She shrugged, turned back and pushed the glass door. The portfolio banged against the doorframe. She shuffled sideways into the bright yellow light, the rattle of teacups and cutlery, the hiss of the espresso machine. 'A cup of tea, please,' she said. 'And — and a doughnut.'

She selected an orange formica-topped table nearby, propped her portfolio and her bag against the bench-end and returned to pick up her order. She sat and sipped and shuddered, gazing out of the window. It looked very dark and cold outside.

'Hello. Mind if I sit here?' A gaunt young woman with greying pale-brown hair smiled down at her.

'No.' The blonde girl smiled. 'No, please.'

'You're not an artist, are you?' The woman slid in behind the table and sat down. She wore a thin white cheesecloth shirt and faded jeans. She had sunken cheeks and very large eyes.

'Yes, sort of . . .' the girl said. 'Only a student.'

'Mind if I see?' The woman indicated the portfolio.

'Er — well — no, I suppose not. It's not very good though. Mostly, you know, rather academic stuff . . .' Her voice trailed off.

The woman had already lifted the folder on to her knee and untied the ribbons. 'Hmm,' she said and turned a page. 'Hey!' Then, 'I like that . . . not bad, not bad at all . . .'

'Thanks,' the girl said sullenly.

'No. Really. Listen, would you like to do a little work for us? I really think these are great, honestly. Sorry, my name is Jane . . .'

'Hi,' said the blonde girl, 'Laura.'

'Look. Why don't you think about some ideas for a poster for us? We'd be really grateful, and then perhaps you could drop in on our headquarters in the Exhibition Road — maybe even come down to our place in the country for a few days . . .'

'You really want a poster . . .?'

'Really. Honestly. Look, here's our card. Do come down. Promise? We'd love to have you down there. Please say you will. Please . . .'

PART ONE

CHAPTER ONE

'*No!*'

Her body stiffened and shook. She pummelled at his chest with half-clenched fists. 'No!' she yelled. 'No, no, no, no, no!'

Something twisted and shrank inside him like plastic in the fire. Her blonde hair was splashed out on the sofa. Her eyes were screwed up tight. There were high spots of colour on otherwise white cheeks. 'Please . . .' she gulped. '*Please*, Philip?'

He sighed and pulled his hand from under her thick, ribbed jersey. His breathing was heavy. Every breath, every rustle of clothing seemed suddenly very loud. For a moment he sat there, one hand holding his forehead, his muscles tense and trembling, then he stood. The television whistled quietly on the other side of the room.

He punched the 'Off' button in passing and moved to the window. The only light now came from the little kitchen in the far corner and the lamps in the street below.

From behind him, he heard the rasping sound as her skirt was pulled down over her stockings, the whisper of skin on fabric as she buttoned her shirt. Her scent still filled his nostrils. His right hand clenched and unclenched.

'I'm sorry, Philip,' she said in a small voice. Bare feet padded on the carpet. 'I'm really, really sorry.'

'Nothing . . .' he started, then had to clear his throat. 'Nothing to be sorry about. If you don't want . . . I mean . . .'

'You know it's not that. Oh, Philip, please don't think that. You know how I feel about you. It's just that − oh, I don't *know*.'

He turned. She stood just three feet away, her shoulders hunched. She forced a sad little smile which quickly vanished. Her hand rose as though to give some consoling caress. She checked it. It just remained suspended in the air.

'But it's been six months, Laura. We've been going out for six whole months, and it's not even as though I were a stranger before that.'

Laura did not reply. She looked at him quizzically for a second, then her hand flapped dismissively. She hummed as she walked over to the sofa and picked up two empty glasses.

'Look, Laura,' Philip frowned. 'I don't want to force myself on you — that's the last thing I'd want, but six months! We ought to know by now.'

Glasses clinked. She strolled towards the kitchen door. 'I've tried. You know damn well I've tried. I want to — it's not you, Philip, I know it's not you — but something's obviously not quite right.'

'And I'm meant to live like this . . .?'

She flicked the light switch at the door. Philip stood still, blinking in the sudden cold brightness. Laura turned. 'You can live how you like,' she said coolly. 'I don't care. Go find some little floozie if that's what you want.'

'You know damn well that's not what I want,' he sighed.

'I'm sorry,' she said from the kitchen. Water thudded on steel. A pedal bin clunked. 'It's all my fault and I'm sorry.'

The tap was turned off. She came through from the kitchen and stood close to him. Philip laid a hand on her shoulder. 'It's not your fault,' he croaked. 'Don't worry. I'm sorry if I . . .'

'Oh, don't be silly.' She laughed and wrapped her arms around his waist. 'It'll be all right — just never having ever, it'll take a little time, that's all.' He stroked the back of her neck. 'But it's funny, you know, I never thought it would be you — you were like a big brother — I never thought that one day, well . . .'

'That makes two of us.'

'I've got a surprise for you,' she sang, gave him one last hug and skipped across to the cupboard on the far wall. She knelt down and tugged at the bottom drawer. 'That's if Caroline hasn't found it first. White or brown?'

'White or brown what?' he spluttered.

'Mint cake, silly. It'll build up your energy for the long trek home. It was always your favourite.'

'I was only ten at the time.'

'Well, I still love it. Reminds me of all those hearty walks over the fells you used to drag me on. Your famous emergency rations in case we got stranded. Well, I'm having white.' The paper crackled as she separated two white tablets from the bar. She walked over to Philip, said 'Open wide,' and popped one into his mouth.

He sucked the sugary white cube. 'Rations and marching orders. I'm in court first thing tomorrow. I ought to be going.'

She stood and faced him. 'Oh, hell,' she said softly. 'Look, I know you won't believe me, but I do love you, Philip.' Her fingers stroked his black curly hair. They trembled. He grabbed her hand and kissed it. Then she leaned on tiptoe and quickly kissed his lips. 'Thanks for the evening,' she said.

He grinned. 'Thanks for the mint cake.'

She held out his dark-blue coat. He slung it over his arm and walked briskly down the passage. At the door, he turned and waved once. Laura stood framed in the light from the sitting-room, her shoulders hunched, the nail of her forefinger locked between her teeth. ''Night!' he called. He shut the door before she could answer.

'Bugger!' he said as he pulled open the lift door and stepped in; 'Oh bloody hell!' as he stabbed the button marked 'G' with his forefinger; 'Damn and blast and

19

buggeration,' as he shoved at the glass doors and ran down the steps to the pavement. He and Laura were so close, they had shared so much. Why was love such a complicated business? He pulled on the coat and turned up the velvet collar. He was suddenly very cold.

'And how was last night?' Caroline yelled above the sound of the television.

Laura drew a couple of strokes with a crayon on a large piece of cartridge paper.

'Fine,' she said hesitantly. 'Philip took me to Santa Anna, the new Italian place.'

'And then?'

'We came back here.'

'And then?'

'Yes, well,' she put a pencil between her teeth. 'Then problems.'

Caroline stopped ironing. 'Oh, God, not again. I thought you were all psyched up for the big ravishment scene.'

'Yes, well.'

'That's the last time I stay out for discretion's sake if all you are going to do is gaze into one another's steely greys. Do you realize where I spent the night? On Charlotte's sofa, me back's playing up something dreadful. And all so you could . . .'

Laura's teeth bit into a crayon. 'I couldn't. I just couldn't. I wanted to, I told myself, tonight's the night, but when it came to it . . .'

'Oh, Laura!'

'I know, don't tell me!'

'But as your flatmate . . .'

'As my flatmate, you'll try and cheer me up.' Laura stared blankly at the wall.

Caroline smiled. 'You know, something's got to go; your sanity or your virginity. You mustn't be scared. Take a stiff drink and you'll feel like a new man.'

'It's just not that simple. You know it's not that simple.'

'Of course it's not, Laura, but the hardest part is finding Mr Right, and once you've found him . . .'

Laura pouted. She reached for an old baked-bean can filled with crayons. Her fingers fumbled. 'Damn,' she said and struck the side of the can. 'Damn, damn, damn, I can't concentrate and it's all your fault.'

Caroline tutted. 'Now now, Laura.'

'But it's important. I must get this right. It's a commission, my first commission.'

'But that's wonderful. Why didn't you tell me?' Caroline put the iron up on end and walked over. 'What is it? A poster?'

Laura crossed her arms over the paper. 'Don't look yet. It's not ready.'

'They'll be jealous at St Martin's.'

'You bet they will.'

'Who's it for?'

Laura shrugged. 'The Green Crusaders. Ever heard of them? A conservation group of some sort. Fame at last.'

'Was it from that exhibition?'

'No, luck really. I ran into someone from the group in Covent Garden, and she really liked my work.'

'Fantastic!'

'Well, it's not exactly Shell or Campbell's soup, but it's a start. Look great on the CV.'

'What are they going to pay you?'

Laura frowned. 'Dunno. The money isn't really important. We haven't discussed that yet. They want me to go and stay with them next weekend so that I can find out more about what they do.'

'Are you going?'

'No. Can't. It's the Headen dance.' Laura threw back her head and sighed. 'God, I hate parties.'

'Oh, I know!' Caroline struck her brow with the heel of her hand. 'The poor, weary social butterfly. The constant pressures! The decisions! Should I have asparagus or caviar? The rosé champagne or the white? And should I let Guido Lamborghini drive me home or am I duty bound to go with Prince Andrew? Honestly, Laura, I don't know how you can stand it! Parties, parties, parties, it's just such a strain . . .'

Bumper to bumper, cars weaved slowly down the drive. Flares lit the way to Headen Hall. Its Jacobean chimney stacks and crenellated roof glowed in the fluttering amber light. The giant marquee stood to the left, surrounded by cedars.

Philip wound down his window. The giggles of girls in other cars and the keening of the brakes as they started and stopped reminded him of the chirping of cicadas. A lone statue of Diana the huntress was reflected in the lake to his right. A little breeze ruffled the water's surface, but the air was thick and warm.

A young man leaned from the car ahead. Blond hair flopped over his fine face. His scarf was a streak of flake white on the darkness. 'Hi, Sophie! Tell Bartleet I want to see both hands on the wheel, if you please!'

There was a chorus of jeers and groans. Several female voices called, 'Shut up, Simon!' A couple of horns sounded. Philip whistled silently. His fingers played scales on the steering wheel. He was nervous and aggressive tonight. His neck muscles were tense. This waiting annoyed him.

He left the two girls on the carriage sweep. There was a lot of laughter and shouting down there. Bright white light burst from the open doorway and flowed down the steps on to the polished car roofs. The jaunty young men who bellowed greetings from the porch as though above a gale were just gawky silhouettes, unrecognizable, indistinguishable. The regular throb of the disco music made the night seem hotter. Philip pushed back his hair, sighed and released the handbrake. Up there, a woman's voice called,

'Philip!' He paid no attention, just followed the waving torches to the car-park.

He brushed his sleeve and straightened his tie as he walked back towards the house into the pool of light. His patent slippers crunched on thick gravel. Someone called, 'Hello, Strickland!' He waved absently at the darkness in acknowledgement and trotted up the steps. He was impatient, thirsty. He did not know what for.

A group of men stood at the bottom of the staircase, neighing. Philip remembered one of them from school. A junior. He nodded curtly. His eyes rose to the landing. From two doors a multicoloured stream of girls emerged and, usually in pairs, came down the stairs. It was like a butterflies' maternity ward. Some, like that blonde in green taffeta — a familiar face; no name to it, but he'd met her at other parties — plucked their dresses up above their silk slippers and kept their eyes cast modestly downwards as they descended. Others, like Imogen's younger sister, whatever her name was, with her spiky, dyed white hair, her dress of black-and-scarlet lightning streaks, frankly slouched. One, a slender Italianate beauty in white silk jersey and ostrich feathers, did the full production number. She seemed to glide down, head held high, long fingers caressing the banister. For a second, her eyes met Philip's. He took a deep breath, a step forward, then a tall, elegant man of thirty-five or so appeared from nowhere, took her hand, said, 'Darling,' and kissed her with more than fraternal warmth.

Philip turned away. The big yellow drawing-room hummed and clinked and purred. He strode through the crowd, nodding, smiling, exchanging greetings here and there. He claimed a glass of champagne, then saw Melissa's father, his host, in the corner looking bemused and rather lonely. He walked over and shook his hand. 'Mr Burnett. You won't remember me. Philip Strickland . . .'

'Philip!' Burnett said jovially. 'Of course!'

23

Three minutes later, Philip, who had asked a series of intelligent and searching questions about property development, discovered that Burnett was, in fact, the owner of several thousand launderettes and hot-drink dispensing machines. He stammered his compliments, topped up his glass and headed off in the direction of the music.

He walked down a corridor lined with portraits of stern-looking gentlemen and their sterner-looking wives, through the french windows and into the marquee. The awnings were boldly striped blue and white. There were pink-and-white roses and carnations entwined around the struts and on all the tables. Only a few couples had so far ventured on to the parquet dance floor across the far end of the tent, but the marquee was filling fast. A queue three deep jostled and barked around the buffet. Flustered men in white coats struggled with champagne corks. The wiser guests had appropriated a bottle or two and borne them to their tables.

Philip had no desire to join the scrum. He picked out a table of friends, wandered over and filled and emptied his glass twice more as he stood chatting. The music grew louder. A thick strand of smoke hung just above head height.

Someone tapped his shoulder. 'Hello, you.'

He turned. Laura. She struck a pose, tossed her pearls over her shoulder and pouted. 'You like it?'

He laughed. She was dressed in a black flapper's dress. A thousand little jet beads rattled like a washboard continuo as she moved. 'It's great,' he said. 'Very *Salad Days*.'

They kissed a clumsy hello. 'I bought it in a jumble sale.' She slipped her arm through Philip's. 'Hello, Jo!'

'Hi, Laura, hi, Philip.' A gaunt redhead with her right leg in a plaster cast waved as she hobbled by on a young man's arm.

'Joanna,' Philip nodded once. He steered Laura towards a table in the corner.

'It is good to see you,' Laura told him. 'I hardly know a soul here. Not exactly our crowd, I'm afraid.'

'No,' said Philip. 'I feel distinctly ancient in this company. Melissa was at school with you, wasn't she?'

'Yep, but she was a year my junior. I haven't seen her since. Nor most of this lot.'

'Oh, well.' Philip shrugged. 'At least we can count ourselves amongst her four hundred nearest and dearest.'

'Isn't it touching?' Laura sat in the corner. 'It's so nice to be wanted.'

The corner of Philip's lips twitched. He drained his glass as he sat.

'Oh, look.' She pointed with her pearls over Philip's shoulder. He turned absently. 'See that tall thing with the three chins and the big nose? Wiping his hand on his trousers? That is Mickey. He's the guy that's got this crazy crush on Caroline. He's as good as an alarm call. Rings the flat every morning to ask her out.'

'Does she like him?' asked Philip glumly.

'Can't stand him, but "no" is not in his vocabulary. I told her that she should go out to dinner with him once, order all the most expensive items on the menu, slobber over the food, and pick her teeth.'

'Why doesn't she?'

'She did, but he didn't even notice. He eats like that himself.'

A man with a silver tray passed close by. 'Champagne?' asked Philip.

'Mmmm, please.'

Philip jumped up and, with his back to Laura, conducted a brisk transaction with the waiter. He returned with two glasses and a full bottle. He sat and poured the wine.

Laura leaned towards him. 'Look, I'm sorry about what happened the other night,' she whispered.

'Or rather didn't happen. Don't mention it.' He handed her a glass.

'I just don't want you to think . . .'

'I don't. I understand and I've got the patience of Job.'

'It's just never got this far before. I haven't let it.'

Philip was on the point of drinking. He stopped, lowered his glass. 'Not even with Mungo Braithwait?'

'Good God, no,' she spluttered into her glass and gasped for breath. 'I nearly did the nose trick! He's fun — a lot of fun — but, you know, romantically, he left me cold.'

He looked at her quizzically. 'So cold that you had to warm yourself up at Annabel's night after night?'

'Safety in numbers. Anyway, that's ancient history. Let's talk about something else.'

'OK. So, what's new?'

'I thought you would never ask. Charge your glasses, ladies and gentlemen,' she proclaimed. 'I, Laura Callender, have my first commission!'

'A royal family group or a little church ceiling in Rome?'

'A poster.'

'Congratulations. Who for?'

'A conservation group — they're going to paint the world green, plant trees and things. I thought . . .' She leaned forward, warming to her theme. 'I thought I would do wide-open fields, patchwork cows with great fat udders — and — I don't know, some cute little dicky birds in the corner. Perhaps some endangered species.'

'Like dodos,' said Philip. 'Yes, I can see it all now. An ornamental lake full of whales, perhaps; baby seals playing hopscotch; foxes cuddling hounds; lions rolling over to have antelopes rub their tummies . . .'

'Now now, Philip,' she laughed. 'Just 'cause you spend your weekends massacring poor innocent little birds.'

'Laura, don't start that again . . .'

'Well, you do, don't you?'

He turned his head away. 'Yeah, well, put a few sniper pheasants up in the trees too, taking potshots at men in tweed suits.'

'Don't try to wriggle out of it, Philip. If you're with someone, you take on their way of life. All those shooting weekends — they're just not me!'

'This is a party, Laura, not a bloody revivalist meeting!' He sighed. 'I see I'm in for a great evening.'

'You do what you like,' she said casually. 'You don't have to be with me.'

'How about a dance?'

Laura glanced across at the floor. 'It's so crowded. Not just yet.'

'OK, later then.' Philip glanced at his watch and stood up. 'Anyway, we should make some attempt to circulate. I'll catch up with you anon.'

'Just a moment!' called Laura. She stood too, reached across and straightened the knot of his tie. 'There.' She smiled. 'That's better.'

'Thanks,' said Philip. He filled the glasses again and walked into the crush.

Laura sat down and watched him go. 'See you later,' she said quietly. She saw him nod once, then the crowd opened and swallowed him.

In the thick smoke and the warm red light, dancers leaped and spun and yelled. A lot of the men had now removed their ties. Philip leaned against the festooned strut. He no longer recognized individuals. There was just a seething whirlpool of flesh, floating hair, silk and barathea. Here a smiling face emerged or someone barged his arm in passing. A few people spoke to him. He burbled nonsense back at them. Now the talking all around him grew urgent and higher pitched and the heavy bass rhythm made the pillar throb. Two gorillas ran on to the dance floor. Girls shrieked. A man with no chin reached across his line of vision, said, 'Oops, sorry, old man,' plucked a carnation and put it behind his ear. A lovely young girl with wide grey eyes sat at the table below Philip. She was cool and clean and she looked as though a little light should come on every time she opened her mouth. Instead, a constant flow of matter-of-fact obscenities poured from between her perfect teeth.

Philip turned towards the other end of the marquee. A girl in azure sequins stood alone, her back to the next pillar but one. She had long black hair, very dark lips and dark eyes which very frankly and slowly flickered over his body from head to toe. She raised her champagne glass to her lips with outstretched fingers. She watched him over the rim.

He pulled himself upright and strolled over to her. 'Hi,' he said, 'mind if I share a pillar?'

'Sure.' She shrugged.

'We met before, didn't we? At the Berkeley Square ball?'

'Dunno.' She shrugged again. 'I was there. Must have been smashed if I don't remember you.' A little husky giggle.

'So how do you know Melissa?'

'I don't. Only met her this evening. I'm here with Arturo — you know, the one taking the photos. Sort of assistant, you know?' She stood very close to him. She looked up under eyelids heavy with aquamarine shadow. Her scent was strong. 'Quite a place they have here.'

'Yes,' said Philip, his voice suddenly very deep. 'Jacobean.'

'Oh yeah? Is that Jewish?'

'Er, no. No, it's . . . just . . . a . . . style.' He brushed an imaginary strand of hair from her eyes.

'A thing you know something about,' she purred. Her pupils grew larger. Her stomach moved against his.

'A little.'

An amused smirk tugged at her lips. She ran a finger along the back of her earlobe. The strands of diamanté hanging from her ear shimmered. Her lips opened. He grasped her upper arm hard. 'Christ!' he muttered.

'What say,' she spoke softly into his mouth. He gulped.

'What say you and I leave the little kids to their games, mmm?'

Laura weaved between the tables and looked casually from left to right. The music behind her had turned to thick plush strings and electric organs with a lot of amplified gasping and groaning. Plates clattered on the trestle tables. Flushed and tousled couples sat slumped before kedgeree, scrambled eggs and bacon. Women in black dresses and white pinafores poured coffee with a disapproving air.

Laura clutched her pearls. She glanced from side to side like a spectator at Wimbledon. 'Laura!' A man's voice. She turned with a smile. It was Mickey. He waved his arms and bounced up and down like a tick-tack man. 'Laura! Over here! Come and join us!'

The smile on her face remained fixed. She turned her head slightly to one side, then walked on.

The thin, splayed legs still pumped slowly on either side of him. They looked very white in the dawn half-light. His right hand lay flat on the damp grass, his left still held her smooth flank under the skirt. He panted. Slowly her legs descended. His head fell forward to rest on the curve of her throat. Her hand stroked the nape of his neck.

Her hair was damp against his lips. It suddenly seemed coarse and immovable. The sweat on her skin dried instantly in the cool breeze from across the lake. His mouth and nostrils were full of her cheap perfume and alien scents. Slowly the deep warmth spread and dissipated through his limbs. His breathing steadied, though his heart still thudded against her breast.

'Oh,' he said lamely.

'Mmmm,' she sighed.

He rolled over on his back and gazed up at the stars. They seemed to be spinning.

'Brr.' The girl trembled beside him. She sat up and

pulled up her dress to cover her breasts. 'It's *freezing*. Where are me flippin' tights?'

He sighed and turned his head lazily. The girl pecked him on the cheek and jumped to her feet. 'Where the hell *are* they?' She hopped up and down, one shoe in her hand. The sequins gleamed dimly in the purple light. Two ducks got up on the lake, honking.

Philip grunted and propped himself up on one elbow. He reached into the roots of a rhododendron bush and plucked out the length of nylon. 'Here,' he said.

'Ooh, thanks, darling.'

He lay back again and watched, uninterested, as she smoothed the tights up over her legs. 'Oh, bleeding hell,' she moaned. 'You've ripped 'em to shreds! They would be the seamed ones, too. Come on, lazybones.' She nudged him, none too gently, with her foot. 'Be a love and do me up.'

His breath hissed from the corner of his mouth. He stood and pulled the zip up over the pale white flesh.

'It's bleedin' damp here,' she giggled. She propped herself up on his shoulder and pulled on her right shoe. 'And what with that effing statue, darling, staring down at us like a maiden aunt with bowel problems . . . Jeez!' She threw an arm around his shoulder and quickly pressed her smudged dark lips on his. 'How long's it been, then?' she breathed. 'Come on, you can tell your Jacky.'

Philip shrugged. 'Long enough.' A picture of Laura flashed through his mind. Hell, what this would do to her if she knew.

'Dunno why. You being one of those types — you know, all brawn, like the guys in the deodorant adverts — I'd've thought you'd get plenty, I mean . . .'

'Isn't it time we went back?'

She stiffened. 'All right, be like that then.'

Philip pecked her on the cheek. 'Thanks,' he said, 'you were great.' He turned and strode up the grass bank towards the house.

'Wait for me,' cried Jacky. 'Wait for me!'

The embers were smouldering in the braziers. The tables were scattered with drained and dirty glasses. Four or five men huddled by the bar, alone. He saw Laura at a table in the corner. Her fingers were twisted through her pearls. Her eyes gazed up at the tented ceiling. The man next to her threw his head back, tilted his chair and laughed. Jacky leaned against Philip and squeezed his arm.

'Look,' he said. 'I'll see you later, OK?' He took hold of her hand and gently lifted it off his arm.

She frowned, put it back and clung like a tentacle. 'No, come on, let's have a dance,' she said.

One of the men by the door put his hand over his mouth and ran for the door. 'But what about Arturo?'

'Oh, him! He's probably playing with his enlarger by now. Come on.' Philip's eyes were on Laura. She turned to the man on her right and spoke. Then they both pushed back their chairs and walked towards the dance floor.

'Oh, come on,' urged Jacky, 'they'll've flippin' well packed up.'

Philip walked stiffly on to the parquet floor. The slow beat of the music throbbed in his ears. He put one arm around Jacky's waist, and the other up at his side.

Jacky frowned. 'Darling, this isn't *Come Dancing*.' She threw her arms around his neck, pressed her sequins against his jacket, and pushed her body into his. His nostrils filled again with her scent.

They circled slowly. He saw Laura just two yards away. Her arms rested lightly on her partner's shoulders. He was tall, his hair was greased. He grinned with the complacency of a well-fed cat. Laura smiled. Her eyes casually ran up and down the girl in the sequined dress. They lingered on the black patent shoes, still damp with dew, the ladder in the tights, just above the ankle, and the blades of grass enmeshed in the sequins.

Laura looked up. Their eyes met momentarily. Hers floated on without expression. She whispered something in her partner's ear. He laughed, and held her tighter.

The music changed. 'OK?' said Philip. It was not a question. He left the floor, stood a few paces from the dancers and faced them.

Laura danced on until the music changed again, then freed herself from her partner. She held out her hand. Her partner clasped it. The whites of her knuckles showed. They turned and walked casually off the floor. Her lips were set in a rigid smile. 'Oh Philip, we're off now,' she sighed. 'Only the sweepings left. It's been a lovely party.'

Philip jangled his car keys in his pocket. 'Are you all right for a lift?'

'Yep, Paul's in the same houseparty.' She turned to Jacky. 'Philip, you haven't introduced us . . .'

'Oh, yes . . .'

Jacky stuck out her hand. 'Pleased to meet you,' she said and rolled her lips. 'I'm Jacky.'

Laura stared at her, then shook her hand. 'Oh, such a nice name,' she said, then turned to Philip and kissed him lightly on both cheeks. 'Good night, darling.'

Philip watched her walk away. Jacky's hand slipped into his. Laura waved to someone. She laughed.

'Hey, Philip!' Jacky squealed. 'You're hurting me!'

'Look, it meant nothing. I just can't live like a monk month after month, that's all.'

Caroline ignored the remark, took a mouthful of cold roast beef and chewed it silently, then looked at Philip across the small, cramped table. 'Do a lot of barristers come here?' she asked eventually.

'Yes, and journalists, but mainly upstairs.'

She glanced furtively at the next-door table. A fat man with a very red face was lunching alone off a ham salad and a bottle of Burgundy.

'Do you know him?' whispered Caroline. 'He looks very eminent.'

'No,' said Philip and put down his knife and fork. 'How is she? It's been a fortnight now since I've seen her.'

'Yes, well, she has been rather busy, what with St Martin's and this poster of hers.'

'And somehow always out when I've rung?'

Caroline smiled. 'Well, it happens.' She looked at the ceiling.

'At the risk of sounding like an abandoned maiden, has she — well, said anything about me, I mean?'

'No.'

'But she must have. There isn't — oh, hell — she's not going out with anyone, is she?'

Caroline tilted her head. 'No, I don't think so.'

'What does that mean?'

'Well, no one in particular.'

Philip sighed and looked down at the cold pie on his plate, so far untouched. He picked up his knife and fork, cut off a segment and put it in his mouth. He chewed hard, then forced it down with water.

'Oh, dear,' said Caroline. She frowned. 'Look, Philip, Laura's a very special girl. You're a lucky man, you really are.'

'You mean she'll get over it?'

Caroline nodded. 'Provided you don't rush her. She feels things so deeply that I think she's terrified of letting go. You didn't know her before she moved in with me, did you?'

'I only saw her every single school holidays.'

'What, up in Cumberland? But you were both kids then. No, I mean in London after her father died.'

'Yes, I know his death hit her hard. It was so sudden. I gather though that the good Mrs Callender wasn't so cut up?'

'No. Didn't look like it. Muddy boots and Huskies were never really her scene. And widow's weeds? Forget it. The house in Cumberland went on the market a week after the funeral, and she rented a place in Chelsea "to be close to the heartbeat", as she put it. You should have seen it. Used to give me the creeps. There was a long drawing-room, always immaculate, never a magazine or book out of place as if it was a show house or something. A photograph of Laura in a silver frame stood on the mantelpiece. Typical. It was Laura aged nine in a crinoline frock, all hazy in one of those Lenare mists that come off the fells. Of course nothing else would do, like a picture of a twenty-year-old. Good God, no! Mrs Callender with a grown-up daughter? It would be a biological miracle. Once a week, Mrs Callender held her little dinner parties with an eye for prospective suitors, and Laura was bundled out to the cinema. She lived like that for four years, hardly knowing a soul. She was so shy in those days.'

A waitress came over and cleared away the plates. She looked at Philip's pie, still only half-eaten, framed by tired lettuce and a saw-toothed tomato. 'Didn't you like it then?' she asked.

'I had a large breakfast,' replied Philip.

'Oh, I see. Well now, how about a sweet? We have a very nice apple pie.'

Caroline shook her head. 'Nothing for me. Just coffee, if you'll have some.'

'Two coffees, please.'

'OK, deary.'

'And she was such a bitch about Laura going to art school. She threatened to cut her off unless she did something sensible. It wasn't the way to meet the right sort, she used to say, though one never, never married for money . . .'

Two cups and a saucer full of coffee arrived on the table. 'I'll change the saucer if you like,' said the waitress.

'No, it's all right,' replied Philip. 'So, what happened?'

'Laura took a job as a waitress. She stuck it out for two

months before her mother relented. That was just before Mrs Callender finally nailed her man.'

'What's he like?'

Caroline screwed up her nose. 'Oh, Cordwain? He's all right, I suppose. An innocuous, bland type of chap with glasses like Coca-Cola bottle bottoms. But I don't think she would have married him unless the money had been running out. She's convinced that one day he will be an ambassador. He's a first secretary or something at the moment. It made me laugh when the first posting was Peru. Mrs Callender was appalled. "The heat," she kept shrieking, "Humphrey, you know I can't stand the heat. Can't you arrange it better? What about Rome or Paris?" But Peru it was. They must have been there for two years now.'

Philip caught the waitress's eye. She looked away. 'Bill, please,' he shouted.

'Are you in court this afternoon?' asked Caroline.

'No, just paperwork.'

'Still, it must be exciting being a barrister.' Caroline glanced at her watch, and frowned. 'And I should get back to the office. Trust me to have a boss who always eats sandwiches.'

Philip drained his coffee cup. They rose and walked up the narrow flight of stairs.

'Laura's away this weekend. She's going down to the country to discuss this poster she's doing.'

'Oh, yes, she mentioned something about it at the dance.'

'They sound deliciously mad. I can just imagine Laura sitting in a country pub surrounded by men with beards with a pint of CAMRA-approved real ale at her elbow. They'll be waxing lyrical on the warble of the lesser-crested snot twirler or something, and she will open her eyes wide, and pretend it's the most tantalizing thing she's ever heard. Trust Laura. I never meet people like that.'

They walked through the crowded bar. 'Do you know anything about them?' shouted Philip above the din.

'No, but at least they've got a proper address. Their headquarters are in the Exhibition Road. You can't put up a tent there and huddle around a primus stove without being arrested.'

They passed through the swing doors and out on to the pavement. A light, continuous drizzle fell from a grey sky.

'Rats,' said Caroline and turned to him. 'I must dash. Thanks a million for lunch. Now, when Laura gets back I promise I'll work on her. Oh yes, and by the way, some friends are coming round for a drink next Tuesday. Why not come along? If I've cleared the pitch by then it might be the easiest way to — well, you know . . .'

Philip smiled. 'Thanks,' he said. 'I'll be there.'

He walked along the wet street deep in thought. Laura had had a tough time — much tougher than she had ever let on to him. She was worth waiting for, he knew that now without any doubt. He smiled again, suddenly sure that they could work it out. He was still smiling as he went up the steps to his chambers.

CHAPTER TWO

Six naked light bulbs hung from the high plasterwork ceiling. The shutters were drawn on the Exhibition Road outside. The boy in the Yale T-shirt strummed on his guitar and smiled. 'Ready now?' he said.

'Ready,' the shout came back.

The boy strummed again.

Gonna forge a New Kingdom in Satan's old land,
Gonna forge the New Kingdom with Father's hand . . .

Five groups of eight or ten sat on the bare wooden floor and swayed, clapped and sang. English accents mingled with transatlantic drawl and the sharp, clipped sounds of Asiatics.

Laura broke away from one of the groups and walked towards the formica-topped table at the end of the room. A girl in jeans and a sweatshirt followed. Her skin looked sallow in the harsh light. Lines like saucer marks on a tablecloth hung under her eyes.

Laura reached over the empty plastic coffee cups, picked up a roll of cartridge paper, and unfurled it. 'Well, what do you think, Jane? It's only the first rough sketch.' Her voice quavered.

The girl smiled. 'Yeah, a lot of consciousness. I'm sure it's going to be great. Hey, Jimmy,' she shouted.

A thin, lanky man turned round. He clutched a silver pendant hanging around his neck. 'What is it?' he asked. 'The bus should be here any minute.'

'Come over here.'

He left his group and walked over. His eyes were ringed like Jane's.

'Laura, this is Jimmy.' The man smiled. His lips slid back and the gums showed. 'Laura's done this poster for us.'

He let go of the pendant. It had seven interlocking stars. 'Wow,' he said. 'Laura, you've sure got talent. How long have you been doing this?'

'I'm only in my second year.'

'Is she coming with us, Jane?'

'Yes.'

'Well, that's great. See you later.' He nodded to Jane and walked away. Jane held up the poster and twisted her head to one side.

'You know, I think it should be something like Dali — I like the fields, but green fields everywhere, and no clouds, and then something coming at you out of a haze in the distance — something wonderful and mysterious like a great walled city made out of crystal with a light around it, a brilliant shining light, a light so bright that it scorches the ground it passes. Then a few stray figures. You know, those thin little Dali people, all bone with limbs like frogs' legs, shielding their eyes and trying to shout something — But Laura, you are the artist, you must tell us what's right.'

Laura frowned. 'I'm still not sure what you do. I listened to the lecture but I'm afraid I still don't understand.'

Jane's hand flapped. 'It will all be explained over the weekend. It's so great you're coming.'

A man bumped into her. She turned. Jimmy was behind the man, gesturing like a waiter with burnt fingers. 'Look,' Jimmy was saying, 'it's really nice down there. The air is fresh and there are wonderful walks . . .'

'No,' the man shouted above the music. 'Stop pressurizing me. I don't want to come on your damn weekend.'

Jimmy put his hand on the man's shoulder, but the man brushed it off, took hold of the girl on his right and darted out of the door. Two others followed.

A plump boy with slanted eyes waved.

'That's the bus,' said Jane.

'Everyone follow me,' shouted Jimmy.

Laura slowly rolled up her poster while the others filtered past her. She turned to Jane, then lowered her eyes. 'I'm not really sure if I . . .'

Jane grabbed her hand. 'Oh, come on! It's going to be such fun. Just wait and see!'

'Sun, sun, sun, here it comes . . .'

Laura groaned. Her eyes opened stickily. A pale purple light filtered through tiny windows cut in the corrugated iron high above her. She rolled over, shielding her ears, and snuggled down in her sleeping bag.

'Come on, time to get up!' yelled Jane.

Laura did not move. 'What time is it?' she murmured.

'Five.'

'God! Wake me up when it's time for breakfast.'

Jane leaned over her. 'Now, now, Laura. We don't want to miss the fun!'

Laura pushed her face into the pillow. 'Leave me alone.' Her voice was muffled. 'We didn't get to bed until two.'

Laura's arms were lifted into the air. Her sleeping bag was unzipped, the soft down pillow pulled away. She lay on the concrete floor in her T-shirt and panties. She shivered.

'There!' said Jane and folded up the bag.

Laura yawned and rubbed her eyes. 'Some Saturday lie-in,' she muttered. 'This'd better be good.'

In the hall of the farmhouse, sleeping bags were stacked against the walls. Fluorescent tubes buzzed and shed a bland white light. Jane ushered Laura on to one of the forty folding chairs facing a blackboard, and sat down next to her. Eager, smiling faces stared ahead.

Jimmy walked up to the podium and raised his arms. 'Let's have a sing-song,' he shouted. 'Let's show how great it is to be alive!'

The shout came back, 'Yes, yes!' in quadraphonic sound. Laura bristled. She leaned across to Jane. 'I don't want to seem like a party pooper,' she yelled above the music, 'but it is five-thirty in the morning, and I might just slip back to bed for a while and join you later.'

Jane put her hand on Laura's. 'No, no, love, you can't, you really can't! You'll miss everything. Please, for me,' she pleaded. 'Laura, please! Dr Singleton will be here any moment now.'

The singing stopped and a middle-aged man walked up to the blackboard. His thin brown hair was brushed sideways over the crown. He wore corduroy trousers and a tweed jacket. His old brown brogues carried a high polish. They squeaked as he walked.

Jane leaned over again. 'He was a very eminent economist before he joined us,' she whispered. 'United Nations.'

Dr Singleton wiped the blackboard with a duster, then turned and cleared his throat. 'I am going to explain why the world is presently in such confusion . . . '

The voice was quiet and urbane. Laura's eyelids sank and snapped open again and again.

'Economists and politicians have searched . . . failed to find an answer . . . I too failed before I joined the Movement . . . failed because I was scratching the surface . . .'

Laura shook her head and looked around her. Her fellow inmates perched on their chairs, their heads slightly forward, spellbound.

'. . . society's ills . . . one common cause . . . lack of love and compassion . . . not enough love in the world . . .'

Laura raised her hand to her face as if scratching an itch. She glanced at her watch. Dr Singleton had been talking for an hour without any sign of inhaling. 'When's breakfast?' she asked.

Jane froze. 'Shh!'

Another hour passed before Dr Singleton stopped talking and a tea urn arrived.

'Is this all?' said Laura. 'Tea and biscuits?' She took a sip from the plastic cup. 'Yuk! Herb tea.' She turned to Jane. 'When are we going to get down to the poster?'

'Oh, soon, Laura, soon, but first you must understand what we do.'

Laura looked at her quizzically. 'Why all this talk of the New Kingdom? You told me you were a community, a conservation group, but you're not, are you? You're some kind of religious movement.'

Jane smiled. 'Well, sometimes, you know, it's not possible to divorce the two.'

Laura frowned. 'Then we discuss the poster today, this afternoon. Otherwise I'm leaving now, OK?'

'But there isn't a bus until Sunday.'

'Look, train, bus — I'll walk if I have to.' Laura took another sip of herb tea and winced. 'This stuff is terrible.'

'Laura, of course we'll discuss the poster just as soon as we can get Jimmy and Dr Singleton and the others together. Please, just give us a chance!' Jane picked up a Rich Tea biscuit, blew across it, and handed it to Laura.

'What did you do that for?'

Jane shrugged. 'Just a custom. Frightens away evil spirits.'

'Nuts.'

'Oh, Laura, if only you would lift those blinkers, you would find that anything is possible, and I mean anything!'

'Yep, like what? More lectures.'

'To start with, yes. It's like — I don't know — being born. It's not easy, but oh, it is worth it once you understand!'

★

Seven of them sat grouped on an old army blanket in the tall grass. Dr Singleton leaned forward. 'We really want to help you, Laura. There is something cutting you off, isn't there, hmm? You are not at peace with yourself?'

'No, it's nothing. Don't be silly. I'm fine.' His brown eyes stared hard at her, and she looked away, up at the overcast sky.

Jane squeezed her gently on the shoulder. 'Laura, we can't help you if you will not help yourself. You're such a wonderful girl, I just know it. You've got a heart. If only you would give a little more. Free yourself. Tell Dr Singleton what you told me about your father.'

Laura bit her lip. 'I don't — I don't see what . . .'

'Tell him,' said Jane. 'Just tell him. It'll make it easier for you.'

Laura's fingers slowly scratched the blanket. 'Well, he died of a heart attack when I was sixteen. It was very sudden.'

Dr Singleton nodded. 'And did you love him?'

Laura looked at him, slightly startled. 'Yes. Of course.'

'Deeply?'

'Yes.'

'And your mother? Were you close to her?'

Laura spoke very quietly. 'We never really got on.'

'Even before the tragedy?'

Laura nodded.

A guitar strummed in the distance. Dr Singleton paused for a moment and stroked his jaw. 'Have you ever thought how much that must have hurt him? Hmm? Your jealousy for her. Your resentment that she would always be closer to him. Because that's what it was, wasn't it, Laura? Resentment and jealousy?'

'No, we just didn't get on. We saw life differently, that's all.'

'Don't you see, it was you? You just would not give,

bitter, envious as you were. You drove your mother away from you. You closed your heart to her love. It was you, Laura, it was you!'

'No! No!'

'You must face the truth,' whispered Jane in her ear. 'None of us is perfect, but you must face it, Laura, and you will feel better for it.'

'But . . . but,' said Laura, 'it just wasn't like that.'

Dr Singleton stabbed a finger at her. 'Think about it, Laura, think about it. Your father paid for an expensive education for you, did he not?'

'Yes.'

'And he had to work hard? All to pay for your education, hmm? And he died of a heart attack. A stress-related disease. Maybe if he hadn't pushed himself so hard out of love for you, he would still be alive today.' His eyes glared at her. 'He died for you, Laura, a father for his child. And how did you repay him? With jealousy and spite.'

Laura's nostrils flared. Her body shook. 'It's lies!' she cried. 'Lies.'

Jane put her arm around her. 'Don't worry, Laura. We are here to help you. Here to help you.'

Philip shaved twice on Tuesday, the day of Caroline's party. He wore an Hermès tie which Laura had given him for his birthday. He might as well not have bothered. Laura was still down in the country.

'So who the hell are these weirdos she's with?' he asked when at last he cornered Caroline.

'Can't remember.' Caroline shrugged. 'Green something. That's all I know.'

'Greenpeace?'

'No, they're the ones with sou'westers, aren't they? These ones have trowels.'

'Not Greenham Common?'

'Good God, no! Oh, I remember, it's the Green Crusaders.'

'Green Crusaders?' Philip frowned. 'Never heard of them.'

'I *am* sorry, Philip,' said Caroline. 'I promise I'll work on her just as soon as she's back. Now there's someone I want you to meet. Fiona — Fiona, this is Philip . . .'

But Philip made his excuses soon afterwards and returned to his bedsit. He kicked several articles of furniture and drank the better part of a half-bottle of Scotch before at last he could sleep.

'Somehow,' Laura stretched and yawned, 'I don't think that I can be the stuff of which saints are made. I thought nine to five must be bad enough, but five in the morning till two in the morning is murder!' The barn was cold. She shivered and bent to unroll her sleeping bag in the narrow space between Jane's bag and the others. 'Four days like that, and already I'm beginning to see things. I just don't know how you do it.'

'The body must be your servant, not your master,' said Jane. 'It's incredible how quickly you get used to it once you truly realize the importance of what you're doing. I mean, to bring love into the world, to banish fear and hatred — it's such a huge job, such a vital mission, and there is so little time.' For a moment her gaunt face vanished and her voice was muffled as she pulled off her green T-shirt. 'Once you get there, once you see, you have no idea how all-embracing, how exciting it all becomes. You just don't want to stop for a moment.' Her head emerged in a cloud of tousled mousy hair. She wore no bra. Her breasts were small and sunken and pointed. The white skin clutched at her ribs.

'I still don't understand — not really — what you're getting at.' Laura pulled off her jumper and shook her head. 'I mean, I can see some of it. It's just — I don't see how you intend to achieve all this perfection.'

'I know, I know,' Jane soothed. 'Don't worry. Vision

comes to you. You cannot reach out and grab it like a child with a toy. It's all so revolutionary, so different from anything you've ever known. Just let the lectures work in your mind. Keep your mind open. It'll come. Truly it will. Oh, Laura! We've got so much living to do, so much to achieve. We *can* change the world. We *will*.'

Laura unfastened her belt. 'Yes, well,' she said. She kicked off her jeans.

Jane stared at her. 'Look, I know it sounds mad, and crazy, but do you think we would all be here if we didn't believe it was possible? It is! It is! And in time we will be able to tell you why and how. But not just yet. First we must be sure that we can trust you.' Jane stepped over her sleeping bag. Her arms went round Laura, and she hugged her. 'But I'm sure it will be all right,' she said, 'you're such a real person.'

Laura's head fell on Jane's shoulder. She yawned and looked up. Her eyes skirted the dimly lit iron walls of the barn. 'It's funny,' she said, 'there are no mirrors anywhere, not even in the Honey-Wagon. Could I borrow yours?'

Jane tutted. 'Vanity, vanity, Laura.'

Laura frowned, then gently pushed Jane away. 'Hang on, I might just have one . . .' She lifted her bag off a rusty nail protruding from the corrugated iron.

'Lights out, everybody!' shouted a high-pitched voice. 'Sweet dreams!'

Laura took out a little mirror, smeared with lipstick and powder. She wiped it on her nightdress and peered into it. 'My God!' she said. Her head shot backwards. The veins in her eyes were swollen and her pupils were the size of aniseed balls.

'Good morning, Thomas,' said Philip. 'Anything for me?'

The clerk peered through his bifocals at his watch. It was just ten o'clock. 'Good afternoon, sir.'

Thomas shuffled through a pile of papers neatly wrapped

in red tape. Some were as thick as a telephone directory. He picked one out, no more than two sheets of foolscap, and dangled it in his fingers. 'Now, what have we here?' he said. 'A traffic offence at West London Magistrates' Court. Should keep the wolf from the door.'

Philip nodded. The corner of his mouth twitched. 'Thank you, Thomas.'

He trotted down the stairs to the small room that he shared with Petherbridge, the junior tenant. He opened the door a fraction and squeezed through. For all his care, he heard the habitual bovine groan as the doorknob pressed into Petherbridge's back. 'Sorry,' he said weakly.

Petherbridge was scribbling away like a man possessed; no flair, but the perseverance of a ticket tout in a thunderstorm. 'Hello, Philip,' he said, mincing his words, 'just dashing these off. Before the Registrar in half an hour. Nasty divorce, loads of money, only married two years. Terrible bitch.'

Philip squeezed past and sat down at his desk. Yellowing papers were stacked high all around him: old cases, very old cases, long dead or settled, but useful decoration for the clients. He stared for a moment out of the window at the white basement wall opposite. Then he picked up the telephone and dialled.

'ITN,' said a girl's voice.

'Could I speak to Bill Peters?'

'Who?'

'Bill Peters, he's one of the script writers.'

'It's ringing for you.' The line went dead. 'Peters.' Typewriters clattered like gunfire in the background.

'Bill, it's Philip Strickland. How are things?'

'Frantic, I'm on the early bulletin.'

'When you've got a moment, could you do me a favour?'

'Is there a story in it?'

'No, but there's a drink.'

'Yeah. Well, provided it's not that nail polish you used to serve at Magdalene.'

'Have you heard of a community group called the Green Crusaders?'

'Oh, Philip, I am touched. We will make a concerned citizen out of you yet. What have they done — frightened the grouse?'

'I just wondered whether you have anything on them.'

'Doesn't ring a bell — but I'll check the files when I've got a moment and let you know. OK?'

'Thanks. We'll make it Krug.'

'Jeez! What have these people done to you?'

Dr Singleton clenched his fist and punched the air. 'Man,' he yelled, 'has deceived God. He has turned his face from love, that love pure and rich, that all consuming divine love, and embraced sin. He has fallen, fallen into a dark and empty place, a place where . . .'

The boy in front of Laura left his seat and stood alone in the aisle. His body trembled, his eyelids were half-closed, his eyes and nose red and shining. Tears streamed down his cheeks. He knelt down slowly with arms outstretched, and then suddenly lunged forward. His head cracked against the floorboards like a mallet. It thudded three, four, five times, then he cried out, 'How could I forsake him! I love you, Father, I love you!'

For a moment there was a strange hush, as if the room was still reverberating with the raw pain in that cry, and then the shout came out from every corner, every mouth, until the walls were singing and shaking and rumbling: 'I LOVE YOU, FATHER! I LOVE YOU!'

All around her were standing and shouting. Laura hesitated. She sat rigidly in her chair. Her hands clenched into white fists. Then her body trembled too. She mouthed the words silently, then just audibly. She shook her fists. She laughed. Kicked back the chair, and hugged Jane.

Then she yelled, 'I LOVE YOU, FATHER! I LOVE YOU!'

Petherbridge was picking his nails when the telephone rang. Philip lifted the receiver.

'Philip? It's Bill. I've traced the file.'

'So, what've you got?'

'Mind telling me why you're so interested?'

Philip sighed. 'Cut the investigative reporter bit, Bill. Can't you just tell me?'

'The Green Crusaders are a front for the Children of Light. They're used for fund-raising and recruiting.'

'And who the hell are the Children of Light?'

A groan came down the telephone. 'Don't you read the papers? They're one of the biggest in the cult business. Their leader is a Dr Sananda, a Nepali self-styled messiah, who claims over one hundred thousand full-time disciples world-wide. The guy's said to be worth over thirty million dollars. I always knew I was in the wrong business. So what's your interest, Philip? Come clean. Is it a girl? For a bottle of Krug, it has to be a girl.'

'Warm. She's been down with them for a week, but she's not a disciple or anything.'

'Not yet, but I warn you, they'll use any excuse to get them in. Does she really matter to you? I mean really matter?'

'Yes. She matters.'

A little wheezy laugh came from Petherbridge, and a chuckle down the line. 'Well, in that case,' Bill said crisply, 'Mike did a story on one of the cults a few months back. I'll try and twist his arm, but I warn you he's got one hell of a thirst.'

'A magnum?'

'Jeroboam.'

'Laura,' said Jane, 'there is really nothing to be frightened of, you're among friends. We all really care for you. Just stand up and say whatever you feel, you've heard the others. Go on!'

Laura looked down the long trestle tables. Everyone was there. Dr Singleton sat at the centre of the horseshoe, beneath a banner with seven interlocking stars. Jimmy was at his side. Mouths munched beans and toast. Knives and forks clattered.

Dr Singleton craned forward and looked down the table at Laura in a kindly way, like a headmaster at a prize-giving. She gulped, rose to her feet, and pushed her chair back. It squeaked on the bare boards. All the group turned to look at her. All were smiling. There was silence.

She took a deep breath. 'Well, I'm Laura, but I guess you all know that by now as we have been together for six whole days. I would like to say how great it is to be here with you all. You've all been so friendly and nice and I would specially like to thank Jane who has been by my side every day and . . . '

Jane nudged her. 'Your life, Laura, tell them about your life.'

'Oh, yes, my life. Well, there's nothing much to tell really. I suppose it's been what Dr Singleton would call a chant to self, a psalm to trivia; yes, a round of parties and weekends in the pursuit of pleasure. Not that it was that much fun really; sometimes it was, but often it was a real bore, and I could not understand why. People were sometimes so cold, and those you really trusted, those you thought were really special, just let you down, walked away when you needed them most. They pretended that they really liked you, but if you were not prepared to, or just felt you couldn't give them what they wanted, they . . .' Laura clutched the back of her chair. 'Well, they just weren't your friends any more.' Laura looked quickly at Jane, and began to sit down.

'Go on,' urged Jane, 'you're doing fine, just fine.'

Laura stood up straight. She glanced at Dr Singleton. He nodded back to her. 'Well, I am an art student, and I hope to do you a really good poster. When I was there — St Martin's, I mean — I spent a lot of time on life class, and I would see the pain and suffering in the eyes of models. Drink and loneliness, I suppose, but I would never really look upon them as people, you know? They were just still life. I suppose I just did not have heart.

'And then good works. To me that meant charity balls. People sitting around in dinner jackets and long dresses checking the numbers on their lucky programmes, raising a thousand pounds for stray pets and,' she giggled, 'four thousand for the caterers. Everything around me seemed so superficial, so uncaring, so empty, as if between money and sex, real love — love without self-interest or design — had been squeezed out like the ketchup in a hot-dog. As if the bond between human being and human being had been severed, and everyone just had to survive as best they could.' Laura paused and took a deep breath. 'I have taken so much from life, from my family.' She lowered her eyes, and sat down quickly.

They clapped. Quietly at first and then louder. They banged knives on the table. 'Laura! We love you! Laura! Laura!'

She looked around her, smiling, breathing in tiny gasps. A tear trickled down her face on to the table below. She gulped and wiped her face with the back of her hand.

The thumping and clapping went on and on. Laura looked around, blinking and bewildered. 'Oh,' she said. 'Oh, Jane!' She threw her arm around the other girl's neck and hid her face as she cried.

Jane's hand stroked her hair. She said, 'Laura, I'm so happy!' Her eyes rose above the shaking blonde head and met Singleton's, querying. He nodded and smiled.

CHAPTER THREE

'Just in case things go sour,' said Bill, 'I thought you should have some idea of what it's about. Got your security pass?'

Philip nodded, and followed Bill Peters along the corridor. 'This is kind of you.'

Bill brushed some ash off his trousers. 'Don't mention it. Who knows? There might be a story in it. We have never been able to bring a film crew inside one of Sananda's communes — it's really features, anyway — but we do have some archive material on a self-styled "mind experience" group. Mike's dug it out.'

Bill's eyes were half-closed. He took another drag on his cigarette, and ushered Philip into the lift. It stopped at the first floor. They walked through two swing doors and into the clatter of typewriters. There were rows of them, with word processors and high-tech knick-knacks spilling over the desks. Their human operators huddled over them, flicking the keys like concert pianists with a train to catch.

Bill led Philip along the rows to a fat man with a loud check jacket. 'Philip, meet Mike.'

The man stopped typing. He rubbed his neck with the palm of his hand and shook his head. 'Good to meet you, Philip.' He quickly glanced at his watch, then held out his hand. Philip shook it. It felt as though he were wearing gardening gloves. 'I'm afraid I've only got about a quarter of an hour, so let's get cracking.'

Bill patted Philip on the back. 'I'll leave you to it, OK?'

Mike threw some papers in a wire tray, then led the way to a small glass cubicle at the far end of the room. It was cool inside. He handed a video cassette to a man hunched over a metal monster. 'Duggie, my boy, run this, will you?'

The machine swallowed the cassette. The man fiddled with knobs on the control panel. The tape whirred. A picture of a velveteen-lined hall appeared on the monitor. About a hundred people with name tabs on their chests sat uneasily in plastic chairs.

The shot changed to a close-up of a man at a lectern. 'Thinking is the greatest block, arseholes,' he shouted.

'OK, let's start here,' said Mike. The technician ran the tape back, then pressed a key.

The man at the lectern started again. 'Thinking is the greatest block, arseholes . . .'

'This is a three-day course on mind expansion,' said Mike, 'at two hundred pounds a shot. All the participants agreed beforehand not to leave the room, eat, drink or piss without permission. The group leader's commands are to be obeyed without question.' He chuckled. 'All that abuse, insults and ridicule in the hope of enlightenment.'

On the screen, the participants were now standing and waving their hands in the air, playing some type of game. Only one man still sat. His arms were folded and he had a grim expression on his face. Two men in electric-blue suits walked behind him, pulled away his chair and pushed him towards the others. They grabbed hold of his wrists and waved his arms for him, then smiled benignly and pushed him again.

'No pussyfooting, as you can see,' said Mike. 'The first step in the process is to break down inhibitions and disorient the person, create an environment in which his previous code of conduct no longer applies. He is forced to act out elaborate charades, given contradictory commands, and shouted at and sworn at until resistance ceases. He is not allowed to make any decision, however basic, without referring to a higher authority. He is made to perform tasks with inadequate information, so that he must constantly rely on the group leader. In the jargon, that's applying "peer pressure". Mike rubbed his neck. 'Gradually, as a means to survival in this new environment, the subject takes for granted the authority of the group leader, and will follow his commands, however unreasonable.'

'How long would that take?' asked Philip.

'I don't know. With a susceptible subject, maybe as little as twenty-four hours. I'll run the tape on to the second day. You'll see what I mean.' He kept his finger on a button. When he released it, a middle-aged woman in floral maternity dress was skipping in the air playing hopscotch with all the exuberance of a performing seal. '*Dormez-vous? Dormez-vous? Sonnez les matines . . .*'

'You see? Dignity gone and little embarrassment. The process precipitates a regression akin to childhood. The participants are relieved of all responsibility. All they have to do is what they are told. If they follow the commands, they are allowed small favours and shown affection. If not, they are assaulted either physically or emotionally, and deprived of necessities.' Mike looked quickly at his watch. 'We'll move on now to the second stage: catharsis.' He pressed the button again. 'This is the third day.'

A man with a beard and deep-set eyes lay on the floor. An attendant in blue kneeled beside him pressing down on his thin outstretched arms. A second held his thighs. A third stood over him, legs astride. The man on the ground was breathing in long, deep gasps. 'Faster!' commanded a voice, 'faster!' The man inhaled more rapidly. His nostrils flared and his stomach quivered. 'Faster!' shouted the voice. 'Faster! Now think of the person you most hate, the person you're most frightened of, the one person you would like to see dead.'

The bearded man's body shook, then he screamed. It was a high-pitched wail like a cat's mating call. His lips gibbered. He screamed again. For a full minute he writhed on the floor shrieking, shouting, twisting his body, and then he was still. His eyelids closed and a little impudent smile plucked at his lips.

Mike pressed a button and the frame froze. 'What you have just seen is a rather crude exercise in hyperventilation. Rapid breathing over-oxygenates the blood, which in turn causes confusion in the mind. It is not difficult to induce, as you see. Once a subject has left all decisions to others, the reserve normally necessary for day-to-day survival can be abandoned and all the long-suppressed feelings and fears are allowed to drift to the surface. His identity can be stripped down by playing on his secret doubts and fears. It's a type of steamroller psychoanalysis. Strip 'em down, get rid of the old prejudices, then build 'em up again.' He nodded and frowned. 'But often those old prejudices were there for one hell of a good reason.'

Philip breathed in deeply, his mind full of Laura. 'Do the Children of Light use the same techniques?'

Mike's checked shoulders rose an inch. 'I don't know, you can get to this point by other routes. This course was for people in a hurry. Three days to get rid of a code for survival that took a lifetime to build.

'Of course, it is open to abuse. Once you have got them to that critical point, they are emotionally naked, and that can lead to a dogmatic acceptance of a cause which they would not otherwise tolerate. Reasoning will not persuade them otherwise, because they did not adopt the cause through rational considerations, but through a gut feeling at a time of emotional vulnerability.

'Having abandoned his old ways, the subject is dependent upon the group for survival. They can impose their own code of ethics and their beliefs. If a person resists, sanctions are imposed. But by then it is unlikely that the indoctrinee has either the will or the strength to resist.' Mike smiled. 'The beliefs come from the same authority as he turns to for his every need. Just as any other pack animal will blindly obey the man who feeds him and dominates him.' Mike lit a cigarette and glanced at his watch again. 'Well, Philip, there you are. The techniques of spiritual persuasion have come a fair old way from Sunday school.'

'Thanks, Mike,' said Philip, 'but I assume that this is a thing for cranks and social casualties. Ordinary people wouldn't fall for it.'

'Don't you believe it, lad.' Mike stood and waved his cigarette like a conductor's baton. 'The more ordinary the better! Why the hell do you think people are ordinary? It is their ability to adapt to the rules of their society. They conform. It's the weirdos, those with a strong, resilient self-image, who remain aloof. All the research conducted into brainwashing after the Korean war pointed to the same conclusion. If you don't believe me, look at any office. See how the employees get into the routine, how they fawn to their superiors, how much they care if someone has a cushier chair, if their office is a fraction larger, if the telephone is a different colour. It's all part of building up a set of rules, a code of preference, a peer structure. The things themselves mean very little.

'In the cults, the same game is played for all it's worth. But don't ask me where brainwashing begins and social adjustment ends. I just don't know. We're all so damn smug, we think that it would never happen to us. But I tell you, lad, it scares me shitless. We all have our breaking point. It's only a matter of degree, but I wouldn't spend a day in one of those places for a lifetime pass to every watering hole in London.' He looked at his watch again. 'Now, if you'll excuse me, I really must get back.

'Thanks,' said Philip. 'Very kind of you to spare the time.'

Mike led Philip back through the news-room to Bill's desk. 'Hope I have been some use. Whatever you do, don't do anything rash. You could push her straight into their arms. It's like a boozer, a junkie, you know? They have to find their own reasons for giving it up.' He winked, slapped Philip on the back and bustled off, glancing at his watch every three paces.

Bill rose to his feet, looked at Philip, then grimaced. 'These things happen,' he said. 'It's not your baby. If I was you I would forget all about it. You have the whole of London. What's so special about one girl?'

The telephone rang on Saturday evening.

'Philip, it's Caroline.' She sounded unnaturally cool. 'Come round quickly. Please . . . now.' Philip had told Caroline about his session at ITN and what it had revealed. Apparently, Laura had rung her, but left no address or telephone number.

'Has she come back?'

'Yes, she arrived a few minutes ago with some people from the commune. She's paid a month's rent in lieu of notice. She's packing her things.'

'Good God! Keep her there until I come. Do anything.' He slammed down the receiver, raced down the stairs and into the street. He was in luck. A cab was shedding its customer nearby. He jumped in and asked the driver to hurry. If the lights were with him he should be at Caroline's flat in ten minutes. He made it in twelve.

His fingers jabbed at the entry-phone. He ran up the stairs two at a time. The door of the flat was ajar. He walked in. The drawing-room was empty. Two cushions and a pair of black tights lay on the floor. A sound of sobbing came from beyond. 'Laura!' called Philip.

'Hello, is that you, Philip?' Caroline pushed open the kitchen door. Her face was red and blotchy and streaked with tears. Her hands shook. She walked over to the sofa and sat down. 'She's gone,' she said. Her voice trembled. 'I tried, really, I tried, but while I was ringing you, one of those bastards was listening in on the extension. They just upped and left. I could do nothing to stop them! Laura only took a couple of pairs of jeans and her passport. That was — that was all!'

'Her passport?' he stammered, his fists clenched. He

felt sick. 'Oh, Jesus, no. Did she say where she was going?'

'No, I don't think she even knew herself. When she came in, it was horrible. Her eyes seemed to pass straight through me as if I were a perfect stranger. "It's Caroline, your flatmate, remember me?" I shouted sort of half-jokingly, you know? She just smiled inanely and backed away as if I were unclean or something, then went to her room. One of the others stayed with me, but I gave him the slip and locked myself in my bedroom. That's when I rang you.'

'You're sure she took her passport?'

'For God's sake, I told you!' she barked ferociously. 'I saw it! In her hand! Oh, damn it, Philip, I'm sorry.' She slumped back on to the sofa. 'I just couldn't do *anything*! What in God's name do we do now?'

'Steady.' Philip sat on the sofa beside her. He took her hand. 'You did everything you could.' But his body was tense. He leaped to his feet a moment later. 'Jesus,' he mused. 'What the hell *can* we do?'

'But it's not her, I know it's not her. They must have done something to her. Can't we go to the police or something?'

'And say what?' Philip snapped. 'That we've got a friend who has been brainwashed? Forget it. There's no proof of physical coercion, no assault, nothing tangible. If Laura was put in the witness box she would swear that she wanted to stay with the Crusaders.'

'You know the way she has sudden enthusiasms. This could be one of them.' Caroline blinked and smiled. She talked very fast. 'I can't believe that she will stay away from St Martin's for long. She loves it so, and she worked so hard to get in. That will be the crunch. That'll bring her back if nothing else does.'

'And if it doesn't, what then?' His fists clenched and unclenched. 'If only I'd been with her these last few weeks . . .'

'Don't blame yourself, Philip. You couldn't have known.

But if only there was something we could do. Maybe . . . maybe if she saw you, if she knew that you really cared, maybe then she'd see reason.'

'She's been avoiding me. She never once returned my calls. Remember?'

'But don't you see? That's only because she cared so deeply about you. You were part of her dreams.'

Philip snorted like a bull. 'That's great. So it was my fault, was it? None of this would've happened if it wasn't for me?'

'No, Philip. I'm not saying that. What's past is past. All I'm saying is that if anybody can make her see reason, then you can. I don't know,' she shrugged, 'maybe she doesn't mean that much to you, maybe you don't think she's worth the trouble. Maybe it was just curiosity. Once you'd had your evil way with her, maybe you were planning . . .'

'Stop it, Caroline! Even if I tried to find her, what good would it do? We can't even have a civilized discussion about field sports. You just can't argue with her. And what do I know about this kind of thing?'

Caroline looked down at the carpet. She shrugged. 'You're right, Philip. You're absolutely right. It was her choice. If that's the way you feel about it, let her stew.' Philip still paced the room. Caroline shot a quick glance at him, then looked away. A little satisfied smile puckered her lips.

25 Exhibition Road was an unprepossessing terraced house. Stucco peeled off the front, and wooden boards were nailed over the ground-floor windows. A plump boy with slant eyes stood on the porch scratching his crotch.

As Philip walked up to the door, the boy took his hand out of his pocket. 'Do you have business here?'

'A meeting. This is the headquarters of the Green Crusaders, isn't it?'

'Yes.' The boy pushed open the door and followed him. 'Please leave shoes.'

A line of plimsolls stretched far down the long, dark corridor. A burble of voices came from within.

'Jimmy,' the boy shouted.

A thin man appeared. A silver pendant with seven interlocking stars hung over his T-shirt. He bared his gums. 'Hi, what can I do for you?'

'I've just stopped by to see an old friend, Laura Callender.'

The man's smile dropped. He frowned. 'Who?'

'Laura Callender, blonde shoulder-length hair, steel-blue eyes, medium height.'

'Are you a relative?' he asked.

'No.'

The man rubbed his chin. 'Don't remember her at all. Maybe she came once or twice, but she is not with us now.'

Philip's eyes narrowed. 'She's not with you, huh? She went down to your place in the country, came back a week ago, and packed her things.'

Jimmy backed away and waved his hands. 'Jesus, a lot can happen in a week. Don't worry. She will probably write. OK?'

'Can I have a look around?'

'Sure,' said Jimmy. He opened the door on his right. Philip looked in. He smelt feet and fried onions. The stars design was painted in the centre of the floorboards. About sixty people sat around it, talking excitedly. A few were asleep by the walls. No Laura.

'You see?' said Jimmy. 'No need to get heavy. I wouldn't lie to you.' Philip stood still for a moment. His teeth were clenched. His right fist struck his thigh. Jimmy smiled nervously. 'I'm sorry about your friend,' he said. 'Er . . . would you like to read . . . er, something about the Green Crusaders? I mean . . .' He edged around the room towards a desk.

Philip took a deep breath and turned on his heel.

Every evening after work for the next four days, Philip stood on the corner of Exhibition Road and watched the doorway of the Green Crusaders' headquarters. He had no great hope that he would see Laura coming in or out, but it was a distant possibility and the only hope he had. It also helped to ease the guilt that dogged him when he thought of his last evening with her.

On the fifth day it became clear just how futile these vigils had been. The postcard bore a sepia print with the legend, THE GOLDEN TEMPLE, BENARES, INDIA. On the back, Laura's familiar, unmistakable scrawl:

> Sorry could not stay to say goodbye, but there's work to be done. So much to do. There is not enough love in the world. This change has come so quickly, I know you will find it difficult to understand as I do myself, but I know what I am doing must be right. We must forge the New Kingdom. Don't worry, Father will protect me. Remember you always.
>
> Laura

Philip read the card twice, rubbed his neck, then read it again. He looked at the postmark. It was 10 May, two weeks after she had left the flat. A desperate numbness spread through his body.

He walked upstairs and into the kitchen, put the milk on the draining board, and kicked the fridge. He filled up the kettle and switched it on. 'Damn, damn, damn,' he yelled. 'Why? Why?' But beneath his anger was a terrible suspicion. With his blindness to her sensitivity, to her hurt, he had helped to push Laura into their arms. Damn his work, damn everything — he was going to find her.

*

'Thomas,' said Philip, 'that case I'm on at the moment, it should only run for another three days.'

The old clerk put his mug of coffee down on a pile of papers. 'If you say so, sir,' he sighed.

Philip took a deep breath. 'Well, if there is nothing particularly urgent, I thought I might take a holiday.'

Thomas peered through his bifocals. His nose twitched. 'What? Aren't we keeping you busy enough, sir?'

'It's not that.'

Thomas shook his head. 'That's no way to build up a practice, sir. A young man like yourself, sir, should stay around in the vacation, pick up whatever's going.'

'It will probably only be a couple of weeks.'

'Very well, sir.'

As Philip was leaving the room, he heard Thomas's voice barely above a whisper: 'A matter of the heart, I would not doubt.'

Philip turned. 'Thomas, I think that is out of order.'

'I'm sorry, sir, just mumbling to myself.'

PART TWO

CHAPTER FOUR

Philip stood in the queue at the ticket office. A turbaned porter waited by his side with a single battered suitcase. Matchstick fingers plucked at Philip's arm. Upturned palms hovered and fluttered on either side. He stared fixedly ahead.

The yawning masonry of the railway hall only partly smothered the bright, searching light of a Delhi morning. Tea-sellers, tiffin-bearers, cooks, touts and porters picked their way through sleeping bodies which lay randomly scattered, like corpses on a battlefield. Immediately in front of Philip, a child spluttered thick white phlegm over his mother's dark-brown nipple. Farmyard noises and the simian chatter of tinkers melded with the clanking of the trolleys, the hissing and low thunder of the trains.

Philip stooped. 'Benares, please.'

'Sir will be wanting return, yes?'

He frowned. Suddenly the absurdity of his quest struck him. He did not know where the trail would lead. He did not even know if he would pick up a trail at all. If the scent was cold in Benares, would he give up and go home or would he continue through every city in the continent, looking amidst all these millions of human beings, for one? He shook his head, shrugged and smiled. 'What the hell,' he said. 'Single.'

Philip struggled through the seething, sweating mob towards his train, found his compartment and tugged at the sliding door. The base jolted out of its runner and stuck. He put down his suitcase and kicked the door back. An excited chatter came from within. He pulled the door open.

The chatter stopped abruptly. Sweat dribbled cold down his back and his sides. He picked up his case, banged his knee on the door-frame and sidestepped in.

The carriage was unbelievably full. On his left was a very dark man with close-cropped hair and an unshaven jaw. Three girls, one a fine-featured beauty, sat straight-backed and silent, their hands in their laps, like star students of decorum at a finishing school. A small girl child in a Juicy Fruit T-shirt and knee-length corduroy shorts sat on the furthest girl's lap. She sucked her thumb and stared hard at Philip with serious brown eyes. A boy with long skinny legs and a bang of black hair over his face stood with his back to the window. His head was bowed low, as though he awaited the pronouncement of sentence from this strange white intruder.

On the right sat an old man. His skin was powdered with the dry white dust of age. His head rested on the window. The skin at his neck was as loose and flaccid as a plucked chicken's crop. Only his eyes swivelled round to watch Philip. They did not blink or move. His breath came in a series of clogged whistles. Each inhalation seemed an immense effort, each exhalation a release.

Ranged along Philip's seat amidst half-empty tiffin trays and cardboard boxes sat a lean crone, then a plump middle-aged woman with an Indira Gandhi streak of white in her hair, and, finally, a round-faced man in pinstripe bell-bottoms, his greying hair smoothed tightly over his scalp.

'Oh,' said Philip, confused. 'Sorry. I'll find another carriage.'

'Nonono, please, kind sir. You are most welcome.' The man in pinstripes stood and placed a hand on his arm. 'Please. Allow me to make you comfortable.'

'No, honestly. Really, I'm sure I'll find another seat.'

The beautiful girl suddenly lost her composure. A little high-pitched giggle trickled from her lips. She looked away, coyly shielding her face with her hand. The others followed suit.

The man frowned, reproving, then turned back to Philip. 'But this is your seat. The train will be all full up.' He picked up a couple of cardboard boxes and pushed them on to the luggage rack. There was a lot of muffled clucking from whatever was inside.

'Well — thank you.' Philip sat and squeezed the suitcase between his knees. The girls giggled again. The man very slowly and solemnly picked up a newspaper full of gleaming, glutinous rice, placed it carefully on the floor and sat again, pressed close to Philip.

'I am Gautam,' he said. He leaned over to make this pronouncement. His breath was as thick and hot as mulligatawny. 'And this is my papa.' He bowed towards the old man. 'My mother, my wife, her sisters Geeta, Manjeet, Ameeta, and her brother Rakesh, and my children.' Each nodded in turn, save the girls, who were too busy being shy, and the old man whose breathing was as persistent as the rasping of a saw. 'We are all going to Benares.'

Philip's heart sank. He squeezed with some difficulty out of his crumpled and sticky linen coat and sat back again. 'So am I,' he said.

'You have been before?'

'No. No, it's my first time in India.'

'Ah. Benares, you know,' Gautam expounded keenly, 'is the most holy city, the city of the great god Shiva. Most holy. You are sightseeing?'

'Er, yes, sort of.'

Gautam's voice dropped. He laid his hand on Philip's forearm again. 'We are on very urgent, important business. My father's time has come. But do not be sad or sorry. We will not be sad.' He shrugged. 'For happy is the Hindu who dies in Shiva's city. His karma is cleansed.'

The train jolted. Philip's body was thrown back against

the seat and a cardboard box landed with a thump on his lap. He looked down. The agitated chicken looked up. It bobbed its head up and down and clucked its disapproval.

'Oh, I am most sorry,' said Gautam. He picked the box up by the string and shoved it hard into the rack. He wagged a finger at it. 'You stay there,' he commanded. 'Be good. And not too much clucky cluck. We have a guest.' He turned and sat again and helped Philip to sweep three or four feathers from his trousers. 'Most sorry,' he said again.

'Oh, it's quite all right,' Philip assured him. 'Don't worry, really.'

'Yes,' Gautam continued, 'if you have bad karma, you know, you might be a toad, an insect, a low-caste individual in the next life. But if you die in Benares, your karma is all clean and good and you go all at once to Shiva's paradise on Mount Kailasa. It is very good to die in Benares.'

'Yes,' said Philip vaguely. 'It must be.'

Doors slammed in rapid succession. A whistle blew. The train jolted again and slid slowly forward. Hands waved on the other side of the window. A puff of black smoke obscured them for a second. When it passed, they were gone. Two men taking a shower under a water hydrant covered their privates. The train gathered speed. The flaking facades of the houses blurred.

Philip drew out a paperback Dick Francis novel that he had bought on the station bookstall. He glanced at the first page and realized that he had read it before. He pretended to concentrate on it all the same. Every time he looked up, the Indian was ready with further information about Benares or questions about London or English literature. Outside, gleaming, flat expanses of rice-fields flashed by, then a great ornate mausoleum on a rise. There were little suburban shanty towns, too, largely composed, so far as he could see, of cardboard boxes and corrugated iron.

The train trundled on. Twilight closed in. The Indians produced food and offered it to him. He refused and pretending to perform a very precise practical criticism of two lines of Dick Francis as the old woman spooned some white pulp into and all over the old man's face. Night fell. Philip had bought a half-bottle of vodka in the hope that it might enable him to sleep. He swigged it down slowly. The girls held a long, excited conversation in whispers in the corner, still giggling whenever they caught Philip's eye. At last they turned out the carriage light. The old man's whistling and gulping were louder than ever in the darkness. It was another hour before Philip nodded off. By then, the children had lost their nervousness. The little girl came over to paw Philip's clothes, inspect his shoes. Gautam had to switch the light on and rattle off a lengthy lecture in Hindi. Throughout the night, the brother-in-law, the unshaven one, leaned forward with his forearms on his knees and stared intently at Philip, his mouth a grim, narrow line. The girls slept with their heads on each other's shoulders. It was five in the morning when at last Philip slept.

'Hotel? Hotel?' the boy seized the handle of Philip's suitcase. 'I take you to hotel, yes?'

Before Philip could speak, the boy was off, nipping in and out of the legs on either side. It was all that Philip could do to keep his suitcase in sight.

'It is a very good hotel,' the boy called over his shoulder. 'Very good, very cheap. Only twenty rupees a night!'

'Yes, but hold on . . .' The boy sidestepped and led Philip out into hot, heavy sunlight. He trotted through a maze of narrow streets strewn with shop-waste and the rotting remnants of food. Everywhere the stench of decay mingled with the sweetness of jasmine and scented oil. Philip almost tripped over a skeletal dog which scavenged in the gutter. It looked up and snarled at him, its eyes dull and grey. Its haunches twitched and trembled. Some white stuff dribbled from its teeth. A cow with a garland of jasmine and marigolds around her neck lounged across the street. She was the only creature that appeared to have leisure. Pilgrims bustled by clutching rosary beads, pots, fruit and flowers. Stalls groaned with souvenirs and the paraphernalia of ritual: ochre shawls stamped with strange devices, plastic *linga*, plastic gods.

The boy stopped, panting, outside a decrepit wooden door. Above hung a crudely painted placard. The letters concertinaed at the end of the line — 'Grand Imperial Guest House.'

'Here,' said the boy. Philip nodded and wiped his brow with his sleeve. The boy grinned and dashed inside. He rang a bell in the entrance hall. There was a strong smell of urine and tobacco. A man with a heavy gut appeared from the shadows at the back. He tucked in his shirt and beamed betel at Philip. 'A room, sir?' He wiped his mouth and swallowed. 'Most fortunately we have a vacancy.' He opened the register with a flourish.

Philip signed where the stubby brown finger pointed. 'Tell me,' he said casually. 'Have you heard of a group that calls itself the Children of Light?'

The man looked up at the ceiling, sucked through the side of his mouth, then shook his head. 'No, sir, it is not at all known to me.'

'They might have a commune here.'

The man shrugged. 'Try the tourist office?'

Philip drew a total blank at the tourist office — and at every one of the forty-three hotels on the official list. No one had heard of the Children of Light, and no one could identify Laura from the photograph he showed them. If he left for Delhi tomorrow morning, he could be back in London, feeling rather foolish, in four days' time. There was nothing to keep him here. He sat down on the battery of stone steps leading to the water's edge and breathed in the rich, sweet spices that filled the evening air. He sighed, and ran his fingers through his hair.

The wind changed. An acrid smell now filled his nostrils and his eyes stung. A pyramid of smoke rose from the neighbouring ghat. A woman wailed. Philip groaned and stood. Death and superstition permeated every brick, every stone.

He walked down to the water's edge. A pilgrim stood waist-deep in the water, his body smeared with ash, his face glowing with a beatific smile. To his left, a flotilla of tiny boats bobbed up and down in the water. Each was made of twisted leaves, and in the centre a small flame flickered around a marigold petal.

A little boy ran down the steps carrying another boat in his hands. He stepped into the water, put the boat down carefully, set the ghee alight, and pushed it. He stood upright and grinned as he watched it float out into the current. He was proud of his handiwork.

He turned then and walked past Philip, no more than a couple of feet away. His silver pendant gleamed brightly on his brown skin. Philip looked back at the leaf boat which listed and spun in an eddy. Then he frowned. 'Hold it,' he said under his breath, then, out loud, 'Hold it! You!' He leaped to his feet and ran up the steps two at a time after the boy. 'Hey, you! Come here!'

The boy turned for a second, then ran. His spidery legs scurried up the steps. His arms worked like pistons. His head jerked from side to side as he looked for somewhere to run, somewhere to hide. On the fourth step from the top, one thin brown arm came in range. Philip lunged for it. The boy spun round, jabbering his fear, pummelling at Philip with his tiny fists.

Philip held him hard. He panted as he pulled himself upright and caught one of the flailing arms. 'Where . . .' he panted. 'Where did you get that?'

The boy looked where he pointed. The pendant on his chest was of seven interlocking stars.

Philip sighed. 'Look. Don't be frightened. Where

did you get that pendant? That's all I want to know.'

The boy shouted something. Spectators rushed to the scene. Little boys punched at Philip's thighs. Adult voices bellowed incomprehensible expostulations. A man with a huge purple lump on his forehead clicked his tongue and attempted to loosen Philip's grip. 'This boy says he is most definitely not stealing from you,' he said in English, shaking his head. 'You are most mistaken.'

'Where did he get the *pendant*?' Philip almost shrieked. Arms waved now. The little boys at his knees yapped like terriers. More people ran up to find out what was going on. The boy, delighted with all this sympathy, put his fist in his eye and wailed like a banshee.

'*Che c'è*?' said a soft voice behind him. 'Whass the problem?'

Philip turned round to confront a face that must once have been European. Dark-brown eyes, deeply tanned and dimpled cheeks. It was a humorous face, the face of a grown-up cherub. 'Is it the pendant?' he asked.

Philip nodded. The man questioned the boy fluently. The boy muttered a few resentful words in reply. 'He said he found it a month ago.' The man smiled. He had very white teeth. '*Chi lo sa*?' He shrugged. 'Maybe he did, maybe he didn't. I dunno.'

'I'm . . . I've been looking for the Children of Light, you see, and . . .'

'Yeah, yeah, OK. I thought as much.' The man flapped a long, elegant hand. 'Let the boy go. He knows nothing.'

'Well, can you tell me . . .?'

Philip relaxed his hold. The boy hesitated, then darted off through the crowd like a fish returned to water.

The man with the dimples beckoned. 'Come on,' he said. 'Let's go somewhere a little quieter.' He turned. A dhoti hung from his narrow shoulders like an empty potato sack. Philip fell in at his side.

'So,' the man said after a while. 'You have lost someone? A brother? A sister? A lover?'

'A friend.'

'A girl.' It was not a question.

'Yes.'

'And from England.'

'Yes. My name's Philip.'

The man smiled. 'And I,' he said, extending a hand, 'I am Pietro, formerly of Milano.'

'Can you tell me where I can find them?'

Pietro did not answer. He just walked on, eyes turned earthwards, that little smile still tugging at the corners of his mouth.

'Look.' Philip spoke through clenched teeth. 'Look, this is important . . .'

'Hey!' Pietro held up his left hand in a halting gesture. 'Easy, huh? Where is your English diplomacy?'

'Time is short,' Philip protested. 'I'm trying to save someone's life, for God's sake.'

'Hah! Listen to the big English bull!' Pietro laughed. 'I find you charging through the streets beating up children and demanding answers to your questions. You know what people do when you behave so? They shut up like *vongole*, like mussels. They laugh at you. Now, if you'd just spent five minutes talking about the weather back there, you'd have learned a great deal. You might even have learned what you want to know. You would certainly have learned something about these people in whose country you come, about the way they think, the way they see. You are going to need all this if you are to help your friend. At the moment, you are looking for — how do you say? A needle in the haystack, no?'

'Oh, Jesus,' Philip muttered under his breath. His fingers opened and closed at his sides. 'Look, can you help?'

'I think yes, maybe,' said Pietro equably. 'But you cannot stamp your foot and demand service and go all crazy when you don't get it. If you want to help your friend, you gotta learn. Keep your eyes and your ears and your mind open. That way, you will understand the people that she has gone to, understand why she has gone, what she is seeking. You will never get her back any other way. Or were you intending to go in with the machine guns and the grenades and pull her away on your horse, huh? 'Cos you know what happens then? She just say, "Thank you very much for a lotta nothin'. *Ciao, bello*," and back she goes again. For good.'

Pietro led the way down some steps to the water's edge. A boatman sat beneath an umbrella. Pietro spoke to him, then turned to Philip. 'Give me twenty rupees,' he said.

'Where are we going?' Philip growled, still faintly embarrassed.

'Sightseeing,' said Pietro jauntily.

They boarded an old wooden barge. It rocked in the water. The boatman loosened the moorings, threw the rope across and jumped aboard. His bare feet landed with a thud as the boat drew away from the bank.

The current carried them slowly down the Ganges. A lone leaf boat of burning petals shimmered unsteadily beside them. '*Ram! Ram! Sita Ram!*' echoed over the water.

The moon and the pilgrims' candles cast a ghostly light on the temples and spires on the bank. Purple smoke surged upwards then stuck, stacked in layers against the blackness. The flames of the cremation pyres quivered with a life of their own, fuelled on the tired limbs they consumed. '*Ram! Ram! Sita Ram!*'

Pietro stood at the bow of the barge, raised his arms and breathed deeply. 'Now, what do you see? Just look and feel. Take it from the air. Can't you sense the magnificence? Can't you see it?' He waved his arms extravagantly. 'It is — it is — as if the cycle of life and death has been brought within the focus of an afternoon.'

Pietro paused and stared at Philip. 'You don't, do you?

Until you do, you will understand nothing. What is the name of the girl?'

'Laura.'

'And you have come to bring her back. For what? To breed babies in surburbia? To be a housewife?' he asked scornfully. 'She has left your world because she has found out much about herself. She has found freedom, she has found compassion, she has felt the call of the spirit. So why should she go back? What can you say to her?'

'Well — er — I'll tell her the facts.'

Pietro laughed. 'I talk of the spirit, and you talk of facts. What facts? I myself have been on the long, lonely search for the last eight years. I'll tell you the facts. While the spirit still burns, how can you waste your time on other things? Once your stomach is full, what more of the material world do you need? The spirit calls. Deny it and you are as dust.'

'But Sananda . . .'

'I know his message is not that of the mystics, but do not underestimate his power. Once someone has found the spirit within themselves, they will not be quick to bite the hand that showed them the way. Some of his followers passed through here a month ago, all smiles and expectation. Maybe *la tua fidanzata*, your lady friend, was with them.'

'But where — where will they be going?'

Pietro shrugged. 'Maybe they go to his commune in Madras, but I think not. If they came this way, I think they go to Nepal, to Pokhara in the foothills of the Himalayas.'

Philip struck the side of the barge with his fist. He stood. 'Well, for God's sake . . . What am I doing here in that case? Every day that passes she's more in their power. I must go there. Now.'

A bird of prey hovered overhead. Something white and gnarled like a yuletide log floated in the water. The bird swooped down and bit into decayed, bloodless flesh.

'*Senti*,' Pietro laughed. 'I will help you, if you will be

helped. I like to travel. I like you, even though you are a bigoted English pig — no, prig. I don't like Sananda, either. He gives out meths and calls it champagne, and after a few weeks on the meths, his followers can no longer tell the difference. I wander, so why should I not wander for a while with you? It is unimportant,' he smiled happily, 'that you will have to pay for all my travel and for very good food and, at least once, for some of your Scotch whisky. All this is quite irrelevant.'

'Whisky?' Philip spluttered. 'What's a would-be mystic doing pining for Scotch, for Christ's sake?'

'And why not?' Pietro shrugged ingenuously. 'Asceticism is very useful sometimes, but it is a very foolish person who turns his back on the finest things of creation. I learned to like whisky when I was in the army. Sometimes I still find myself dreaming of it.'

Philip laughed. 'I'll bet.' He held out his hand. 'All right, you crazy wop bastard. You've got a deal.'

Pietro grasped the hand. 'So now the first thing we do is eat. OK? Then we wait two days. There are things to be done. Then we go.'

CHAPTER FIVE

The bus dipped suddenly and stopped. A cloud of dust came in through the open window, then the flies. Philip wiped his face with a handkerchief, picked up his suitcase and climbed out. He blinked in the strong light, then sighed and nodded.

The air was menthol, sharp and rare. The mountains were perfectly reflected in the glassy lake. Swarming trees and giant cascades looked like mere children's toys amid the massive rockfaces here in the Olympus of Eastern gods, the graveyard of so many mountaineers.

'Some spot for an ashram,' said Philip, as Pietro clambered out of the bus behind him.

Pietro smiled sadly. '*Si, si*. It is beautiful. So the seekers come here. They lose their way. I tell you, here there are more lost souls per metre than almost anywhere on earth.' He shrugged and pointed along the dirt track. 'Needle kids,' he sighed. 'Come on.'

Half a mile down the dusty track, Pietro stopped outside a green breeze-block bungalow. 'We stay here,' he said. 'The Babu Lodge. It is simple, yes, but the food is the best in Pokhara.' A few late-afternoon diners sat silently on benches on the lawn. A white canvas awning flapped gently above them.

'OK,' said Philip, 'let's book in.'

Pietro raised a finger. 'You English! No, first we eat, then we book in.'

They passed a stack of dirty plates and sat at a trestle table. Pietro picked up the menu and studied it.

Opposite Philip, a girl lay slumped over a plate of noodles. Her eyes were closed. A groan came from somewhere deep inside her.

'The man next to her grinned at Philip. His long, greasy hair was scooped up in an elastic band at the back of his head. This is what swung it,' he said proudly. He thumped a lump of hashish resin on the table. It was the size of a cricket ball. 'Some of the best goddamn shit I've ever smoked. Takes you straight there.' He picked up a sheath knife and spread the ball. 'In New Zealand it must have been cowshit, man. You hear that? Cowshit.'

Pietro ignored the man. He waved to a waiter and spoke rapidly in Gurkhali. The waiter took a notebook out of a dirty apron and wrote slowly and deliberately with a stubby pencil. He filled two pages before Pietro stopped speaking, smiled complacently and turned to Philip. 'And what would you like?' he said. He fanned himself with the menu. 'I recommend the *bollito misto di bufalone*. I have just given them the recipe.'

'And how much is that going to cost?'

Pietro shrugged. 'Only money.'

'Yeah,' said Philip. 'My money. In future we stick to the menu, OK?' He frowned testily and leaned across the table towards the New Zealander. 'The Children of Light's commune. Know where it is?'

The New Zealander stabbed his knife deeper into the ball of resin. 'Sure,' he said. 'One of my best mates went and joined 'em. Stupid git. Gets high on scrubbing dishes now. On the far side of the lake. 'Bout four miles from here. Just follow the track round and you can't miss it.'

Philip took the photograph of Laura out of his back trouser pocket and handed it to the man. 'You haven't seen this girl, have you?'

The New Zealander studied it. 'Not a face you'd forget, but they change once they're in that place. Your girl?'

'A friend. Thanks all the same.' Philip turned to Pietro. 'I'm going to take a look.'

Pietro curled his lips and waved dismissively. 'OK, so go. But just remember, you are stumbling in the dark. You don't know anything about these people. We are talking about the spirit, my friend, and we are talking about the East, so just go softly, huh?'

Philip followed the track past the village with its squat, terraced restaurants and cheap lodging houses. After half an hour, the track grew faint and the ground underfoot marshy. He kept close to the side of the lake. His feet squelched in the soft, clinging mud.

A few miles on, he came upon a newly erected barbed-wire fence. It marked a plot around a large, ramshackle wooden house, set on the hillside sixty yards from the lake. Forty or fifty people sat on a clipped lawn on the far side of the fence. Philip heard the sound of a man's voice. He stopped, retraced his steps and climbed up a hillock overlooking the garden. He crawled the last hundred feet and focused his binoculars.

A tall, gaunt Negro sat at the head of the group in a long white kaftan. A silver amulet and a shark's tooth hung around his neck. The rise and fall of his voice floated clearly to Philip's ears on the still air. 'We have been blessed by another day . . . another day in which we brought Father's work closer to fulfilment . . . It was truly a gift from Father . . . a gift of such magnificence that we can never repay, a gift of which we are unworthy . . . But Father in his magnanimity does not ask us to repay, but merely help him through our love and loyalty and our work . . .'

Not a murmur came from the Children as they sat cross-legged in rows, listening. Philip swivelled the binoculars towards the audience. A young girl's face filled the lens. She was European or maybe American, a brunette. A drained, tired, strained face. She closed her eyes as if to blink, but the eyes stayed shut for a moment, then opened only with effort.

Philip scanned the faces. Some were turned away from

him or obscured by others. Some he looked at twice. There was a sameness about them, about the dead, forced expressions, about the dark, heavy rings around the eyes, about the jeans and T-shirts. They were almost impossible to distinguish. But of one thing he was sure. No Laura.

The Negro stopped talking. The Children stretched, stood, and formed a ragged line by a trestle table in the garden. A girl with a large behind waddled out of the house carrying a large tureen. A blonde girl followed with both hands around the handle of a steaming bucket, her shoulders hunched forward. The top of her head was not consistently blonde. The first three inches from the roots were a mousy brown, then the hair changed suddenly to a streaked straw. She put down the bucket and looked towards the table on the lawn. The nose, too prominent for the face, cast a sharp profile.

Philip clutched the binoculars tighter. Deep, cruel rings hung beneath her steel-blue eyes and stained the still-white skin. It could be her, only she was skeletally thin now. Her worn jeans hung loosely on her body. Her hand brushed her forehead, the corners of her mouth turned down. She bent and lifted up the bucket. It was her. Surely. It had to be her. He gulped. His mouth was very dry.

Philip put the binoculars back into their case, stood up straight and took a deep breath. None of the listening disciples seemed to notice him, but two tall men on either side of the gate looked up sharply and moved into the centre. They put their hands on their hips, their weight on one leg, watching his approach calmly, sardonically.

They too wore the statutory faded jeans and T-shirt. The taller and darker of the two wore a gold ring in his left ear. Philip walked straight up to them, nodded in casual greeting and made as though to walk past them into the camp. A brown forearm with thick sun-bleached hairs reached out and held his upper arm. 'Hold it.' The voice was deep, the accent from the southern states. 'C'n we help you, friend?'

'I've come to see someone,' said Philip, 'a friend.'

'Who's the friend, then, friend?'

'An English girl. I've come from England to see her. Laura Callender.'

'Well now.' The man pulled up his jeans with his right hand. 'We gotta problem here. See, no visitors are allowed without the man's say so. Best thing you c'n do's to leave your name an' where we c'n git ahold of you. That way, if the man says OK an' if your friend wants to come out an' see you, we c'n make an appointment for you, you know?'

'That's right,' said the shorter man. He had thin sandy hair and a red bull neck. 'No outsiders are allowed actually into the ashram. Disturbs the vibes, diminishes the concentration of energy.'

'Yes, well.' Philip grabbed the wrist and attempted to pull off the hand. 'I'm not actually leaving until I have seen Miss Callender and she has assured me that she's happy to stay.'

'Listen, friend.' The fingers merely tightened on his biceps. 'I don't think mebbe you heard us right. This here's private property an' we don't allow unauthorized visitors. You jus' leave us your name, huh? Don't make waves.'

'And I have told you.' Philip's voice strained. 'I have told you that I am not leaving. If there's someone you've got to ask, go and ask them now. OK?'

The two guards nodded to one another. The sandy-haired man turned and walked towards the main ashram building. The ring of disciples had dispersed now. The girl with the bucket had gone. There were just a few people going about their business. In the far right-hand corner, by the wooden porch, two men worked a double-handed saw. A girl with sloped shoulders and thin, lanky hair picked up the logs as they dropped. Over to the left, a man and a girl, both naked to the waist, played catch with a softball. A machine — a generator, perhaps — hummed inside the house.

The man returned. 'Guthro says he don't remember the name. Try the village.'

'But I saw her, I'm sure I saw her, not five minutes ago,' said Philip.

The sandy-haired man tightened his hold. 'Look, are you going to go peaceful like or are we going to have to throw you out?'

'All right,' said Philip. He half turned as though to walk away. The Southerner loosened his grip. Philip suddenly ducked down and swung like a discus thrower. The man was thrown off-balance. His arms flailed. Philip's right foot caught him hard in the groin. He grunted, 'Shit!' and jack-knifed. Philip's right forearm smashed into the underside of his nose. As he reeled, doubled up, and fell to his hands and knees, his companion turned and scurried flat out for the house. 'Guthro!' he yelled. 'Guthro!'

Philip walked after him. His eyes were hard and expressionless. His mouth was set. The man and the woman playing catch had stopped now. They stood stock still and watched Philip progress across the compound. His heels kicked up a wake of dust. He reached the porch and placed one foot on the step. Then the door swung outwards fast.

The lean black man loped out. He slammed the door behind him. His shoulders were down, his fists clenched. His eyes were staring and bloodshot. He was a good two inches taller than Philip. He looked sleek and fit and angry. 'Who are you?' he snapped, 'an' what you think you're doin' here?'

'I — I've come to see Laura Callender.' Philip licked his lips. 'Those — those men refused to let me in. Now, can I see Laura or not?'

'I asked you who you are,' the Negro snarled.

'My name is Philip Strickland. I've come all the way from

England to see Laura and I'm not going home till I've seen her.'

'Laura, Laura . . .' The Negro rolled his eyes. 'Think you got the wrong place. Can't remember no Laura.'

'I saw her not five minutes ago,' said Philip calmly, 'and I'll make as much trouble as may be necessary to get to see her. I warn you, I'm a barrister-at-law and I've got friends and colleagues who could make life very, very difficult for your so-called recruitment agencies on both sides of the Atlantic. The law may not touch you here, but it can crush the Green Crusaders in Exhibition Road or their equivalent in New York like swatting flies. We can ban your organization's personnel just like we did with Scientology.'

The black man frowned. Philip heard a movement behind him. The dark Southerner had recovered from his injuries. The blood on his face was clogged with dust. He limped. His teeth showed in a savage snarl. 'I'll get rid of him, Guthro,' he spat. 'Let me deal with him, the *bastard*.'

Guthro raised a huge hand. 'Peace!' he growled. 'Get inside and clean yourself up. And don't attack our visitors. Violence ain't part of our code. Get inside!'

The Southerner's cocky air vanished. His blood-spattered face crumpled like a burst balloon.

'In,' said the Negro. He turned back to Philip. 'Look,' he said, 'I'm sorry if our brothers got a little over-excited. They are only trying to protect our home, same as you would. Listen, if you say this girl is here, of course you can see her. She's not held here. She's not here against her will. She'll tell you that herself. This is just one big family. Everyone's free to come and go as they please. It's just — you must understand — there's so much work to do in the cause that most of us don't like to spend a moment away from the ashram. Still. I'll try and persuade her. Seeing as how you've come all the way from England — hell, you *deserve* to see her . . .' He raised a hand as though to place it on Philip's shoulder. Philip sidestepped. 'Thing is, though,'

Guthro went on, 'you must realize that people change once they have dedicated their lives to others. She must have time to prepare herself. OK? So, where are you staying?'

'The Babu Lodge.'

'So be under the tree in the village square tomorrow — at noon, shall we say? You'll be met.'

'Is that a promise?'

'Hey! Hey!' The Negro exuded bonhomie. 'Stay loose, huh? Guthro always keeps his word. The village square at noon, OK?'

Philip smiled. 'I'll be there.'

CHAPTER SIX

Philip shared the shade of the banyan tree with some water buffaloes, a dozen small children and a couple of trippers. A water buffalo screwed up its nose as a fly came in to land. A child asked for chewing gum. One of the dreamers exposed a dentist's nightmare in a yawn. Philip glanced at his watch, and sighed. 12.30. Laura was late. He knew what he had to do, but the plan he and Pietro had agreed was going to be both difficult and dangerous and the waiting wasn't helping his nerves. Was he going to be able to convince the commune that he wanted to join them — and would he be able to withstand their techniques?

A buffalo enriched the soil and a haze of bobbing flies descended instantly. A tripper opened his eyes, put a tablet in his mouth, groaned and closed his eyes again.

A girl arrived. Shiny black hair hung down to her waist and rippled as she walked. Her thin, elegant fingers tapped quickly against her black cotton trousers. She went up to Philip. Green eyes stared down at him. 'Are you the one who has come to see Laura?' Philip nodded and smiled. He stood. 'I'm Cristiana.' She flicked her head towards a thin Indian boy carrying a basket. His hair was greased back with a neat parting. 'And this is Krishna.'

Philip nodded again. 'But where is Laura? Isn't she with you?'

Cristiana breathed deeply. The outline of her nipples showed through her thin black cotton blouse. 'Oh, she's running late. She'll join us at the picnic site. Are you ready to set off?'

'Er — OK, yes, sure.'

'Laura knows the place. It's not far from the commune. Don't worry.'

They walked some two miles to the north-west in silence until they came to a small grassy shelf overlooking the lake. A slight breeze riffled the grass.

'We'll have lunch here,' she said. 'Krishna, set out the things.' Krishna put the wicker basket under the tree and wiped his forehead.

Philip looked around him. Below, the side of the hill was broken into steps with narrow earth walls. The lower steps were flooded and shone like copper in the bright light. The commune building was just visible in the distance. The track leading from the commune was deserted except for one man with an ox and cart. 'When's Laura coming?' he asked.

'Presently,' said Cristiana sharply. Her fingers were tapping again. She sat down in the sun, ran her hand around the back of her neck and flicked her head. Her hair swooshed out, then fell back. The ends almost touched the grass. Krishna spread a tartan blanket under the tree and laid out papaya, nuts, and miniature mushroom quiches.

Philip sat down next to Cristiana. There was a strong musky scent about her. It was not a perfume. 'Where are you from?' he asked.

Cristiana turned and scowled at him. 'It is not important. Now, I am here.' She put the small finger of her left hand in her mouth and bit the nail with white uneven teeth. The nail was ragged, and the cuticle torn. The others on the hand were long, manicured and unvarnished. 'Eat,' she said. 'Eat.'

Philip picked up one of the mushroom quiches. It was still warm. He bit into it and the pastry crumbled down his chin.

'Drink!' said Cristiana. Krishna reached into the basket, unscrewed a Thermos and handed Philip a cup. His mouth twitched nervously. He did not look up.

'Thank you,' said Philip, and sipped. It tasted like a fruit juice. No sting of alcohol. He turned to Cristiana. 'And what do you do in the commune?'

Cristiana's head turned suddenly. Her green eyes glared at him witheringly. 'Questions? So many questions? It's no business of yours what I do.'

Krishna half smiled, then closed his lips tightly together. He reached forward and picked up a nut.

'Eat,' said Cristiana.

'Please,' said Philip and gestured with his hand. 'After you.'

Cristiana pulled a knife from her pocket. Her arm went back. The blade flickered and thudded into a papaya three feet away. She leaned forward and grabbed the ivory handle, pulled off the papaya, blew over it and ripped the fruit open with her thumb. Her mouth lunged towards it. She pulled at the stringy flesh with her teeth like a hyena at its victim's stomach. Her full lips shone with papaya juice. She pulled again, then purred and licked her fingers one at a time. 'Now, you eat,' she said.

Philip swallowed. 'Right. I eat.' He took a papaya and another quiche. 'When *is* Laura coming?' he asked again.

'She comes,' said Cristiana and stabbed the knife into the earth.

'You know, I would like to learn more about your movement,' said Philip. Cristiana sighed and turned her head away. Krishna nodded, but did not speak. 'I would like to learn. Do you think it might be possible to spend a few days at the commune?'

'You will have to ask Guthro,' she said and began to unbutton her blouse. The dip between her full brown breasts showed, then dark, neat, pointed nipples. She unbuttoned the cuffs, slipped off the shirt and lay back in the sun. A silver amulet rested on her left breast and sparkled as it slowly rose and fell. Philip gulped the fruit juice. Sweat broke out on his forehead. 'Guthro, you say?'

Cristiana's hand reached out towards him, and stroked his trouser leg. Her fingers slowly caressed the cotton. He felt their warmth on his skin. She wriggled closer and looked up at him. Her fingers slid under the cotton and moved slowly and sensuously over his calf. 'You will eat some more. Laura made them, she will be so disappointed.'

A lump stuck in Philip's throat. He cleared it. 'Well — maybe — if Laura made them – just one more.' He reached out for one clumsily. His head spun as he brought the quiche to his lips. The taste somehow exploded and spread through his mouth like a bursting grape.

'There are still four left,' purred Cristiana.

Philip's hands lay heavily by his sides. He felt as if he had lead weights tied to his wrists. 'No, I can't — I couldn't. They are good but . . .'

Fingers reached down his open shirt, and rubbed the hairs on his chest. As they moved, his whole body seemed to move. He gasped and shook his head. The tree swayed, the valley swayed. His lips moved.

Hot breath rasped in his ears. 'Y-you-u w-will-l e-eat-t. T-they-y a-are g-good-d, n-no?'

He coughed. Crumbs of pastry and gobs of egg flew out of his mouth. 'No,' he said, 'no . . .' He flexed his shoulders and pushed at the warm, soft mass on his back. Suddenly it wasn't there any more. His back muscles felt cold and naked, as though they had stripped away the skin. He turned. Cristiana lay on her back. Her eyes were on his face. She smiled. Her hair was deep apricot, her hair was on fire. He blinked, said, 'Oh . . .Oh, God!', blinked again. Her hair was amethyst, a throbbing, pulsing disco light. Philip's heart thudded in time with it like the sound of a basement party. Sweat was very cold on his hot brow, but when he reached up to wipe it away, his skin was soft and dry.

He looked down and gasped. Where before there had

been skin and clothes, now he could see his rib cage; not the outline, but the actual bone. It was greyer than he had expected and covered in little glistening lumps like barnacles. The skin had been peeled back. No, it had become transparent, for nothing was out of place. Within the cage, a thick, deep crimson-and-yellow mass of offal pounded away. It had a strange beauty as it gulped and pumped, sieved, filtered and absorbed. Each moist-lipped mouth that pouted and sucked, swallowed and spat, had its rhythmical place, its role, and above them all, the great heart contracted and spread, shaking the hillside with its insistent beat. 'This is me.' Philip tapped the rib cage and smiled proudly. 'This is me.'

He tried to get to his feet. There was cement in his veins. Slowly now, slowly. The palm trees, the great leafy bushes, even the grasses were dancing just for him in vibrant greens and yellows. 'It's the bossa nova,' he said happily. He tried to click his fingers. 'Yes, definitely. Definitely the bossa nova.'

A butterfly passed by his nose. It flapped its wings very loudly and ponderously as if it were teasing him. Of all the butterflies he had seen, this one was the most perfect and beautifully formed. Red, or was it green, or yellow? A tie-dyed admiral among admirals — the supreme commander of the fleet.

Philip stretched out his arms and hugged the air. He felt a strange affinity for all about him whether it was a pebble, mud or a lonesome leaf. Beneath his right foot he saw a broken blade of grass. He crouched, crooning. He felt as if his own finger had been crushed. The mountains soared above like icicles on fire. The lake flashed turquoise, then aquamarine, then purple.

He shielded his eyes. He could not look any longer. It was blowing his mind. Too much beauty, too fast. Was this what they had been talking about: this sense of oneness; a dissolution of the body, mind and spirit into nature; the rhythmic harmony of all things? Philip threw back his head and laughed out loud. He laughed until he cried, and then he laughed some more.

The girl with green hair laughed too, but it was not really a laugh. It was a cackle. The sound went on and on. Ugly and rasping, it would not stop. Philip covered his ears, and still it went round and round in his skull like the ball in a roulette wheel, clattering. Then her mouth opened, and those teeth seemed everywhere, like a ragged townscape carved of ivory with canine towers and molar motels around a setting tonsillar sun.

A gale blew musk and papaya juice and a voice like a mechanical toy said, 'P-present-t, p-present-t f-for-r y-you.' A jagged nail waved, pointed.

Philip looked down. A black tarry substance covered his legs and rose slowly up towards his trunk. He looked again. It was alive. A thousand little hairy legs crawled over his skin. Ants, hundreds of them, thousands, up, up they came. He shook his legs. Still they came on. His hands beat against his legs and came back dripping with this living liquid. His hands were black, then his arms.

His body shook. His stomach lurched. The muscles in his neck tightened and his jaw locked. He screamed. He screamed again, but no sound came out. All he could hear was the low hiss of the ants' slow advance, and his own heart, pounding.

Only his head was not black now. His body was frozen. None of the limbs would move. Sweat poured off his body, and the ants slurped it up as it fell. An axe cleaved his head at the temples and he closed his eyes. Still they came. They tickled his lips, they ate through his lips. They crawled under his eyelids. They pierced the balloons that once were his eyes. They devoured the grey sponge of his brain.

Vulture's wings flapped above his head. A snake with a

fish's head crawled from his bowels. A man with a wooden leg did a somersault, and he fell to the grass clutching great clumps of it, moaning as though the earth could hide him.

Philip groaned and opened his eyes. Everything around him was black except for a dark-grey haze coming through a barred window. His hands fumbled in something soft. Sheets. A pillow.

A disembodied voice rasped in his ears. 'I, Dr Sananda, am your Father . . . You have been chosen from many to help prepare the path with your love . . .'

Philip's gut shook. His stomach was stuck in a centrifuge. The muscles in his neck tightened, then suddenly they released and a purée of three weeks' dinners poured out on to the pillow. It splashed his hand, his chin. He couldn't move.

Where am I? What's happening? Then it came back: the agonizing torture and that strange elation before the nightmare began, the sense of harmony which had encompassed all about him. It was almost as if – as if he had found a whole new way of seeing. He had felt a profound feeling of peace, a sublime escape, lost in and as one with an order far greater than the parts.

'. . . There is not enough love in the world . . . You the chosen ones will bring about the New Order through your compassion and understanding . . . There is work to be done.

The words rang in his ears. 'Give it a try,' a siren called. 'At least give it a try, if only to understand. You could always leave. Give it a try . . . Give it a try . . .'

'You!' Cristiana prodded the body on the bed. 'Hey, you!' It did not move. She prodded it again. The bloated puff-ball eyes half opened. They blinked at the bright sunlight coming in through the window, closed again. 'Wake up!'

she said, 'Wake up!' and stripped back the bed sheets. They were damp and transparent with sweat.

Philip's hands trembled. He groaned and clutched his belly. His lips quivered. 'B-bitch!' he gasped.

Cristiana threw back her head and laughed. 'Are you ready? Someone's coming to see you.' She nodded to Krishna who stood to attention by the door.

The door creaked and a wedge of brilliant light crossed the room and covered the bed. Philip winced and screwed up his eyes. Then a shadow passed across the doorway. Laura walked in.

Her lips were curved in a parody of a smile; the inanimate rubbery mouth of a bendy doll. Her eyes too were like those of a doll — bright, glazed. They stared in on themselves to some secret place.

The air was foul and stale. Laura looked down momentarily at the vomit-stained pillow on the floor, then turned towards him. 'Hello, Philip,' she said coldly. Her voice was as expressive as a metronome.

Philip stared at her. He strained to sit up. 'Laura,' he said, 'Laura,' then the words broke up into meaningless drooling.

Laura came closer. 'Look, you see me, Philip?' she said. 'Can you see me? You wanted to see me, didn't you? Well, here I am. Here I am.'

Philip shook his head and gulped. 'L-Laura, I w-wanted to . . . I only w-wanted to ask you . . .'

'Whether I'm happy? Just look at me!' She laughed and turned, mocking, to Cristiana. 'Yep, I'm happy. Just go back and tell everyone how happy I am. OK?' She nodded to Cristiana. 'And don't go on bugging me. Leave me alone. I'm not a child any more.'

'Look,' said Philip. 'Oh, Christ!' He pushed himself to the side of the bed. His hand trembled on the mattress. 'I'm getting up. We must talk.'

The door handle rattled. The door swung inwards with a

bang. The Negro strode in. His white kaftan billowed around him in the breeze from the fan. He smiled. 'Hi,' he said. 'Everything all right now?' Then he saw Philip on the bed. He frowned. 'Cristiana, what goes on here?' he demanded, bewildered.

'Nothing, honey,' she shrugged, suddenly full of defensive bravado.

Guthro cast her a heavy look then walked over to the bed. 'What you mean, nothing?' he barked. 'Look at him. What the hell have you done to him?'

Her mouth curled. She put her hand on his back. 'Come on, honey,' she wheedled. 'I just gave him a few nice mushrooms. Open up his mind, you know?'

Guthro's breathing made a deep rhythmical growling sound. 'I told you,' he said between gritted teeth, 'to bring her to him. Let him see that she was OK, and you have to play your damn fool games. What's the matter with you, girl? You could have killed this guy. Do you want us to lose everything, for God's sake? Hey, you.' He nudged Philip with his right fist. Philip stirred. His eyes opened, apparently unfocusing. 'Look, we gotta get rid of him. You've seen enough, Laura? Sorry about this, I really am. You know we don't use drugs and things.'

'I don't mind,' Laura said. 'He shouldn't have followed me. He shouldn't have tried to harm us. Cristiana's right. Maybe it will open up his mind.'

'I'd like to join the commune. Please,' gasped the voice from the bed. It was so unexpected that everyone jumped and turned to look. Philip lay flat on his back still staring at the ceiling.

'No,' said Laura.

Guthro looked up at her, then turned, walked up to her and put his arm around her. Laura leaned back against his chest and smiled. 'No,' he said, 'we're just one happy family here. 'Fraid there ain't no room for no barristers-at-law.'

Philip's heavy breathing suddenly seemed to stop. His

eyes narrowed. Very slowly, as though moving through thick liquid, he pushed himself up and off the bed. He stood rocking for a second, then lunged in a slow-motion haymaker at the Negro's jaw.

Guthro stepped backwards. His eyes flashed white. His right hand jerked up and rammed down on Philip's shoulder. Philip shuddered, reeled slowly round like a top on its last spin and fell loose-limbed on to the concrete floor. He lay there, one eye staring blearily up at Laura, his upper lip pushed back by the concrete. 'Don't much like your friend's manners, Laura,' said Guthro. Cristiana giggled. Guthro's deep, soft laugh rocked through the silence.

'Laura, for God's sake . . .' Philip's knees rose towards his chest. His left hand reached out to her. '*Please*,' he whispered.

Laura looked down at him as though studying a rare, if rather repulsive insect. She took Guthro's arm and leaned up against him. 'You're ridiculous, Philip,' she said. 'Look at you. Just go away and leave us alone.'

Philip raised himself on one elbow. He shook his head rapidly, then stared at her. 'Laura?' he gasped. She looked him straight in the eye. Her expression did not change. Her blue eyes were cold and scornful. Cristiana giggled again. Philip's head shook. He raised a hand to his brow. Then Guthro stepped forward again and his foot struck out. It caught Philip in the lower ribs. He grunted and fell backwards. His crown hit the concrete hard.

'Hey now, brother,' drawled Guthro. 'I don't like to have to do this, but you ought to show some respect for folks' intelligence − not to mention their property − all this shit around here. That's ugly, man, and we don't like ugly.'

Cristiana's fingers tapped against Guthro's arm. Her green eyes stared up at him. 'We did well, huh?'

Guthro's jaw hardened. He slapped her hard across the cheek. 'You went too far. You rubbed your body in dung.'

She did not flinch. Her cheeks slowly reddened and her eyes shone. 'But I did it for you, honey.'

Guthro glowered at her. 'Yeah, like hell, you did. Brimstone and ashes going to eat up your ass.' Cristiana smirked. They both laughed.

Guthro turned and watched Philip as he slowly rose to his feet again. 'Now what are we going to do with him, our barrister-at-law? We don't want him telling tales about your crazy games. He can make trouble, real trouble.'

'So we make sure he doesn't remember anything.' Cristiana smiled. She opened her hand. On her palm lay three yellow tablets, one cube of sugar.

'OK,' Guthro said. 'We got to. Come on! Let's get it over with.'

Philip was not struggling now. Guthro moved behind him, locked his forearm around his neck and pulled his trunk from the floor. Krishna held Philip's dropped lower jaw. Cristiana popped the pills in, one by one.

'Right.' Guthro stood. 'Take him away, Krishna. A good long way away. Give him a walk in the mountains.'

Nightfall was near. Dusk gathered in caves and under boulders and swarmed up the chimneys in the rock. A lone white figure reeled along the narrow path in the foothills beneath Machha Puchhare. His hair was tousled. His fists and his knees were scratched and bleeding. He was naked but for a pair of underpants on his head.

'Bring me my bow of burning gold,' he drooled. Tears streamed down his face. 'Bring me my arrows of desire . . .' He flailed his arms like a crazed conductor. He lost balance, stumbled, fell to his hands and knees. His whole body shook with sobs. 'Bring me my spear . . . Oh, *Christ!*' He sprawled out flat, then rolled over on to his back and gazed up at the iron-grey sky. His chest rose and fell very fast. A black vulture circled high above. 'Hello, bird,' he said, and giggled. 'Bring me my spear . . .' he breathed. A shadow fell over him. 'Oh, clouds unfold . . .'

Soft, warm wool was wrapped around his shoulders. He tried to shrug it off, but firm hands replaced it. Warm, acrid liquid jolted down his throat, dribbled down his chin and chest. 'Bring me my chariot . . .' he blubbered. Then warm, strong arms were around him, raising him easily from the ground. Like a child, he turned his head and shook it as though to make a niche for his head in the other man's chest. 'Laura.' A sob bubbled up through his chest. 'Laura . . .'

'*Stai fermo*,' purred the voice. '*Dormi adesso*, sleep now, *amico*. There is nothing you can do. They have taken her away.' There was a deep sigh. 'English bull. *Grazie a Dio*, I knew I could not let you out alone . . .'

CHAPTER SEVEN

Burp burp . . . burp burp.

'*Pronto*? Signor Strickland's clerk, please.'

'Speaking.'

'I am ringing on behalf of Signor Strickland.

'Has something happened, sir? He's been gone some five weeks. We were getting concerned.'

'He's been ill, very ill.'

'Delhi belly, I suppose. Ate something that didn't agree with him?'

'Er — yes.'

'It's always the problem with foreign food. It's the grease you know.'

'*Porca miseria!*'

'Oh sorry, sir, I was forgetting myself. Italian? Yes. No offence meant. Brenda, my better half, is very partial to your native dishes. Particularly the spaghetti. She goes for the rings in tomato sauce herself. Not so messy. Now you were saying. When can we expect Mr Strickland back in the land of the living?'

'He is still very weak. He must rest. Maybe two weeks.'

'Two weeks! Oh dear, oh dear. And I had a nice case lined up for him. Would run four or five weeks in the High Court. Well, I dare say Mr Petherbridge won't be objecting. Send Mr Strickland my condolences, sir, and kindly ask him to ring me once he's on the mend. Where is he, by the way?'

'Madras.'

'Oh yes, where the curry comes from. Well, sir, thanks for calling.'

'Goodbye.' Pietro put down the receiver, paid the girl behind the desk, and walked out into the bright sunlight. He crossed the road and walked along the beachside esplanade.

A gentle breeze wafted through the palm trees on the fine powder sand. Great rollers from the Bay of Bengal rose and broke on the beach. They swept up the driftwood in their undertow, sucked it out to sea, then propelled it forward as the next great wave tore on to the beach with a shuddering roar. Two small children sifted through the refuse, dark silhouettes in the brilliant light.

Pietro fanned himself with a copy of the Veda, and smiled. He walked over a bridge, turned right and stopped. The gates of the Theosophical Society stood before him. Inscribed on the sandstone wall of the gatehouse were the three Objects of the Society:

To form a nucleus of the Universal Brotherhood of Humanity without distinction of race, creed, sex, caste or colour;

To encourage the study of Comparative Religion, Philosophy and Science;

To investigate unexplained laws of Nature and the powers latent in man.

A chocolate-skinned Tamil with a white turban nodded to him as he passed through the gates. Pietro stopped to sniff the bougainvillaea, then sauntered down a drive lined with palm trees. He passed the red-brick Headquarters Hall, the publishing house and the great banyan tree whose branches could give shade to three thousand people. He walked on through a coconut grove until he reached an old, white colonial-style house set in a shadow-dappled clearing.

A man with a well-tended waxed moustache sat in a rocking chair on the veranda. Only a loincloth covered his wrinkled, parched skin. He looked up as Pietro approached and put down his book. 'Pietro, dear fellow, back already?' he said in clipped, military English. 'Take a pew.' He pointed towards a bamboo armchair with a faded chintz cushion.

Pietro smiled. The bamboo squeaked as he sat down.

'I was just reading a romantic novel. Read quite a lot of them, you know. Terrific stuff. You might think it's rather a cop out, but I reckon I've reached the end of my spiritual development for this lifetime, feel free now to amuse myself with something in a lighter vein. Find the post office OK?'

Pietro nodded.

'Silly of me. As you were going into town I should have asked you to pick up a copy of *The Times*. Test scores, you know. Wireless's on the blink again. How about some tea, mmm? Nitya!' he shouted. 'Nitya!'

A boy shuffled through the french windows out on to the veranda. 'Yes, sahib.'

The man's head turned. 'There you are. Tea for two and some of Mrs Arbuthnot's biscuits, please. And do pick up your feet!'

'Yes, sahib,' the boy smirked and shuffled out.

The man with the moustache pushed down with his heels. The chair rocked. The boards creaked to its rhythm. 'Good to have you back, Pietro, it really is. It's been years. Now, first things first. Did they have room for you both in the Leadbeater Lodge?'

'Yes, Robert.'

'Good. There's a girl staying there who may be worth talking to. A refugee from this Children of Light ashram. We get quite a few of them since they started their Madras shop two years ago.'

Pietro nodded. 'I thought as much. Their natural refuge.'

Robert Yates curled his lip and blew air up through his moustache.

'So that's why you've come here. Can't say they're the sort of people you would choose as neighbours. From what I hear it's more like a sweatshop than a place of the spirit. Gives us occidentals a bad name.'

China clinked. Nitya shuffled forward. He balanced a tray with cups and saucers on a small table. Robert poured out a strong army brew and handed Pietro a cup. 'Sugar?' he asked.

'Thank you,' said Pietro, 'one lump.'

'Quite right. You need it in this heat.' He put four lumps in his own cup. 'This Sananda chap, though, he knows his stuff. Studied under Kailash Baba, no less.'

Pietro whistled silently. '*The* Kailash Baba?'

'The very same. And those daily discourses he used to give in New York were quite something, so I'm told. Used to talk for two or three hours without notes, plucking the words off the ceiling. Broad in knowledge too. Tantra, Yoga, Vedanta, Sufism, all covered. No slouch as a biblical scholar either. I read his translation of the Bhagavad-Gita. Damn good. Excellent notes.' He sat back and raised the cup. 'Now what makes you think this girl you are looking for is in Madras?'

'Well, we know she is no longer in Pokhara. Of that I am certain. Neither is the tall black man. A busload of them left the day after we came down off the mountain. Here to see Father, I assume. Sananda has just been in Madras, no?'

Robert nodded. 'Yes. He was here for some kind of group marriage ceremony, so I'm told.'

'Group marriage ceremony, eh?' Pietro's cup rattled against its saucer. 'I wish we could have come here sooner, but Philip was in no state to travel.'

'Mmm.' Robert twisted the end of his moustache. 'You know, this drugs business surprises me. None of the refugees who have come here have ever been given drugs in the ashram. They don't drink alcohol, they eat little. It's a spartan regime. Nothing but work, sleep and prayer.'

'Yes, but Philip was an outsider. To them he was a non-person, a vassal of Satan, and he came on heavy, eh? He was interfering. He was a threat.' Pietro shrugged. 'If he had died of exposure up on the mountainside — only the jackals would have known.'

'Mmm, just one more European junkie.' A bell rang. Robert shouted. 'Heavens, six already, dinner time. Mrs Arbuthnot won't be best pleased if you're late. She may be a little severe, but she's a goodly soul at heart. You'd better go. You know the way, don't you? Down the path, keep right.'

'Yup. *A presto*. See you soon.' Pietro rose and walked down the path until he reached a squat, white-washed building with a long columned veranda on the upper floor. He walked into a small, dark office. A scratched and dented anglepoise lamp stood on an empty desk. He turned and walked out.

'Pietro, is that you?' called a sharp voice. A door opened. A woman in a brightly coloured dress stepped on to the portico. Cotton carnations swelled over her massive bodice. A steel ring with fifty keys jangled from her belt. 'You're late, Pietro. You're late.'

'Yes, Mrs Arbuthnot. I'm sorry, Mrs Arbuthnot,' he said meekly.

She patted her short grey hair. 'Well, don't just stand there. The dinner's getting cold.'

Pietro followed Mrs Arbuthnot into the dining room where Philip sat at a large circular table flanked by three men and a girl. He looked tired and drawn, his skin sallow.

The man next to him was clad in a black habit. He glanced up as they entered, pushed his heavy black framed glasses further up the bridge of his nose, then turned back to Philip: 'As I was saying, we Esoteric Theosophists believe in the Mahatmas, the custodians of divine wisdom.'

101

Philip nodded listlessly and ate without appetite.

Pietro walked over to the sideboard, speared two sausage-shaped things in batter, took some yoghurt and chopped cucumber and returned to the table. He sat down opposite the girl.

She was plump and pale. Short blonde hair framed her round face. Her eyes were cast downwards. Methodically, she cut the lengths of batter on her plate into tiny pieces, then put down her knife and fork and stared at her plate. For twenty minutes or more, she stayed thus. She did not say a word.

At last the Theosophists left. Mrs Arbuthnot went through to the kitchen with a jangle of keys and a boy cleared the sideboard. The girl still picked silently at her food. Only then did Pietro lean across the table. 'How long have you been here?' he asked.

The girl did not look up. 'Er . . . yeah, a couple of days.' She rested her elbows on the table. Her round face perched on her palms.

'How are you finding it?'

'They have all been very kind, especially Robert Yates. You wouldn't believe it. Bless them. But it's, you know, it's really just a transit stop for me. I'll be going back to the States as soon as some money's wired over. Hey, but, come on. I'm Tammy by the way. What about you guys?'

'We have just arrived after a long journey, and long journeys make the mouth very dry.' He pushed away the glass of water in front of him and nudged Philip. 'Maybe we find some whisky.'

'Pietro, you're incorrigible.'

'Look! The *ragazza*'s mouth is turned down. She is sad. We make her smile, eh?' He leaned across towards her. 'You come with us? We go into Madras.'

She sighed. 'I haven't had a smoke or a drink, a proper drink, in three years.' Suddenly she smiled. 'Yeah, what the hell.'

*

Only three men stood at the copper-topped bar that ran the length of the small cramped room. Their eyes flickered over Tammy as she entered, then flashed at Philip and Pietro. They turned and drank in silence.

'Have you a permit?' asked the barman.

Philip showed him his passport. The man opened it. He smiled and pocketed two bank notes. 'And what is your liking?'

'A large neat gin for me,' said Tammy.

'And two whiskies . . .' said Pietro.

Philip took the drinks over to a table in the corner. Tammy squeezed on to the squeaking banquette. Philip and Pietro sat either side. A freezing draught from the air-conditioning unit hit Philip's back.

'Well, I suppose there is nothing else to do here but get smashed,' said Tammy. She raised her glass, downed the drink in one, and coughed. 'Hey, after so long you forget what it tastes like. Kind of weird.'

Pietro leaned forward and smiled. 'Why all this noble abstention?'

Tammy picked up her second glass. 'I was a member of this group that didn't believe in it. Didn't believe in nicotine either, or drugs, or any of those things that most people go for. Big on work though, and big on spiritual development.'

'In Madras?'

'Well, I joined in the States but was then transferred out here. The Children of Light.'

Philip started.

Pietro glared at him. 'How did you come to join these Children? That's if you don't mind talking about it.'

Tammy took another sip of gin. 'No, it's racing around in my head anyway. Tom met one of them in the street . . .'

'Not so fast,' said Pietro. 'Who is this Tom?'

'Guy I was dating. I met him when he was a rising young star at Harvard Business School,' she sighed. 'Life was different then. I suppose, without realizing it, I was preparing myself for a role as the executive's dream girl.' She giggled. 'My teeth were fixed. My hair looked terrific even in a gale. You could take me anywhere. A man with a martini in one hand and me in the other just had it made.

'One evening while he was studying, we went round the block for some fast food. It was just the same as usual. He was talking about cost-effective displacement of personnel and I was struggling to get my triple-thick milkshake up the straw, when suddenly he flipped. "I've lost my *raison d'être*," he said. I knew something was wrong. It was the first time he had spoken French. Harvard had given him negative feedback.

'We drifted around for a while, thought of joining the Maharishi's levitation course for two thousand dollars a shot. We began saving, but it was a lot of money, and there was no money-back guarantee if we didn't make a millimetre.'

Pietro nodded. 'A trampoline is cheaper, no?' They all laughed. The men at the bar turned and stared as though levity was somehow in bad taste. 'So how did you meet the Children?'

Tammy drained her glass. 'Of course, when Tom met this guy in the street we didn't know then that he was from the Movement, but we went and had dinner with them and later spent a fortnight at their farm in the country. I wasn't too sure about it all – really I wasn't, but Tom was hooked so I went along. No money, no bourgeois conventions, just dedication to the cause; it seemed all right. I felt sure that Tom knew best.' She sighed. 'He was a Harvard man, after all.

'Once we were in, the party was over. We sold stationery,

distributed leaflets, even made some conversions. I don't know how I did it. I didn't even really believe in what we stood for. I guess it was for Tom, and then after a while I did it automatically. It just became a way of life, day after day. I never questioned it.'

Pietro raised his hand. The barman nodded. 'So how come you left the States?'

'Well, one day we were told that Tom had been specially selected by Father to take part in a vital new project in India and would be leaving the next day. They wouldn't let me go too. I pleaded with them. I threatened to leave them, tell my story, and eventually they agreed. Everything was arranged for us. We were taken to the airport, given a couple of charter tickets, and met at the other end.

'I learnt how to embroider belts which were shipped back to the States and sold on the streets. Tom has always been good with his hands and so he was put in charge of the furniture workshop. He began to do some really good stuff. Some of the big department stores have taken it. I was really proud. If only . . .'

The barman came over carrying a copper tray. 'Another drink?' asked Pietro.

Tammy nodded and smiled. A soft, seductive glow had entered her eyes. She seemed to have forgotten Philip altogether. 'I suppose nothing went wrong with our relationship. Just nothing right. It was kind of on automatic pilot. There was no sex in the commune, but I suppose I just got used to that. I guess you can get used to anything. I always thought one day we would get married. Father believes in marriage. He believes in babies for a new race worthy of the New Kingdom. Some day, I thought. Then the day came. Guthro announced that Father had examined the signs. The auspices were right for a mass marriage of his Madras Children.'

'When was this?' asked Philip nervously.

'The ceremony? Father arrived just a few days ago. The longest four days of my life. His jet landed. We all paraded in the assembly hall. Father spoke to each of us for a few minutes — I was so excited my tongue was all twisted — then he slowly walked down the line and began the pairing. When he reached Tom, he pointed to some Swedish bitch who had only just arrived. And me — me he put with a pimply Frenchman.

'I was nearly hysterical. I went up to Tom and asked him whether he was really going to marry that bitch. I had stayed with him for three years in that living hell, and now he was going to throw me over.'

She rested her head on Pietro's shoulder. 'I couldn't believe it! It wasn't for love! "What about me?" I yelled. "You're not going to go with her." He just pointed to the Frenchman. "Father knows best," she mimicked. "He knows who I should marry. I thought I loved you but I was mistaken. We must not think of ourselves, but the future of mankind. We must be thankful. Without divine guidance we would have made a terrible mistake. With our God-given partners we will make babies worthy of the new race!"

'Babies!' she squeaked. 'It just grossed me out. Tom screwing that Swedish bitch for Sananda so that a whole new generation could be plagued by his plastic busts! It was just too much. I didn't think that he would go through with it. I mean, how *could* he? Love, if nothing else, must win through. The ceremony was the next day. When it came to the crunch, I thought he'd feel it. I knew it.' She closed her eyes. Her torso swayed.

'Sananda presided. The assembly hall was decked with the garlands we had painstakingly tacked together the week before. Twenty couples lined up. Twenty, for God's sake! Next to me was this pimply Frenchman grinning away. The nearest he had ever got to an orgasm was squeezing his zits. Tom and the Swede were in the line just before us.

'Sananda went through the preliminaries, then turned to Tom. "My child, to you I give your sister Elsa as wife to cherish and to hold according to the laws of the New Kingdom. Do you take this woman?" "I do," said Tom. He didn't even gulp. "Tom!" I cried, "Tom you filthy . . .!" I forget now what I called him, then I ran from the hall. What could I do? It wasn't a lawful marriage — Dr Sananda has never been ordained or anything — but I had lost Tom.

'I felt sure that he would come to his senses in the cold light of the morning. That's why I stuck around here, so that I could be near him — so that he could come to me. Some hope.'

Tammy drained her third glass, then lay back on Pietro's shoulder again. 'It was me in the end that made the final gesture. I went back there today to say goodbye. Tom was so offhand. After all the years we had spent together. I was like a stranger. He just stood there chiselling away at a coffee table, making polite conversation as if nothing had happened. He said that Father had complimented him personally on the tables and that there would be a display of them at the special exhibition at Madison Square Garden in September — as if I cared.

'I told him that I was going back to the States.' She laughed. 'And would you believe it, he shook my hand. He actually stopped work and pushed out a sawdust paw at me. I thought I was going to throw up. "I wish you every happiness and Father's blessing," he said. I laughed in his face. It's funny. In a way it made it easier. He killed it stone dead. There was nothing of that impetuous college boy left. I guess in a way it was the memory of those times in Cambridge that had really kept us together. That and my idiocy.'

The bar was empty now except for the barman. He slowly polished a glass. Philip moved uneasily on the banquette.

'There wasn't a girl there, an English girl, L-Laura Callender, was there?'

Tammy started. 'Laura? Sure. You know her? Hey, what are you guys playing at?'

'We were hoping to see her. This ceremony, did — er, was Laura paired off?'

'So that's it!' Her mouth hardened.

'I've got to know!' pleaded Philip.

Tammy smiled then shook her head. 'No, Laura wasn't married to anyone, though I thought she was going to be. Father talked to her for nearly twenty minutes. They seemed to get on real well and that was that.'

Philip sighed with relief. He wiped a bead of sweat from his forehead. 'How's she getting on?'

'I didn't know her that well. She was one of the new recruits that came down with Guthro and Cristiana from Pokhara. She was in the workroom with us, embroidering dresses, making belts. Seemed to get the hang of it quite quickly. That's really all I know.'

'Does she ever go outside the commune?'

'She didn't, not while I was there. Only Children on special details go outside. She's still too new.'

'So how can I reach her?'

'Knock on the door and they'll never let you near her.'

'But what she needs is time away from all that pressure.' Philip paused. 'Look, Tammy, we couldn't ask you a favour, could we? You wouldn't draw us a map of the commune?'

Tammy smiled drunkenly. Her fingers pawed Pietro's thigh. 'A map. Hey, that's a funny thing to ask a girl, isn't it?'

Philip paced up and down the veranda. Sweat stained his shirt. 'What *else* do you suggest?' he asked angrily.

Robert Yates rocked back in his chair. Pietro took a sip of

lime soda. 'It's the brutality of the thing,' said Yates. 'If only you could just talk to her normally, sound out her feelings.'

'But how?' He turned. 'For God's sake, how? I tried in Pokhara. They would never let me see her alone, and even if they did, what could we do? She has been with them now for nearly three months. We must get her thinking for herself again. We won't do that, we can't do it, unless we can get her away from them.'

Yates twisted the end of his moustache. 'But not everyone believes in the Mahatmas. Imagine — just imagine — if each time someone came down here, parents and friends sent *kidnappers* to rescue them. You must allow freedom of religious thought, freedom of expression. What you are suggesting is some kind of inquisitorial denial of such freedoms.'

'No, it's not the same,' said Philip. 'You don't take potential converts to camps, deprive them of proteins and sugars, deny them sleep, subject them to weeks of lectures, never even telling them you are Theosophists. It's that type of pressure which creates Children of Light, not the creed. In that environment, it is the techniques that are all important, not the message.'

'It's dangerous ground, Philip, dangerous ground. What would you have done if Laura had joined a closed order of nuns?'

'You don't join them overnight. There is a long period of preparation without pressure, which is as it should be. Anyway,' he shrugged. 'Laura wasn't the type.'

Yates smiled. 'I didn't think I was the type either, and I heard the call. What do you think, Pietro?'

Pietro leaned forward hunched up on his chair. 'There is a smell about the Children and it is not the smell of enlightenment, but of spirits crushed. But coercion, that's the very thing of which we accuse Sananda. How would you feel if you were kidnapped? Your one thought would be to get back to your friends. If ever before she had doubt, it would be squashed. I don't like it. If something went wrong, that would be the end. We would be cutting off her one line of escape.'

'So what do we do?' said Philip. 'Leave her there and hope that one day she'll ring home? Christ! Every day she is with them their hold over her is stronger. I saw her in Pokhara, for God's sake. She was a shell, a monster. And you witter about sensibilities? We owe it to her to try.'

'Philip,' said Pietro, 'you are still not well.'

Philip's fists slammed against the side of the house. 'I don't care. I'm going in to get her. I'll get her tonight. All I want is three days. Just three days. If, after that, she still wants to stay with the Children, she will be free to leave.'

'It is brain surgery with a trowel,' said Pietro, 'but if you have nothing else . . .'

Yates stood. 'Only three days. You promise that? Scout's honour?'

'I think,' said Pietro, 'that will be all we will need. In three days, we will know whether she has truly found her chosen path, however tawdry and rotten it may seem to us. And in three days you, Philip, must accept her decision, whatever it may be.'

'Done,' said Philip. 'I will accept it. Whatever it may be.'

The Lodge bungalow stood by the beach about a mile from the Society's grounds. In the cool of the evening, Philip and Pietro set to work. They stripped the bedroom of all its contents except for the two beds and four chairs. They removed the electrical fittings. Only one overhead light remained, taped to the ceiling out of reach. They boarded up the windows, then fixed an outside bolt on the bedroom door.

'All ready,' said Philip.

Pietro nodded. 'Now we sleep. We sleep four hours. Then we go visiting.'

110

CHAPTER EIGHT

Light burned in only one room in the Leadbeater Lodge. A regular snore rattled through the wall.

Philip stood in front of the mirror with a row of small pots by his side. He covered his fingers with Vaseline and ran them through his hair. He darkened his skin with shoe polish and face cream until it was black and shiny, then smeared the mixture over his arms, chest and legs. He checked the result in the mirror, then donned a polyester half-sleeve shirt and a pair of loose, ill-fitting trousers. 'Pietro? How do I look?' he asked.

Pietro was as black as he. His eyes glinted against his wetsuit skin. 'Hey, what you think this is, the *commedia dell'arte*? Devote a little more care, a little more imagination.'

'But this fancy dress was your idea.'

'Of course it was my idea. It is a good idea. Who else goes into the ashram except for local craftsmen, huh? And a black face — no European looks so closely at a black face, and if we go in at night . . . we are camouflaged. So, a good idea? *Certo*. More polish. More Vaseline.'

Philip returned to the mirror and rubbed more make-up into his skin.

A car crunched and rumbled, waiting outside. 'Good. You have the map?' asked Pietro.

'Yes.'

'So, let me look at you. Oh, yes. Very beautiful. Now, we go.' Pietro picked up a small canvas bag, switched off the light, and they clattered down the outside staircase.

Yates was at the wheel of the black car in the driveway. 'I hope you didn't wake Mrs Arbuthnot or there'll be hell to pay in the morning.'

111

Pietro climbed in the front of the car, Philip in the back. 'I think she sleeps soundly, no? Only the Mahatmas could wake her. I hope sleep comes so easily to Guthro and the Children.'

Yates nodded, lowered the handbrake and drove off without a word.

After nine or ten miles the car turned off the tarmac and bumped along a narrow dirt track. Fifty yards on, the headlights caught a modern brick wall in their beam. The car stopped. Pietro and Philip got out and untied a ladder from the roof-rack. A gentle breeze carried the soft sounds of the surf in the salty air. Cicadas creaked like rocking chairs. Silently, Philip placed the ladder up against the wall. Pietro pushed against it and nodded.

'Good luck,' whispered Yates.

Philip was the first to climb. The ladder was some eight feet long; the wall another two. Jagged green glass crowned the top. Philip stood on the last rung and leaned back. Pietro threw up a blanket. Philip folded it and smothered the spikes, then put his left foot on the rung and pulled himself up. He felt a sharp pressure on the ball of his foot. He jumped quickly, bending his knees as the earth came to meet him. He made little sound. He turned, caught the canvas bag, then Pietro landed lightly by his side. 'OK?' he murmured.

The moon was in its last quarter. It was very dark, and a heavy mist made the garden murkier still. Ahead, there was the diffuse outline of a building. They made their way slowly towards it, their feet rustling in the long grass. They stopped once as something howled not a hundred yards away, then Philip tapped Pietro's arm and they moved on side by side.

They almost bumped into a wide, heavy form in front of them. Philip paused, then switched on a small flashlight. Its beam broke on a shiny, polished bumper and black metal. He went closer, pressed his face against a side window and ran the beam over the old-fashioned wooden facia. He smiled and nodded.

They tiptoed on for ten yards to the wall of the building. A window stood to their left. Philip flickered torchlight over the map and pointed to the right. They slid around the side of the building, staying close to the wall.

They reached a small door. The smell of cold cooking fat came from inside. Philip stopped, crouched, and laid his ear against the door. Silence. After half a minute, he clutched the iron knob and turned it a fraction, then a fraction more. It grated. He clenched his teeth, turned it quickly and pushed. He leaned against it. The wood groaned and the sound seemed to splinter the air. Still the door did not give. 'Come,' he whispered.

There was still no sound from within. Not a snore. Not a murmur. Only the chirp of the cicados. After a couple of minutes' deep breathing, they retraced their steps. A small window stood at shoulder height: wire mesh mounted on a wooden frame. Philip checked the map again, then flashed the light inside. A large steel machine filled the centre of the room. Cartons lay on the floor. No sleeping bags. No faces.

Philip unzipped the canvas bag and pulled out a pair of wire cutters. He clipped the bottom of the mesh close to the wood, then nodded, clipped again. It was a crisp, quick sound. He cut the mesh on two sides and pulled it back.

Pietro crouched, and made a cradle with his hands. Philip pulled himself up on to the window ledge. He climbed through the ragged mesh, then twisted his body round, held on to the frame and slowly lowered himself on to the wooden floor. Pietro followed.

In the quick flash of the torch they saw hundreds of plastic models of Sananda, a foot high, lining the shelves all round the room. Some were plain shiny white, others painted and mounted on purple velveteen bases. Each had a hand raised in blessing. 'Some little army,' murmured Pietro.

In the centre of the room, a long corrugated intestine ran from the top of the machine into a metal box filled with deformed embryos; Sananda without arms, Sananda with misshapen feet, with stretch-mark smears across the face, with no face at all.

Philip pushed the wire mesh back into place, and crept over to the door in the right-hand wall. He turned the handle. He hesitated for a moment, then swung round it into the darkness.

The air was dusty with wood shavings. There was a strong smell of glue and polyurethane. Blocks of treated timber stood against the wall. On benches lay chisels, hammers and planes. Finished coffee tables were stacked at the end of the room.

His foot struck something hard. He breathed a curse as the echo died. He cut off the torch. A cough came through the wall, then a creak and a yawn. The back of his collar was damp now. He waited a minute more. Silence again. He flashed the torch over the low, packed wooden crate in front of him it was stencilled *Bloomingdales, New York*.

Pietro crept across to the door set in the left-hand wall and opened it an inch. He gasped as the latch clicked shut. He paused for a moment. He was breathing fast. 'They're in here,' he whispered. 'Boys' dormitory. The assembly hall.'

Philip sighed and flashed his light on the map again. He moved over to the second door. He bent down, turned the handle carefully, slowly. The hinges squeaked. In front of him was a passage wall. He looked down the corridor, then again beckoned to Pietro.

A grey band of light crossed the passage on the right. A door was ajar. There was a sound of slow, rhythmical breathing. Beneath grey mosquito netting a black head lay on a pillow facing him. The eyes were closed, the mouth slightly open. A girl slept on the far side of the bed. Her back was turned to Guthro, but her hand reached back to rest on his thigh. Her long blue-black hair sprayed over the sheets. She groaned and rolled over. Cristiana. Philip stepped quickly back. He followed Pietro's silhouette at the end of the passage.

He reached a staircase. The banisters were warped and bent, the stairs bleached and worn by countless feet. He put a foot on the bottom step and the wood seemed to cry out in protest. Each step creaked as Pietro followed. In the still air, their progress sounded like a gaggle of geese in conference.

Suddenly the honking stopped with one little squeak. There was the sound of humming above. A high-pitched girl's hum. Philip heard footfalls at the top of the stairs. Ceramic struck tin. Water slopped, swirled. They waited. The footsteps receded. A door shut. They went on.

They reached a landing. A door stood to the left. Philip opened it a fraction. Bodies everywhere. All girls. The girl closest to him lay on top of her sleeping bag in a long white nightdress. Her arms were entwined around a pillow as if it were a lover. Rows of sewing machines split the room. Racks of dresses in polythene bags lined its walls. But the faces were indistinguishable; all the same anonymous grey.

Philip closed the door. He put a finger to his lips. They walked a few paces down the passage. 'She must be in there,' he whispered.

'I know, but we can't go in.' Pietro glowered at him. 'It will be like *carnevale*.'

Philip clenched his fist. The palm was moist. 'We've got to, though. It's our only chance . . .'

'Be reasonable,' said Pietro. 'We are trying to bring her out, not get ourselves killed.' He bit a nail. 'No, we must choose our time.' He turned away and walked down the passage to the last door. He stopped, sniffed, then pushed the door open. Two primitive latrines led off from a cloakroom with washbasins and a cupboard. Pietro opened

115

the cupboard. A few brooms and mops stood in the corner. Buckets lay on the floor.

'Look,' whispered Pietro. 'When will Laura be alone? Not in the machine-room. This is the only place.'

'For Christ's sake! Not here.'

'It's not how you saw it, eh? It's not romantic, so what did you want? You wave a rose in front of her nose, you whisper, "Laura, my darling," and stars come in her eyes and she follows you to the end of the earth. Is that what you see? This may not be romantic, but it is practical, very practical.' His voice sharpened. 'Now what is it to be? The latrine or the cupboard?'

'OK,' said Philip. He reached into the bag, pulled out a marlinspike and cut a small hole in the cupboard door at head height. Pietro rearranged the brooms, then made an extravagant courtly gesture and followed Philip in.

Philip stood with his eye pressed to the spyhole. He watched throughout the night as the girls shuffled in and out in their nightdresses and long white T-shirts, while Pietro sat, eyes half-closed, hunched up on the floor among the brooms. The air in the cupboard grew fetid and stale. Twice he shook Pietro and they changed places, but neither time could he sleep. Though his eyelids were heavy, his blood raced, his body was tense.

The only sounds he heard were the dribbling and hissing of a tap and Pietro's slow, regular breathing, until suddenly, at first light, the twang and strumming of a guitar broke the silence. He heard yawns, moans and high-pitched chatter. An amplified recorded voice rose above the guitar. 'Welcome, my Children, to another day. Each minute is precious to us, each minute brings the New Kingdom closer . . .'

Footsteps came nearer. A girl yawned and switched on the light. Her dark hair fell over her cotton nightdress. 'I hate mornings, I just can't help it,' she said to another girl. The latrine doors closed.

Five other girls passed through before Philip caught sight of a mane of streaked straw and three inches of mousy root. The head turned. Laura. His mouth went dry. No one made a sound, but it seemed that someone shrieked inside his skull. This was such a distant and sad place. Laura. His Laura.

'Hurry up in there,' she said, and banged on the door. 'We'll be late for dedication.'

'Hang on a minute.'

Laura hovered impatiently by the door alone.

Philip nudged Pietro. Pietro nodded, pulled the cork from a bottle and covered the neck with a rag. He upturned the bottle twice and handed the rag to Philip.

Slowly, silently, Philip pushed open the cupboard door. Laura turned around lazily, relaxed.

Her eyes snapped open, her skin went pale, her lips white. 'No,' she yelled. 'No, no, no!' She threw back her head and screwed up her eyes. Her mouth opened. One sharp cry shuddered from her dry lips, then Philip pushed the damp rag on to her face, swung his arm around her neck. She strained against the rag. Her head lurched sideways. She spat something.

'Are you all right?' The voice came from the latrine. 'Is that you, Laura?'

Her body went limp and heavy. He slipped his arms under hers and dragged her towards the cupboard. Her heels scraped the floor.

'Is that you, Laura?'

Philip closed the cupboard door. He crouched down, squeezed her tight to him and muttered a prayer. Her tired, strained face was still, her breathing slow, her body warm. He ran his hand across her face. He stroked it very gently.

The door of the latrine clicked open. 'Laura? Laura?'

The other door clicked. 'Where is she?'

'Dunno. Do you think it's that rat again?'

'God, I hope not.'

A gong sounded. Feet ran down the stairs. 'Come on, we're late for dedication.'

'But . . . Laura . . .'

'She must have gone on ahead, come on.'

Philip nudged Pietro and nodded. He opened the door and together they carried Laura out into the cloakroom.

'Where do we go now?' whispered Pietro. 'Same way as we came in?'

Guthro's voice came through the wall, then the singing. Philip grinned. 'Why? There's a car out front. Meet you round the back in five minutes exactly. OK?'

He crept down the stairs and turned left. Two girls were in the kitchen to the right. One glanced at him. She stiffened. 'Just a moment.' Philip nodded reassuringly and walked straight past her out into the sunlight. He saw his sleeve now. It was streaked with black dye. He quickened his pace.

The black car stood ahead of him, its bumpers gleaming in the sun. Fifty yards away, four or five dark-skinned workmen were walking up the drive. He pressed the button on the handle of the car. Locked. He looked for a stone, found one and threw it against the side window. The window shattered. The workmen turned. One of them shouted 'Hey?' and started running towards him. The singing inside stopped.

Quickly he pushed his hand through the hole in the broken window. Then he looked up and saw another car, a delivery van, twenty paces away. He ran across to it. A key was in the ignition. He jumped inside and turned the key. The engine rumbled, died, rumbled again, then roared.

He released the handbrake and slammed the van into reverse. It jolted, then spun and bumped over the grass towards the back door. It stalled, Pietro emerged and ran. He reached the van just as the engine coughed back into life. He pushed a large shape wrapped in a blanket into the back, slammed the door and jumped in.

His back hit the car seat hard. The van growled, spat, roared and leaped towards the ashram gates. A crowd stood before them. Brown and white faces, arms waving. He put his foot down. A dozen of them rushed at the van. He swerved. The suspension clanked. He smelled burning rubber. The van skidded past them on to the dirt track leading to the gates. It was before them now — a barrier across the road. The Children ran waving and shouting down the drive after them. In the mirror, he saw Guthro standing alone on the ashram steps.

The guard standing in front of the barrier stopped flapping his hands and somersaulted into the bushes. Philip kept his foot hard down. On the straight they were gaining speed — forty, fifty, sixty; it was as much as they could do. Any second now. He gritted his teeth and pressed down hard on the steering wheel. The metal dented. Wood cracked. The van shook. He was flung forward. His chest smashed against the steering wheel. His lungs emptied. Then the barrier swept along the bonnet and struck the windscreen. He raised his arm, ducked and closed his eyes. Glass flew in tiny pieces like a hailstorm. It struck his face and his hair. He looked up, and opened his smarting eyes. The road was ahead of them. He whooped. 'Jesus!' he laughed and pushed back his hair. 'We did it!'

'Yes,' Pietro said quietly. 'God save us. We did it.'

CHAPTER NINE

Laura lay asleep on the bed. Her blonde hair, tousled on the pillow, framed her face like a halo. Her white cotton nightdress rose and fell at each breath.

Philip paced up and down the room. His footfalls rattled and rang on the bare bleached boards. A white bandage was wrapped tightly about his left wrist. Pietro sat in a chair in the corner. He was reading. A small cut crossed his right cheek. Narrow shafts of light slid between the boards nailed over the windows. The rollers smashed on the sand outside.

Laura stirred. She turned over, stretched her legs and rubbed the back of her hand against her forehead. Her eyes snapped open. She blinked, looked around her, then sat up suddenly.

Philip turned. Their eyes met. He took two steps towards her. 'Now, Laura . . .'

She closed her eyes and screamed. She lifted her hands to her bloodless face and screamed again. 'No, no, no. Get away from me! Don't come near me! No! Devils!'

He stood his ground. 'Laura, there are no devils here, only friends.'

Her wide white eyes swivelled quickly around the room. She took a deep breath and muttered, 'Father, give me strength.' She jumped off the bed and raced to the door. Her hand grabbed and twisted the handle. 'Damn! Damn!' She cried. Her fists beat against the wood. Her body buckled and slid to the floor. 'My God, what are you trying to do to me?'

Philip still stood on the far side of the room, hands uselessly outstretched. 'Laura, we are trying to help you . . .'

120

'Help!' she cried. 'You call this help? It's kidnap! It's rape! For Christ's sake, there are homes for people like you. My God!' She swallowed. 'Look, why don't you just let me go back to my friends. I promise we won't bring any charges, OK?'

Philip walked towards her. 'You must understand . . .'

Her hands shot out. 'Stay away from me. Stay away! Who do you think you are? God, Satan, the Angel Gabriel? Just look at yourself, Strickland! Ignorant, unimaginative, boring little arsehole! What right — what fucking right have you to barge in like a little boy playing soldiers? This isn't games we're playing, Philip. This is *life*. Can't you grow up? Can't you leave me alone? If you don't open that door this minute and let me go, I'll make sure you spend the next three years mouldering and sweating in an Indian jail. Do you understand? Guthro's got influence. Open that door! Open it now!' She pointed imperiously. Her fist beat against it.

'No, Laura.' Philip shook his head. 'No, I'm sorry.'

'And I'll get you disbarred. No more cosy cases. No more Inner Temple. This is assault, Philip. Kidnap and assault.'

'Laura . . . you are among friends.'

'My friends are at the commune. My life is there. Let me go back. Let me go. Dear God, you are going to regret this. Look — look, what do you want of me? What's going on in your warped little mind? Is it my body? Is that it? Has your poncy little ego been bruised? Is that why you have been following me? OK, so I'll strip off, let's do it. Then I can go back, OK?' Laura stared at him, her eyes hard as crystal, her lips clenched tight.

Philip felt he was going to retch. 'All we want to do is talk, Laura, talk. No one is going to harm you.' He pointed to a chair. 'Why don't you sit down? Make yourself comfortable. Would you like a cup of tea?'

She did not move. 'You're not going to turn me over to the deprogrammers, are you? Please, whatever you do.'

'No,' said Philip. 'Just talk.'

There was a knock on the door. Pietro laid down his book and walked over. 'Who is it?'

'Tammy. I've brought some tea.'

'OK,' he said. 'Philip, hold her.' He pulled a key from his pocket and unlocked the door. Tammy came in with a tray. Pietro pushed it quickly shut again.

Laura looked at Tammy with raw hate. 'Oh, yeah,' she sneered, 'I should've known you'd be here. Traitor! Satan's handmaiden. Huh! We all know how he got to you. Lust! So Father's choice was not good enough for you. Little bourgeoise.' She spat on the floor.

Philip took a cup off the tray. 'Sugar?' he asked Laura. She did not reply. 'Oh yes, one lump, that's right, isn't it?' He handed the cup and saucer to Laura. She took it with a shaking hand. Philip smiled and squatted down beside her. She returned the smile, then suddenly her arm jerked back. The china saucer spun and shattered. She dived down after it. She grabbed a fragment. She lunged at his throat.

He fell back gasping. He caught her wrist when the little china dagger was just inches from his neck. Her thighs were warm through his shirt, her breath on his face. Her eyes were flecked with red. Blonde hair masked his vision. He pushed upwards. There was force in her trembling arm. Unnatural force. He gritted his teeth and pushed it slowly back.

Suddenly he was gazing up at the light bulb, the criss-cross beams. He pulled himself up. Laura sat at his feet. Her hair covered her face. Her legs were obscenely splayed. 'Father,' she whispered. Tammy yelped. Laura's right hand moved up towards her own neck. 'Father, help me . . .' she said again.

'No!' cried Philip. His hand shot forward. He could not reach her.

But a large brown hand wrapped tightly round her wrist and squeezed. Laura's fingers opened slowly. The green sliver of china fell from her hand. '*Basta, bimba*, enough, child,' said Pietro. 'Whatever you want to do with your body. Whatever you want to do with your soul. That is not the way. Better to go to the wrong place than to go nowhere.'

A huge sob corkscrewed up from Laura's stomach and forced its way through her open lips. She covered her face with her hands and her body curled slowly into a foetal position on the floor.

'My God.' Philip sat there staring at her jerking form. 'My God. She's sick!'

Laura did not speak again that day. She would not eat. She would not move off the floor. Her eyes lost their focus and she chanted to herself. When it grew dark, she curled up on the bed. Tammy stayed with her. Philip and Pietro went through into the adjoining room.

'I can't believe it,' said Philip. 'It's not the same girl.'

'What did you expect? We must be gentle.'

'But those things she said — that's not Laura.'

Pietro smiled. 'Not the girl of your dreams? Come, Philip, don't tell me you are having doubts. What do you want, a robot? Let her sleep, that is the most important. Food and sleep, the only miracle-workers I know. Oh yes, and drink. Maybe I could manage some whisky.'

Tammy banged on the door at eight-thirty the next morning. 'Laura's awake.'

Philip rose and stretched, picked up the bundle of papers on the table and went into the room. Laura was sitting up on the bed in her cotton nightdress. 'Did you sleep well?' he asked.

'Twelve hours,' whispered Tammy on the way out.

'I want to go back,' Laura recited dully. 'I want to go back. How long are you going to keep me here?'

'Just as long as it takes to talk this thing through. We've got all the time in the world. If you want to sit there and chant, it's fine by me, but you will just be here that much longer. Will you talk?'

'There is nothing to talk about.'

'Come on.'

'You've got no right.'

'Look, Laura, Pietro and I have risked our necks to get you here. We're not going to brainwash you or assault you. All we want is to talk. You have heard only what Guthro and the Children wanted you to hear for the last three months. You are an intelligent girl, Laura. All we want to do is put the other side of the argument. If at the end you still believe Dr Sananda is the Messiah and want to devote your life to him, that's fine by us, just fine. We will unlock the door and you will be free to go. All we ask is a chance. Is that a deal?' She did not reply. She just stared at him. 'Is that a deal?'

'Philip,' she said hesitantly, 'if only you understood. I've changed. I'm not the girl you used to take out in London, the shy little art student. I'm a new person and a far happier one than I ever was before . . . until yesterday. But I'm not afraid. Father will save me.'

'But, Laura.' Philip sat on the end of the bed. 'Please just believe that we want what's best. Maybe you are right, but just give us a chance.'

'You are trying to pull me back to my old ways. I don't want it. It's so distant now I can laugh at how foolish I was, and how aimless and arid my life was before I found Father. If only you understood, if only you could see the futility of your own life. I pray for you sometimes, Philip, I pray for you. How can you live with your soul black with guilt, fallen, lost, without feeling it?'

'It's just your imagination, Laura. I know I'm far from perfect, but . . .'

'You're ridiculous, Philip,' she snapped. 'You're ridiculous. Get out, can't you! Just get out and leave me alone!'

Philip stood and sighed. He walked over to the boarded window and looked out through a crack. The tide was out. The air was still. A gull called. 'I rang your mother before I left,' he said without turning.

'How was she?'

Philip turned. 'Busy, but she sends you her love.'

'Huh. Did you mention the Children?'

'Yes, she said that she had toyed with the idea of becoming a nun when she was your age.'

Laura laughed. 'Mummy a nun? I don't believe it. She never cared for anyone but herself. Not even Daddy. He was a meal ticket to her. Sometimes, sometimes I wonder why she went through the pain and suffering of childbirth all for me. She wasn't the maternal type. I see that now. Not her fault. It was just her soulless, middle-class upbringing.'

'But she did love you. I know she did.'

She stared straight at Philip. 'What love? She's incapable of love. If she did love me, do you think she would have gone off to Peru leaving me in London? Is that love?'

'But she didn't know Cordwain was going to be posted abroad when she married him. You're being unreasonable.'

'Look, it doesn't matter. She means nothing to me now. I have been brought into the world and that's that. Natural parents are instruments of procreation. That's all.'

'That is Sananda's creed. But why do you think he wants his followers to sever all ties with their families? They pose a threat. They offer a bond outside his sphere of influence, restricting his power over your mind. They offer a taste of the real world.'

'Stop it! Stop it!' Laura screamed. Her eyes seemed to close in on themselves. She started chanting.

'That's right,' shouted Philip. 'Shut out reason with gobbledegook. Sometime in your life you are going to have to face the facts and think the thing through for yourself. It could be now, tomorrow, next year, or it could be in twenty years when you are washed out and Sananda no longer has any use for you. Look.' He thumbed through some papers. 'I brought with me from London some photocopies of newsclippings that might interest you. This one comes from an American regional newspaper. It was written last year. Are you listening, Laura?' She did not respond. He read out loud.

' "Nan Oakrine was united with her son Patrick last week after ten years. Patrick had joined the religious cult known as the Children of Light from high school and had travelled around the country soliciting funds for the organization. Last week, two cult members left him on his mother's doorstep and ran away before they could be questioned.

"Patrick had always been remembered by his friends as an intelligent, lively boy who took an active interest in sports. He is now reported to be physically weak and suffering incontinency. His speech is slurred and even simple decisions are beyond him, bringing on crippling headaches.

"Mrs Oakrine is seeking medical and psychiatric help. When asked to comment she replied: 'Sure I'm bitter, I can't believe the change in him. I had always hoped that one day he would return home, but I have only got him back because they can't use him any longer. They took my son and gave me back a vegetable.' "

'Well, there is one case for you of a disciple who couldn't stand the pace. He could no longer generate the donations. He was thrown out of the New Kingdom, poor guy. Is that Sananda's type of love?'

Laura sat silently. She did not react. Her lips just moved in a continuous silent chant.

'How are you standing the pace, Laura? After six months in the cult, it is quite normal for the boys' beards to stop growing and girls to cease menstruating. Are you still troubled with the curse?'

'Stop it,' she cried. 'Stop it.'

'Don't worry, Laura, just keep chanting. You're not a

vegetable yet. Those fair hands are still good for many thousand belts and some fine embroidery. Just don't be too hard on your mother. One afternoon, she might receive an unexpected visitor.'

'You're doomed, Philip. Don't you realize you are all doomed? When the New Order comes you will rot in hell. Only the Children will be saved.'

There was a knock on the door. 'They've come for me,' Laura laughed. 'You see! You see!'

'Who is it?' asked Philip without turning.

'Pietro.' Philip walked over to the door and let him in. He smelt freshly baked bread. Rolls, yoghurt, boiled eggs, tea and three chocolate milkshakes were laid out on a tray. 'Breakfast,' said Pietro. 'A magnificent breakfast for the beautiful Laura. Waiter service.' He flourished a starched napkin over his arm, carried the tray over to Laura's bedside. 'And what would the *signorina* desire?'

'I'm not hungry.'

'Oh, come, you ate nothing yesterday. You must build up your strength.'

'No.'

Pietro frowned. 'OK.' He shrugged. 'So starve.' He put the tray down by the side of the bed and pulled up two chairs. Philip and Pietro began to eat. 'You know,' said Pietro. 'I admire you. Few people have your courage.' He scooped up some mango. 'I come from Milano. It is a beautiful city, the city of my birth, and very rich. I left there seven years ago for a holiday in India. I thought I would go and see the Taj Mahal, say "*Che bello*! How lovely!" and go back. I stayed three months, then went back to Milano only to pack my bags and sell my flat. Mmmm, this mango is *stupendo*. They said, "Pietro, you are crazy, you have had too much sun. Why do you want to go back?" Philip, the yoghurt. "Here life is good, the wine is excellent, the food and the women the best in the world. All this talk of the spirit and enlightenment, leave it to *Il Papa*." ' He pointed

127

to the ceiling. ' "He understands." But something drove me on. I had to go back. I had to try for myself, learn and watch.'

'And have you found whatever it was?' asked Laura, hesitantly.

'Sometimes I feel I am getting there. I have crawled a millimetre in a year. But how can I say? An egg, Philip. I have been with three different gurus. One of them helped me much, the other two I am not so sure. That's why Dr Sananda interests me. He must have some power. A hundred thousand disciples, eh? Maybe he is the one I am seeking?'

'He is more than a guru,' said Laura, excited now. 'If you knew him you would understand.'

'You sure you don't want any breakfast?'

Laura tossed her head to one side. 'Well, maybe a little.'

Pietro grinned and brought the tray over to the bed. Laura sipped the milkshake through the straw. 'As you know, Laura,' he said tenderly, 'there are many paths to an enlightened spirit. Which one has Dr Sananda chosen for you?'

'Well, we never really looked at it as a path.'

'So what do you do each day? Work?'

'Mostly I make belts. Sometimes in the afternoon we play games or look after the vegetable garden, but usually we continue working. It is a terrible rush at the moment. The designs for the autumn collection have arrived from New York and there's this big exhibition in Madison Square Garden in September.'

Pietro rubbed his chin. 'It is a novel approach. My gurus were perhaps too old-fashioned. We used to spend our days in meditation and reading the great texts. We did a little manual work, but only what was necessary. Do you feel that making belts helps you get closer to whatever you believe?'

'Well, it's not so much that. It's that we are doing it for him. Each stitch brings the New Kingdom closer.'

'What? By raising funds?'

'I guess so.'

'Have you met Dr Sananda?'

'When he came down for the ceremony.'

'And what did you think?'

'It was the greatest moment in my life. He sort of glowed. There I was, face to face with the most important man in history. I couldn't believe it. He even spoke to me. He asked me all about myself — as if I mattered. It was funny. He was smaller than I expected but he had this aura about him and he was so gentle. No one who ever met him could doubt that he was the Messiah.'

'Well, maybe he is,' said Pietro. 'Wouldn't it be wonderful? We have been waiting for this to happen, some sign from the skies. But there have been many men before who claimed such things. How can you be sure Dr Sananda is the one?'

'I just know it in my bones, in my heart. Then there are the signs of his birth. And he has done so much to make the world a better place.'

'What has he done?'

'He has smothered the world with love. There is not enough love in the world.'

'True, Laura, but what do you mean by love? Give me some concrete examples.'

Laura moved uneasily. 'Get that scumbag out of here,' she said quietly. Pietro nodded. Philip smothered his wounded pride, rose and left.

Pietro was with Laura all day. At times Philip heard her shouting the old commune slogans through the wall. Then there were long periods, half an hour or more, when he only heard Pietro's voice. It was never raised, always firm. Occasionally, he heard Pietro's laugh. Once Laura laughed too. A tray went in at lunchtime. It came back empty. Mrs Arbuthnot brought a clean set of clothes. Robert Yates came three times during the afternoon to ask how it was going.

A tray with dinner went in at six and at seven Pietro came out and asked Tammy to go in. Laura was ready for bed. 'How's it going?' asked Philip nervously.

Pietro looked drained. He shrugged and poured out half a tumblerful of Scotch. He drank it before he replied. 'She talks now, that is good. But she can't concentrate for long. We argue for fifteen minutes, then she drifts off and you are talking to a wall. But she talks, and sometimes, sometimes she listens. Still all is Father, Father this, Father that. She is blind to all but Father. I have done what I can but I have not helped her.' Pietro shrugged. 'But it does not matter.'

'What do you mean it does not matter? Tomorrow is the third day.'

'She is beginning to think for herself. That is what matters.'

The next morning Laura was strangely silent. She was already dressed when Tammy knocked on the door and called Philip and Pietro in. Laura smiled at Pietro. Her eyes skirted around Philip. She turned away and kicked the wall, but she did not ask him to leave.

Philip and Pietro argued with her all morning and over lunch Tammy recounted her experiences in the Movement. Laura still mouthed slogans and answered questions with stereotyped phrases, but she seemed less assertive than the day before. Her tone was more hesitant.

After lunch Pietro brought Robert Yates to see Laura. He introduced himself and sat down on the side of the bed. Laura sat beside him on a hard chair as he recounted his own search for the truth that had brought him to India and made him stay. He had been an engineer in Hyderabad, yet drawn and fascinated by mysticism.

'My dear,' he said at last, taking her hand. 'I'm an old man now and you might think it strange that someone of my age can give advice to one so young, but we are of the same kind, you and I.' She looked up at him like a little child.

130

'There is a divine spark in all of us. The answer to your search lies inside yourself, not in others. Seek their guidance and learn from their experience, but do not expect *them* to find what you alone can seek.'

'But that's where I know it,' whispered Laura, 'inside myself. Father holds the truth. I know it.'

Philip flicked through a dossier on his knee. 'Laura, do you know how many religious cults there are in the States?' he asked.

She did not reply.

'Over two thousand. Have you thought about the Moonies, the Divine Light Mission, the Children of God, Hare Krishna, Scientology? Many have their own Messiah. All believe that only they hold the truth. Think about it, Laura.' Laura shrugged. 'Why the Children of Light? Why Dr Sananda? How much do you know of the man you believe is the Messiah? Look, here in this dossier I have what is known of his early history.' Philip reached into the folder and pulled out a piece of foolscap. He read it out and handed a copy to Laura. It made strangely contradictory reading. She glanced at it, then crumpled it up into a ball and stood up.

'Sit down, Laura,' said Philip. 'You have got to ask yourself some hard questions. Look, maybe you have the answers. If so it's fine by us and you will be free to go.'

'I don't want . . .'

'We are talking about your life, Laura, maybe your whole life. Sit down.'

Laura slipped a thumb in her mouth and screwed up her eyes. 'I want to go back,' she mumbled.

'Sit down.' Slowly she moved towards the bed, dragging her feet. She hunched up her shoulders and sat down next to Yates. 'Let's look at what the Children of Light actually do,' Philip went on. 'You say they are bringing love to mankind, but how, Laura? Why the lies and deception? Were you told about the Children of Light when you went down to stay with the Green Crusaders? Why do they lie

131

when they are fund-raising, pretending they are a charity for the poor and the sick? If Sananda holds the truth and salvation for the world, why does he have to resort to lies? Is that giving love to mankind?' Laura stared at him, mute. 'And what about your allowance?'

'I signed a banker's order. It goes to the Movement, but it's not a lot.'

'And where does the money go? You've got a right to know. And what about the rest?' Philip turned to Tammy. 'When you were out fund-raising on the streets, how much money did you raise on average each day?'

'We were expected to collect at least one hundred dollars each. If we failed consistently we were put on a "condition". Most of us raised more.'

'And how much time was spent fund-raising?'

'After the first month of training, we were on the streets for about fifty per cent of the time.'

'Laura, Sananda now claims over one hundred thousand active followers. If a tenth of those collected an average of fifty dollars a day, Sananda's income would be in excess of one hundred and eighty million dollars a year from fund-raising alone. One hundred and eighty million dollars! His labour force is free, his profit exempt from tax, and the communes' expenses kept to a minimum.

'Think about it and ask yourself where are these great projects which will bring benefit to mankind. You talk of love. Why then isn't the money spent on schools, hospitals and the poor instead of just enriching Sananda's private empire? While you are working eighteen hours a day, Sananda and his entourage are living in the height of luxury savouring the material fruits you have abandoned. Your selfless work isn't going to feed hungry mouths or bring love to mankind, but add one more crystal decanter to his table. Will that be your life's work?'

'But he is the Messiah, he must want for nothing the world can offer,' replied Laura, her eyes glazing over.

'Laura,' Philip said urgently. 'You work hard to collect the money and give it to this guy so he can build a New Kingdom, and what does he do with it? He buys a large estate in Connecticut, an executive jet, a newspaper, a munitions factory, some industrial plant and a few hotels. "Thank you very much," he says. "Your soul is in a fallen state, but if you keep working like that, I'm sure it will get much better." '

Laura covered her face with her hands.

'Laura,' said Philip, 'when you left for India you had never met Dr Sananda and yet you were prepared to sacrifice your life for him. What happened down at that farm in the country?'

'Nothing.'

'Think, Laura. Your case is not unique. Tens of thousands of people, sharing no more than a mild dissatisfaction with the ways of the world, have ended up believing Sananda is the Messiah after a few weeks of so-called instruction. Their whole personalities have undergone a radical shift in a matter of days.'

'Through seeing the light.'

'Come off it, they have not even read the texts. As with you, something inside snapped.'

Tammy leaned forward. 'Laura,' she said. 'I joined on the other side of the pond, but if it was anything like my experience, we were never told about Dr Sananda until the second week, and we were never left alone for a minute, even in the rest-room. You know, I used to go out witnessing, finding new recruits. I must have recruited fifteen, twenty. It was always the same. Love-bombing we called it. It didn't mean anything, it was something to switch on, but it worked like a charm. Get them down to the farm, use any method you can, that's what we were told. Then the machine takes over.'

Laura ran her hand across her forehead. 'What are you trying to tell me?' she shouted. 'That it's some kind of psychological trick? Huh! That's what you would like to believe, but it's not, I know it's not. Only I know how I feel, only I know that!'

Philip knelt down beside her. 'Why then do you think they take you to isolated camps, give you little protein and little sleep? Why do you think there is something planned for every moment of the day and you are never left alone? Why do you think they play on your doubts and fears and undermine your self-confidence in any way they can?

'You didn't come to believe that Sananda was the Messiah through a conscious act of will. After a couple of weeks in that hell-hole of a camp, it was an act of animal survival. Unless you believed, the strains and stresses of life there would have been too much to bear. Sooner or later you would have had a nervous breakdown.'

'Sure, I was tired, but that doesn't mean . . .'

'You were more than tired. Your mind was numbed. Yet in that state you took the decision to abandon your life to Sananda. From the first day you were there, the Children began the process of breaking down your confidence in yourself. And then they gave you hope for the future, hinting at great things, and gave you love, affection and acceptance. More and more you grew dependent upon them.

'But as time went on that love and affection became conditional. To be accepted, you must embrace the doctrine, you must become one of them. You must share their enthusiasm for the Movement and its ideals. At first you just payed lip-service to humour them as an interested observer, but then it became for real. You needed them. You were too tired and too drained to act and think for yourself. Something snapped. The human mind can only take so much.

'Is that how it happened, Laura? If so, it's the same story as for thousands of other converts — the formula works like clockwork. After what you had been through you would have believed Mickey Mouse was the Messiah if they had told you so. Can't you see that now?'

Laura's head shook violently from side to side. Her face was flushed. Her hands were trembling. 'No, no, no. Please, tell me. Christ. Please let me think. No, no, no.' She threw herself down on the bed and smothered her face in the pillow. Her fist beat against the mattress, then she sniffed. Her body went still and she cried. 'Leave me,' her muffled voice whimpered. 'Please leave me. Let me think.'

Laura was left alone for half an hour, then Yates went back into the room. He stayed with her for four hours. When he returned, he was smiling. He closed the door quietly behind him. 'My God. I think we've done it,' he said. 'She seems much more settled. We argued the toss, and came to the conclusion that Sananda could be the Messiah, but the evidence was rather flimsy. She is doubting herself now, but her mind is still drifting. She says that at times she can see, actually see, that black man, Guthro, in the room and his eyes are calling her. She can see the New Kingdom, and Sananda on a jewelled gold throne and the Children kneeling at his feet. Rather graphic, if unoriginal.' He shrugged. 'But that's only to be expected. Tammy has nightmares too and she's been away from them for nearly two weeks. Laura had one rather odd request though. She wondered whether you had any of that Kendal Mint Cake?'

Philip laughed. 'Shall I go in?'

Yates shook his head. 'She's been through a lot and she's tired now. Let Tammy go. They can have a quiet supper together and an early night. Tomorrow she starts her new life.'

It was still dark when Philip awoke. He had a drink of water and lay back on his camp-bed. When he awoke the second time, Pietro was sitting by the window in the lotus position. Philip lowered himself off the bed, went into the bathroom

135

and splashed his face with water, brushed his teeth and shaved. He looked at his watch — 8.10. He walked over to Laura and Tammy's bedroom door and pressed his ear against it. Not a sound.

'Let them sleep,' said Pietro. He breathed in deeply, then slowly exhaled.

Philip dressed quickly, then lay down on the bed and picked up a book. He turned a dozen pages, then got up and returned to Laura and Tammy's bedroom door. He knocked lightly. No reply. He knocked again. 'Everything OK?' he asked. 'Tammy! Laura!' Only the waves answered. He walked over to the table by the window, picked up a key, walked back to the door and unlocked it.

The beds were empty. The boards that had covered the windows lay scattered on the floor.

'What has happened?' asked Pietro from behind him. He was already out of the door. They ran around to the side of the bungalow. Footsteps in the sand led to and away from the window. 'We have had visitors,' said Pietro, stooping. 'Maybe five, maybe six. They were as quiet as the night. We must hurry.' He turned and ran towards the Society compound.

Yates was sitting on his veranda in his rocking chair. 'Quick!' Philip shouted when he was in earshot. 'Get your car.'

Robert's eyebrows rose. He slipped inside the house, returned with a set of keys and a sun hat, and walked down the veranda steps. 'What's the rush?' he asked. 'Where to?'

'The airport. She has been abducted.'

They jumped in the car and Yates turned on the ignition. The engine rattled, then stalled. 'Against her will?' He turned the key again.

'Tammy's not there either. I don't know.'

The engine chugged, then rumbled. 'Tammy, too? But I thought she was shot of them.'

'Look, I don't know, but if there had been a struggle, we

136

would have heard it. We were next door. We heard nothing.'

They passed the gatehouse. The porter nodded. Yates turned left on to the open road. 'So what now?'

Philip struck the dashboard with the heel of his hand as though it would make the car go faster. 'The airport's our best bet. Get her arrested at Immigration, alleging theft, anything.

Yates's moustache twitched. 'We were close, I could have sworn she was coming to her senses. Just one more day, one more day.'

Twenty minutes later, Robert drew up in front of a brown concrete slab. Five porters surrounded the car and peered through the windows. Philip leaped out and darted through the door marked 'Departures'.

To the left of him, five businessmen crowded around the Air India desk. Philip pushed his way through. 'I'm sorry,' he said, 'when is the next flight to the States?'

A girl in a sari stood behind the desk. She looked up at him angrily. 'If you would be good enough to wait a moment . . .'

Philip's fist thumped on the desk. 'I've got to know now.'

The girl started. 'Please, sir, you have plenty of time. You will be going via Bombay. Now if you will wait for a moment until I have sorted out this gentleman's ticketing . . .'

'Was there an earlier flight?'

'Only a connection via Delhi, that left at six. That you have missed.'

'Have you a passenger list?' She muttered something, reached under the desk and pulled out two sheets of tissue-thin paper. Philip scanned the names. All were Indian, except Buckmeyer and Cranshaw. 'And this was the only flight?' asked Philip. 'Are you sure?'

The girl looked up and nodded, but it was Pietro who

replied from behind him. 'Except one. A private plane from New York.'

Philip gasped. 'Sananda's?'

CHAPTER TEN

Burp burp . . . burp burp.

'Thomas, Philip Strickland.'

'I'm afraid Mr Strickland is in hospital, but Mr Pether-bridge is available.'

'Thomas, it's me.'

'Oh, *you*, sir! Better now?'

'Yes, what *have* you been saying about me?'

'Well sir, it has been two months. That's not easy to explain. People begin talking, they begin to think that a young man who goes swanning off to all sorts of places isn't perhaps taking his career seriously, that maybe he does not fit in. It's not some holiday camp we're running here, you know, sir. Still you're better now. When can we expect you back, sir?'

'I can't be sure. I'm looking for someone.'

'Aren't we all?'

'No, Thomas. Someone who's in deep trouble.'

'Look, sir, we all want to do what we can for others, but there is no point in you sacrificing your career like this. We would not have taken you on unless we thought you had a bright future. But now this rescue mission or whatever it is has gone on for two whole months. You can't win 'em all. I wish you could, sir, or we would be milking it in here, but there comes a time when you have to cut your losses, and call it a day, and your number, sir, to put it crudely, has come up.'

'But Thomas, it's a life that is being thrown away!'

'Yes,' said Thomas laconically. 'Yours. If I may say so, sir. Don't say I didn't warn you. We have got a couple of very bright pupils here at the moment. I don't know what they are going to decide at the Chambers meeting next week. I think they want to take at least one of them on. The work's here, but we haven't the space. They've been eyeing your desk as if it were the House of Lords. That empty space could be earning good fees. This isn't a Clapham omnibus, sir, we can't carry passengers. I'll do my best, but that is all I can say.'

'Hell, they're not going to throw me out, are they, Thomas? They can't!'

'Oh, sir, who am I to say what is going on behind their learned brows?'

'Maybe I should talk to Sir Lionel?'

'I would not do that. You know what a temper our learned Head of Chambers possesses. When he was a young man, he used to sleep on a camp-bed in Chambers. I don't think he would quite see it your way. It would be the poisoned chalice. No, sir, as far as he is concerned you are still in quarantine for your rare tropical disease. Can't say that you got much sympathy. Sir Lionel's not one for foreign travel himself.'

'Thank you, Thomas, thank you.'

'I'm sticking my neck out for you, mind. Right under the chopper it is, and if I was you I'd come out of quarantine in time for the Chambers meeting next week.'

'I won't be back in time.'

'Where are you?'

'Nepal. The foothills of the Himalayas. Have any fees come in?'

'You have to earn them first, sir. I've sent what there was to your bank. About three hundred.'

'Thomas, thank you, I won't forget this.'

'Nor, sir, I assure you, will I.'

Heavy globules of rain tumbled out of a lead-coloured sky. They slapped down on to the dark-green leaves and poured off them in streams. The deep puddles in the mud track spat back at the clouds. Water thudded on Philip's umbrella, snagged on his eyelashes, trickled down his nose, his cheeks. His gym shoes squelched with every step. 'I'm still not sure what the hell we're doing here,' he said.

'Grumble, grumble, grumble,' Pietro said blithely. 'You are here to learn. Keep your brain open and your mouth a little more shut and you will understand things about your Laura, about the East, about your enemy.'

'You don't need to psychoanalyse a rat before you poison it, for Christ's sake.'

'*È vero*, very true, but one rat is smaller than you. When all the rats get together, it is as well to know rat psychology. What we are facing here is very big, very powerful . . .'

'Damn!' Philip started and looked down at his left leg. 'What's that?'

'A leech,' said Pietro calmly. 'No, don't knock it off. It'll leave its horns inside you and it'll go septic. Let it enjoy its meal. It is not greedy, and you have plenty to spare.'

'Great.' Philip shuddered. 'That's all I need.' He trudged on grimly, cursing as his feet slipped in the mud. A dozen wooden shacks perched high on the hill ahead of them. 'Is that the place, then?'

'I think so, yes.'

'About bloody time too. I could have spent the last week in the States looking for Laura or in London trying to patch up my career, but no, I have to listen to you. I'm also soaking wet, covered in leeches . . .'

'Covered in one leech, to be precise,' said Pietro drily. 'Listen. For the last time. We are not just looking for Laura. We are looking for a means to understand her, to offer her a reasonable alternative to Sananda's candyfloss nirvana.'

Philip licked rain from his lips. He said nothing, just trudged on up the hill in silence. Only as he heaved himself up on to the path where the shacks stood did he puff, 'Well, it damned nearly worked, didn't it? We were close. So close.'

'Maybe, maybe, or maybe she was just playing us along. But all right, say it was sincere. What then, *caro*? How long would it be before she felt the need again, the need for something indefinable which she feels to be missing in her life?'

'Never,' said Philip sharply. 'Never again. I'll see to that.'

Pietro knocked on the door of a shack with smoke pouring from its chimney. An old Nepali appeared in the entrance. A thin clay pipe hung from his lower jaw. His long slanted eyes narrowed still further. Pietro spoke to him in Gurkhali. 'Kailash Baba,' the man muttered, bowed his head slightly, and beckoned them in.

Philp shook his umbrella and followed. The inside of the shack was thick with smoke and smelt of fresh dung. A woman and three children sat around the open fire. She smiled at them warily as she worked dough with her fingers on a wooden board.

The old man drew the cork from a dusty bottle and filled three small cups with cloudy white liquid. He offered one to Philip, who thanked him and joined Pietro by the fire. Steam came off their bodies as they dried off. 'Kailash Baba's messenger will meet us here,' said Pietro. 'I still can't get over our luck.'

'We know that Sananda studied there,' replied Philip, 'but what's the big deal? With all the mystics in the Himalayas, you could fill an entire new town.'

'But Kailash Baba is different. He is a legend.'

The rain stopped suddenly. There was a knock on the door. A young man dressed in a saffron robe stood in the entrance. The harsh sunlight shone in from behind him and framed his body with a brilliant glow. 'I come for the friends of Mr Yates.'

*

At first light they came across a lone figure on a hill, a Buddha carved out of brick. The erosion of time had long since caused its head to crumble and had torn a cleft in its chest. Only fragments of plaster remained to give it human form over the loose brickwork. Grass and mountain flowers grew over the limbs and out of the crevices.

Philip stopped and looked down at the open palm of the Buddha with its mesh of cracked lines, and the small seeds of grass that sprouted between them. 'Oh,' he said quietly. Pietro said nothing but a little smile tugged at his lips.

Their guide reached into the bag that hung over his shoulder. He drew out two black silk blindfolds. 'From here,' he said, 'I am afraid that you must wear these.' Their guide tied the silk carefully around their heads, then tapped Philip's side with a staff. 'Hold on to this,' he said. Philip reached for it. He felt it twist as Pietro took hold of it from behind him. 'Ready,' said the guide, and they started walking.

'You can take the blindfolds off now.' Philip ripped his off. His eyes smarted at the light. They had been walking for two, maybe three hours. He stared about him. By the side of a waterfall stood a three-tiered pagoda with strange mythical beasts guarding its entrance, and next to it, a palace with an intricately carved facade. The sun glistened on its gold-studded roof.

'This isn't human,' exclaimed Pietro. 'It is nirvana.' The guide smiled sheepishly.

On a neighbouring hill stood an egg-shaped dome like an astronomer's tower but in shining gold. 'What is that?' asked Philip.

'On the hill? That's the wave tower. From there Master sends force waves to the outside world for the welfare of mankind. That has been his role for centuries. The tower acts as an amplifier, I think you would say.'

'Does he ever leave the valley?'

'No, his body is now too sensitive to withstand the impact of everyday life. Such energy as he has left is directed to the higher consciousness. Soon, though, he will have to adopt a new body as he has used the present one for over one hundred and fifty years. He would have left his present one decades ago, but the world is now passing through a critical era. A change takes time, and who can foretell what havoc the forces of darkness might cause in the interim.

'In the fourteenth century he renounced his right to merge with the oneness. Each time his present body grows too fragile, he is reincarnated and the search to find his new incarnation must begin again. The guardians from the palace question all the mothers in the valley until they find the child. Sometimes fifteen or twenty years elapse, but once they find him there can be no mistake. Master has a blue birthmark at the base of his spine and knows the secret mantras preserved in vaults of the palace.'

They walked towards the palace. The wooden beams and the roof struts were carved with ways of lovemaking, each one different. 'Until the seventeenth century,' said the guide, 'many of Master's disciples followed the Tantric path to enlightenment. Now we no longer do so, but the tradition has never died in these parts.'

Pietro smiled. 'The Tantric path is a difficult one for us Italians too.'

The guide led them through the palace gates into a stone courtyard where twenty or thirty men sat in rows, their bodies motionless. Philip watched closely, but he could see no signs of inhalation. Their faces were drained of all blood. Their skin was a pale shade of green. It was like the aftermath of a mass ritual suicide.

'These are Master's most advanced students,' said the guide. 'Their spirits have temporarily left their bodies. They have mastered the art of breath control to such a degree that the respiratory process is suspended. The *asana* is not for novices. The tongue is turned backwards behind the tonsils to stop the passage of air, and the heel of the left foot is pressed against the anus. All the body's orifices are closed so that the vital fluid is preserved.'

An old bald man with thick circular glasses came towards them. He stooped as he walked and clutched his hands tightly together in front of his robe. The guide bowed his head quickly. 'Welcome,' said the old man. 'You must be our guests. I am Colishan, Master's Comptroller. It is a rare privilege for us to have guests here, and rarer still for me to be able to practise my English.' He smiled smugly.

'It is a great honour for us to be here,' said Pietro.

'I am sure Master would wish for news of his wayward son, bitter though it might be. He has been journeying out of his body for the past two days, but when he returns, he will receive you. You must be prepared. He is no longer strong. The time cannot be far off when he will have to surrender his present frame for one that is younger. Ang will show you to your room, then come, join me in the library.' He turned on his heels and went back into the palace.

Their guide took them to a room overlooking the courtyard. Two low beds were the only furniture. The walls were white and unadorned. A bowl of water sat by a jug in the corner. He bowed. 'Have you all you need?'

'Thank you,' said Pietro. 'And thank you for bringing us here.'

'I only do my duty.' He bowed again and left.

Philip went over to the shutters and opened them. Sunlight filled the room. He moved over to the bed nearest the window and pressed his hand down on the mattress. Wooden boards.

Pietro turned. His eyes sparkled. 'This is quite simply the greatest moment of my life,' he exclaimed. 'I can't believe it. It's all true! For years I thought the great Kailash Baba was just a legend. This, I am sure, this is what I've been waiting for. Here you can — you can *feel* the spirit move. Come, Philip, even you must feel it!'

Philip sat down on the bed. 'Yes, well, I've got to admit, it's got something.'

'Oh, you English, take them to nirvana and they would complain that there was no television, the plumbing was not British, they did not like the food. Your Laura, now she would understand. Right here, Philip, it's right here in the spirit in the air. All you have to do is grab hold of it and not let go until you and it are one.'

'So why then did Sananda ever leave this place?'

'Ah now, that is an interesting question. That is what we are here to find out.'

The Comptroller sat at the far end of the library at a long polished table. He was reading a brightly coloured manuscript. There were books and parchments everywhere; stacked on the floor, piled high on the tables, lining every inch of the walls. A thin haze of dust filled the room. As Philip and Pietro entered, he rose. 'Come in,' he said. 'You have had a long journey. You must be tired.'

'Not at all,' replied Pietro. 'This is — this is quite remarkable.'

'Yes, I believe it is the finest library of its kind anywhere. We have all Master's teachings dating back to the fourteenth century when he reached the enlightened state, and all the great classic texts, of course.'

'Would you allow me to look through some of them?' asked Pietro.

'Of course, but they are in Sanskrit and medieval Parbatia.'

'I am lucky to have studied both under my guru.'

The Comptroller quickly closed the manuscript in front of him. 'Then we will see.'

A boy came in with small cups of tea on a tray. Colishan signalled to Philip and Pietro to sit down on the floor around a low table, and they were each handed a cup.

Colishan stared into space and pursed his lips. 'Mingma Sananda, yes, I remember him.'

'How long did he study here?' asked Philip.

'About ten, maybe eleven years. He came from a poor family from the village of Dzemu in the Solu valley in the east. His father was a farmer, I think, and he had two brothers. Mingma was the youngest. As usually happens here, when the family plot of land is too small to be divided among all the sons, the family make provision for the youngest so that he can take the ochre robe.

'We first heard about Mingma from the Head Lama of the Tengboche monastery where he had been enrolled as a novice. By then Mingma must have been there for some fifteen years. I'd never seen the Head Lama so excited before. He said that Mingma was a prodigy. After only a year's study he had mastered the texts of the Tripitaka by heart, and could argue each interpretation with the lamas. There was nothing more that they could teach him. He was now convinced that Mingma's young body held a much-reincarnated spirit that would soon be ready for its final journey.'

The boy reappeared. He bowed as he presented Philip and Pietro with bowls of noodles in clear vegetable broth. 'Eat,' said Colishan, 'you must be hungry.'

'And how did you find Sananda?' asked Philip.

'He was everything that we had been told. How can I explain it to you? In your words, there was a saintliness about him. He was quiet and reserved, but there was an aura about him, even here, something different. We had no doubt that one day he would become a great ascetic. Master took him under his wing, and after the first five years none of the secret teachings were kept from him. That was our greatest mistake.' The corners of Colishan's lips turned down. Suddenly he looked very old.

'It must have been a great disappointment for you?' said Pietro.

Colishan's head shot up like that of a startled ferret. 'It's not that, it is the danger. The route to the esoteric discipline is not an easy one. It requires single-mindedness, discipline and self-denial beyond the capabilities of most mortals. For the others, there are less demanding, different routes. But for the chosen few, with time, the disciplines can yield great power.

'Stories abound in the West about the powers which develop once the lower *siddhis* have been mastered. These are exaggerated nonsense, but a man who has opened the third eye does wield a special power unlike any other, for he can communicate directly with the essence of things. That is why these disciplines are kept secret. They must not be taught until the pupil is ready, until we can be sure that he will not abuse these powers, and will use them only for good.

'In our enthusiasm, we taught Mingma too much too soon. He learned so fast, so very fast. We should perhaps have recognized the lust for knowledge, so different from the love of understanding. He mastered the lower *siddhis* before he had exorcized the evil from his mind, before he had destroyed self and worldly ambition.'

'Mmmm,' murmured Philip.

Pietro shot him a look that would have skinned a rabbit. 'And you are sure that Sananda had mastered the techniques?'

'I don't doubt it.'

'*Dio mio*. Dangerous indeed.'

'Maybe none of this would have happened if we had not made one further mistake, and that is entirely my responsibility. One afternoon, a young Negro half-caste knocked on our gate. As you know, the whereabouts of the ashram is a secret shared only by the few, and this is imperative if our work is to continue undisturbed.'

'Was his name Guthro?' asked Philip.

Colishan nodded. 'How he found us we still are not sure. He would not tell us. However much they were bribed, no

148

one in the valley would reveal our whereabouts as it would set back their spirits countless lives. He murmured something about airforce surveillance photographs. That could have just been a cover.'

'Did you let him stay?'

'We did not want him. He said that he was on a quest for enlightenment, but he did not have the training or the discipline. He had just read some book or other, and thought all you had to do was stare into space for a few hours like a basking toad and mutter a few mantras and you were a mystic. What could we do with him? We asked him to leave, but he threatened to reveal our whereabouts, get it printed in every tourist handbook. It was the early sixties then. From what I hear, Kathmandu was like a circus with mysticism and drugs sold like ice cream. Imagine what would have happened here.'

'So you let him stay?' asked Philip.

'Only as a helper. There is a lot of work to do here. The novices do most of it between tuition, but few of us here are still young.'

'But he was not a Nepali,' said Pietro.

'That does not matter. We have never closed our doors to those of other cultures if they can show the qualities we are looking for. They are rare enough in themselves.' Pietro nodded pensively, then for a second his dimples showed in a contented smile. 'And he worked well,' Colishan continued, 'and hard. He never complained, though I can't say I totally trusted him. For the first time I locked the library every night.'

Colishan pushed his horn-rimmed glasses up his squat nose. 'Mingma left with Guthro three months later. He told Master that there was a great country across the oceans which was waiting for enlightenment, that his destiny was to show them the light and awaken their spirits. Of course it was Guthro who had filled him with these ridiculous ideas. Master told him that this was not the way of the spirit, and

149

that he was not ready. He forbade him to go and sent him up into the hills to meditate, but it was no good. Later, we heard reports of the commune Mingma and Guthro started in the United States and our worst fears were confirmed.

'Of course, once we had seen that Mingma was not ready for the powers he had attained, we should have terminated the experiment forthwith and drawn his spirit from his mortal frame. The sacrificial pyre would have cleansed his body and left his spirit free to progress in his next incarnation. Death would have been but a minor inconvenience to his progress. As it is, he is doing untold damage to himself and his disciples, the poor misguided creatures. But what can they do against the powers of the lower *siddhis*? They would be clay to be moulded, nothing but clay.'

There was a knock on the door. A young acolyte entered silently, bowed before Colishan and spoke to him. Colishan nodded. 'Master has returned to his body. He will see you now.'

It was a steep climb up smooth grass to the tower with the egg-shaped dome. The sound of the waterfall, previously a constant deep roar, faded to a gentle lapping sound as they neared the top. Philip squinted up at the great golden orb at the top of the dome. It gleamed like a second sun, dazzling Philip so that when he looked away, coloured specks circled behind his eyelids.

Six strange beasts of painted stone guarded the entrance. They were twice the size of a man, and their noses were wrinkled back in snarls, baring glittering white canines. They were of uncertain, decidedly mongrel ancestry; the head of a lion, the wings of an eagle, the tail of a snake; a dog's maw with an elephant's trunk and a twisted reptilian body. Their eyes were of different coloured veined agates.

Colishan led the way up the stone steps to a door of beaten bronze. Six golden bells surmounted the architrave. As they reached the door, it swung inwards, though Philip could see neither spyhole nor window through which their approach could be seen.

The vast circular hall was dark but for the dusty, pale light which stabbed in sharp, crisp shafts through the six small windows around the dome. The shafts met, their first brilliance dissipated, in the centre of the hall where a bundle of cloth and skin huddled on the mosaic floor.

As Philip's eyes adjusted to the darkness, he saw the gleaming pate of a man who sat cross-legged and wrapped in a tiger skin. The man sat almost as still as those who had practised their *asanas* beneath the window, but two long bony fingers stroked a silvery beard which spread out on the floor before him like a bridal train.

The old man smiled. The gums were without teeth. 'Come in, my children,' he said, and his frail, quavering voice seemed powerful and portentous as it echoed around that still, silent place. They came closer to him. It was cool in the darkness. The sweat of the climb froze on Philip's shirt.

First Colishan, then Philip and Pietro bowed. Kailash Baba motioned with one hand. They sat on the rug before him. Colishan leaned forward and whispered something in his ear. The old man turned to Philip and Pietro. Only then did they see that his eyes were pale-blue agate like those of the lion's head outside. Kailash Baba was totally blind.

He started to talk very slowly, very quietly, as if communing only with himself. Colishan listened attentively and translated in quick staccato bursts of words.

'Welcome, Colishan has told me of Mingma's doings. He has reaped a harvest of young fresh flowers, growing buds that have yet to bloom, and wound them into a crown about his head. He cares not that these buds will wilt, and the petals turn brown, that they will never live to bloom, that they will be dead long before their scent will cast its spell upon the air. I am tired now.' Kailash Baba raised his hand. 'Look at this hand.' Colishan pointed. 'It is emaciated.

Blood hardly trickles through these limbs. Soon, I will not be able to operate through this form, and it will have to be put to sleep. I pray that it will last until the spiritual crisis in the West is over.

'Seekers come to these hills in search of the ancient wisdom. Disillusioned and discontented with the West, they travel East to escape the dirty, dusty treadmills of their lives. They tell themselves there must be something more. They seek nirvana. What do they find? Poverty and disease. They come to a society much more fragile than their own. We cannot even feed our people. Why turn to us for help? I hold no key to life's problems, and can offer no solution. For the problems of the external world, they must turn to the scientists. For the problems of the soul, they must look inside themselves. It is inside themselves that the answer will be found.

'A will is not enough. Without an iron discipline, the seed will be crushed in the meanderings of self. All worldly ambitions and hopes, all passions and desires, must be quelled. Only then can I help. How can they know the divine if they do not know themselves?'

'Master, could I ask what you intend to do?' asked Philip.

'Do not expect the miraculous,' said Kailash Baba. 'The laws of causality which bind the universe must not be disturbed. There will only be repercussions in other times and in other places. Whatever is done will happen unseen and unsung through the agency of others. I only hope that I still have the strength.'

There was silence then. Pietro lowered his head and almost whispered, 'Master . . .?'

'Yes, Pietro.' Kailash Baba raised his hand and gave his toothless smile. He spoke in tremulous but faultless English. 'Yes, you may stay. When the moon is in its last quarter, Colishan will bring you to see me again and we shall talk.'

Pietro blinked. Although he smiled, his eyes filled with

water and reflected the mellow light more softly. For a moment it seemed that he too had his master's eyes. 'Master . . .' he said again, and Philip grinned to see his friend's happiness.

'Do not thank me,' the old man trilled, 'but wear the robe with humility.'

'And now,' again Colishan spoke for him, 'you must say goodbye to your friend, for Philip too has much to do and must start tonight.'

Pietro stood. Philip still watched the old man. He heard Pietro's footfalls come closer, felt his hand grasp his shoulder. 'I am happy,' said Pietro.

'I know. I am glad.'

'And you too, English bull, be happy. Find peace. I will be praying for you.'

'Curious as it may seem, I'll miss you.'

'So I should think . . .'

Philip looked up with a smile, but before he could catch his friend's eye, Pietro gave his shoulder a quick, hard squeeze and turned away. Philip watched as he walked towards the door.

''Bye, Pietro,' he said quietly. 'And thank you.'

'*Ciao*, Philip,' the deep voice echoed softly. 'Go with God.'

As soon as the door had closed, Kailash Baba turned his sightless eyes on Philip. 'Come closer,' he said. 'Come closer.'

Philip rose and walked two paces nearer. He knelt and lowered his head before he had realized what he was doing. Kailash Baba reached inside the tiger skin and drew out a silver amulet in his trembling hand. For a moment Philip thought it was Sananda's logo, then he saw that there were only six interlocking stars, not seven. Kailash Baba spoke.

'The seventh, you see,' droned Colishan, 'represents a power that we would never use. It springs from the very bowels of the earth, the depths of the mind.' Kailash Baba fumbled slightly as he lowered the amulet over Philip's neck. 'Let this be your protection and your strength,' he said, 'though you will never have protection and strength other than your own. I will be with you. You have a task before you. It is not a pleasant task. It is not even, perhaps, a good task, but it must be done because of who you are and because no new buds must be shorn from their stems to fill Mingma's crown. Never fear. Listen only to the small voice in your heart. Now go. Your guide awaits you.'

Philip raised his head slowly. 'I . . .' he started, then, 'Master, I will do whatever must be done.'

PART THREE

CHAPTER ELEVEN

Connecticut, USA

'You mean this is "New Kingdom"?' exclaimed Laura. She turned away from the car window and looked at Sananda. The soft leather upholstery squeaked.

Sananda waved his hand dismissively. 'We all need somewhere to relax. I wish it could still be the Himalayas, with the stars as my roof and the mountains my bed, but then how could I give my love to those in need? And there are mountains in Connecticut. At least, they call them mountains.'

Four security guards in dark-blue uniforms saluted, and the great wrought-iron gates shuddered and opened. The fleur-de-lys finials cast an arc twenty feet in the air. The front of the Pontiac turned slowly on to the thick gravel of the driveway. They passed through a wood so dense that the yellow light barely flickered through, then into a park of lawns and flowering shrubs.

Laura cleared her throat. 'Father, it really is a great honour to be brought here.'

Sananda looked at Laura and smiled fondly. He put his hand on hers. Laura inhaled sharply.

'My child, you have suffered much. But not in vain. You were being tested. The powers of darkness tried to claim your spirit for their own. They knew its true worth. Now you know what is meant by the dark night of the soul.'

'And Tammy? Is she coming too?'

'Tammy?' he said absently. 'Oh, the Jones girl! No, for her there are other duties.'

'Father, I hope I prove worthy.'

Sananda smiled again. 'Just open up your heart. Let love and truth pour in. That's all you have to do.'

A white wooden house shaped like a horseshoe was ahead of them now. Some twenty people waited in the forecourt beneath marble torsos twice their size. Faces and hands squashed up against the windows, cutting out the light. Sananda bowed his head slightly. His lips curled in a happy smile. The chauffeur opened the door and the Children screamed. 'Welcome home, Father, welcome home!' A girl reached out and touched his robe. Another fell to her knees. A third touched the ground where he had just stood then lifted her hand to her breast.

'Come, my Children,' beamed Sananda, 'I have only been away for two quarters of the moon, and I left my heart with you.' He beckoned to Laura. She slid awkwardly out of the car. 'I want you all to meet Laura,' he said. He turned to a well-built redhead in a bikini. 'Andy, will you look after her? Oh, it is so good to be home,' sighed Sananda, 'but now . . . now I must rest.' He nodded to them all, then swept past the pool into the house. Two of the girls followed.

Andy stared at Laura for a moment, then ran her finger along the top strap of her bikini. A trickle of water ran out between her cleavage. 'You're English, aren't you?'

'Yes.' Laura grinned.

'Where are you from?'

'Cumberland.'

Andy smiled. 'I'm from Ruislip.'

'No kidding!'

'First thing is to get you something to wear. We got a message over the telex that you were a size ten.'

Laura giggled. 'I was a twelve when I left for India.'

'Well, honeybunch, you've lost a bit since then. I think ten's right. And your hair – my God, we'll have to do something about that. What've you been combing it with? A combine harvester?'

158

'That wasn't — that wasn't what we thought about in India.'

Andy sidled up to Laura and touched her hair. 'And those streaks,' she tutted. 'Right down to your ears! But don't worry, we'll get them seen to.'

Laura shrugged. 'That sort of thing doesn't matter to me any more. There are more important things — like work. I'd prefer just to be natural.'

Andy squeezed her hand. 'Honeybunch, that's what we all want to be, and boyo, that is work.'

A splash of water hit them. A dark tanned girl in a topless bikini surfaced nearby. She looked up casually. 'Sorry,' she said.

'Laura, how about a dip?' asked Andy. 'There's time before dinner, and it is the greatest pool.'

'Oh, God, yes. I'd love that.'

'I'll get you a costume. Hang on a moment. Oh, yeah, and I must get your room fixed up.'

Laura looked down at the pool. It was shaped like a classic feminine nose, with some sixty feet from nostril to bridge. Six marble statues surrounded it, twice life size, casting a clear reflection on the water. Laura looked again. It was not a reflection. The images refracted by the water were of the same figures and were upright. There were identical statues submerged beneath the pool.

'It's the best I can do,' said Andy. She handed Laura a wet green bikini and a towel. Laura wrapped the towel around her and changed quickly. 'So, how good are you on religion?'

The towel slipped six inches. Laura grabbed it. 'What?'

Andy laughed. 'No, silly, the religious heavyweights around the pool. How many do you recognize?' Andy ran off and stood by the one nearest to Laura. 'Buddha,' she said, and ran on to the next. 'Zoroaster . . . Mohammed . . . Jesus . . . Moses . . . And, of course, Father.' She wrapped her arms around Sananda's statue and hugged it. Her breasts pressed against the marble torso. She fluttered her eyelashes in self-mocking adoration, then suddenly turned and dived. It was a neat dive, the dive of an athlete. Her head broke the surface. She opened her eyes and shook her head. Her rich red hair hung heavily about her face. 'It's really great,' she said. 'Come on in.'

'Coming,' said Laura. She threw off her towel and plunged in. Laura's head bobbed up and she swam towards Andy. 'What a pool! But why the shape?'

'It was like that when Father bought the place. The previous owner was a plastic surgeon, and I guess he did it for a laugh. Father used to use the pool for mass baptisms, but with all those bodies passing through, and all that chlorine, it was like a sheep dip. Now we have got it to ourselves. Hold your breath. I'll take you on an underwater magical mystical tour.' Laura inhaled deeply and they both duck-dived underneath the surface. After a tour of the underwater statues, Laura clambered up the stone steps out of the pool. She panted.

'I'll take you to your room,' said Andy. They both wrapped themselves in towels and Andy led Laura across the patio. She slid back a glass door and passed through. Brightly coloured country chintz covered the double bed, the tablecloth, the festoon blinds. The only decoration on the walls was a huge photograph of Dr Sananda in a watergilt frame. It hung above the bed.

Andy beamed and waved expansively. 'Well, what do you think?'

Laura gasped. 'Is this for me?'

'Yup, and wait, you haven't see the best of it yet.' She threw open the cupboard doors. Dresses bulged out: silk taffeta and silk jersey in all different colours; embroidered black lace; crepe de Chine; gold lamé; a silver fox jacket; two mink coats and an ermine muff. Beneath, matching shoes were crammed on four gilt racks.

160

Laura started. 'But none of this stuff is made by the communes.'

'Honeybunch, if it was, every designer from New York to Paris would be drinking hot cocoa on a park bench. Dinner's in an hour, just flick through and wear whatever you feel like.' Andy ran her fingers along the coathangers and pulled out a mid-length emerald dress with wide silk taffeta frills. She held it up against Laura's wet body. 'Mmmm,' she said. 'It's kinda cute. But choose for yourself.' She threw the dress down on the bed and walked towards the glass door.

Laura did not smile. She sat down on the bed and stared ahead of her with a fixed expression of bewilderment in her wide eyes. 'Curiouser and curiouser,' she said. She shook her head. A small smile tugged at the corner of her mouth. 'And not what I was expecting at all.'

An hour later, she stepped out on to the patio in a simple white cotton dress. She wore no make-up. Her hair was combed neatly from a centre parting. Laura looked around her nervously, bit her lip, then straightened her shoulders and walked along the courtyard.

The air was warm and still. The pool was lit from beneath and the water shone a rich bright blue. The marble statues stood like sentinels clad in brilliant white. Before her, a table was set for dinner. Twenty candles flickered in smoked-glass balloons. Long dresses rustled on the flag-stones. There was the rattle of chat and of laughter.

Andy broke away from the group and came towards her. Her auburn hair was gathered in a bun behind her head. A ruby-and-diamond necklace sparkled as she walked. 'My,' she said, 'the waif look, that's different. Didn't we get your size right?'

'Yep, it's just that I wouldn't feel comfortable in all that . . .'

'Laura, just whatever you feel. Come and meet the

others.' They walked over to a group of four girls. Two stood. Two sat. Each wore a long dress. Each held a cocktail. 'Mary, Jo, Louise, Ingrid,' said Andy, 'meet Laura. A new arrival.' Painted lips, painted cheeks, painted eyes smiled back.

Sananda swept across the courtyard, his head slightly bowed. Eight men in pinstriped suits walked behind. Sananda sat at the head of the table and spread open his hands in a sacramental gesture of welcome. Andy and Mary sat on either side of him, then Laura, Louise, Jo and Ingrid. The eight men in pinstripes sat together at the end. Sananda raised a finger. Two men in crisp white jackets poured wine. 'Well now, girls,' asked Sananda, 'what have you been doing while I have been away?'

Andy sighed. It was the type of theatrical sigh that would be at home in a village hall on a frosty evening. 'Waiting for you, counting the days.'

'And I've been trying the new *asanas*,' said Mary in a little voice. She did a wide-eyed Shirley Temple number. 'You know, the one where you stand on your head. It's a great way to meditate and tone yourself at the same time.'

'The new jacuzzi's great,' said Andy. 'You never know which jet is going to start up next.'

'I will try it after dinner,' said Sananda.

The waiter brought in a plate piled high with cold asparagus. Sananda looked Laura warmly in the eye, then tapped a fork on the glass table-top. He spoke in a loud, clear voice. 'My Children, you will all have seen that we have a new sister among us. My recent trip to the communes has done much to bring the New Order closer to fruition, and yet it is nothing compared to the jewel we have found in this girl.

'She was prised from us by the powers of darkness. The harmony of our commune in Madras was savaged by intruders, who tore her, screaming and unwilling, from the bosom of the family. We can understand why they wanted to make such a jewel their own, but how foolish of them to think that they could thwart our great work by force. From my heart, I welcome you, Laura. From all our hearts. We all open them to you.'

Laura blushed. Glasses chinked and rose. All eyes stared at her. 'To Laura.'

She clutched the side of the table with both hands. She cleared her throat. 'Th-thank you, thank you,' she said.

Sananda picked up two spears of asparagus, dipped them in hollandaise, and bit off both heads simultaneously.

'You're a lucky girl,' whispered Andy. 'He likes you.'

'Me?'

She nodded. 'I can tell.'

Laura frowned. She left the asparagus untouched.

Laura slept for ten hours. When Andy shook her awake the sun was already high. 'Come on,' she said, 'wake up. They want to see you.'

Laura sat up startled and wiped the sleepy dust from her eyes. 'Who?'

'Father and the wallahs. They are in the library.'

'Christ!' Laura leaped out of bed, splashed her face with cold water, and threw on a dress. Andy led her through a marble hallway and knocked loudly on a mahogany door. A muffled sound came from within.

'Good luck,' whispered Andy.

Laura ran her fingers through her hair, nodded at Andy, then pushed open the heavy door. Around a long polished table sat the eight men in pinstripes. Sananda sat at the end furthest from Laura. He smiled at her. 'Laura, my dear child,' he said. 'There is nothing to be frightened of. There are just a few questions we would like to ask you.' One of the men clicked a gold ballpoint pen.

'Of course, Father,' said Laura.

'Sit down at the end of the table.' A Hepplewhite armchair stood in front of her. Sananda glared at the man in

163

pinstripes on her immediate right. 'You are forgetting your manners.' The man got up and pulled the chair out for her. It slid noiselessly over the Persian carpet.

'Thank you,' said Laura primly and sat down.

The man on her left clicked his pen again. 'We would like to ask you about Brother Guthro,' he said in an emotionless drawl. 'How did you find him?'

Laura moved in her chair. 'Well . . . um . . . fine. What do you mean?'

'Did he always put forward Father's message, and Father's message alone?'

'Well, yes. I mean, we were all working for the New Kingdom together.'

'But it is a question of allegiance. Who did Guthro put forward as the number one? Was it Father or himself?'

'Well, Guthro *was* the head of the commune, so of course we did owe allegiance to him as well. But it was to Father, I think, always to Father.'

'You don't seem too sure.'

'No, I am sure. It was always Father.'

'Did he always play tapes of Father's speeches?' asked a man on the other side of the table.

'Yes, always, while we worked.' Laura swallowed. Her voice wavered, became intense. 'They were an inspiration to us all.' Sananda smiled.

'But how would you — how would you classify Guthro's attitude?' asked the man on Laura's right. 'Co-operative, resentful, lackadaisical? Did he ever refer to Father or any of the rest of us in the Movement in a derogatory way?'

'He did blow his top at times, but I suppose that is only natural.'

The man turned over a sheet of doodles, clicked his pen again, and began writing on a fresh page. 'So how exactly did he blow his top?'

'He swore and shouted at everybody and everything.'

'Including us, including Father?'

'Once or twice maybe. But I was up in the machine-room most of the time so I'm not really the one to ask.'

'And the Cristiana woman, was she still with him?'

'Y-yes.'

'And their relationship was . . .' The pen tapped against the table-top. '. . . intimate?'

'They were certainly close. It was — I always imagined — but I really would not know.'

The man frowned and faced the others. 'Any other questions, gentlemen?' Heads shook, answers were mumbled, the pen clicked again. 'Thank you, Laura,' said the man, 'you have been very helpful.'

'Thank you, my dear child,' echoed Sananda. 'You may go now to your duties. Join Andy in the rose garden.'

Laura found Andy at the back of the house beneath a high brick wall. Old-fashioned roses covered bowers, wooden trestles and the fallen trunk of an old apple tree. A maze of arbours crossed and interlinked. Rosebeds divided them, each of a single colour.

Andy was tending the icebergs. A floppy hat hung over her face. Her gloved hand held a pair of secateurs. She looked up as Laura approached. Only her freckled mouth showed beneath the shadow. 'Oh, there you are. Haven't you a hat?'

'No.'

'Then watch out for the sun.'

'I have been in India.'

'Well, it's up to you. Have you done much gardening before?'

'Not a lot. Daddy only trusted us with clearing away the leaves.'

'Pity, but you should get the hang of it quite quickly. You'll get a fair bit of practice here.' The lips beneath the hat smiled. 'We don't do much else, apart from entertaining a few ageing congressmen. We'll start with a little gentle dead-heading.' She reached in the wicker basket over her

165

arm and took out another pair of secateurs and a pair of thick gloves. 'Put these on. Now, be careful,' said Andy, 'only dead ones. No buds. So what did they want to see you about?'

Laura pulled on the gloves. She shrugged. 'Nothing, really. They just asked me a few questions about Guthro. You know, motivation, that kind of thing.'

'That black guy, you mean? The half-caste? Oh, yes, I remember him. He used to be out here a lot when I first arrived. That was a couple of years ago. He more or less lived here.'

'What did you make of him?'

'Not a lot. He had a mouth like a loudhailer. Anybody would have thought he owned the place. Then one day, silence. He never came back. That girl of his went too, thank God. That Puerto Rican.'

'Cristiana?'

'That's the one.' A brown bloom, dry as rice paper, fell to the ground.

'Still, it was Guthro that rescued me. Guthro and Cristiana.'

'Yes, that must have been pretty bad. The deprogramming, I mean. Did they tie you up, give you drugs and things?'

'Well, they did knock me out, but it wasn't the obvious things that were really frightening. It was like the most terrifying nightmare. You know, faces you once knew coming out at you, but all distorted, warped, full of hate. Shadows, but shadows with flesh. Father always said that when Satan comes, he will attack your most vulnerable point. He will come in the guise of someone familiar to you, someone you once cared about. You pinch yourself, open your eyes, and expect to wake up back at the commune, but they are still there. It's like a nightmare that never ends.' Laura stared straight ahead of her. A thin trail of sweat trickled down her neck.

166

'But you knew it would end. They wouldn't have left you there.'

'Yes, that's what kept me going. I knew they would come and save me. You can bear anything, I suppose, if you know it's going to end. I just played them along. Let them think they were winning through. Stopped them doing anything desperate.'

Andy stroked Laura's cheek with a gloved hand. 'We're all so proud of you, Laura. But how did they get you out?'

Laura smiled. 'Oh, that was easy really. They left me with Tammy, this girl who thought she knew better than Father whom she should marry. Well, Tom, the boy she had a crush on, came and tapped the window. He told her that Father had annulled his marriage to Elsa, wanted him to marry her instead, but she must come now.'

'So what did you do, rush up and overpower her?' Andy took a swipe at a bee with her secateurs.

'No, it wasn't quite like that,' she laughed. 'It was Tammy that let them in.'

'And this Tammy — she get her man?'

'You must be kidding! After what she did! No, she's over here now at one of the training camps on "condition". I am sure she'll be grateful in the end. Poor girl. By the way, what's that hideous great wall for?' Laura gestured.

'Oh, that! That's to ensure that Father's safe and that everything we do in here is very, very private. The administrators work over on that side.'

'Where were you before?'

'A commune in southern California. Father spotted me on one of his routine visits and transferred me here. I was never really cut out for street selling.'

'Were you told why you were being transferred?'

'Father said that he wanted someone who knew about roses, but they had been pretty well cared for before I arrived. Another of the plastic surgeon's obsessions.'

'What about the other girls?'

'Oh, there's always something to do, and it's a great privilege to be so close to Father.' She smirked. 'And I can tell you, you can't get much closer than some of us have got.'

The secateurs froze in Laura's hand. 'You mean he's tried things?'

'Well, try isn't the word, honeybunch. Father does not have to try, it's his anyway. The whole universe is his. He doesn't have to ask. There's part of him in everything. It's almost,' she smiled, 'as if he was doing it to himself.'

'But . . .'

'Hey, open your mind, Laura. Where's your cosmic consciousness?'

'It wasn't so much my mind I was worried about,' Laura said wryly.

'Don't be such a *prude*. OK, so we're stuck in these bodies for a while, but there's no need to get too possessive about them. Like all things, they change.' Andy pointed to a tired bloom, and slowly clipped it off. 'That too was beautiful once.'

Laura stared at the dead bloom on the dark soil. Then she knelt down and picked it up. She turned it slowly in her fingers.

'You are going to have to face it, Laura. What's the big deal? I'd give you a diamond to a doughnut that at the next full moon Father will enrol you as an Elder Sister of the New Order, with all that that entails.'

'With all that that entails,' Laura repeated softly.

'It's a great honour. Most of the girls in the Movement would give their porcelain caps to be an Elder Sister. You are really someone then.'

'So — um, when is the next full moon?'

'A week, ten days.'

'But why me?'

'Because you, honeybunch, have been chosen. That's all there is to it. You're a lucky girl.' Laura's mouth twitched,

168

then she turned and walked away from the rosebed, the dead bloom still in her hand. 'Hey, Laura, is anything the matter?' shouted Andy to her back.

Laura did not turn. 'No, nothing. Nothing at all.'

CHAPTER TWELVE

Bangkok, Thailand

In the entrance hall of the concrete block, two plastic nymphets sported beneath a battery-operated waterfall. A trickle of water splashed their moulded smiles. They clutched a sign illuminated by a lime-green light: 'Meet the girl of your dreams at the Julie Massage Parlour, 4th Floor. Best girls in Bangkok. No credit cards.'

The lift doors slid open and a man with thin, wispy grey hair walked out. He hitched his belt up to his bulging gut, sighed and looked at his watch. 'Strewth!' he muttered, wiped his large hand against his cotton trousers and passed through the glass swing doors into the noise, heat and neon of the Suriwongsee Road.

The evening traffic was stationary. The air was leaden with exhaust fumes. Horns hooted in ragged discord. The man weaved between the cars and jumped in the back of an empty taxi. The driver turned and leered. 'You want girl? You want boy?'

'You want knuckle sandwich?' said the man. 'Take me to the bar of the Oriental, and step on it.'

Five minutes of cursing and sweating later, the man swaggered up to the bar, and perched his swollen rump on a padded bar stool. Liquor bottles gleamed in front of a mirrored wall. He wetted his lips and tapped on the counter. 'Service, Henri, service.'

A small Thai in an immaculate white coat looked up from behind the bar. 'Ah, Mr Rich, the usual?'

'No, one of your specials. I've company.'

The barman moved down the counter until he was opposite Rich. 'Yes. He has arrived. He has been asking for you.'

'Which one is he?' The barman pointed along the counter. 'Oh, that one,' said Rich. 'Show him over.'

The barman whisked along the shelves, swooping on bottles. He shook the concoction and put a tumbler down in front of Rich. Rich took a long swig, then clutched the glass with the care usually reserved for babes in arms.

'Excuse me,' said Philip. 'Are you Rich Alcott?'

'The same, and you must be Bill Peters' mate. G'd-day and welcome to the Front.' He sounded as if he had spent a lifetime torturing innocent vowels. 'That's what I call this place, as some of the best eye-witness accounts of the troubles in south-east Asia from Korea, Laos, Vietnam and Cambodia have been written in this very room. It's part of history. Here, my friend, you see before you the scene of devastation and mortal horror left by one of the most lethal weapons ever to be unleashed upon the West.'

'What?' asked Philip.

'Henri's special. My shout.' Rich slammed down his empty glass on the counter. 'Another napalm, Henri, and one for my good friend here.' He turned to Philip. 'So how are the boys at ITN? I haven't seen them for a while.'

'Fine, I think. I spoke to Bill last week over the telephone, but I have been travelling for the last three months.'

'Where've you been?'

'India.'

'Your drinks, Mr Rich,' said Henri, and placed them on the counter. 'Shall I put them on your slate?' Rich's thumb pointed towards Philip. The barman nodded.

'India,' said Rich. 'You know, one of the great unsung heroes is the cobber who dreamed up the Indian rope trick. Deserved a Pulitzer in creative journalism. He was a pommy hack on an Indian colonial rag at the end of the last century, stuck with the perennial problem. Some weeks damn all happens. You've got the lingerie adverts, in the best possible taste, mind, and a few local tradesmen flogging the latest in tiffin boxes, but what are you going to do with the Gobi Desert in between?

'So, in a moment of inspiration, the Indian rope trick was born. It came straight out of his head, and he wrote it as fact. I bet you could have knocked him down with a chapati when the letters flooded in. Every memsahib this side of the Khyber had a friend or relation who had seen it. But no first-hand accounts, mind. The poor shy hack kept mum until his retirement party, but once the gold-plated pocket watch was in his sweaty hand, he could contain himself no longer. Spilled the beans. No one paid any attention, though. That's history for you.'

Philip took a sip of Henri's special. 'What the hell goes into this?' he spluttered.

Rich smiled. 'The whole shelf, then Henri spits in it. So what took you to India?'

'The Children of Light.'

Rich's fist hit the table. 'Oh, shit!' he sighed. 'Why don't you just clear the hell out of here.' He got up and steadied himself with his hand on the stool. 'Yeah, go on, clear the hell out, damn you.'

'Look,' said Philip seriously, 'I've come to Bangkok specially to see you.'

'That's not my problem. Can't you see I'm busy? I've a story to file.' He walked towards the door. His head was lost in the leaves of a huge kentia palm. 'Damn foliage,' he muttered. 'Like fighting through the fucking jungle.'

'Mr Alcott,' pleaded Philip. 'Please help, you know more about the Children than anybody.'

Rich did not turn. 'Look, I'm sick and tired of wallies coming to me with their hard-luck stories. Go and cry on another drip-dry shirt. I have written attacks on Sananda until I am spare. And what's happened? Fuck all.'

'So? Your conscience is salved. Now you can forget. Families are being broken up every day. Lives are being ruined. Mr Alcott, I need your help.' Rich turned, his fleshy face quivering. His mouth hardened. 'I've got an idea,' Philip added.

'Congratulations, mate.' Rich looked at his watch and sighed. 'OK, I'll give you half an hour, but let's go somewhere else. Here there are ears that make sonar obsolete. Settle up with Henri. We'll go down to Patpong.'

A heavy disco beat reverberated through the crowded pavements. Neon signs flashed the names of bars. Rich stopped at the entrance to 'Hank's Place'. A dwarf pulled back a plastic beaded curtain and beckoned them inside. Rich turned to Philip. 'Don't you ever talk to me of social responsibility again. You haven't been through what I have. You don't know what it means.'

The curtain jangled behind him. Philip pushed through. It was dark and noisy. A smell of musk hung in the thick, smoky air. A go-go dancer in a G-string gyrated her groin on a tiny stage above the bar. Beyond, on a small dance floor, couples clutched each other in a slow grind. The flickering disco lights painted their dead expressions the colours of the rainbow.

A short girl with a wide, open smile came towards them and put her arm around Rich. Her sequined bikini sparkled. 'Ah, Mr Rich,' she said, 'my number one man. You want table?'

'Hey, Jiri,' said Rich. 'Why aren't you up on the platform wriggling your guts?'

She frowned. 'No good today. I've got a stitch. What's the use of a go-go dancer with a stitch? You sorry for me? You buy me drink?'

'What, some of that green slime at thirty bucks a glass? Later, maybe. First, get us a table, will you, sweetie? Time to share a few jokes with the whisky bottle.'

'OK.' Jiri took them to a small table in the corner away from the dance floor.

'What's yours?' Rich asked Philip.

'Whisky.'

'I hope you like it with water. They add it anyway.' He turned to the girl. 'Two whiskies. Jiri, you know? That brown stuff that comes out of a bottle, not that clear stuff out of the tap.'

'Very good, Mr Rich.' The girl turned, teetering on her high heels.

Rich leered across the table. 'So what's yours like, preppy? Eh? She must be one hell of a sheila for you to be poncing off halfway round the globe.'

Philip bristled. 'It's not that. She . . .'

'Don't tell me. She's got a beautiful mind. Light shining out of her whatever. Like it. A lovesick pommy. India, you say? Was Guthro still there?'

'Yeah.'

'You know he used to be the most powerful guy in the whole movement. Sananda would still be muttering mantras on some mountaintop if it wasn't for him. They were partners, and it was Guthro who handled the cash, lucky sod. But he blew it. He was so damn greedy. That and the tart he was hanging out with. The wallahs ousted him.'

'I don't get it.'

'Preppy, try not to be naive. We are talking about a financial conglomerate that would shame a multinational. And where there's that type of money, the MBAs move in. The irony was that Guthro hired them in the first place. The funds were getting too big for one man to control, and Guthro wanted to play the stock market, buy real estate, start a newspaper, make the Movement a political force, find new outlets for the communes' products. The boy thought big and hired well, too damn well for his own good. What he hadn't reckoned with was their sheer professionalism. Ask them to guard a honeypot and they won't be happy until they are swimming about inside.'

'So they ousted him?'

'You can just imagine it, can't you? The board meeting of

"The New Kingdom Central Committee" held in some fancy attorney's office with fifteen men in immaculately pressed pinstripe suits, Sananda in his robes muttering some Eastern wisdom about the sea and the sky, and Guthro bad mouthing it, like a black mafioso with money to burn. Of course, it couldn't last. They needed Sananda, but Guthro was expendable. He was blocking their way.'

'Sananda didn't stand by him?'

'He tried, I think, in a half-hearted sort of way but, in the end, they made Guthro so hot, he couldn't. It was easy for them. Guthro had a record from the old days, anyhow, and used the Movement's funds like his own bankroll. Two or three million dollars were missing. He had bought a place in Florida as a retirement home, that sort of thing, and the cash had just gone to his head. They had not been properly advised, and the IRS were breathing down their necks. The accounts were a shambles. The wallahs made it clear that unless Guthro went, the Movement would lose its status as a church and there was no way they could square the IRS. Sananda had no alternative.'

'So Guthro went.'

Rich smiled. 'They played him along, sent him on tours of the communes and asked him to supervise a new crusade in India. It was conveniently far away. He returned to find his cheques on the Movement funds bounced like a rubber ball. Tough titty.'

'How did you find all this out?' asked Philip.

Rich raised an eyebrow. 'Now that's not a question to ask a journalist. I got interested early on as Judy got involved with them when Sananda first came to Manhattan. She took me to see him a few times when I was over there to kiss the feet of my bounteous editor.'

'She's your daughter?'

'Was.' Jiri arrived with the drinks. 'About bloody time,' said Rich. 'Bring the bottle, will you?'

The girl giggled. 'Oh, Mr Rich, you are such a man.'

'OK, and one green slime for you. Put it on the check.'

'Thank you, Mr Rich, thank you.' She left.

Rich's eyes followed her, then he downed the whisky in one. 'You wouldn't believe it, in those days Sananda held his meetings in a small flat on Manhattan's west side. You had to fight your way through the garbage and climb up some stone steps to the fifth floor. There in front of grubby sheers draped with garlands of plastic flowers, stood the self-acclaimed "Enlightened One from Nepal". Guthro always stood by his side, protecting his investment. He was meant to be translating, though I think he made up a lot of it himself. It was the usual tosh about harmony and the spirit.'

'Did they attract much of a crowd?'

'Well, the first time I went they were talking to the cockroaches, but soon it was standing room only. Predominantly older women with loose flowery skirts, bloody great sunglasses and hairy armpits. Then the young came. Remember, it was the early seventies. People were still looking for things. Themselves, for example. The old hippy dreams were still alive. Judy was hooked, but it didn't worry me then. She was a qualified dental hygienist, and had a good job waiting for her back in Sydney. But God, she was a pain in the arse at dinner. She tried to persuade me to become a vegetarian, and burst into tears about the poor cows. It was very seriously boring. I suppose I shouldn't say it now, but I was counting the minutes to get away. Hell, I had a fucking war to report. I had seen men mangled into summer pudding. I wasn't going to turn soppy for the sake of a few cows.'

'Didn't you think she was at risk?'

'Sananda and Guthro had nothing then. They were just peddling words — mystic masturbation. They had no organization, no cash. It was innocuous enough. The problems really started when they hooked Ethyl Brankhead, an old society broad with real money. The kind that speaks. After old Mr Brankhead died, she got religion, and adopted Sananda as her personal guru. She lent him a house in New Jersey, and they started their first commune, and their damn courses. Then the spotty rock stars joined in and they were away.' Rich refilled his glass and downed a slug of whisky, then rubbed his cheek with his hand. His face was jelly.

'But you couldn't have known,' said Philip.

Rich did not look up from the table. 'What difference does it make now? You can't wrap your daughter up in mothballs. She had never shown any signs of instability, though it must have been there somewhere. They broke her, those bastards broke her. We never found out what it was. Some damn therapy. Been in the funny farm now for seven years. Shits in her pants and doesn't even recognize me. And she howls – God she howls.'

'I'm sorry,' said Philip.

Rich glared back. 'Look, preppy, I don't want your sympathy. I just did what I could and hell, there was a good story in it. Still is, if you like tilting at windmills, but I'm too old.' Rich took another gulp of whisky. He slammed down the glass on the table-top.

Philip felt a girl's hand on his shoulder, long black hair on his cheek. 'Hi,' said the girl. 'Which ship you on?' Philip pushed her hand away.

'Piss off,' said Rich. He leaned back on his chair and crossed his legs. 'Have you tried deprogramming, preppy?'

Philip lowered his eyes. 'Yes.'

'And you cocked it up.' Rich frowned. 'Then I think you've blown it. Might as well drown your sorrows. I'll get Jiri to fix you up.'

Philip's eyes narrowed. 'Christ! What sort of man are you? You can't just give up – not once you've seen what they do to people.'

'Hey, keep your cool, preppy. What are you planning to do? Expose them to the world? I tried it. I, the best goddamn professional in the business. So what can a lovelorn pommy preppy do that I can't, eh? Sananda's press makes Nixon look like Mother Teresa, but the shit washes off like in biological soap powder. He has money, he has friends, expensive friends, and he has the law behind him. His affairs have been investigated five times by government bodies in the States, yes, five times, and all they have found is the occasional street-selling offence, and minor abuses of the charity laws. And each time an investigation has been announced, the civil liberty boys have kicked up a stink. They say Congress is interfering with the constitutional right of all Americans to religious freedom, and Sananda's expensive friends all nod.

'The politicians are frightened of him. Just imagine; as one man he can mobilize tens of thousands of supporters, who vote the way he wants, feed the party machine, are there to stage a rally, a demonstration — what have you. That's even more valuable than the money. And Sananda asks for very little in return. What do you think you can do? You're dreaming, preppy, you're dreaming.'

'But it's a scandal. It's evil. Lives are being destroyed . . .'

'I know that, you know that, but no one who hasn't been through it believes that brainwashing crap. It's too hot to touch. Ask any congressman — religion is a political graveyard. They like their liberties clean and simple.'

'Then somebody's got to do something. It's up to us.'

'Look, preppy, where did you get this "us"? Whatever cockeyed scheme is running through that love-crazed head of yours, leave me out of it, OK?'

'I know we can do it. We can destroy them. Really.'

'That's big talk, preppy.'

'All Sananda's enemies need is a lever to crucify him, and it's so simple . . .'

'Yeah, yeah, sure. Tell me about it.'

Philip leaned towards Rich and whispered in his ear.

Rich nodded, and took another slug of whisky. He waved the empty glass dismissively and mumbled something. Three more girls approached them, sinuous and smiling, during the next fifteen minutes. All left, sullen and slouching. Rich recharged his own glass five times, Philip only once.

'So?' said Philip, at last.

'So what?'

'Will you help?'

Rich sat back in his chair and crossed his legs. 'Look, preppy, I don't think you understand what you're getting yourself into. You are taking the law into your own hands. It's dirty, messy. Why not cool down, think about it. Relax. Take a few days' holiday, then think some more.'

'Can you forget? And what about the others still in there? Don't we owe it to them?'

'I could not give a monkey's for them. If I were to do it at all, I'd do it for myself, for Judy. Nothing but nice, healthy, clean revenge.'

'Could you fix up the New York end?'

'I would have to talk to a few people.'

'And the blueprints?'

'They could be sent over. What about the date?'

'September first. The date of the mass rally at Madison Square Garden. The climax of his Pilgrimage for Peace. Then it would hurt, really hurt. In the middle of August Sananda is going on a world tour of his communes. He will pick up the commune heads and bring them to New York for the convention. They'll all be there. All the worms in the same tin.'

'Look, I don't like it. I don't think it will work.'

'So what are we going to do? Let Sananda get away with it? How many more girls are going to end up like Judy and Laura? There *is* something we can do, Rich. You and I can stop it forever.'

'Skip the histrionics, you Stone Age bastard. OK, if you

can pull off the dirty bit, you can count on me in New York. But just remember, Rich Alcott always comes up smelling of roses. If you louse it up, you're on your own.'

'Thanks, Rich, thanks a lot.'

Rich smiled and handed him a folded slip of paper. 'Thank me after you have seen your check.'

CHAPTER THIRTEEN

Laura paced up and down her room. She wore only a blue silk dressing gown. The roots of her hair were blonde now, her fingers and toes manicured, her legs waxed.

There was a knock on the glass door. It slid back and Andy entered. A long red robe hung over her arm. 'Honeybunch, I've brought you your ceremonial robe.'

Laura glanced at her, then lowered her head. 'I just can't go through with it. I can't.'

'Laura, you can't back out now. It's all prepared. Dinner's over, everyone's waiting.'

'Let them wait.'

A gong sounded three times. 'That's your cue. You're on.'

'I said let them wait.'

Andy carefully laid the robe down on the bed. 'Don't be so nervous,' she said. 'You're covered in blotches.'

'Oh, God, am I?' Laura quickly pulled open the wardrobe door and looked in the mirror.

'Don't worry. It won't show in the candlelight. Now pull yourself together. I'm sure you are going to be great. There is nothing to be frightened of. Look upon it as a baptism into the mystic order, a fusing of mind, body and spirit.'

'Oh, yeah!'

'Look, we're talking about Father, for God's sake, the greatest man who ever lived, the man who is going to bring the New Kingdom on earth, not some pimp from off the street.'

Laura was still looking at herself in the mirror. Despite the tan, her skin seemed blue-white. She patted her face distractedly.

The gong sounded again. 'Last orders!' shouted Andy, then took hold of Laura's shoulder and spun her round so that she faced her. Laura glared at her. 'Look,' said Andy, 'do you want to become an Elder Sister or don't you? It's up to you, entirely up to you.'

Laura's lips trembled. She lowered her eyes. 'Yes, I do,' she said softly.

'Then get off your butt and get out there.'

Laura clenched her fists. 'I know you're right. Yes, of course you are. OK, Andy. I've just got so many — I don't know — so many silly egotistical hang-ups to overcome. But don't worry. I will go through with it, I will, I will, I will!'

'Attagirl.' Andy took her hand and squeezed it. 'It'll be easy, really it will.'

Laura stepped out into the courtyard. The long red robe hung loosely from her breasts and swept lightly over the flagstones. There was a circle of light in front of the house. She swallowed twice and walked towards it. She drew closer and gasped.

In front of her the Children squatted around a painted parchment scroll, some twenty feet square depicting a man's open palm. Grotesque models stood on each finger. Candles flickered on small golden shrines bedecked with fruit and flowers. Emeralds glinted.

Laura's eyes were fixed on the effigy standing in the centre of the palm. It had blonde hair down to the shoulder, the same nose as her, the same mouth, the same jaw, the same lips, the same red robe. Only the eyes were different. Two small diamonds sparkled in the yellow wax.

Andy came up behind her. 'Don't worry,' she said, 'there is nothing to fear. The ceremony is based on the *gyepshi*, an old Sherpa rite of purification. The powers of darkness are offered jewels and fruit if they will accept the effigy instead of your soul.' Laura made no reply. Andy pointed to the wrist of the hand. 'Sit there,' she said, 'facing sideways.'

Laura passed through the group, rearranged her robe and

squatted on the roll. The Children did not look at her. They stared steadfastly in front of them.

The gong sounded again. Sananda bustled into the circle, white robe billowing out behind him. He sat down opposite Laura, no more than a foot away. Suddenly the air was filled with a rich sweet smell. Smoke rose up around the circle. She caught his eye. He gave a little consoling smile.

A deep booming sound seemed to come from beneath the earth. The effigy shook. The candles guttered and flickered. Voices chanted. 'Sananda, Doevo, Sananda, Kanticasta, Sananda Paripashan; Pankiparatin Dusan. Sananda, Doevo . . .'

Sananda took a large silver goblet in his hands, held it above his head, then handed it to Laura. 'Sip this,' he said softly. 'Let the nectar course through your veins until each corpuscle is awakened. Let the petals open. It is the koumiss of the New Kingdom.'

Laura took hold of the goblet and raised it to her lips. She sipped.

'More, my child, more.' Sananda smiled gently.

Laura sipped again. She swayed slightly. Sananda took the goblet from her. Their fingers touched. Then he sipped from it himself.

'Sananda, Doevo, Sananda, Kanticasta, Sananda Paripashan; Pankiparatin Dusan.'

Kernels of grain and rose petals pattered over the effigy. Sananda held Laura's head in his hands. He stared into her eyes. Her lips trembled. The Children grouped around her. They were close now. In the candlelight, their faces quivered like ghostly images in a fire. Their bodies swayed rhythmically.

Laura's eyes were fixed on his. She did not blink. Her pupils grew like inkstains on blotting paper. Drums sounded. A sitar played. The smell of incense grew stronger, heavier.

He stared. Her nostrils twitched. Her skin turned grey.

Fine bands of sweat gathered on her brow. A mesh of red wires spliced the whites of her eyes. Hands went out to her, caressed her thighs, her back, her neck, her hair.

'Sananda, Doevo, Sananda, Kanticasta, Sananda Paripashan; Pankiparatin Dusan.'

The corners of Laura's mouth turned down. Her eyes closed, her body went limp. Sananda signalled. The chanting stopped instantly. 'Laura is cleansed!' he shouted. 'She is ready and worthy to become an Elder Sister of the New Kingdom.' He turned to her. 'Come, my child.' He spoke softly. 'Now we must wash away the scars of your previous life. Only then will you be free.' Laura did not react. Sananda rose to his feet. 'Come,' he said again.

Laura opened her eyes lazily and looked up at him. A small voice whispered, 'Yes, Father.'

Sananda offered her his hand. She took it. She stumbled, clutched his hand tightly, and he pulled her to her feet.

They entered through a door on the right of the house. They were in a cavern. The low roof looked as if it had been chiselled out of black rock. Only a dull shine betrayed it as fibreglass. Narrow beams of light shone down from the tips of a stalactite on to a pool of green whirling water. Boulders stood around the pool; empty glasses sat on some, cushions on others.

Sananda was the first in the water. Wearing only a cotton loincloth, he walked down the steps to the centre of the pool. The water swirled about his short brown legs. A smile formed on his lips. 'Laura,' he called. 'Your inner body has been cleansed. Now let the water free you.'

Laura bent down and raised her arms. Andy pulled off the ceremonial robe. Laura rose and stood at the water's edge. She wore only a pair of white knickers. Her arms crossed and covered her breasts. She stepped down into the jacuzzi, hesitated for a moment, then walked up to Sananda. She was a foot taller. Softly the Children chanted. Their voices carried over the water.

Sananda placed the palms of his hands on Laura's shoulder blades, and pushed down. Laura's head disappeared beneath the surface. 'First you lose your scars,' said Sananda.

Her head reappeared and he pushed again. 'Then you die a death.'

He pushed again. 'The third time, you are reborn.'

'Praise be to Father!' the Children cried. 'Praise be to Father!' A white mist spewed out of ducts around the pool and covered the water.

Laura surfaced and spluttered. She held her hand to her mouth and coughed. She nodded and whispered, 'Thank you, Father, thank you.'

Sananda smiled, then, without a word, walked up the steps and out of the jacuzzi. Andy handed him a white towelling bathrobe. He beckoned to Laura. She followed. Andy held out an identical bathrobe, quickly wrapped it around Laura's wet body and scooped her hair up over the collar. 'Good luck,' she whispered. Laura swallowed.

Sananda led the way two paces in front of her. She followed him along the courtyard, past the swimming pool, past her room, and through a glass door into the west wing of the house. They crossed a small corridor, then Sananda turned the knob on a mahogany door. He waited for Laura, ushered her in, and closed the door behind him.

Heavy red velvet curtains hung from heavy scalloped pelmets. Tibetan paintings framed on silk rolls covered the walls. Bronzes of Eastern gods crowded the tables. At the far end of the room stood a large swivel chair and an imposing mahogany desk covered with photograph frames. The only light in the room came from one standard lamp by the desk and down-lighters and up-lighters around the treasures.

Laura breathed in deeply. There was a sweet smell of flowers and spices in the air. Sananda touched her lightly on the shoulder and pointed towards the sofa. It was a bed of tulsi leaves. Garlands of hibiscus were strewn over the armrests. A dozen pots lay on the floor beside it. 'You are soon to be an Elder Sister. You have been cleansed and you are free. Now you are worthy to receive the message of the New Kingdom. Sit down, my child.'

Laura perched on the edge of the sofa. She clutched her knees with her hands. Sananda sat down beside her, a foot away. She turned only her head towards him. 'There are things,' said Sananda, 'which are not yet ripe to put into words.' His hand flapped. 'And things which will be forever outside their ambit. They must be learnt in other ways.' His head bowed slightly. 'Such is the seed of knowledge of the New Kingdom.'

Laura swallowed, and she clutched her knees tighter. 'You mean, Father . . .'

Sananda put a finger to his lips. 'I can teach you,' he said, 'and only I. The seed of the New Kingdom will be yours, but first you must relax. Put your mind at peace. Lie down, my child, lie down.' He rose.

Laura tightened the knot on her bathrobe, and lay stiffly on the sofa. The leaves crackled. Her arms were folded under her chin, her legs pressed together so that her ankles met. Drops of water trickled down the strands of her hair on to the leaves.

Sananda knelt down by Laura's side, took hold of the collar of her bathrobe, turned it in his fingers, then gently lowered it over her shoulder blades. She did not react. He ran outstretched dark-brown fingers across her white skin. Then the fingers pressed hard into the little dips around the nape of her long neck. Laura sighed. 'You like that?' said Sananda softly.

'It makes me feel sleepy.' His hands lingered there. 'Father,' she said dreamily, 'being an Elder Sister. What does it mean, actually mean?'

'Relax, my child, relax. When the great day comes and

the New Kingdom stretches across the globe, you will be a queen, because you will have knowledge of the seed. Is that what you want, my queen?'

'Father, I w-w-want nothing. Just whatever will bring love to the world. Whatever you want. Whatever you want of me.' She lifted her head off the side of the sofa, and turned on to her back. She bit her lip. 'But, Father, does it — does it have to be so soon?'

Sananda's hand waved. 'Tonight it is a full moon. Tonight it is ordained. My queen, since the beginning of time, the great mysteries have been the preserve of the Tantrists. And they knew, yes, they knew the ultimate cannot be taught through the mind.' He pressed his hands together in an arc. 'Only through a meeting of the body and spirit on the night of the full moon when Shakti and Shiva are one.

'First your neck and cheeks must be anointed with keora; your hands with jasmine; your hair with spikenard; your stomach with musk; your thighs with sandal paste; your feet with khus; and your breasts with champa and hina. Only then will you be ready for your journey down the river to samarasa.'

Laura's shoulders were hunched forward. Her foot beat against the sofa. 'And it is the only way,' she whispered.

'The only way.' Sananda bent down and put his finger under Laura's chin. He lifted up her head and gazed into her eyes. A cruel line crossed her forehead. 'What is the matter, my queen? Do your eyes not like what they see?'

'No, Father, it's not that.'

'Then what is it, my child?'

Laura twisted her fingers around the cord on her bathrobe. 'Father, what would you say if I told you . . .' Suddenly she stopped.

'What, Laura?'

'No, it's nothing, Father.'

Sananda put his hand on hers. 'Come, my child, we must have no secrets between us.'

'Father, no man on earth has your warmth, your heart. No man. Take me down the river to samarasa. Anoint me, Father. Anoint me.'

'So be it, child.' He smiled with childish delight. 'My Elder Sister, my queen.' Sananda went over to the side of the sofa and dipped his fingers in a pot resting on a small burner, then ran his fingers through Laura's hair. Laura smiled, traced her hair with her fingers, and smelt the rich scent on her hands. Sananda anointed her neck and cheeks. 'Such beauty,' he whispered.

Laura lay lazily sprawled on the sofa. Her hands hung loosely at her sides. The warm oils soaked into her skin. Sananda poured khus over her feet and rubbed sandal paste over her legs. He reached over and gently untied the knot in her bathrobe. Laura closed her eyes. He lifted one side of the gown. Her hand quickly covered her breast. Sananda lifted the other flap, leaned towards her, put his arms around her shoulders and lifted her arms out of the bathrobe. Laura waved her head listlessly and lay back.

The light trickled over her soft white skin, splashed on to the Persian rug, now strewn with scattered petals. Her stomach shifted slightly with every breath. Her breasts rose and fell.

Sananda stared at her, motionless, then smiled and poured oil on his hands. He knelt at the edge of the sofa. Oil dribbled on to her breasts, her stomach. 'Mmm,' she said and smiled. Her left hand rose and rested without pressure on his shoulder.

His hands started working just below her right breast. Laura shuddered. Her eyes opened slowly, lazily. She stretched, looked down at his hand, then into his eyes. She continued to smile and to watch him, eyes wide and expressionless as marble, as the hand slowly massaged the soft white flesh of her breasts. As it brushed, flicked and teased her hard nipples, her fingers tightened on the nape of his neck, fluttering and stroking over his hair.

There was silence then, but for the gentle hissing and slapping sounds of his wet hands on her skin and their quickening breath. Somewhere outside, a dog barked. Distant voices laughed and chatted.

'Such tenderness,' Sananda breathed in a clogged whisper. 'The tenderness of a goddess at one with all nature. A beautiful, beautiful queen. My queen.' He leaned towards her now. His breath was warm on her throat. The robe for a moment obscured her sight. His hand kept working. 'Trust me, my child,' he said huskily. 'Trust me. You are the future, the source and the spring of life for me, and for the New Kingdom. Trust me. Laura . . .'

Their lips met. He kissed her lightly at first and her lips barely moved. He stroked her cheek softly. Then his arm went round her neck and pulled her hard against him. Her lips opened. Her teeth separated and her body arched upwards. 'Master,' she gasped. 'Father . . .'

For a full minute then there was no sound but Laura's gasps and groans and their ever-quickening breath. When at last she pushed gently at his chest and lay back, she said, 'Father, I've never felt so secure, you know. I haven't felt so safe since I was a little girl.' Her voice was slurred. Her eyelids were heavy again.

Above her, Sananda grinned. His breath was heavy now. Sweat pearled his temples. He untied his bathrobe and shrugged it off his shoulders. He turned a switch on his left. The lights dimmed.

'So safe . . .' Laura's forefinger ran over his shoulders, his chest. 'So protected . . .' Sananda's hand trembled as it pushed up her inner thigh and rested on the thin wet cotton at her crotch. One finger slipped inside.

Laura's body jack-knifed. A sound like a cat's snarl came from the back of her throat. 'Please,

Father,' she said quickly, crisply. 'Please don't spoil it.'

A deep gravelly sound was Sananda's only reply. His shoulder muscles tightened around Laura's neck. His tongue was on her face, her throat. His left hand gripped the top of her knickers. He pulled. The fabric ripped. Her hand darted to her crotch. 'No!' She pushed him. 'No, Father, please don't spoil it, please, don't. Please!'

Her fist pummelled against the sweat-soaked flesh. Something hard pushed at her stomach. 'Oh, oh, oh, oh,' she whimpered. 'No . . .?'

Then, suddenly, above the rhythmical sound of her sobbing, there was a howl of pain. It was not a girl's high-pitched shriek. It was the voice of a man.

Sananda slumped forward writhing and gasping for breath. For a moment, the sofa was still, then Laura slid out from under him and stood, moist petals sticking to her skin and pattering on to the carpet. She grabbed the bathrobe and wrapped it around her. 'I'm – I'm sorry, Father,' she sobbed as she walked slowly backwards towards the door. 'I really am. I didn't mean to do that, really I'm sorry.'

She turned and ran to the door. 'Laura!' The voice that followed her was weak and high. 'Laura!'

She did not turn. The door slammed behind her.

CHAPTER FOURTEEN

Madras, India

Philip slammed the door behind him and flung his suitcase down on the little truckle bed. He threw off his jacket and mopped his brow. Sweat ran in rivulets down the side of his nose and glistened on the thick blue stubble on his jaw. His eyes were dull yellow and bloodshot, his hair matted and unkempt.

He looked around the room and sniffed. There were no sheets on the bed. Dry black hair curled out through the broken seams of a thin mattress. The sink in the corner was small and dirty. The wallpaper was of three shades of green — pea, olive and vivid electric — punctuated at irregular intervals by huge orange flowers. The unshaded light bulb hung from a cracked and blistered ceiling. He flicked a switch. A fan turned slowly and very noisily.

Philip unbuttoned his shirt as he walked towards the window. He squinted in the dark-yellow evening sunlight. The hotel stood at the end of a row of peeling beige houses. Immediately opposite the window, a dark alleyway led to the corner of the market square. He heard the constant seething, the rattle of bickering and barter.

On the far left, a group of beautiful dark-skinned Tamil women twittered over lengths of floral prints. Skinny boys, no more than thirteen or fourteen, stood guard over piles of Colgate toothpaste, Marvel dried milk and Lucozade bottles on a breeze-block stall. Dogs and beggars lined the wall, waiting for alms in cash or kind. Philip smiled humourlessly. He stripped off his shirt and turned back to the basin. 'Perfect,' he said. 'Absolutely perfect.'

An hour later, Philip clattered down the stairs and

stepped out into the thick smells and sounds of a bazaar evening. As he started down the dark alleyway towards the square, a husky voice behind him said, 'Howdy, mister. You American?'

He turned. A slim brown boy leaned in the hotel doorway, a long American cigarette unlit in his hand. The boy's skinny legs and arms were those of a twelve- or thirteen-year old, but the face was older. 'No,' Philip grinned, 'English.'

'Gee.' The boy shrugged. 'You gotta light, if you please . . . man?' he added as an afterthought.

'Er – no, sorry. Don't smoke,' Philip replied and walked on.

'Hotel belongs to my father.' The boy trotted along beside him. He puffed out his chest. 'Very fine hotel, no? Television. I can see Westerns from America. One day I am going to America.'

'Good,' said Philip.

'Anything you want, ask Ravi.' The boy strutted. 'My name is Ravi, but here I am called Ronnie, like Reagan. I am a cowboy too.'

Philip smiled and turned briefly to look down a long straight street to his left. Craftsmen sat on the ground or worked at their benches amongst statues, furniture, racks of clothes and trays of jewellery.

The boy tapped his arm and said, 'So what can I be doing for you, mister? You want a girl?'

'No, thanks.'

'A boy? I've lots of friends.'

'No, no thanks.'

'Alcohol? Opium? Hashish?'

'Look, Ravi, Ronnie, I'm busy right now. See you later, OK?' Philip moved on into the square. Suddenly, all around him, there was shouting and argument. He was surrounded by the brilliant colours of silks, cottons and the polyesters which the Indians so prize. Spangled saris and the Polynesian-style lungis rustled as they brushed by.

Black, brown and yellow faces bobbed into view then vanished into the seething crowd.

Smells clashed and merged. The acrid odour of fish spread out to dry on rush matting made way for fluffy clouds of cardamon and coriander, cumin, saffron, dill, the familiar whiff of marijuana, flowers, fruit and faeces.

Philip followed the smell of marijuana. It came from a man standing in the lane between the stalls. He had greasy, curly hair and a thin moustache. One hand held a reefer, the other waved at two tourists. The tourists walked past. The man returned Philip's gaze. 'Hey!' he said, 'you want hashish? Malawi, Afghani black, Nepali gold? Top quality.'

Philip stopped. 'What else've you got?' A lump formed in his throat. 'Have you got, have you got . . . heroin?' he whispered.

The man's fingers reached out and grabbed Philip's arm. They held on tight. The man smiled. 'Smack, best quality. Yes, we have smack.' He beckoned with his head. 'Come.'

'You no go with him,' yelled a high, husky voice from below. 'You no go.' A small fist beat against his ribs. Philip looked down. Ravi. 'Come away, come.'

Philip looked at both of them, freed his arm and followed Ravi.

'Hey,' said the boy. 'Ronnie's your friend. You need something, you ask Ronnie, OK?' He stopped and turned to him. 'So you want smack. You ask man in bazaar and what happens? He takes your money and you buy world's most expensive talcum powder. Ask Ronnie. He knows.'

'So,' asked Philip casually, 'where would someone go if they wanted heroin? A lot of it.'

The boy frowned. 'I cannot get someone a lot. I can get someone only a little. If someone want a lot, I know however whom to see.' He leaned back and nodded smugly. There was silence for a moment.

'So?' said Philip.

'So it is very difficult information to remember.'

'What would ten rupees do for your memory, tough boy?'

'Very much good.' The boy held out his hand. 'All right. In the bazaar, further down.' He pointed. 'Ask for Mr Husani. He will find you the right persons.'

'Can you show me where to go?'

'Sorry, no. In the bazaar they know me. My mother would beat me if she were knowing I ask for Mr Husani.'

'OK.' Philip wandered off along the lane. 'I'll see you later, Ronnie. Thanks.'

He pressed through a fleshy forest, a jungle of thin, wiry limbs. A huge, teetering pile of old tins and oil cans clanked and clattered past. Beneath it, two small eyes stared rigidly ahead. Sacks of fruit passed, bags spilling grain, bald lorry tyres, more cans.

On Philip's right, a stall sold plastic goods. Brightly coloured water bottles hung from the roof. A man stood by them, brandishing a feather duster. 'Please,' said Philip, 'I'm looking for . . . er, Husani, Mr Husani?'

The man looked at Philip disdainfully, then scowled. He pointed the duster at a shack two along on the other side of the alley, and turned his back.

Philip walked across. Suitcases and trunks were stacked up to the roof in front of the shack and spilled out on to the dirt forecourt. All were faced with metal from recycled cans: Pepsi, 7UP, Mobil. A thin dark man hammered an already flattened oil can on a table. He wore a grubby loincloth and a baseball cap. 'Is there a Mr Husani here?' asked Philip.

The man's eyes swivelled. His head did not move. 'Who wants him?' he replied.

'Someone with a business proposition.'

The man shouted something over his shoulder then resumed his hammering. A door at the back of the shop creaked. A tiny head with a huge moustache peered around the jamb. It gabbled a question. The man in the baseball cap grunted his reply between hammer blows. The moustache bobbed twice. 'You come.' A hand grabbed Philip's sleeve and pulled.

He passed through a narrow corridor lit by a single naked light bulb, then into the back room. The man closed the door behind him and crossed his hands behind his back.

A large man sat behind a rough wooden desk at the other end of the room. He was fat and yellow, more Arab than Indian, with a bushy black beard and a balding head. His face was in shadow. One hand rested on the desk turning a string of amber beads the size of strawberries. The other held a telephone. He spoke rapidly in Hindi, then bellowed and slammed down the receiver. He squeezed the beads in his hand. Philip stepped forward. 'Mr Husani?'

'Mr Husani is not here,' the fat man said in a deep voice which made the walls hum. 'What do you want?'

'I have a business proposition for him. When will he be here?'

The man shrugged. 'Who knows? Only Mr Husani knows. But anything you want to say to him you can say to me.' The man glanced at his watch. 'Sit down.' A spindly chair hit the back of Philip's calves. He sat. 'So, what is it?'

'I was looking for some special merchandise. I understand — well, I was told that Mr Husani might be able to help.'

The beads whirled around the man's pudgy fingers. 'What do you want?'

'They're — um, pharmaceuticals. You could call them recreational pharmaceuticals.'

'We sell trunks.'

'Yes, but . . . I thought maybe Mr Husani might know . . . maybe he has a friend who could help.'

The man shook his head. 'No.'

'Then I'm . . . I'm sorry,' said Philip. 'I was misinformed.' He rose.

The man's hand flapped. He leaned back in his chair.

'Haste is such an unattractive thing. And so dangerous. I do not like sudden movements, Mr . . .?'

'Smith.'

'Of course, of course. Ritual makes life safe, Mr Smith. Sit down. Let us talk slowly, calmly. Now, first we must establish what we are talking about, hmm?' A hand pressed down on Philip's shoulder. He sat. 'So, what are we talking about?'

The hammering outside stopped. Philip waited until it had begun again before he spoke. 'Heroin. Five kilos. Processed.'

'Five kilos.' The man fingered his beard, shifted his weight from one buttock to the other and sighed. 'Five kilos, and processed. Now. Arithmetic. I hate arithmetic, don't you, Mr Smith? Five kilos at six thousand dollars a kilo makes . . .'

'I can make the arithmetic easier.' Philip smiled. 'Five kilos at one thousand dollars a kilo. That's a much nicer sum.'

'Oh, yes, yes.' The stomach shook. The eyebrows bobbed. 'Easier but unrealistic. The street price in Europe is two hundred a kilo.' A silhouette of a man passed across the drawn curtain.

'Yeah, but we are not on the street. Will you be able to help me or not?'

'I don't know, Mr Smith. We don't know you. We don't know you at all. You come to us without an introduction. How much money do you have? US dollars or sterling.'

'Enough.'

'Show me the money. Then we talk.' The man dropped the beads on the table. Philip's chair was pulled away from under him. A hand gripped his shoulder and pushed him along the passage and out into the bazaar.

As soon as he stepped out he saw them. A group of five tanned Europeans distributing leaflets, strolling slope-shouldered through the bazaar towards him. All had dark, sunken eyes. They wore the uniform T-shirts and faded jeans. One of them wore a silver pendant around his neck.

He darted into the next doorway along and waited there with a foul-smelling goat until they had passed. There were two young men and three girls. He recognized none of them, but that did not mean that they couldn't recognize him.

There was no avoiding them, though. Three times more, he managed to hide before they saw him in his wanderings through the bazaar. On the third day, however, as he returned to the hotel from breakfast with his now firm friend, Ravi, he turned a corner and walked straight into a group of ten or more.

He stopped for a second, then walked on with studied casualness. A tall blonde girl with a big jaw turned and hissed something to the group. They planted their feet apart then and the girl droned, 'Satan out! Satan out!' The chant was taken up by the others. 'Satan *out*! Satan *out*!'

'What are these persons doing?' Ravi followed Philip, plucking at his trousers. 'What have you done, Philip?'

'Nothing.' Philip set his jaw and weaved his way through the chanting group. 'Let's get out of here.'

'National Westminster. Hello?'

'Hello, this is Philip Strickland. I am calling from Madras, India. Could you tell me how much I've got in my account?'

'That will be the correspondence department, sir,' said a girl's voice. 'We'll put you through.' The line went dead.

The glass booth was like a greenhouse. Philip wiped his forehead and pushed open the sliding door. No draught came through. A child screamed. A man read out a telegram in Hindi very slowly and loudly. The telex machine started. 'Correspondence here.'

He closed the door. 'Hello, this is Philip Strickland. I'm

calling from India. Could you tell me how much I've got in my account?'

'For purposes of identification would you tell us for how many years you have been banking with us?'

'Christ! Well, my father opened the account for me after I left prep school. That must have been seventeen, eighteen years at least. Look, I don't know. How long was it?'

'Sir, we could not possibly divulge that type of information until we are sure that you are indeed our Mr Strickland. We will have to ask you another question. What is your mother's maiden name?'

'Slingsby.'

'Good. Well, sir, you are one thousand, two hundred and three pounds and sixty-two pence overdrawn.'

'Shit. Look, I've got some certificates in a unit trust. I'd like to sell them.'

'That'll be stocks and shares. I'll put you through.' The line went dead again.

Philip sighed and pushed open the sliding door. A limousine had stopped outside the main entrance of the post office. A dark, tall, thin man got out. He peered through the doorway, looked at Philip, then walked across to the fruit bar opposite. Guthro. The offside door of the car opened, Cristiana climbed out and followed. Guthro tilted the sunglasses on his nose. She laughed.

'Stocks and shares, can I help you? Hello? Hello? Cynthia, I think we've lost him.'

'Hello,' said Philip. He pushed back the sliding door. His eyes still watched Guthro and Cristiana as they strolled to a table in the sunlight and sat down on either side. 'This is Philip Strickland. You are holding for me three thousand units in the Alpha Consolidated Fund. I'd like to sell some. How much are they worth?'

'I'm afraid it's a bad time to sell. Just under six and a half thousand.'

Philip's fingers tapped against the glass. 'Sell the lot,' he said, 'and get the money sent out to me here, care of the Standard Chartered, Madras.'

'Very well, sir. Will you confirm that in writing for us, sir?' A small boy arrived at Guthro's table. He brought two long green drinks with straws. The limousine was still parked outside. Philip could not see the driver. 'Hello, Mr Strickland?'

'Yes. I'll confirm. When can I expect the money?'

'Well, if we telegraph it, a week, ten days. Trust that is acceptable, sir, and that you are enjoying your holiday.'

'Yes,' said Philip. 'Yes, thank you.' He put down the receiver, left the booth, went across to the desk, queued and paid for the call. Then he queued again and checked the poste restante box. Nothing.

There was only one way out of the building. Philip took three deep breaths, turned and walked out quickly with a firm military step.

'Well, now!' Guthro uncrossed his legs and stood as Philip emerged on the sun-soaked street. The green drink clinked in his hand. 'If it ain't our friend the barrister-at-law. I heard tell that you were still around.'

'Guthro.' Philip nodded and gritted his teeth. The black hand fell gently on his shoulder and held hard.

'You know, of course, my friend Cristiana.' Guthro made an exaggerated courtly gesture.

Philip looked down at the table. Cristiana's Oxford shirt was open to the middle of her cleavage. Her white shorts showed a lot of golden leg. She looked up under heavy raised eyebrows and smiled without moving her mouth from the straw. 'Yes,' Philip said. 'Thanks. We've met.'

'So. Now. Why don't you just sit down an' talk to us for a little while, hmm? Have a drink, why not?'

Philip shrugged, pulled out a chair and sat down. Cristiana turned towards him and spread her legs. Her shorts were very tight. 'Get us a drink, honey,' she told Guthro without turning.

'Of course, of course! Same again,' he told the waiter without moving, 'for three.'

'No,' said Philip. 'I'll have a mineral water, please. In a closed bottle.'

'Hey . . .' Guthro's lips drew back in a broad white smile. 'Par-a-noi-a. Be cool, man. Take it easy.'

'You've changed a bit,' Cristiana purred.

'Yes, well . . .' Philip shrugged. 'I learned.'

'That's right! That's right!' Guthro slapped the table and sat up straight. His eyes oscillated very rapidly from side to side over Philip's face. 'You got to learn! Over here in the East, you learn, huh? There are different values, different ways of seeing.'

'Yes,' said Philip. 'I realize that now.'

'And you see, man, Cristiana and I, we couldn't afford to have you comin' in and ruining everything just because you hadn't yet understood, right? We — we had problems enough. I mean, the way the big guys back in the States have it in for us at the moment, we just could not afford hassles.'

'Bastards,' spat Cristiana. 'Guthro made the Movement. Guthro made all of them. They pretend it's 'cos of me, but it ain't true. That's not the real reason. It's 'cos they know Guthro is the real boss, the natural boss, and they're scared, man, they're scared. And it's 'cos Guthro's black and them mean honky bastards are racists through an' through.' She thumped the table. A bubble of spittle appeared at the corner of her mouth.

'Shut it,' said Guthro. He reached up casually and threw some notes on to the drinks tray. 'Just shut it, you hear?'

She shivered and smiled. 'That's right, honey,' she hummed. 'You're the boss. See?' She nodded at Philip.

Guthro shot her a look steeped in curare. 'So.' He picked up his drink and swirled it round. 'You know that Laura's no longer here, man?'

'I guessed as much.'

'So, what you doin' here now?'

'Oh.' Philip shrugged. He held his glass up against the pale-blue sky. He squinted at it closely. 'Oh, just enjoying the sunshine, the atmosphere. I like it here.'

Guthro's eyes narrowed. 'Yeah, like hell. What are you playing at, man?'

'I said, I like it here. I'm taking a break, a holiday.'

'I think it's time you went back to being a barrister-at-law. Look at you, man. You're cracking up. Really. Take my advice. Go back to England.'

'Yes.' Cristiana leaned forward and stroked Philip's thigh. 'Listen to the man. Go back to England. It's really dangerous here.'

'Am I to understand . . .' Philip wiped his upper lip. 'Am I to understand that you are threatening me?'

'No, man, no! I told you, no paranoia! It's just that we're worried for you. I mean, you got a lot of backs up when you did all that number and the Nazi stuff, the kidnapping. I understand, Cristiana understands, but there's a lot of people that don't, you know? And life is cheap around here, you dig?'

'I'll go when I'm good and ready,' said Philip casually.

'*Now*,' said Guthro, suddenly very angry, very cold. 'Go now. You make everyone feel uneasy. You made enemies. Go now. OK?'

'I'll take my time.' Philip's lips twitched. 'I make my own decisions, in my own time.'

Cristiana snarled. Guthro said, 'Now,' very quietly. 'Whatever you're doin', we don't like it. Do it somewhere else.'

'Yeah.' Cristiana uncurled her body. She thrust her hips forward at him. 'Anywhere else. Not here.'

She and Guthro looked at one another and smiled, then linked arms and walked away, down the steps on to the esplanade. Philip watched them go. They were still smiling as they climbed into a dark-blue car. Philip saw the bright flash of teeth as they drove off.

He sipped his drink slowly. Despite the sunshine, he felt very cold. He looked anxiously over his shoulder as he stood and headed back into the dark network of streets which were now his home.

Every day Philip checked the poste restante. Every day Ravi saw him return, hands in pockets, dragging his feet despondently in the dust. On the sixth day, however, Philip strode jauntily past with a wave. 'Here, Ronnie!' he called. 'A present for you.'

Ravi ran over to him where he stood at the junction of the alleyway and the street of the craftsmen. 'Here you go, Ron.' Philip tore the thick A4 envelope in his right hand. 'Five genuine American stamps complete with portraits of George Washington and fresh New York postmarks.'

Ravi gazed at the scrap of paper wide-eyed. 'Gee whiz, Philip sahib,' he said. 'Thank you most very much.'

Philip smiled happily. 'I've got a little business to do,' he said. 'I'll see you at supper, OK?'

He strolled off down the street adjoining the bazaar. He passed metal-workers, jewellers, potters. Then there were five carpenters' shops, all together. Chairs, tables and bed frames were stacked outside. He stopped at each shop and examined the merchandise. Most were crudely made utilitarian pieces, though some were carved, a few inlaid.

At last, Philip nodded and returned to the second of the shops: 'Marapana's high-class furniture emporium.' He strolled in through the rattling bead curtain. Two men worked at a long carpenter's bench. One leaned over a vice, cutting a dovetail joint with a hacksaw. The other planed a long plank of what looked like deal.

'Hello,' he said. 'Good afternoon.'

The older man put down the hacksaw and shuffled into the light. He had a long, hooked nose and wild, staring, pale-blue eyes. His grey hair and beard were thick and matted. He limped heavily, and rowed himself across the room with his right hand on the furniture.

'What can we be doing for you, sir?' His voice was a high-pitched gargle. His elbows twitched. 'We have very nice fine souvenirs. Beautiful inlay. Onyx, agate, mother-of-pearl. Much prized by maharajahs and gentlemen of quality.' He beckoned. 'Come, I show you.'

'Um, no thank you.' Philip smiled weakly. 'Perhaps another time. I was thinking of having something made, antually.' Philip stepped past him and opened the envelope with his thumb. He pulled out four glossy black-and-white photographs and laid them out on the bench; a top view and three elevations of a brass-inlaid coffee table.

The carpenter fingered the photographs with a trembling hand. 'Oh dear, oh dear,' he muttered. 'Much work. Yes. Much work. When will sir be wishing it done?'

'It must be ready by the twenty-fifth of August at the latest.'

'Two weeks!' The pale eyes rolled upwards. 'Two *weeks*! Normally, you understand, we would be wanting a full month. It is not *easy*. It is not at all *easy*, and the inlay, the work. But if, *if* we work night and day, maybe, *maybe* in two weeks we can do it for you.'

'And how much?' Philip sighed.

The man bobbed up and down and took a deep sucking breath. He screwed up his mouth and frowned at the ceiling. 'Two thousand, five hundred rupees.' He shook his head. The matted, grime-stained curls flapped. 'Not possible one rupee cheaper.'

Philip had become used to the haggling routine. It was ten minutes before they at last settled on one thousand rupees and shook hands.

Philip left wearily and turned back towards his hotel. A girl lounging in the doorway opposite stepped into the street as he emerged and followed him. She made no effort to conceal herself. She simply followed at fifteen yards distance. Whenever he stopped and turned, she too stopped and met his gaze with a sneer.

She took up a position against the wall opposite the front door of the hotel. Twice Philip sent Ravi down to shoo her away, but she was not to be moved. She just stared up at Philip's window. She was there when he switched off the light and tried to sleep. She was there, just a dark shadow, when, at two o'clock, he got up, unable to sleep, and gazed out of the window. She was there, still staring straight at him, when at last the morning came. She had shaggy blonde hair and yellowish-white skin. She had wide, staring eyes. She wore a white T-shirt and faded jeans.

In the days that followed the girls changed, blonde, brunette, white, tanned, but there was always someone standing there. They ran when Philip ran, they walked when he walked, they stopped when he stopped. They never smiled.

'Hey, Philip!' Ravi rapped on the door. 'Hey! Two men asking for Mr Smith.'

Philip unlocked the door. The boy bounced in. 'Where?'

'Downstairs. Say they are friends of Mr Husani. Come, I show you.'

Philip followed Ravi to the top of the stairs and looked down the well. Two men stood by the reception desk. Both were Indian. Both were large. 'Seen them before?' Philip whispered.

Ravi shook his head. 'No. You going to see them? Maybe better if Mr Smith not in? Eh?'

'No.' Philip frowned. 'No, I'll go.' The men watched him descend the stairs, then moved to stand on either side of the banisters.

'Mr Smith?' asked the man on the left. He was built to be a bouncer's bouncer, but his hands were surprisingly fine.

He wore a gold ring on each finger. 'A friend of Mr Husani would like to meet you.'

'Who?' The man did not reply. He just nodded towards the door. Philip sighed and followed.

The girl on duty that day was the same shaggy blonde who had waited for him outside the carpenter's shop. She moved off as Philip and the two Indians walked out of the hotel and followed them along the alleyway. A car stood at the kerb, engine running. The man with the rings opened the door for Philip and nodded once. Philip got in, the men on either side. The car drove off. The girl on the pavement scowled.

Soon they were in the suburbs. The plastic car seat stuck to Philip's back. The men's shoulders pressed hard against his. No one spoke. A small doll of Kali, the destroyer, red tongue extended from a tar-black face, bobbed up and down in the windscreen. They passed the white rails of the racecourse, the brown hillocks of a golf course, then turned right through white marble gateposts. The house was white too, but had a nacreous lustre. It glistened in the bright sunlight. Only when the car drew up before the portico did Philip realize that the facade was of crushed mother-of-pearl set in plaster.

The man with the rings got out and held the door open. Philip's sandals sank into hot, sticky tarmac. The three men trotted up the steps side by side. A bell tinkled and echoed inside, and a man in a white tunic opened the door almost immediately.

It was cool inside. An air-conditioning unit purred softly. The floor was of black-and-white marble. There was a huge circular marble table inlaid with malachite, lapis lazuli, rhodochrosite and jades. The furniture was all European and Empire – walnut tallboys and satinwood gilt chairs. A huge stuffed bear flashed nicotine-stained teeth in the corner.

The Brylcreem-sleek, white-coated man led Philip down

a dark red passage. A tiger stood there, snarling. Above it hung two framed sepia photographs of the kill.

'If you will please wait in here,' said the man. He held open a white door. Philip stepped into a pale-blue circular room festooned with plants. The light came from a great cupola forty feet above a circular pond filled with water-lilies. Faded frescoes, Italian, surely, surrounded the room behind white marble pillars. Philip sat on a low green sofa.

'Ah, Mr Smith, jolly good.' The voice struck the pillars one by one and rang around the great glass dome.

Philip turned. The tallest Indian that he had ever seen stood in the french windows. He wore a perfectly pressed blue mohair suit. He tugged at his shirt cuffs as he spoke. Oblong, black-rimmed glasses flashed. 'The sun is not quite over the yardarm, but I think a snort will do us good, no? I have finally taught Ram to make an excellent White Lady.'

The steel-tipped ox-blood brogues clicked on the marble floor. Philip stood. The man was a good six inches taller than he. 'Er, thank you,' he said. He held out his hand. 'Philip.'

'Smith, I believe.' The tall man smiled and took his hand. His handshake was soft. 'Just like Brighton hotel reservations, what?' he said slyly. 'Please be seated, old chap.'

Philip sat again. The tall man folded his lean frame into the cane chair on the other side of the table. 'I thought maybe we should have a little chinwag. We have, I think, a mutual acquaintance, have we not? An unfortunate little person called Husani?'

Philip nodded. 'Yes.'

'I'm sorry that you have to deal with such people. Not exactly PLU. He told me, however, that you were in commerce, that you were looking, shall we say, to enter the import-export business. Is that so, Mr Smith?'

Philip leaned forward. 'I don't yet know whom I'm talking to,' he said amiably.

The tall man yawned and smiled. 'Neither do I, Mr

Smith, do I? Cigarette?' He held out a gold cigarette case. 'Turkish on your right, Virginia on your left.'

'No, thank you.' Philip sat back and crossed his legs. 'I don't.'

'Very wise, very wise.' The case snapped shut. The tall man tapped the end of an oval cigarette on the gold. 'No, you see, I am by nature a shy man, Mr Smith. I don't like people I don't know, and I know very few people. It is difficult to trust people you don't know, isn't it? Everybody has his territory. It may not be a beautiful territory, it may not be large, but it is theirs, hmm?'

The drinks arrived, though Philip had not seen his host so much as press a bell. The rim of the cocktail glass was frosted with sugar. Philip sipped, shuddered. 'Good,' he said, 'very good.'

'Chin chin.' The glasses flashed. 'We make the gin ourselves, as a matter of fact. Not quite Gordon's, perhaps, but we're rather proud of it.' The man narrowed his eyes as he inhaled. He sucked the smoke in, then blew it out slowly through his nose. 'I would say, in fact, that you, like me, Mr Smith, probably prefer the simpler delights of grape and grain to the more esoteric concoctions of chemicals.'

'Maybe so.' Philip nodded. 'But that doesn't stop you, Mr . . .?'

'Mr Singh.' The thin lips twitched.

'That does not stop you or me from having some interest in such concoctions.'

'True. True. But I am a businessman, Mr Smith. You are not. Nor are you an addict. Nor, I think, are you so stupid or greedy as to try to break into a closed market on impulse. So what is your interest, old boy?'

Philip shifted his weight from one buttock to the other. 'I just want them for export, that's all.'

'So I supply you with, let's say, five kilos of the very finest example of the filthy muck, made from Calcuttan pre-cursors and Burmese opium, processed in the Shan states.

Ninety per cent pure. That would have a street value in the United States of, say, three-quarters of a million, maybe a million dollars. Tell me, Mr Smith, how do you cut this large quantity of high-class poison?'

Philip sipped his White Lady and waved a hand. 'Well,' he said, 'standard techniques.'

'Of course, of course.' Singh nodded and smiled. His eyes were invisible behind those glasses. He leaned forward and tipped ash into a rose quartz ashtray. 'You came to India — how long ago, Mr Smith?'

'Three months.' Philip shrugged.

'And you came, of course, on holiday?'

'Yes. Well . . .'

'And it would be absurd to suggest that you had anything to do with a certain young English gentleman who organized the kidnapping of a certain young English lady from the ashram of a group calling itself the Children of Light weeks ago?'

'Quite absurd.'

'I thought so. Yes. Pity. I'd like to have shaken his hand. Yes, these Children of Light. Very near here. Surprised you haven't run into them. There's this fellow called — what is it? Guthro, that's it. He comes to our home and thinks he can do what he likes. He corrupts the young *dishonestly*, you know what I mean? Yes, I'd like to have shaken this Strickland chap's hand.'

'Oh,' said Philip. He drained his glass. 'It seems that we have much in common, Mr Singh. Do you think we can do business?'

'Oh, I think so, Mr Smith.' Singh grinned broadly. 'I think so. One thousand a kilo, you said, I think? No need to barter. Very vulgar. Nasty stuff, money . . .' He stubbed out his cigarette. His suit rustled. 'Yes, I think we can do business.'

'And I'd like to — have you friends at the airport, Mr Singh?'

Singh nodded slowly. 'I have creditors, at least. You push your luck, Mr Smith, but we are both on the same side, and I have no desire to see you ending up as a statistic. My friends tell me that you are already being followed.'

'Your friends get about.'

'They do indeed, Mr Smith. So, tell me where you want the stuff delivered. What?'

'Thank you, Mr Singh.' Philip smiled a one-sided smile.

'Don't mention it, old chap. Now, let's have another drink and talk no more about it, what? I say, you don't play snooker, do you?'

Ravi was waiting at the reception desk when Philip returned that evening. 'Hey, Philip!' he said. 'OK? OK?' He raised his arm in a military salute.

Philip returned the salute. 'Fine, I'm fine,' he replied.

'Another package arrived for you.' Ravi reached into the desk and pulled out a large stiff envelope. 'More New York pictures.'

Philip looked at it. 'More designs,' he said. 'I'll have to go out again. To the carpenter's.' He walked to the entrance and glanced outside. The brunette with the roman nose was on duty now. Her eyes looked up at him but she did not move.

He went back to the reception desk. 'Ravi,' he said, 'it'll have to be the usual way.'

Ravi nodded. Philip crossed the hall, turned left, passed through two reception rooms and into a small kitchen. A man heaved and sweated by a wood-fire stove. Philip smiled at him and, without a word, climbed through the open window.

It was dusk. The fading sun was behind the houses now. The shadows were uneven. Shafts of light crossed the street. The sound of a sitar drifted down from an upstairs window.

Philip's sandals thudded lightly on the hard-packed mud. An old woman passed him, muttering, then a skulking man in a flat cap who clung to the walls like last summer's fly. He glanced over his shoulder as he scuttled past. He looked scared.

There were four people at the end of the street now. They had no faces. They were just silhouettes against the dull yellow light from the bazaar, which seemed to flicker like candlelight beneath a huge moth's wings. Philip pursed his lips to whistle, but no sound emerged. The four people were not moving. He could see the light between their wide-set legs. They were standing still, blocking the alleyway, waiting for him.

He quickly thrust the envelope into his open-necked shirt. He turned. Another group of four stood ten yards behind him. A man stepped slowly out of a dark doorway on his left, another on his right, no more than six feet away. He could not see their eyes, but he could feel them watching him.

Philip turned back up the street.

'Satan out!' said a man's voice.

'Satan out!' Another's.

Then the resonant voice of a girl. 'He who standeth in the way of the Kingdom, let him be cast out.'

Philip spun, arms extended, like a blind man in an unfamiliar room. 'Satan out!' said a deep Asian voice behind him. Glass crunched as both groups came nearer.

'More, I say,' that same thrilling woman's voice, 'if he repenteth not, let limb be hewn from limb.'

'Let the birds of the air and the jackals feed on the flesh of the man whose soul is already dead . . .'

'Let dead blood be shed to give new life . . .'

The voices were very close now. Someone kicked a can. Philip gritted his teeth and strode up the alley towards the first group that he had seen. They barred his path, hissing, 'Satan out! Satan out!' He shoved between two of them. They fell aside without resistance. The voices just continued behind him, thudding like muffled drums.

'Jesus,' he breathed, and broke into a trot. Then a slim figure in breeches and gleaming boots stepped out into the light ahead of him. She pushed the thick black hair off her face. Philip stopped. The green eyes were opalescent and cloudy in the half-light.

'This is your last warning, Philip Strickland. Go home now!' Cristiana's voice was clear above the chanting. Her black-gloved body hardly seemed to move. He saw a flash of teeth. Something flickered, hissed in the air, thudded, glittering, into the earth at his feet.

Philip had ducked automatically. He lost his balance and fell forward. His hand shook as he reached across and plucked the blade from the dust. The chanting was distant now. All that he could hear was his own short, fast breathing. His lungs seemed to have shrunk. He could not get enough air.

'Oh, Christ,' he said softly. He looked up. The alleyway was deserted. The shadows were gone. Somewhere in a neighbouring street, like an unoiled seesaw, there was the cackle of high-pitched laughter.

'Hey, Philip.' Ravi's voice from the corner was suddenly high and timorous. 'You OK?'

'Yes, yes, I think so,' he replied huskily.

'Who *is* that woman?' Ravi's little hand slipped into his. 'Who are these peoples?'

Philip squeezed the hand and pulled himself to his feet. 'Strange people, Ronnie. Dangerous people. Better you don't know too much.' He dusted down his trousers and gulped deep draughts of air. 'Whew!' he said, then, 'Listen, Ronnie, I think I'd better stay in the hotel from now on. In my room. You and your friends know these streets, don't you? Can you keep an eye out, check who's coming and going, who's watching the hotel, that sort of thing? I'll give you thirty rupees a day.'

Ravi whistled. 'There is no need, really,' he said seriously. 'For thirty rupees I think I could buy assassins.'

211

'No need for that yet awhile,' Philip laughed. 'But I think it's time Brer Fox lay low.' They turned and walked back down the alley.

'Don't worry, you will be safe as houses. You will see.'

'Good man, Ronnie.' Philip slapped his shoulder and stepped into the hotel lobby. 'These things have to go down to Mr Marapana's furniture shop. Can you take them?'

'Sure.' Ravi took the package and held it very firmly in his two tight fists. His eyes glinted fiercely. 'No one will take it away from Ronnie.'

Philip smiled and called from the bottom stair, 'See you later then.' He turned back and trudged wearily up the stairs. His legs were still weak. He clung on to the rickety banister and unlocked the door to his room. 'Well.' He smiled. 'Home, Sweet Home.' And the door slammed shut behind him.

CHAPTER FIFTEEN

Laura knocked on the door of Sananda's study.

'Who is it now?' asked a muffled voice from within.

'Father, it's me, Laura.'

'Come in.' Laura pushed open the door. Sananda's head peered above the huge mahogany desk at the far end of the room. A brilliant light shone through the large open windows. 'What is it, my child?' he asked.

Laura glanced at the sofa, then walked up to the desk. 'Well, Father, I don't know quite how to say this. I've been thinking . . .' she started nervously.

Sananda pointed to a low carved chair in front of the desk. Laura sat. 'About what happened the other night, my dear?'

'Yes, Father, and — and other things.'

Sananda waved his hand dismissively. 'Don't worry, my child, don't worry. What are we but one big family? It was I who was mistaken. I thought you were ready. I thought you had freed yourself.' He shrugged. 'But then I did not know . . .'

'Father, I'm sorry, I've — I've come to say goodbye.'

Sananda tilted back in his chair. He nodded slowly. He straightened, stood, and walked round to Laura. His hand fell on her shoulder. She stiffened. 'Laura, my child, I think you misunderstood what we were doing. When Shakti and Shiva met, do you think that was something crude? Listen to the music of the spheres, and tell me what you hear. You do not hear the ranting of men. You do not hear words. You do not even hear the harp or the sitar. But you hear music like no other. Such are the *asanas*, and such are the ways of knowledge.'

213

'It's no good, Father. I can't do it. I just can't. God knows I tried . . .'

'And your purpose, my child. What about the great works we have yet to accomplish? Our mission to bring love to the world. What about that?'

'Yes, Father.'

'There is still so much to be done.'

'Yes, Father, but what — I mean, really — what are we doing?'

'My child, just look around you, look at the world, look at the needless pain, the anguish, the mindless craving for baubles that mean nothing, look at man's inhumanity to man. You ask what we are doing? We preach harmony. A world of love where hate is unknown, where compassion is unthinking, automatic, a world at peace with itself. A world where all nature is one. Is that not what you want, Laura?'

'Of course, Father. In principle, of course I do. But how can we achieve it?'

'I can't do it alone.' He walked back to the desk and sat down. 'I need others, and above all — understand what I am saying, Laura — above all, I need you.' Laura stared at him and slowly shook her head.

'You don't know yourself, my child. Your spirit is as pure as the snow that drifts from the peaks of Annapurna. The lotus is still closed, but I know,' he nodded, 'when the petals open, it will bloom into a flower that will make nature cry out with anguish because all are not as you. You, my child, are the spirit of the New Kingdom. You will be the guiding light. I felt that when first I saw you in Madras. I knew then that you must come here. Together, we can do it, Laura, I know we can. But only together. Without you, what am I? Without you, I am infertile, I am nothing!'

Laura shivered. 'Father, look, I mean, I am honoured, really I am. Thank you, but no. It's just — I'm not made that way. I can't.'

'Laura, Laura, you are still so young! There are many

things you do not yet understand. Don't be so quick to judge. You have a great and glorious role to play in history.'

She looked Sananda straight in the eye. Her mouth hardened. 'Father, I am going.'

His fist slammed down on the desk. 'I forbid it,' he said. 'You behave as if evil forces are still rampant within you. You are confused. You don't know your own mind.' He wagged a finger. 'But I know it is Devi. Devi up to her old tricks. Devi the great. Devi the conqueror. Devi the source of feminine guile. Don't tease me, Devi. Do not tease me. The spirit of Devi rests in you, Laura. Of that now I am sure. I was blind not to see it before.'

'The what?' stammered Laura, wide-eyed.

'Oh, my child, this is glorious for all of us.' Sananda clapped his hands and leaped to his feet. 'You have been blessed as no others have been blessed. There is much now that we must get ready.' He jumped up and down like an excited child. 'First I must call together the Committee and tell them the news. And still you do not understand? Laura, oh, Laura, come to me at midday tomorrow.'

Laura sighed, exasperated. 'I have told you . . . .' she started.

'I order it, my child. I order it. You cannot cry in the face of destiny.'

'Yes, Father,' she said curtly. There was no respect now in that 'Father'.

Sananda's little legs raced to the door. He opened it for her, and smiled a broad smile. Laura stood and looked at him. For several seconds she did not move, just gazed at him with an expression of bemusement and annoyance. Then she shook her head again and strode past him with a deep sigh.

Mary lay on a Lilo with a drink in one hand. Ingrid pushed an inflated plastic shark through the water. 'Laura, come on in!' she shouted.

'No thanks,' Laura replied. She strode on, along the edge of the courtyard, then out on to the lawns beyond. She walked briskly down the drive through the lush green bushes of the park. Sprinklers showered the grass. A gardener in the distance stopped and stared, wiped his hand across his forehead, then bent down and prodded a sapling.

She was sweating slightly by the time she reached the wood. She slowed her pace in the shade of the trees. The great wrought-iron gates were ahead of her. They were shut. Two men in blue uniforms stood on the far side of the gates, their backs turned to her.

She walked straight up to the gates. Her hands gripped the bars. One of the men spun round, then the other followed. The first one spoke. He had a match in his mouth. 'What do you want, lady?'

Laura straightened. 'Kindly open the gates. I'm going for a walk.' She spoke like a schoolma'am.

The match moved a centimetre towards the corner of his mouth. 'You got a permit? No one allowed out without a permit.'

'What the hell are you talking about?' she demanded. 'I can leave when I please. You will let me out.'

''Fraid not, lady,' the man droned. 'We got our orders. You gotta get a permit.'

'Let me get this straight.' Laura's voice was hard-edged and imperious. 'You are telling me — I'm sorry, but I'd like to get this clear for the judge — you are telling me that you are preventing me from exercising my constitutional freedom to go where I will when I will. Is that right?'

''S'right.' The man smiled and leaned back on the gate.

'You are, in other words, party to a — to a kidnapping.'

''Fyou say so, lady.' The other guard grinned.

Laura nodded slowly. Her eyes narrowed. 'What is the penalty for kidnap in this state?' she hissed.

'Hey.' The man turned. The match jerked upwards. 'You just listen, girl. We just doin' our job. Security, eh? No one goes in or out without a permit. Those are our orders. Right? So don't you come the limey duchess, OK? You stay till I hear otherwise.'

'Oh, for Christ's sake!' Laura stamped and turned. Her fist struck her thigh as she walked back up the drive. She muttered continually. There was laughter behind her.

As she rounded the bend she looked quickly back, then cut into the darkness of the wood. There was a strong smell of wild garlic. She pushed branches aside with her forearm and ducked and wove through the trees. Twigs rustled and crackled beneath her feet. Near the boundary fence the trees were less dense, the light stronger. There was a ditch there. She slid down it, then pulled herself up on the other side.

Above her twelve feet of close-mesh chicken netting hung on a framework of steel props set six feet apart. The whole structure was crowned with tangled curls of barbed wire. She pushed at the netting. It was rigid. It did not give an inch. There were no signs of rust on the wire or the props. Her shoulders sank. Just ten yards away ran the gleaming tarmac road.

She turned, disconsolate, and walked along the side of the wood between the fence and the ditch. Occasionally she stumbled. Once she fell forward on to her knees and struck the ground again and again with her clenched fists. When she pulled herself to her feet, tears were dripping from her jawbone.

She was ten yards past the oak tree when she stopped. Blinking, sniffing, she turned and looked up with red eyes, taking it in. It was a big, old oak. One branch overhung the fence. It passed a good six feet above the barbed-wire curls. On the far side, the drop was perhaps eighteen feet on to the verge of the road. Laura walked back and fingered the tree trunk. She pulled at the bark. It came away easily and flaked in her hands. If not dead, the tree was none too healthy. She sniffed once, very hard, looked up at the branch again, pursed her lips and said, 'Right.' She hugged the trunk and pulled.

The first knot was at shoulder height. Her plimsolls slid on the bark. She levered her body up with her right hand and quickly transferred her weight. Standing now on the knot, she could just reach the first of the lower branches on her left. She stood still, panting, for a moment, then swung her body up and over. Her stomach was now across the branch. Her right hand had caught on something and was bleeding. She sucked it, then pulled herself sideways towards the trunk again. The other branch, her branch, was four feet above her.

With the trunk hard against her back, she stood slowly. Her arms flailed at her sides like those of a tightrope walker. Once standing, she leaned forward and slid full length on to the bough. She half grinned and muttered, 'Damn the lot of them!'

She moved forward. The branch groaned but held. She was halfway along it now and only four feet from the fence. Suddenly, there was a crack like a bullwhip. She closed her eyes and hugged the branch. The jolt almost knocked her flying. The branch rocked, steadied. She gasped for breath and looked down. The ground was still far beneath her. The branch had come to rest on the very top of the fence.

She whistled, sighed, wiped the hair from her eyes. 'OK,' she whispered, 'all well. Come on, girl.'

'Now then,' a deep voice drawled below her. 'What are we doing up there, eh, lady?'

She looked down. A black Dobermann snuffled at the trunk of the tree. Beside it, looking straight up at her, was a man in a blue uniform. She did not reply. She just wriggled a little further along the branch.

'I reckon you'd better come down, lady,' the man sighed. 'You ain't going nowhere, sorry.'

'Oh, just leave me alone!' she snarled. 'I'll go where I please. Go away, will you?'

'Well, no one can say as I haven't given you fair warning,' the man sang out. There was a loud crack as he snapped a sapling with his foot. ''Course, if you go on, we'll just pick you up on the other side of the fence. Case you didn't know, this whole scene's being watched up at the house on closed circuit. Smile, honey, you're on candid camera.' Laura groaned. 'But I reckon I'd rather save the effort and have you come down right here on this side, huh?'

He jabbed with the sapling. Laura yelped as it struck her in the ribs. She half rolled, then righted herself. It struck her again, this time harder and just below the hip. This time she rolled over to her right. 'Oh, damn! Damn, damn, damn, damn!' she sobbed as she hung for a moment upside down like a moth, clinging on with her hands and knees.

Her legs dropped first. Suddenly there was hot breath on her ankles and her calves. The dog whimpered excitedly. 'Sit!' the man ordered. 'Sit, boy!' The whimpering did not stop. 'Come on, girl,' the man said laconically. A hand wrapped around her ankle and pulled.

'You bastards!' she yelled as her arms slid from the branch and she fell. 'Bastards!' She landed on her knees and fell forward sobbing on the crisp dead leaves. 'What is this place, for Christ's sake? You bastards!' She rolled over on to her side. Her shoulders heaved and she struggled for breath. 'You, you — you kidnapping, criminal Nazi bastards!'

'That's right, doll.' The man grabbed her right arm and pulled her up. 'Now you just calm down, you hear?'

'Get your hands off me, you — you . . .!' Laura shrieked. 'How dare you touch me, how dare you? Let me go! Let me go!'

The blue arms wrapped around her and held her tight. She wriggled and kicked, grunted and sobbed, but the man laughed softly in her ear and held her hard.

'Having trouble, Chuck?' Two other guards came through the undergrowth and stood smiling, legs planted apart.

'She's a bit of a kicker, that's all,' the man laughed. 'Bucks, too.'

'Needs a red ribbon on her tail,' one of them laughed.

'Let me go!' Laura squeaked. She half turned. Her hand reached up like a claw. The nails dug deep into the man's smiling face and pulled downwards. 'Let me go!'

'Jesus! I'll kill her!' The man pushed her away from him. She stumbled and fell forward on the edge of the ditch. 'You little bitch. Look what she done!' He pulled his hand away from his face. It was covered in blood. 'Look!'

'Steady, Chuck.' The other men moved forward. One grabbed his arm. 'Steady, man. You don't wanna blow this job by scarring the old man's favourite bit of ass, do you? We'll get her back to the nurse. She's hysterical. Leave her be.'

The man trembled but nodded. 'OK. Yeah. Just get her outa my sight, that's all.'

'Sure, Chuck.' The two men put their hands beneath Laura's arms and heaved her up. 'Come on, bitch.'

'Good afternoon, gentlemen.' The eight men sat around the table mumbled their replies. Sananda walked to the far end of the room, patted the carved back of the empty chair, then leaned against it. 'Gentlemen, I have called this special meeting of the New Kingdom Central Committee because something wonderful has happened. Something we have been waiting for for a long time.' All the heads turned towards him. He smiled.

'For four years — or is it five — you keep telling me that what our great Movement needs is a Divine Mother. Someone American or European who could interpret our message, someone with whom the seekers in the West could identify.'

Sananda shrugged. 'You keep telling me about Sri Aurobindo and the Mother, and without the Mother, you

say, Aurobindo's teachings would not have had the following they had, and Auroville would never have been built.'
Two of the men nodded. Sananda shrugged again. 'And you keep telling me about the line, that there must be someone to take over when my spirit leaves my body, someone of my blood, a caretaker.' A biro clicked.

'And I have told you that that was impossible until the spirit of Devi made herself incarnate and came down to this earth. Only then would I find a consort.' The fat man closest to the door frowned and sighed.

Sananda raised his hand. 'Well, that day has come. Devi has found a cloth to clothe her spirit, and as I told you it would be, the cloth is pure and untouched.'

A bald man next to him waved a cigar. 'Father, you mean the girl's a virgin?'

Sananda straightened and nodded smugly. 'She is untouched.'

The little dark man nearest the door whistled. His bald colleague cast a heavy reproving gaze in his direction, flicked ash on to the floor and turned, smiling, to Sananda. 'Well,' he said, 'I think I speak for all of us when I say good on you, and many congratulations.'

A deep mumble of agreement shook the table.

'I hope that we've got it right this time,' said the small dark man. 'I mean, we all understood that Devi was damn particular. It had to be a virgin. Only question was, where in hell were we gonna find one? Who's the lucky girl, Father?'

'The chosen one is Laura Callender.'

'The English girl we saw the other day?' The bald man raised his eyebrows and nodded appraisingly. 'Hmmm.'

'Yeah. There are possibilities there.' The dark man spoke in machine-gun bursts. 'But, you know, Father, we were all kind of hoping for an American.'

Sananda said nothing. He drew out the chair in front of him and sat down stiffly.

'Well now, what do you guys think? Is English OK for a Divine Mother?'

There was a short silence. The pen clicked again. A man in the middle leaned forward keenly. 'Well, we are essentially multinational — international, now. It should pull some weight in Europe.'

'Yup,' said another. 'And that's the area where we've been seeing our main expansion. She speaks pretty fancy, too. Give us added credibility. A little class.'

'Might be a little too upmarket. She hasn't got any Irish blood, has she?'

'We'll find some,' said the dark man. 'No problem. And it seems to me the most important thing is that we secure the line. We've got to think about the twenty-first century and we got to think insurance. This girl's young. She can have five, six kids. We've got a good chance of raising another leader, huh?'

'What Charomski means, Father,' the bald man leaned over, his red silk handkerchief cascading from his breast pocket, 'is that it would be beneficial to have a caretaker of your own blood to tend the Movement until we can find your reincarnated spirit.'

'Yeah.' Charomski chopped at the air with an open palm. 'Yeah, that's right. Sure. That's what I mean.'

'But I don't think we should be too hasty, Father.' A grizzled man tapped his teeth with his pen. 'The first thing is to check her out, and thoroughly.'

'You bet your ass.' Charomski nodded.

Sananda looked around the table, bemused. 'But I tell you, she is the one,' he almost whined.

'Hey now, look, Father,' Charomski blurted. 'Don't get us wrong! We are two hundred per cent behind you. We've been waiting for this for a long time. Didn't I say — what, five years ago? Didn't I say, Father, we need a mother figure? Didn't I say that? But let's face it, Father, we've made a few little mistakes in our time, haven't we? Marty's dead right. Of course we got to check her out. We're a clean Movement. Everything about us is clean. It's got to be. So what we don't need is some jerk suddenly springing up and revealing that the virgin Divine Mother used to be a number-one attraction in a Liverpool cathouse, right? Or that she's a card-carrying party member. Just as a for instance. Right?'

There was silence. The men looked down at their blotters or up at the ceiling. 'I mean, am I right or am I right?' Charomski persisted.

'Sometimes, Charomski,' Sananda said through clenched teeth. 'Sometimes I think you have no place with us. Yours is an arid spirit.'

Charomski struck his own chest. 'Look, please don't misunderstand me. We've got to consider the marketing angle. Someone's got to put it across. Right? That's the job I'm paid to do, and if you ask me whether this girl could harm us if she didn't smell too good, I'd tell you straight, she could hurt and hurt real bad.'

'Her stepfather is a British diplomat,' said Sananda proudly, 'a Commander of the British Empire, made by Her Majesty the Queen. Soon he will be an ambassador. A Sir.'

'Yes, absolutely, absolutely. One splendid girl.' The bald man smiled soothingly. 'What Charomski means, though, is that Devi would never choose as her earthly mouthpiece a girl whose life was tarnished. Of course not. But devils, as we all know, as you have taught us, Father, can adopt the guise even of a goddess. You, of course, are the only one who can judge, but we must be able to reassure our followers. So just as a matter of form,' he pulled out the silk handkerchief and patted his forehead, 'just as a matter of form, I suggest that we might collect a few biographical details from independent sources. This would be a formality, of course, Father, only a formality.'

Charomski raised a small aerosol can to his mouth and pressed the button twice. He exhaled and smelled the back of his hand. 'Yeah,' he said. 'Yeah. That's right.'

'Very well,' said Sananda. 'If that will satisfy you, I am content.'

'And if everything works out OK,' said the grizzled man, 'when shall we hold the big ceremony?'

'When do you think, for God's sake?' snapped Charomski. 'There is only one date. The climax of the biggest spiritual cavalcade ever mounted, the high point of the Pilgrimage for Peace, September first, Madison Square Garden. First day of the convention. We'll have the media coverage, we'll have the audience of millions, and there it is, this great spontaneous love scene that seals the future of the Movement. It's a dream. Satisfy the female element, too. Am I right or am I right? Does the Committee agree?'

Two rows of heads nodded. 'September first it is, then,' the bald man rumbled. 'On September first, we will declare the Divine Mother of us all. Now, we'd better talk budget . . .'

CHAPTER SIXTEEN

Already in July Sananda's great Pilgrimage for Peace had visited Montreal, Los Angeles and Mexico City. The second stage, which was to culminate in the four rallies at Madison Square Garden, began in London on 10 August with three consecutive nights at Earls Court. The British press were hostile but capacity audiences filled the hall each night. A huge orange airship bearing the legends, 'Children of Light' and 'Pilgrimage for Peace' was visible all over south and west London. In Paris, the response was disappointing. In Bonn, ninety thousand gathered to cheer Sananda at a candlelit rally. The rock band 'Coalescence' played. Over three hundred new recruits were made, including a princess and the eldest son of the Minister for Trade. In Tokyo, Sananda was mobbed with garlands, in Sydney with eggs. By any standard, the tour was a success.

At ten minutes to midday on Friday, 30 August, Sananda's aeroplane landed at Madras Airport. He was scheduled to address a meeting at the University Hall, not a mile from Philip's hotel, at five o'clock.

A fist pummelled so hard on Philip's door that the wood shook. 'Hey, Philip,' said a high voice. 'Let me in. It's me.'

Philip was lying on the bed reading the Bhagavad-Gita. His dull yellow eyes were half-closed. Sweat marks stained his shirt. The window was wide open, but the air in the room was still stale with the smell of two weeks' habitation. Philip got up, walked over to the door and unlocked it.

Ravi bounced in. 'He's here,' he said, 'he's here. Sananda. Outside the university. Many, many people.'

Philip nodded and smiled. He clenched his fist, turned

away from Ravi and walked over to the window. 'And what did they tell you at the airport? When's the plane scheduled to leave?'

'Tomorrow morning. Dawn,' replied Ravi behind him. A foot stamped. 'Hey, why you waiting? We move now, eh! You been telling me two weeks, the toad comes, we move.'

Philip stared out of the window. Down below, heads bobbed and weaved along the alleyway leading to the market square. The shaggy blonde with the silver pendant around her neck leaned against the wall opposite. She was a familiar figure now. Philip knew when she washed her hair, when she changed her T-shirt. Four girls had been detailed to watch him in shifts of twelve hours. They had been part of his life. They had been his calendar.

He had been waiting for this moment for two weeks. Yet now it had come, he felt crumpled and listless. He faced Ravi. 'Got your friends lined up?'

'Sure, chief.' Ravi winked.

Philip reached under the bed and pulled out an Air India bag. He flung it over his shoulder and patted it. He switched on the light by the bed, then felt under the mattress and put a thick wodge of notes in his pocket. 'OK, Ronnie, let's move.'

They left quickly and locked the door behind them. Even the dark wooden staircase seemed strange to Philip now. Down the stairwell he could see three people leaning against the reception desk. Their very presence seemed threatening.

Ravi went ahead down to the hall, looked around him, then waved Philip on. Philip crept down the stairs and stopped on the last step, out of sight of the girl with the pendant.

Ravi whistled. Four small boys came from nowhere. He gave them each a five-rupee note, nodded at Philip, then whistled again. The boys ran down the hall and out into the street. 'Ahhh!' a girl screamed. 'Hey! You give me that back! Gimme back, you thieving . . .' A boy laughed. Feet scampered outside.

Philip clutched the Air India bag tightly, peered along the hallway and out through the door. The girl was gone. He raced out into the street, kicking up a wake of dust, looked about him, then ducked and scuttled along the alleyway towards the market square. The crowd burbled about him and pulled him along in its flow. He turned left again, passed the metal-workers, jewellers and potters, then sidestepped quickly in through the bead curtain.

The bearded man with the long, hooked nose was bent double over the workbench. He crooned and gibbered as he worked. The wooden frame of a coffee table lay upside down on the bench before him. The brass inlay glinted. The man's head jerked sideways as Philip entered. 'Ah, your table.' The man's fingers caressed the wood. A black thumbnail ran over the inlay. 'Much work, much work, and where else can you find such work in days like today? Nobody craftsman. They think they glue chipboard and call that a table, eh? Beautiful, eh? And for one thousand rupees . . .'

'Er, yes,' said Philip. 'Thank you, Mr Marapana. You have done a good job.' Marapana took hold of one end of the table, Philip the other. They turned it over. The underside was hollow as Philip had instructed. A long pole with a hook rested against the wall. Philip took hold of it, went back out to the front of the shop and pulled down the corrugated steel shutters. They rattled and screeched as they descended. When there was only a foot to go, Philip ducked underneath.

It was dark now inside the shop, except for the band of light coming from below the blind. 'It's too early to close,' the old man trilled, 'too early.'

'Stop jabbering,' said Philip curtly. He picked some matches off the table and lit the oil lamp on the bench. Its smoky light spread slowly through the room. Philip pulled down the last foot of blind. The noise from the bazaar was suddenly very distant. 'Now look,' he said. 'I want these bags packed into the base of the table.'

The man's pale-blue eyes stared at him. His elbows twitched. 'Shiva save me! You think I'm crazy?'

'I'll make it worth your while,' said Philip softly. 'I will pay you three thousand rupees. That is my last offer. Now get down to work.' His hand tightened around a chisel on the bench.

Muttering irritably, the old man packed the five one-kilogram packets of white powder into the table. He filled up the hole with wood composite and covered the bottom with a square of black veneer. Finally, it was loaded into a wooden crate and the sides were nailed down.

Philip strolled over and peered through the blinds. The sky had turned from black velvet to dark-blue silk. 'It won't be long now,' he said.

'Naughty, naughty man,' Marapana scolded Philip's back. 'Fvil, go away.'

Philip turned. The old man stood six feet away, acting like an egg-bound hen. He had a long steel knife in his hand. He scowled at Philip and turned away mumbling. 'You've done a good job,' Philip said calmly, 'you'll be wanting your money . . .' The man laid down the knife and nodded. Philip slowly counted out the notes. 'I'm sure you weren't thinking of ingratiating yourself with the authorities or claiming a little reward on top of this, hmm? But just in case such a thought should cross your mind, my friend Mr Singh will be paying you a visit. Understood?'

The pale-blue eyes turned heavenwards. 'Oh, my God, please no,' he dribbled. 'I would do no such thing. Please no.'

There was a rap on the shutters. 'Good,' said Philip, 'my friend's here. Take your money.' He handed it to him and pulled up the shutters. Ravi stood waiting in the head-light beams of an old white van. There was a small cold wind. The pitted tarmac gave off a grey glow of its own.

'OK,' said Philip. 'All done.'

A swarthy, squat man with a dead-mouse moustache moved sideways into the doorway behind the boy. 'This is my Uncle Ram,' whispered Ravi.

The man shook Philip's hand very formally. 'Where is the object?' he asked. 'Is that it?'

'Yup,' Philip whispered. 'Think we can manage it?'

'Easy. Ravi, open the back of the van. *Quietly* now. OK, Mr Strickland? One, two, three . . .'

Harsh sodium lights lit the wire-mesh fence and the forecourt of the airport buildings. The yellow beams were strong at first, but, after twenty yards or so, broke up and dissipated in the mist. The buildings themselves were almost invisible, just formless blue-black hulks. Small coloured lights twinkled and flashed in the emptiness beyond.

The van bounced in and stopped in the centre of the forecourt. Three porters in identical red turbans squatted in the headlight beams. A flaky yellow forklift truck waited on their right. The man in the middle stirred, rubbed his eyes and rose to his feet. Every movement seemed very slow, every sound very intense in the mist and the stillness. Ram kept the van's engine running.

The man came round to the driver's door. Ram wound down the window. 'Mr Smith?' the man hissed. His eyes were like marbles. His porter's badge glinted.

Philip nodded. 'Yes. They haven't loaded yet, have they?'

The man glanced over his shoulder towards the dark expanse of the runway. 'No,' he said. 'You have the special cargo?'

'In the back,' whispered Philip. 'All right to unload here?'

'Yes. Here no one will see us.'

'Right.' Philip nodded to Ram. The two men got down from the cab and walked round to the rear of the van. The exhaust pumped out yellow smoke. Ram opened the door very carefully, very quietly.

'You understand precisely what you have to do?' asked Philip. The porter nodded and signalled to his colleagues. One slid the forklift into gear. It whined as it slid across the asphalt towards them. The other limped over. Together, the four men levered the crate out and laid it softly down. As the forklift's headlight beams came closer, Philip saw Ravi's handiwork. THE CHILDREN OF LIGHT it said on the crate in large red stencilled letters, EXHIBITION HALL, MADISON SQUARE GARDEN, NEW YORK, and, stamped on all six sides, FRAGILE, HANDLE WITH CARE.

The crate rose. The head porter waved. The forklift wheeled on its own axis and drifted off through the mist towards the airport building. The driver looked very grim. Without a word, the other two walked alongside, flanking its progress.

'All OK?' asked Ravi as Philip climbed into the cab again.

'Fine. We've done it.'

Ravi whooped in a whisper. He bounced up and down on the seat, his short legs waggling on either side of the gear stick. 'Yippee! Now we have big celebration breakfast, no?'

'Yup, Ronnie.' Philip exchanged a quick smile with Ram. 'I reckon you've deserved it. But first let's just wait and see the stuff loaded.'

Ram released the handbrake. The van chugged out through the fence and a couple of hundred yards along the perimeter road. It stopped on the verge overlooking the runways.

The stocking-mask mist was lifting now. The light grew. The air was still cold, but occasional shafts of sunlight touched Philip's bare forearms as he held the binoculars to his eyes. The trunks of the aeroplanes glistened in the lemon light of dawn. A sloping cockpit gave off a sudden yellow flash.

There were four planes parked there on the left of the beige concrete slab of the terminal building. Philip looked at each in turn, the orange-and-green flags of Air Lanka, the red-and-white of Air India and, furthest away, jutting out beyond a giant MAS jumbo, a tailplane decorated with seven interlocking stars.

They waited for three-quarters of an hour before there was any movement. A plane thundered overhead and landed on another runway, out of sight. Then a motorized cart emerged from the building, pulling eight laden trolleys across the tarmac. It stopped at the rear of Sananda's plane. A small orange figure unhitched the trolleys, waved and called something. It was a tiny, distant sound. The cart drove back to the terminal building.

It returned three times. A whole gypsy encampment of crates and suitcases soon surrounded the tailplane. 'They travel heavy, hey?' piped Ravi at Philip's elbow. 'They movin' out, mebbe?'

'No, Ronnie.' Philip shook his head. 'It's for this exhibition they're having. All the communes are showing their best stuff, their latest designs.'

Four orange men busied themselves with ropes. Two mounted an hydraulic platform and disappeared into the body of the aircraft. Philip watched as the platform went up and down. For the most part, he could see only the men's legs and the base of each crate as it was shifted along, loaded and raised. There were four crates half-visible beneath the jumbo now, two behind the tail. The platform went up. It came down still laden. Behind the plane, one man shrugged and pointed back towards the terminal. Another slouched and leaned back against a crate. Work had stopped.

'Hey,' said Ravi. 'They gone on strike.'

'Oh, Christ,' Philip breathed. 'They can't be full, they can't be . . .'

The remaining trolleys were hitched up again and driven back to the terminal. The orange men rode perched on the packing-cases. They gestured and laughed. The cart vanished into the terminal building.

'Shit!' Philip seethed. 'They're leaving some!'

'Don't worry,' said Ravi. 'They have ours. I am sure of it.'

'Let's get back and find out.' Philip turned to climb back into the van.

'Wait!' Ram pointed. Philip turned back. A school-like crocodile of Children now made its way from the terminal towards the aeroplane. A huddle of teachers strode at its head. One of them was a tall black man in a sleeveless white shirt. Beside him, looking downwards, a girl with a heavy mane of black hair. Then came the school governors, all in dark suits, then the pupils.

The black man stood with a gallant bow to let the woman pass. Under the jumbo's belly, Philip saw the feet trotting up the gangway — first, pale cotton, bare calves. Fluttering robes, then black mohair, then faded jeans. The gangway rose.

The plane sighed and then whistled like a dentist's drill. Orange men waved orange ping-pong bats. A tractor pulled slowly forward.

'Why are they leaving those things behind?' Ravi asked.

'How the hell do I know?' Philip snapped. 'I don't know. They've been to five, six communes before this one, picking up their precious exhibits. They must just be full up.'

Five figures in jeans and T-shirts stood now on the tarmac before the taxi-ing plane. As it went by, they bowed low. The plane gathered speed, shooting off a slipstream of pale light. Philip thought he saw a flash of white, a waving hand from the rear porthole. Then the nose went up and the plane slid smoothly into the shimmering air.

'Right,' he said. 'For God's sake let's get back and see that porter.'

He was not to find the porter again for another half-hour. There were crowds in the airport now, Europeans looking Oriental in white suits and panamas, Indians trying to look European in dark-brown suits and ties. The porter leaned against a trolley in the arrivals hall.

Philip strode across the hall dodging bleary-eyed travellers. Ravi trotted at his heels. The porter looked up and backed away, putting the trolley between him and Philip. 'Porter, are you free?' asked Philip, then quieter, glancing over his shoulder, 'Was our crate loaded for God's sake?'

The man shrugged. 'I put it on the right trolley,' he said. 'What more could I do, sahib? Loading is another department. Ground staff department. I do not know. Plane very full already, chock-a-block so they say. But you need not be worrying yourself, sahib — rest go air freight to New York. Next flight. All well. No cause for concerning.'

Philip muttered something to himself. 'But it has to be that flight. Can you find out — quietly?'

'Maybe they find question very interesting. Maybe they ask why cargo so important. Maybe then cargo never arrive.'

Philip snarled. 'Oh, bloody hell!' He swung into a glass telephone booth, ground his teeth and spun the dial with rapid, vicious strokes of his forefinger.

'Rich here . . .' said the voice in Philip's ear.

'Hello, Rich?' Philip barked.

'I'm out. If you've got anything funny to say, speak after the repulsive noise. If not, sod off.'

'Oh, *Christ*,' Philip muttered, then, 'Cautiously optimistic that everything's OK. Stick with it. Merchandise left Madras 6.20 local. A little late. Taking the next scheduled flight. Changing planes at Bombay and London.

Should arrive New York 9.35 tomorrow just in time for the fireworks. OK? See you there . . .' He slammed the telephone down. Now it was time for that breakfast.

PART FOUR

CHAPTER SEVENTEEN

'With regard to the recent press report, Father . . .' The man with the pink shirt raised his voice above the hum of the engines. He had glossy, slicked-back fair hair. Steel suspenders glinted on his shirt-sleeves. 'I wondered if you wanted any further statements made.'

'I haven't seen your reply to those absurd allegations.' Sananda leaned back in the needlework armchair, pushed aside the safety-belt and crossed his legs.

'Absurd allegations. Were our very words, Father.' The man bared his teeth in a conciliatory smile. 'This is the report in yesterday's *Herald Tribune*. Shall I read it to you?'

Sananda nodded. 'Please, Frederick.'

' "Following allegations of regular drug-taking at the communes of the Oriental religious sect, the Children of Light, a spokesman for the cult's founder, Dr Mingma Sananda, told a press conference yesterday: 'These trumped-up allegations are absurd and unfounded. Spiritual development is impeded, not enhanced, by the use of narcotics. They are never used at our communes. Anyone found buying, selling or using them in our communes would be expelled.'

"The denial follows assertions in the *New York Times* and the London *Daily Express* that two girls, Cheryl Clarke, 27, and Esther Goodman, 24, were forcibly addicted to hallucinogenic drugs during their recruitment to the Children of Light and subsequently found readily available stocks of narcotics in the Australia and New Mexico communes. 'There was a roaring trade in heroin at the ashram,' Miss Clarke is alleged to have said.

" 'This is a typically vindictive press slur,' said the

spokesman. 'We are discussing the possibility of legal action with our advisers.'

"The Children of Light first came to public attention when actor Conway Torvill abandoned his career to join their ashram in New Jersey. Last year, the Children won a two hundred thousand dollar libel suit against the London *Star* following a story headed 'Homebreakers and Fraudsters'.

"Dr Sananda was yesterday reported to be visiting one of his communes in India in the course of his 'Great Pilgrimage for Peace'." '

'Very good,' said Sananda. 'Excellent. I'd leave it at that. No more trouble. Not with the convention coming up. What does Charomski say?'

'He agrees. We all agree.'

'Fine.' Sananda nodded. 'So. Now. Tell me what happens at Kennedy tomorrow morning . . .'

Heathrow Airport, London. Seven o'clock in the morning, local time. 'Good on Rich,' Philip murmured. He folded his *Herald Tribune*, drained his teacup and left the table. He trotted down the steps to the concourse. He was home again.

He looked at his watch, then blinked out through the plate-glass windows at the morning light. His flat was just miles away. He could ring a few friends, but he could not think of anyone that he wanted to ring. Tanned and tousle-haired in his crumpled cotton trousers and his tennis shoes, he felt alien here amongst the suited businessmen, the tawny-maned women with their well-cut faces and their frosted smiles. There seemed no purpose, no joy in their precise eating, their jovial drinking, their buying and their bright display.

A beige-and-golden woman in tailored black sat opposite him on a low bench. She was, perhaps, thirty, thirty-five. She puffed smoke rings at the ceiling, crossed her legs and smiled at him in frank appraisal. Philip looked away.

A tall, grey-haired man in an aluminium suit smiled exuberantly and roared with laughter. He slapped his little Japanese companion on the shoulder, quickly looked up at the clock, pursed his lips and was laughing again at nothing in particular.

Philip shook his head and pushed the hair back off his brow. He had not expected his homecoming to be thus. He was a stranger here, among these people.

'Passengers for the delayed flight to New York, TW 439, please make your way to departure gate 7 for immediate boarding.'

Philip turned, whistling. He'd left Bombay ten hours ago. There'd been over an hour's delay here in London. Maybe Sananda would have been delayed too. He still might be there in time.

As Philip unfastened his seat-belt and ordered a large whisky, Sananda's plane sped like a silver fish through the moonlit coral reefs of cloud, twenty thousand feet above Ireland.

In the back, behind the gold brocade curtains, Sananda slept. A single blue silk sheet covered his body. There were pages of typescript on the great circular bed beside him. A silver-framed photograph of a blonde girl stood on the bedside table beside a Mogadon bottle. Sananda muttered. His face twitched. He rolled over and the pages of his speech slid on to the floor.

Up front, men in shirt-sleeves sweated and snarled, smoked and tacked bits of paper to the cork boards on the walls. The commune members sat, heads thrown back, and snored, or nestled up to one another as they gratefully slept.

'Wake the old man at ten,' the young blond man told a girl with beads. 'Send the make-up girl in at ten-thirty. He won't like it, but persuade him. He's got to look great.'

'Christ, my ears hearing right?' Guthro pushed towards them. 'Hey, you making the man a nancy boy? Look, when I was doing the babysitting . . .'

The blond man glowered at him. 'Guthro, we've got it all squared up. Why don't you get some sleep. You've been up all night. It's a big day tomorrow.'

Guthro huffed, 'Now listen you little pimp . . .'

'Please Guthro, please, we got work to do.' He turned his back and talked to the girl. 'ETA is 10.12. Here's a picture of Congressman Behrens. Right? Remember that face. Lead him straight up to him. We don't want to lose a minute. I want everyone up and out of the airport by 11.05, you dig?'

'I dig,' she nodded. 'Keep cool, Frederick, keep cool. There's nothing to worry about, OK?'

'This is your captain speaking. We had a favourable tailwind running behind us and have made up some of the time lost due to technical difficulties in London. We will be beginning our descent to Kennedy in twenty minutes, just fifty-one minutes behind schedule.'

Philip stretched and yawned. He had slept for just two hours. Now he looked out on the gleaming blue water and the brighter blue sky.

'Here we go,' he murmured with a little nervous smile. He struck the arm of his seat three times very slowly with his half-clenched fist. 'Here we go.'

The sound thudded at the windows and flowed in and out of the building like a thick, bubbling tide. 'Father! Father! Heaven in America! Father! Father! Heaven in America!'

'Jeez, Alcott.' The customs officer pushed back his blue-and-gold peaked cap and wiped his forehead. 'This is not exactly low-profile stuff. I hope to hell you're right on this one.'

'Yeah, well.' Rich scratched his crotch and gave a lopsided grin. 'I sure as hell hope so too, Wayne. My source was good, and, as a public-spirited enemy of your country, I thought it only my duty to let you know.'

The officer set his cap straight and faced forward. His hands clutched the red cordon rope. 'A good source?' he said.

Rich slapped him on the back. 'Now, you wouldn't be about to ask a reputable journalist to reveal his sources, would you?' he bellowed above the approaching roar. 'What's happening now?'

'The dogs are in there taking a sniff around.'

'Good, good. Whoops, here come the first of them. Stand to attention, officer. This rabble may be the evangelists of the future.'

Through the open door at the end came twenty or more people, most of them young, in T-shirts and faded jeans. They looked around them as though seeing for the first time after years of blindness. Their sandalled feet clattered and faltered on the polished linoleum. Every sound echoed here as though in a public swimming pool. A tall Indian girl at the front had pink rose petals in her hair.

The red light on Wayne's walkie-talkie flashed. He put it to his ear. 'The dogs haven't found anything,' he said. 'The hold's canine clean.'

Rich shrugged. 'So your dogs got sinus trouble?'

'Yeah, well, the smell can be masked. The real test is the examination. Just puts your arse on the line if we only find baby powder.'

Rich smiled. 'Don't worry. It's there. I told you, I've got a good source.'

The commune members passed through the customs barriers without question, then turned and formed ranks on both sides of the red cordon rope. They smiled. Outside, there was a single shout, then a huge roar. 'Father, Father, heaven in America! Father! Father!'

'First time I ever busted God,' muttered Wayne.

The luggage and the packing-cases were pushed in now

on trolleys. Four men dumped the first few cases on steel inspection benches. The rest were propped against the walls. From the other end of the aisle, another customs officer raised his eyebrows at Wayne. Wayne nodded once. 'OK.' He straightened his shoulders. 'Let's do it.'

'We regret that owing to congestion in the approach lanes, we are still awaiting landing clearance. We anticipate a delay of ten minutes or so.'

Philip shifted in his seat. He had no cigarettes and he had not smoked for five years, but the old craving had returned now, and he resented the 'no smoking' order.

He looked at his watch. It did not seem to have moved in the last five minutes. He listened to it. Still working. Sananda should have landed fourteen minutes ago. 'Oh, God, let me down!' he said aloud like a child on a fairground ride.

The man sitting next to him raised his eyes from *The Times* to look at him suspiciously. Ahead, two young girls turned and tittered.

The plane banked and slowly circled.

The aides came first, clearing a path for their master. Then Guthro, Cristiana, Frederick, a tanned man with a beard, and, walking very slowly, Sananda. Two aides had their arms linked behind him. The roaring from outside swelled and sank. The commune members lining the cordon inside cheered and clapped and called, 'Father! Father!'

Sananda gave his smile as though giving alms to beggars. Behind them now, Rich moved over to the nearside wall, crossed his arms and lounged against it. One of Sananda's aides stepped up to Wayne and handed him a sheaf of dockets. 'Your 6059-Bs,' he said.

242

'Thanks, thanks.' Wayne flicked absently through them. 'Hmmm. Right,' he said.

'Can we get things moving, please?' snapped Frederick. 'We've got a tight schedule. You, pick up these things and let's get them loaded. OK?'

'Hold it, *hold* it.' Wayne raised a hand in a calming gesture. 'Just let's take it easy, shall we?' He strolled over to Sananda. The two aides behind moved in front of him, blocking his path. He smiled and pushed them gently aside. 'Are you Dr Sananda?'

'I am.' Sananda gave a little bow.

'Where have you been on this trip, Doctor?'

'On a pilgrimage to England, France, Germany, Japan, Australia and India.'

Wayne nodded towards the cases. 'You've picked up quite a bit of stuff on the way – for a pilgrim. Is it all here?'

'Look.' Frederick strode back and faced Wayne. 'Father has a rally to address at Madison Square Garden tonight. He's had a long journey. There is absolutely no call for this bureaucratic shit.'

'Yeah, right. Do you know who this is, man?' said Guthro.

'Dr Mingma Sananda,' said Wayne calmly. 'A United States citizen, and subject to United States law . . .'

'Look.' Frederick nodded. 'Of course we understand that. We're a law-abiding organization. We make large donations to charity. Isn't that right, Congressman?'

The fat man with the crewcut nodded. 'Sure, officer, these people are friends of mine, good friends. The Doctor needs some rest. Don't you worry, really.'

'It won't take long, Congressman,' said Wayne blithely. 'Now, Doctor. Is all this stuff yours?'

'It belongs to the Children of Light,' snapped Frederick.

'It belongs to the Children,' Sananda repeated wearily.

'But you are responsible for its importation into the United States?'

'Yes,' said Sananda. 'Of course.'

Frederick said, 'Oh, for Chrissakes!' and swung round. He moved over to the inspection bench and sat. Cristiana slouched up behind him, put a hand on his shoulder and smoothed his sleek blond hair.

Two customs men hauled a large whitewood crate from the aisle. MADRAS was stamped on the side. 'So, what's in this, for example?' Wayne tapped it with his clipboard.

'Handicrafts from my commune in India,' Sananda replied.

Wayne took a small book out of his shirt pocket, licked his forefinger and flicked the pages. 'Handicrafts manufactured in India and carried as personal effects are not liable to duty,' he read, and closed the book. Then, 'OK, Alan. Open her up.'

'This is intolerable . . .' Frederick leaped to his feet again.

'Of course.' Sananda waved a hand. 'It is your privilege.'

A young customs officer, with brown hair bubbling over his collar, bent to pick up a large canvas bag. A saw and an axe handle protruded from one end. He threw it down on to the bench with a loud clunk which rang around the vaults of the hall. The officer picked out a jemmy and approached the crate. He moved very slowly, very economically. In a sudden, smooth movement, he prised out one nail, then another. They tinkled as they fell on the floor and rolled.

Rich reached into the capacious pockets of his raincoat and pulled out a little bottle. He covered it with his open hand as he raised it to his lips and, with a jerk, tossed the contents down his throat. He shook his head and made a sound like an astronaut's sigh.

The side of the crate came down. Wayne nodded, stepped forward, reached into the woodshavings and pulled.

*

'Welcome to Kennedy. Local time is ten thirty-eight. The outside air temperature is thirty-seven degrees centigrade. Captain Giordani and his crew hope you enjoyed your flight. Thank you for flying TWA.'

Philip unfastened his seat-belt before the plane had even stopped taxi-ing and braced himself as though to launch himself forward as soon as it stopped.

'Not a number nine bus, old chap,' the man beside him smiled condescendingly. 'Can't jump off between stops, I'm afraid.'

'No,' said Philip lamely. The plane turned slowly.

'Good God,' the man leaned over Philip and squinted at the sunlight. 'We seem to have a reception committee. Very flattering. Friends of yours, are they?'

'What?' Philip turned. Outside, on the rails of the observation deck, stood a hundred or more young people bedecked with garlands or waving bunches of flowers. There were placards, too; huge bobbing pictures of Sananda, and printed posters bearing the legends, 'Welcome Father,' and 'Heaven in America'. At the perimeter fence too, there were robes and placards and flowers, and a huge banner, held by six people, blared in shiny orange letters, 'The Pilgrimage for Peace. Welcome Home Father.' Philip shuddered. 'No friends of mine,' he said. As the plane wheeled, he saw the plane with the interlocking stars on its tailplane. The gangway was down. Philip smiled.

'Always up to something loony and new-fangled,' said the man, 'I don't know. What is it, a pop group or something?'

'No,' said Philip. 'The Messiah.'

'Oh,' said the man, 'jolly good,' and he turned back to his paper.

'We're only making sawdust, chief,' the young customs officer shouted and switched off the drill. 'You want us to go on?'

245

Wayne nodded. 'Yeah,' he said. 'Strip off the black muck.'

'That's lacquer, for God's sake, man.' Frederick jumped up again. 'Do you realize how much labour has gone into that, how much time and money?'

'No,' said Wayne. 'Tell me. We're only doing our job, sir. Any individual has the right to claim against the customs service if his belongings are damaged.'

'But these are works of art,' said Sananda. 'Irreplaceable . . .'

'Sorry about that, Doctor. We won't do any more than is absolutely necessary. Alan.' He nodded. 'Take it off.'

Alan returned to the table with a blowtorch. The strips of brass inlay sprang up as soon as the flames touched them. The lacquer bubbled and seethed. He scraped broad strips in it with a chisel. Then he turned to the legs. He broke them off one by one with a heavy hammer, peered at each in turn and threw them aside. 'Clean,' he said. 'Just chunks of wood.'

Wayne looked down and scowled. He glanced over his shoulder to where Alcott slouched. 'Open the others,' he commanded, 'all the ones from Madras.'

'Hell, there are twenty, thirty!'

'Yeah,' said Wayne. 'Look, I'm not asking you to work 'em all over like this. Just unpack them and we'll take a look, OK?'

'OK.' Alan shrugged.

They no longer bothered now with pulling out nails one by one. They just ripped the sides off the crates with the jemmies.

'But why — why are you doing this?' Sananda asked plaintively.

Wayne shrugged. 'We are acting on information received,' he said. 'Probably nothing in it, but we have to do our job. You know that.'

Sananda nodded and turned to Guthro, questioning.

Guthro shrugged and turned his palms upwards. 'I don't know, Father,' he mouthed.

Sananda shook his head sorrowfully and turned away. Cristiana threw herself forward and grasped his shoulder. An aide put his hand on her breastbone and held her at arm's length. 'Father, really!' she said in an urgent undertone. 'It has nothing to do with us. Really!'

'Gonna forge a New Kingdom in Satan's old land . . .' started one male voice and the other commune members slowly joined in in a ragged chorus. 'Gonna forge the New Kingdom, with Father's hand . . .' Wayne's mouth twitched. He shot another quick glance at Rich, then walked into the centre, set his jaw, picked up an axe and swung it high. It smashed into the side of a crate. The Children sang louder, clapped and danced while wood split and crackled like a forest fire.

Seven coffee tables were now lined along the inspection bench. Wayne shouldered the axe and walked along the row. He tapped each table and listened carefully. He reached the end of the row and returned on the other side. He rubbed his chin, nodded, then stabbed a finger at one of the tables. It looked almost identical to the others but the brass work was simpler, the legs a little thinner. 'That one,' he said. His finger wandered on down the line, 'and that one.'

'Right, chief,' said Alan. The two customs men cleared the bench and set to work.

Even the commune members had slumped down on the inspection benches now. Garlands of honeysuckle and roses around the girls' necks looked dry and wilted. The petals fluttered to the floor as the girls leaned forward to rest their foreheads in their hands or impatiently swept back their hair.

No one spoke now. No one sang. But for the pudder of the blowlamp, and the rustling of woodshavings and the quick, sharp clicking of Frederick's heels, there was silence.

When Alan spoke, it was very quietly, as though in a church. 'Those two are clean, chief,' he said. He switched off the blowlamp, stood and stretched. Sweat dribbled down his temples and on either side of his nose. 'All clean,' he repeated, and sighed.

'Are we now free to leave?' Sananda's echoing voice seemed very loud in the silence. 'Have you finished your business?'

Wayne looked at the four smashed tables. He glanced at Rich, twitched his lips, shrugged. A few commune members stood.

'Sir.' Frederick grabbed Wayne's sleeve. 'This has been an outrage, an unjustified and vindictive act of vandalism. We will be lodging an official complaint against the customs service and we will be claiming substantial damages. Do you understand? And I want your name, sir. I want your name *now*, I'll see that you're dismissed for this.'

'Yeah. Too right,' said Guthro.

'Bureaucratic *bastards*,' said someone in the crowd.

'Fascist!' Cristiana stood and snarled at Wayne. 'Fascist unbeliever!'

Wayne stood stock still as the hissing abuse and the jibes of passers-by grew. Then he muttered, 'What the hell,' and pointed. 'Drill the others as well!' His voice made the skylights buzz.

Rich grinned and nodded.

'What, all of them?' asked Alan.

'Yeah, why not?' said Wayne. 'All of them.'

Alan grinned. 'Anything you say, chief.'

The drill began to whistle again. The children groaned and slumped down on to the benches. Alan and his colleague now worked fast. They bored fifteen holes in the first table. 'Solid,' said Alan. He moved on to the next one.

'This is just wanton destruction, young man.' Congressman Behrens lumbered forward and tapped Wayne's chest.

Suddenly the drill head snapped off. Behrens's words

dissolved into an embarrassed stutter. Hardly anyone heard Alan's quiet, 'Jesus Christ.'

Wayne heard. He was at his side in two paces. He squatted. Both men stared at the bit of the drill as Alan slowly withdrew it. The sawdust was flecked with white powder. Alan stuck the bit back into the hole and prodded. The powder flowed out like sand. Both men simultaneously reached out, dabbed at it, licked their fingers. Both men nodded. 'Goddamn it.' Wayne smiled slowly. 'We've found it.'

Frederick stood watching them. There were bright-pink spots on his cheeks. His eyes were wide and worried.

Guthro stood and said, 'No . . .'

Sananda too pulled himself to his feet and walked three or four steps towards the table. He shook his head. His lips were dry and very white.

Wayne turned, still squatting, and looked up at him. 'Heroin,' he said. 'Lots of it.' He pulled out the walkie-talkie and rapped, 'We've found it. Get the boys over to read 'em their rights.'

'There's been — there must have been some mistake . . .' stammered Frederick.

'No mistake.' Wayne stood.

'No.' Sananda spoke very quietly. He turned and stared straight at Guthro. 'There has been no mistake . . .'

'No, Father.' Guthro licked his lips. 'No, it wasn't me. Don't, Father. It has nothing to do with me.'

'Guthro,' Sananda said pityingly, 'Guthro . . . Never enough, never satisfied, still the slave of material wealth . . .'

'It wasn't me!' Guthro squealed. 'I swear, it wasn't me. Please!' He spun around, huge hands extended, looking for a friendly face. His eyes showed a lot of white.

'Confess now,' Sananda soothed. 'For all our sakes. You will be shown mercy.'

'You bastard!' Cristiana spat. A glistening gob of saliva

slid slowly down the side of Sananda's nose. The commune members hissed.

'Yes, come on, Guthro.' Frederick gulped and laid a hand on his shoulder. 'It's all over, confess.'

'Oh, Christ!' Guthro gave a deep moan. 'Oh, God. This was all planned, wasn't it?' He walked slowly backwards. His head jerked from side to side. 'You set me up, huh? You wanted it all for yourself. You and those arseholes. You set me up! Guthro's an embarrassment, right? He's got a record. Get rid of him permanently, locked outa sight. Well, I ain't goin' no place. Christ, man, is that how you repay me? I made you, Sananda, I made you!'

'OK, man.' A customs officer grabbed Guthro's arm. 'Cool it.'

Three guards stepped up on either side of the inspection bench. 'Let's go through into the office,' said one.

Suddenly Guthro lunged to his left. His right arm shot out. His fingers stretched and grasped. The guard on his left, off-balance, had time to say 'No!' before the axe handle smashed into his mouth. He fell sideways, moaning and spitting blood. Then Guthro's left hand chopped down on his neck hard and fast.

'Jesus!' the other guard yelled. He fumbled with the flap on his holster.

'Don't shoot, for Christ's sake!' someone yelled.

Guthro was running now. Only a few yards separated him from Sananda. The guard took aim, then shook his head and lowered the gun. Sananda, Wayne and Frederick spun round. Sananda's eyes snapped open wide. Guthro made a sound like a weightlifter. He bared his teeth and swung the axe around his head.

'Put it down or I shoot!' another guard barked.

The giant shadow fell over Sananda. 'No . . .' he whimpered.

'Get back!' Wayne's hand rose to parry the axe blow but was swept aside. Sananda dropped to his

250

knees. Frederick whimpered and flung himself sideways.

The swing of the axe seemed so slow. Sananda's arm arose. His lips drew back from his teeth.

A guard on the right aimed and fired quickly, twice. There were screams and whimpers all around. Someone shrieked. 'No! God! Please!' Guthro spun round like a top on its last circuit. His bulging white eyes looked astonished. Dark blood spread from a gash just below his collarbone. The flat of the axe head cracked down on Sananda's shoulder.

Guthro supported himself with one hand on the bench, took one more deep breath with a sound like a sob, and swung again. His head jolted back at the third shot and a great red flower seemed to bloom from his throat just under the jawbone. His huge eyes rolled upwards. The blood jerked out in large dark gouts. He staggered back and raised a hand to his neck. The blood squirted through his fingers in a thin jet and ran down his arm. He made a strange, strangled sound. The axe clattered to the floor. His right hand felt for support, clasped Sananda's head. Then he fell forward and his jaw hit the linoleum with a crunch.

There was screaming all around now. In the opposite aisle, everyone had ducked or dropped, save one plump woman with iron-grey hair who leaned forward, her hands on her thighs, and hurled shrieks at Sananda. The Children clung to one another for safety where they lay on the ground. Some of the white T-shirts were speckled and spattered with blood. One girl knelt, sobbing, and just drooled, 'God, God, God, God,' again and again.

In all the confusion, no one heard the other sound, the savage keening which seeped from Cristiana's mouth as she knelt astride Guthro's body and examined her blood-soaked hands. She rocked back and forth, crooning, her lips twisted into a deep red bow. Saliva dribbled down her chin.

'For God's sake clear the area!' Wayne yelled. He helped Sananda to his feet. 'How many are hit?'

251

Sananda turned to bustle through the door. His robes were torn and stained. He clutched his shoulder where the axe had fallen. Cristiana's whimpers had been as rhythmical as an ill-oiled wheel. No one noticed when it stopped.

She ran a blood-soaked hand across her eyes. The sound seemed to build up inside her, escaping her lips as a screech. She stood. Her eyes blazed. Her hands were claws. Her mouth was open wide in a scream which shivered through the thick-textured babbling like steel. Again Sananda turned like a scared rabbit, and the long, dark-brown, clogged nails dug deep into his flesh below the eyes and pulled and pulled and pulled.

CHAPTER EIGHTEEN

'Eleven thirty-nine and fourteen — fifteen seconds.' The little man in front of him leaned back and spoke over his shoulder. 'I don't know. One gets used to it, but really! Always damned queues. Same in Dar es Salaam, last week. Hello.' He stopped suddenly and Philip almost walked into his back. 'Looks as if there's been a bit of a shindig here . . .'

Philip blinked as he emerged in the porcelain-bright sunlight of the customs hall. Rich stood at the end of the aisle on the right. His hands were forced deep into the pockets of his open brown raincoat. His face was very grey, the lines from nose to jaw deep and dark. He was looking downwards, but his eyes flickered over to Philip as he entered, then returned to a study of his scuffed brown shoes. He half turned away.

A pop and a bright flash made Philip turn back to his left. A row of large, dirty-green screens shielded the two adjacent aisles. Behind them, men talked in low murmurs. Cameras flashed. 'Hell of a shindig, by the look of things,' said the Englishman.

'Yes,' said Philip quietly. As they passed the first screen, he looked back. He could not see much between the gap, just the swell of the breasts under the pink blanket, the wool-covered profile and one small, very pale hand that emerged, clutching at nothing. A garland of honeysuckle and roses lay a yard away, the petals now scattered and stained. The men stood, backs turned, and murmured in a huddle as though afraid to disturb the dead woman.

Philip frowned and turned. Rich had his back to him now. His head was still bowed. 'Your passport, please,' the customs man said for the third time.

Philip jumped. 'Oh, sorry,' he said.

The man inspected the visa and snapped it shut. 'Welcome to New York,' he said. 'Have a nice day.'

Philip nodded. 'Rich,' he said. 'Rich?' His breathing was suddenly very quick and shallow. Things wriggled in his stomach.

'You wanted me, preppy?' Rich did not look up. 'Let's take a walk.'

'What the hell happened?'

'Let's take a walk,' Rich snapped. He pushed the glass door open. 'What d'you wanna know, preppy? Did they find your present? Yeah. Clever boy. They found your present. Did you hurt the Children? Well, yeah, you hurt three of them real bad. Was it a success? Yeah, sure it was a success. You think anyone came home from the theatre the night Lincoln was killed and complained about the play?'

'Rich.' Philip grabbed Alcott's jacket. 'Will you bloody tell me what happened?'

'First let's get a drink,' he said. 'You just killed two people before breakfast. I haven't got that strong a stomach.'

Philip stopped. 'No,' he said, then he shook his head violently. His heart was beating very fast. It seemed the only sound in the world. People sat talking at tables at the bottom of the stairs beneath him, but they made no noise. An oily purple film blurred his vision. He dropped his bag and held on to the railing as though the earth rocked.

'Large whisky.' Rich rested his elbow on the bar. 'Make that two large whiskies. Hell. Quadruples.'

Philip absently said, 'Excuse me,' as he squeezed between two chairs. 'So what happened, Rich?' Philip looked straight at his watery eyes.

'We tried to rewrite history, that's what.' Rich shrugged and drank. 'We tried to make a lie come true. We tried to impose our morality on the course of events. Know what that's called, preppy? It's called cheating. It's also called totalitarianism. Alcott's lesson in politics and morals number one. Text for today: might is right. We may not like it, but if we get beat by Communism, Fascism, or bloody Sanandaism we are wrong and it is right. We fight, we lose — we may even win — but if we cheat, we're no more than bullies, we're King what's his name trying to stem the tide. Jesus, I should have known better . . . '

'You're drunk,' said Philip.

'True, oh wise one, and I shall probably remain so for some days hence. I like it here. Very few quixotic psychos get in. Exclusive sort of joint, drunkenness.'

'Please,' Philip almost sobbed and grabbed Rich's shoulder. 'Please tell me what happened.'

'Sananda blamed Guthro, Guthro freaked and tried to anatomize Sananda. Guards opened fire in a crowded customs hall. Guthro dead. One poor innocent mug of a girl — pretty little blonde thing, all garlands and flowers and happy smiles. Came from my country, actually, a Perth girl, an orphan, joined the cult 'cos it's better than being a junkie. Name of Jenny — also dead. Then there's the English girl . . .'

'What English girl?' Philip's grip tightened. Hot tears stung his eyes.

'Not yours, preppy,' said Rich slowly. 'Not yours. Just another English girl who wanted something new and exciting. She got it, too; a .38 slug in her gut. She'll be OK. Just won't be adding to the British population explosion. They don't do spare wombs.'

Philip felt for a stool behind him and sat. 'But the Children? Sananda?'

'Coming up bright lights and Santa Claus.' Rich sniffed. 'Sananda was released a few minutes ago. Guthro gets the rap, and Guthro's cold meat. There'll be a few more questions, but nothing much. Guthro had a record in the old days anyhow. It's all bloody neat.'

'Then we'll have to think again.' Philip blinked away the tears and hit the bar with his fist.

Rich paid no attention. 'If anything,' he shrugged, 'you've done Sananda a big favour. He's got rid of the one lieutenant who was giving him a headache, the one with a claim to over half the Movement's funds. For that he could live with a few scratches on his cheek. Should've seen that PR girl of Guthro's though,' he continued dreamily. 'Tore little Sananda's face to ribbons. Lovely. Then he came over the magnanimous big daddy. Said they'd look after her. Bet they will.'

'Yes, we'll have to do something,' Philip gulped. He spoke very fast. 'Sananda can't get away with this. Lives are being wasted. Every day more people are being swallowed in. The Movement gets richer and richer, bigger and bigger. We've got to stop it . . .' He could hardly speak.

'Shut it, preppy!' Rich snapped, suddenly fierce. 'Think what's happened, will you, man? Two people dead, one seriously injured. Your work.'

'And − and yours,' Philip stammered.

'Oh, sure, and mine. God save me for a gullible idiot. But don't worry about me, preppy. I've got my friend here,' he patted his glass, 'and I've seen more death than that. People die, people are born, people make life shitty. I just broke one cardinal rule: never get involved. Watch, laugh, cry if you like crying, but never get involved. And I forgot. Won't happen again.'

'You don't care then?'

'That's right, preppy,' Rich snarled. 'Written all over my face, isn't it? I don't care.' He turned back to the bar and hunched his shoulders. 'Now get lost, will you?'

Philip picked up his glass and raised it to his lips before he saw that it was empty. He looked at Rich with an expression of disgust, slammed down the glass and strode towards the staircase and out into the low burble of the traffic. He waved at the nearest yellow cab. 'Take me to a cheap hotel,' he said. 'Somewhere close to Madison Square Garden.'

The pale light turned grey. The streets were soon thick-grained and spangled. Twice it rained. Philip walked without direction or intent. His hair was plastered to his forehead. The water dripped down, snagging his eyelashes, filming his view. He reeled on, barging into corners as he turned them and relishing the pain. Horns blared.

He turned and walked down a narrow street of dirty white cement. In one doorway a young man lay, legs extended. Blank eyes stared up at Philip from the molten wax death mask of the junkie. The soles of his shoes had all but come away from the uppers. His corduroy trousers were spattered with some hard ochre paste. As he saw Philip, he moved his hand slowly to his stomach and slowly rolled on to his side. His shoulders jerked. Philip shook his head. He felt that the man had recognized him, knew him for what he was.

Two doorways on, by a corner which led to a large grey car-park, a lean black man with a frilly shirt and tight yellow trousers reached out a hand and said, 'Hey, man.' Philip smiled and brushed off the hand quite amiably. 'You lookin' for somethin', man?'

Philip shook his head. He was not afraid. He was one of these people. A killer, an outcast.

The church was cool and smoky. Skimmed-milk light spilled through the window and washed the flags. Philip entered and walked slowly up to the altar rails. His right hand ran loosely over the pews. He knelt at the altar with no thought of praying. It was what you did in church, that was all. He had not been in a church since his schooldays.

Above him, between thick-veined marble columns, the crucifix shed lurid blood from the five wounds, impaled hands clutched at nothing.

'Dear Lord,' he blurted, as again tears filled his eyes.

'Oh, *Christ.*' He buried his head in his hands and at last he let go. His whole body shook and he whimpered convulsively. It was a full five minutes before he looked up with a face stained with grime and with tears and stammered, 'Oh, my God, I'm sorry . . .'

It was twilight when he came out. He made some effort to smooth down his hair and straightened the jacket over his shoulders. He glanced at his watch. It was ten past seven. Only twenty minutes to go.

CHAPTER NINETEEN

A thin girl with a fixed expression of sniffing self-righteousness pushed a leaflet into his hand. 'I truly hope and pray that today will be *your* regeneration day. Love you,' she said. She instantly looked away and started the speech again to the man behind him.

Bodies seethed around him. People bared their teeth in directionless smiles. Young workers waved and sold T-shirts, books, amulets and plastic busts of Sananda. Donation buckets rattled.

Philip pressed through the crowd and up the stairs. He reached the third tier, turned and looked down at the thousands of heads below. The stage was washed in a dusky-blue light. There was an air of excitement and anticipation, a constant low growl. They were preparing to roar.

Philip slid sideways to a seat and sat. Swinging search-lights picked out human heads and made them uniform, like studs on black leather. He shielded his eyes as they passed.

For a second the light landed on a girl just two tiers below him. Her hands were full of leaflets. She turned and squinted up the dazzling beam. 'Tammy . . .?' Philip said quietly. She was thinner. Her face was now gaunt and heavily shaded, but the eyes, the expression were hers. 'Tammy!' he yelled. 'Tammy!'

The girl looked up towards him. 'Tammy!' He waved. 'Over here!'

She shook her head. Maybe she could not see him in the dim light. 'Tammy!' he roared. 'It's me, Philip!'

Her head snapped up. She frowned. Her jaw dropped. She edged backwards still shaking her head. Then the lights went out and a single spotlight followed a man across the stage.

'OK, OK!' the microphone belched. The tinny voice twanged from a hundred speakers. The man's hair was brushed forward. His shirt was open and a silver amulet flashed on the black hair on his chest. He waved. The applause rattled at first like pebbles sucked back by the tide, then came in great breakers, crashing through the hall.

Philip flashed a light on the programme. A photograph of the man filled the second page. Pete Jansen, TV personality. 'OK, OK! Alleluia and welcome everyone! Alleluia and welcome! Yes indeed.' The crowd yelled again.

Jansen pulled the microphone from its stand and strolled across the stage. The vertical spotlight stayed with him. Another spot played slowly over the ranks of the Regeneration Choir backstage. There must have been three, four hundred of them, all dressed in green satin robes. Their faces leaped from the darkness, three at a time, then vanished into silhouette as the light passed on.

'I want to give a very special welcome tonight on this the first day of our crusade here, to all of you who are with us for the first time, those of you who have come as our guests, those of you who are just curious, those of you who are not yet a part of this great Movement, this great family that has gathered here together. For you, I am sure, the first of September will be remembered as the day which changed your lives, the day when negativity was thrown out of the window, the day when you realized — truly realized — that you were a force, a great force to bring love and peace to all mankind! The day — your day — of regeneration, of new life! . . .'

Some people stood, clapping their hands above their heads. Some, near the stage, leaped and danced. Some shouted, 'Yeah!' or 'Alleluia!' Others just sat forward and bellowed.

The girl beside Philip turned. 'Your first time?'

she said. Her eyes sparkled. Her red cheeks seemed inflated.

'Yes,' Philip said sourly.

'Oh. I'm so excited for you,' she squeaked. 'It's gonna blow you away!'

'. . . Now in the hall, as some of you will already have seen, there is an exhibition of some of the wonderful things which have been made by our brothers and sisters throughout the world. I hope you'll look at them. I hope you'll reflect on the love and the craftsmanship and the goodwill that went into them. There are some beautiful girls wandering around the Garden tonight ready to take your orders so that you can take a memento of tonight home with you.

'Well, folks, we've got a great evening ahead of us. Give yourselves to it. Become a part of it all. You *are* a vital part. Without you, the Movement is the poorer, the love and the goodness that we are generating is the weaker. Let's make tonight the night that love came to America, an historic night, and then let us go forth and spread the message, let us draw on the deep, deep well of love that we are digging here, together, and let us scatter it far and wide in the cause of a better, richer, finer, and more peaceful world. Thank you.'

The roof rattled now as the crowd cheered.

'And now, let's put our hands together for our own, our very own — Regeneration Choir!'

The green mass of bodies backstage rose. Sheets of music rustled. The choir master, a thickset Negro with a surplice and a sash over his satin robes, tapped a baton and raised his arms. There was a huge amplified intake of breath.

Brilliant light flooded the stage and lit a great cloth painting of Sananda twenty times natural size. The statutory garland was about his neck, touched up in pinks and scarlets. He smiled a broad, blissful smile. A child's smile. 'HEAVEN IN AMERICA, NOW!' read the caption. 'LET SEPTEMBER 1ST BE YOUR REGENERATION DAY.'

The choir began to sing. The green robes swung from side to side. Hands clapped.

Philip scanned the faces. Laura must be there. But somehow the faces just melted into one another along the countless ranked tiers. The smiles were fixed and identical as though they had been moulded in soap. He stood and searched the rows behind him. No Laura. But she must be here, somewhere.

It was an hour and a half later that Sananda at last appeared on stage, an hour and a half of speeches, strumming, singing, and testimonials. Celebrities in the audience were called to stand up and take their bows. Congressman Behrens stretched a few words into half an hour. Two sixties rock stars called David Thomas and Steve Nash mumbled incoherently about their days of decadence, but avowed that their love for Father had given their lives purpose and meaning, that they had found, with the Children, all that they had sought in fame and drugs and cheap sex. They then droned an inharmonious anthem and left the darkened stage waving their guitars and blowing kisses.

Sananda came out quietly and without fanfare. He emerged from the darkness backstage, robes fluttering, like a moth coming closer in the headlight beams. He looked downwards. His arms were folded under his robes. The dull blue spotlight made his bald pate glow. The plain white cotton garment fluttered in a providential cross-stage wind.

There was absolute silence as he reached centre-stage and stood for a moment, still gazing downwards. Then his head rose, his arms extended. Three brilliant white spots flashed on. Footlights like candles came on more slowly, suffusing the great cloth picture above him. The seats snapped back on their hinges. The audience rose, hands raised, and the roar made the whole building shake. 'Father! Father!'

'I love you, Father! I love you!' whined the girl on Philip's right. Then she clasped her hands together between her thighs and bent forward as though suffering cramps. 'Oh, God, oh, God, I can't bear it,' she groaned. 'Father! Oh, Father!'

The roar went on and on. Sananda closed his eyes and stood smiling. It seemed that it was the sound, not the wind machine, which made his robes billow and swept his thin hair back. Philip snarled.

The applause continued for ten minutes before at last, with a damping motion, Sananda quelled it, shaking his head, blinking away tears, saying, 'Children . . . My Children . . . ' He wiped his eyes. 'Oh, my beloved Children and oh, my friends. I am come here to give thanks to you all. It is through you — only through you — that we have brought the New Kingdom so much closer for us all.' His hand reached out, trembling. 'I feel now that I can almost touch it, that we are almost there, that it is materializing before our very eyes, as if the word has indeed been made flesh.

' "A cult", they say, "a passing fad, a movement for the few. Sad people", they say, "misguided, not like others." ' He paused, smiled. 'Look around you. Tell me. How does it feel to be so unique? How does it feel to be so . . . odd? How does it feel to be so loveless? How does it feel, my friends, to be so alone?'

The crowd was on its feet again. Philip remained seated. Four minutes, five minutes passed. The applause pattered now like wet cement. The girl beside him sat and rocked back and forth in her seat and murmured, 'Father, Father, love, love, Father, yes, oh, yes, save me, Father . . . '

Sananda raised his hand. 'Our moment of triumph is nigh — the moment we have been waiting for, working for, praying for — and in this moment of triumph we must not forget those who have shared our love, have renounced all for that love. One man very close to us all, who enshrined that sacrifice, cannot be with us today. In the early days of our great Movement, he stood by my side, his unselfish love was a guiding light, his strength of purpose an inspiration. For such a man there is no such thing as death, the great river still flows onwards though our eyes see it not in the darkness of the night. Your love is his epitaph, your tears his shroud . . .'

His voice was calm, authoritative and melodic. The effect was hypnotic.

'My Children,' he continued, 'when I promised you that the New Kingdom would soon be with us, I knew that there were rumblings within the cosmic order, and that your love would bring about the great changes that were needed.' He raised his hand. 'But I also knew that the New Kingdom would not come into being until one momentous happening, a gift from the heavens, one thing that I could not control. The Divine Mother, known in the East as Devi and to others by countless other names, must make herself incarnate and come down upon this earth so that together we could lead the race that is to follow into the New Kingdom.'

His voice trembled. 'For the last ten years I have been searching for some sign of this great gift to the world, waiting for the day when the Divine Mother would come. My Children, that day — that day has now come! The Divine Mother is now among us and has graciously consented to become my consort on earth. This is a sign, if ever there was need of a sign, that the New Kingdom is not something of the future, but is here and now!'

The girl next to Philip perched on the very edge of her seat. She threw back her head. 'It's all true,' she murmured. 'It's all true. It's happening!'

'Shhh!' said Philip.

'I confess,' continued Sananda, 'that I had no more idea than you of what frame the Divine Mother would adopt for this incarnation until she revealed herself to me. She could have come as a flower in full bloom, but she knew that there was work to be done. That together we must lead the way for the race that is to follow. So she chose to come as a bud bejewelled only by the morning dew, in the guise of a young English girl touched only by the ardour of her purpose. I wanted to share this with you, my Children, because it was your love that brought her here among us. We will be joined in wedlock here and now before you all.'

When the shouting died down, the choir again stood. Trumpets blared in a dissonant fanfare. Sweet singing swirled through the auditorium like smoke. The sound started softly, then swelled. An orchestrated sunrise. The footlights too came up for the first time, casting a pale rose glow throughout the stage.

A girl walked out, stage right, and stood stock still. Her long robe, like Sananda's, was white and fluttered in the wind. The edges of her hair glowed like a fuzzy bright halo. Her hands rubbed against her robe as though wiping off sweat. She looked out into the darkness of the hall with wide, uncomprehending eyes, like a bewildered, wounded fawn, like a little girl, dressed up and left alone at her first party . . .

'Jesus Christ!' Philip gasped. The bitter taste of bile seeped into his mouth. Phlegm bit at the back of his throat. 'No,' he said. 'No, it *can't* be!'

He stood. His seat thudded back. Then suddenly he was moving forward, jumping two steps at a time down the aisle as the crowd too stood and clapped and bellowed.

At the first set of railings he looked round, panting. Beneath him, Laura lurched forward, off-balance and propelled by her own weight. Then again she stopped and covered her ears with her hands. She mouthed something. She shook her head. A man stepped quickly from the wings and took her arm. He smiled and steered her towards

Sananda. A foot turned, a knee buckled. The man muttered something and heaved her up.

Philip turned left. 'No,' he said. 'Jesus, no.' He charged through the swing doors. The grey stone stairs clicked beneath his feet. He hurtled down them like a puppet, bouncing off the bare cement walls at the landings. Behind him, the crowd clapped and cheered.

He was back in a corridor. The sound was louder now and he could pick out individual yells of 'Father!' and 'Mother! Our Divine Mother!' on his right.

He pushed through a doorway and again the sea of sound crashed over him. The stage was to his left now, above the bobbing heads of jumping, dancing Children.

Laura and Sananda stood hand in hand centre-stage in a Hollywood duet pose, a dream of bliss. Sananda waved to the crowd. Laura gazed at him with shining eyes, bemused.

Philip barged through the dancing Children. He could see the thick foundation daubed on Laura's cheeks, the long black artificial eyelashes, clogged with mascara. 'Laura!' he yelled and reached up over the shoulder of a barrel-chested security guard. 'Laura!'

She did not hear him. 'Get back, now,' the guard mumbled. He pushed Philip's chest.

'Let me pass!' Philip grunted. 'Let me pass, damn you!' He bent down. His shoulder rammed into the man's side. A huge forearm curled around Philip's neck. The man's giant weight pulled him off-balance. 'Let me pass!' he shrieked as he was tugged backwards. He kicked like a panicking swimmer.

'Come on, you,' the guard growled, then, 'Sorry, ma'am. Troublemaker,' as he trod on someone's toe.

Philip was dragged back towards the door. The man's clothes rustled in his ears. The crowd still bellowed. The choir still sang. All about him there were bouncing hair and waving arms and wide-open mouths yelling. He saw Laura standing wide-eyed and expressionless as a sleepwalker as

Sananda muttered some inaudible vows. 'Laura!' he screamed. 'Don't! *Laura*!'

Balloons fell from the roof and drifted down above him. Confetti showered his hair and shoulders. A couple of Children embraced and masked his view, then the doors creaked behind him and he was dragged into the cool darkness of the corridor.

The guard released his hold then puffed, 'OK. You goin' quietly?' He fingered the truncheon at his belt.

'Yes, all right,' Philip panted. The guard's shoulders dropped in a sigh. Philip took a deep breath and lunged past him back towards the auditorium, but a hand like a clamp snapped shut on his arm and spun him round.

'You asked for it, son,' the man belched, and his fist went in low. Philip doubled up, retching. Golden snowflakes bobbed and swirled behind his eyelids. His knees hit the ground with a crack. 'Come on, then,' the man breathed. 'Out . . .'

He put an arm around Philip's back and almost gently propelled him up the steps to a push-bar double door. 'Go on, then,' he rasped. 'Sober up.'

He pushed. Philip reeled forward and nearly fell on to the still wet pavement. The air was cold. It had a sharp ether edge to it. He sniffed. His nose was bleeding. His brain spun. He turned, breathing asthmatic chords, in time to see the door swing shut with a clunk.

He bent forward and sat wearily on the cold stone steps. He pressed the palms of his hands hard against his temples. His whole body shook. The Manhattan traffic miaowed by. Shouts, cheers and singing from within now belonged to another world, another time. 'Married,' he said and shuddered. 'She's married . . .'

He pulled himself up. The streetlamps dazzled him. He raised his hand to shield his eyes and staggered weak-kneed around the block, and down Thirty-First Street to the vast gaping hole of the Madison Square Garden garage. There he stopped, propped himself up against a lamppost and waited.

He remained there for an hour, maybe more. The singing stopped. The pavements filled. Engines started. A few cars trundled up the ramp and turned into the street, swinging great lances of light. There was a pause. Shouts echoed up from below. A great black limousine, half the size of a charabanc, purred up the ramp, then another. A moment later he saw seven stars on a white ground fluttering on a bonnet. Sananda's limousine slid out into the street.

Philip lurched forward. He saw the driver first, a burly man in a peaked cap, then, side by side, the flash of a white robe and beyond, blonde hair. Sananda sat back, smiling, hands folded on his stomach. 'I want — I want to talk to you!' Philip called. He bent to look through the window and trotted along by the car. 'Hey! You!' he shouted to Sananda. 'Stop! I've got to talk to you!' The car speeded up. Philip almost stumbled.

Sananda turned, looked at him. His smile did not change. He waved regally. 'Laura!' Philip yelled. 'Laura! Tell him to stop! I've got to talk to you!'

The blonde figure turned behind the beaded smoked glass. For a moment, her eyes met Philip's. Her brows bent. She leaned forward. Her eyes opened wider. Her mouth moved. He thought she said, 'Philip?' Her hand reached out across Sananda, fingers trembling and outstretched. Philip's trot had become a breakneck canter. 'Stop,' he shouted, 'stop!' He strained forward. His hand touched the boot. Then the rear lights passed him. The car was gone.

Philip had seen her for no more than five seconds, but it had been enough. That hand had reached out for him. He knew it. He was sure. His own fingertips tingled as though they had been touched. He could smell the sweetness of her breath in the cold night air. It was her tears, caught up in the wind, which flicked his eyelids and coursed down his cheeks.

Suddenly he laughed. He would get her back. He would find a way.

*

It was very late when he stopped walking and made his way back to the hotel. Every sound seemed very loud at this hour of the morning; the creak of the stairs, the clunk of his footfalls, the rustle of clothing, the click as he switched on the lights.

He threw himself down on the bed and kicked off his shoes. He pulled out the gun he had bought a few hours earlier. It was a small, very square-looking pistol with a white shiny butt of some smooth stuff like bakelite. The name 'Ortgies' was engraved in elegant copperplate on the barrel. He flicked open the chamber. It was loaded. There were four little bullets with hollow lead tips. Their brass cases gleamed as brightly as the gun. He snapped it shut again and nodded, satisfied.

Now he started his preparation.

From his bag he drew the lightweight grey suit that he had bought on his arrival in Delhi. He had one clean white shirt, too. He had been keeping it for a special occasion. This was it. He laid them out on his bed.

He stripped and examined his body in the mirror. He was lean now and tanned. The thickness about his waist was gone, and the sinews at his neck and shoulders were clearly visible. He ran a hand over his chest, his arms. The muscles were tight and hard as cabochon stones.

He picked up his sponge bag and climbed into the shower. He just stood there under the thudding jet for five minutes, then washed his hair three times and soaped his body all over.

Afterwards he rubbed himself with the teacloth they had given him for a bath towel and went back to the mirror. Brave birds were singing now, and the sky outside was pale dappled grey. He shaved three times. The first time he removed the stubble, the second time his face was smooth and juddered to the touch. The third time was just for the sake of it. He had, after all, a date.

He put on the trousers and the shirt. The poplin was cool

269

and crisp on his shoulders. He hung the Kailash Baba amulet around his neck and tucked it under the shirt, next to his skin. He polished his shoes and buffed them until they glowed, and pulled his only tie from the suitcase. Dark blue, with a discreet geometric design. The one Laura had given him. He shrugged on the jacket and put the gun back into his right pocket.

He was ready. All he had to do now was wait. He lay on the bed trying uselessly to read until the rushing of the traffic outside was constant and the light was strong. He switched off the bedside lamp, slipped the binoculars over his shoulders and strapped on his watch. Seven forty-five. Time to go.

He looked at the suitcase, the crumpled clothes on the bed. He would have no further need of them. He shrugged and walked to the door.

CHAPTER TWENTY

You told me goodbye;
How was I to know
You didn't mean goodbye,
You meant please don't let me go . . .

Philip leaned forward and tapped the steering wheel in time with Jerry Garcia's singing and the wail of the steel pedal guitar. It was turning into a beautiful day.

He had hired the green Impala for three days. He had no credit left, but the card still worked. And now he was on his way. He eased the car into fourth gear. Highway 5 to Connecticut was thick with traffic; executives in shiny suits, women with dogs and empty carryalls, lorry drivers in peaked caps, children, delivery men.

Shining cars bounced out of driveways on to the road. Wives in housecoats or in jeans waved. Joggers bounced by, puffing and streaming with grimy sweat.

So many lives. Each of them would have a story if you had a few hours and a bottle of Scotch to spare. Each was potential prey for Sananda and his kind.

Now he was out in the country. Signs read Birlin, New Britain, Plainsville. There were no hedges here, and the great mansions with their well-tended, flowing lawns were of wood, not of stone, but otherwise it could have been an Indian summer's day in England. The sky was cloudless, clear pale blue and sheer as a sheet of ice. The harvest was in, save for a few late cornfields which bowed and rippled below the smoothing hand of a breeze. The lawns were yellowing at the centres but the trees in the orchards were green and laden with fruit. Late roses were out, too, and blue and pale-pink hydrangeas shed showers of dewy diamonds.

Philip reached Granville at eleven-thirty. A hamburger hut stood at the crossroads. He parked, locked the car, checked the boot twice, and walked in.

The hats were jaunty, the yellow overalls spotless. The girl behind the counter had five stars pinned below the name tab on her chest. She was mean with the microphone. 'One Super-Senator,' she purred huskily, 'hold the onions, one French fries, one regular coffee.' She looked up at Philip. 'Is that all?'

'Yeah, but just one thing. Can you direct me to a place called New Kingdom?'

'Never heard of it,' she tutted.

'Religious place. Nepalese guy called Sananda. Big place.'

'Oh.' She bared gleaming white teeth and shook her head. 'Them! Kooks, loonies. Head up to the crossroads an' turn right. 'Bout two miles down the valley. Can't miss it.' Burgers rolled off a conveyor belt behind the counter. A hand dropped on salad, pickle, squirted mayonnaise and ketchup. 'Here you are, enjoy,' said the girl and pushed a plastic tray towards him.

'Thanks a lot.' Philip picked up the tray and sat down on a plastic banquette behind a plastic table. He opened the hamburger box and stared down at the dead, charred flesh with its red, gelatinous halo. He picked out a single chip and put it in his mouth and chewed. A thin film of grease spread over his tongue. He coughed and spat it out. He wiped his lips, carried his tray over to a bin marked THANK YOU and threw the lot inside. 'Enjoy,' he muttered, 'enjoy.'

A mile after the crossroads, the road dipped into a deep, dappled tunnel of trees. A stream rattled somewhere nearby. The road curved round and suddenly the trees on the left were confined by a high wire-mesh fence with a barbed-wire crown of thorns. There were gentle open hills studded with little copses on the right.

He reached the gateway two-thirds of a mile later. He tried to look like a curious tripper and bent low to examine the high white marble pillars, the ornate iron gates, the soaring fleur-de-lys finials. One uniformed guard leaned with his shoulder against the gate. He chatted to another who sat on the gatehouse steps. Philip caught a glimpse of the shifting shadows on the lawns, the curve of the drive beneath the cedars, then he was past.

Another mile further on, Philip found what he was looking for. On his right, a deeply rutted farm track led up the hill. The car bumped and jolted and leaned so far that it almost toppled as he dodged deep potholes and ground along the hard mud ridges.

The track led up to grey stone farm buildings high on the hill, but Philip took a grass track which ran along the hillside to his right. At last, out of sight of the farm buildings, he came to a five-bar gate. Beyond, a green field spotted with yellow flowers sloped down to a wooded dell. Philip parked the car on the bank at the side of the track, locked the doors and the boot and clambered up on to the gate. He pulled out his binoculars.

The wood obscured his view of the gatehouse, but he could see the drive where it split into two, the gardens on every side and, in the centre, slightly raised on the other side of the valley, the house.

It was a single white horseshoe with a roof of crenellated red tiles. Within the horseshoe, a strange-shaped pool shot stars at the limewash sun. A man in a short white coat carried a tray over the gleaming flags to where three girls lay on sunbeds. Two of them wore bikinis. The other, a pale, bubbly blonde, had shed her top. The light was too bright for Philip to see through the plate-glass windows which surrounded them, but curtains were still drawn in the rooms to the left of the pool. He nodded. The morning after.

Philip looked over to the far side where the back drive led to the outside of the horseshoe. More activity there. Several cars came up the drive as he watched. Men in shirt-sleeves bustled in and out. They carried sheaves of papers in their hands or under their arms. This, then, was where the business was done. The plans were made there, the speeches written, the money counted and distributed whilst within, protected by his team like the star player by the ruck, Sananda slept.

Soon after one o'clock, the curtains at the left were drawn open. Philip thought that he saw something white moving around inside the plate-glass doors. He couldn't be sure. It might just be a reflection.

His arms grew weary, and his eyelids heavy. He put the binoculars back in their case, shook himself and jumped down from the gate. He walked down towards the wood, dropped his binoculars in the grass, pulled the gun from his pocket and took off his jacket.

Again he flicked open the chamber, tipped out the bullets and examined them. He slotted them back in again and squinted down the truncated barrel. He pushed the safety-catch on and off twice, then threw himself backwards, arms outstretched, and lay flat on his back. He was exhausted but he could not sleep . . .

A cold breeze aroused him an hour later. He took up his position on the gate once more. The girls had gone inside. The lights were on in the rooms around the pool. He glanced at his watch. Half past three. They'd be setting off for the convention soon.

There was no sign of life outside the house until, simultaneously, the servant in the white coat walked out on to the flags around the pool to clear up the glasses on the tables, and the first of five huge black limousines slid out of the trees below the house and seemed to drift up towards the courtyard and the pool.

First the men came out, now in their suits. As each car was filled, it moved on ten yards to make room for its successor. Then the girls emerged. Philip leaned forward. They wore brightly coloured dresses. The pale blonde that he had seen earlier was now in turquoise. Two more full cars drove ten yards forward and stopped, waiting.

The last car now stood in front of the house. The driver held open the car door. Sananda came out first. Philip saw his brown pate as he ducked into the car. There was a pause then before a small, dumpy woman came down the steps. She stretched her hand out behind her. Laura emerged slowly. She wore a dark-blue coat over the white robe. She leaned on the hand. The woman put her arm around her and pushed her gently into the car beside Sananda.

The door shut. The driver regained his seat. The cortège glided slowly down the drive and vanished from his view beneath the trees. He shivered. The wind had changed and was suddenly cold.

He drove right round the New Kingdom domain. Halfway round, parallel, he assumed, with the house, the wire mesh made way for high old walls, topped with spikes of broken glass. The village of Eastfield stood at the westernmost corner. It was a nice village, full of old colonial mini-mansions of white timber. A perfect bolthole for the world-weary executive; a place, you'd have thought, where he could channel the old aggression against the woodworm and the lawn. But FOR SALE signs littered the verges like mailboxes.

Philip turned left. The wall led on uninterrupted for another half-mile. Then there was another big wrought-iron gate. He looked through. Another two guards lay sprawled on the drive playing cards. Their sleeves were rolled up to their elbows. Their caps and their gunbelts lay several yards away. 'When the cat's away . . .' Philip grinned.

Just seven hundred yards and half a minute later, he found what he was looking for. Another wrought-iron gate, a small one, set into the wall. A standard, old-fashioned kitchen-garden gate. He carefully inspected the black whorls, the spokes which radiated outwards from a leonine-looking sun, its crown of barbed wire.

He found a lay-by a mere hundred yards further on. He parked the car, switched off the ignition and leaned back, suddenly thoughtful. He could still go back. It wasn't too late. He'd get an earful of homespun homilies from Thomas, of course, and a right-royal bollocking from his head of chambers, but they'd take him back. His name was still painted on the staircase wall: P. M. W. Strickland, barrister-at-law. All he had to do was return to the junction and follow the signs to New York. He could be home by tomorrow night.

What was there to keep him, after all? Love? If this was love, he could do without it. There was no transcendental glow in his brain, only a cold, numb sensation not unlike that of panic. No smell of roses in his nostrils, only cow dung and petrol fumes. No bells in his ears, only distant sirens and the heavy pounding at his temples.

Was it just pride, then? An absurd illusion that he could conduct a one-man crusade against evil? When had morals worried him so much? The strong thrived and the weak survived as best they could. Did he really give a damn for those caught in Sananda's giant web? They had found their answers, for better or for worse.

But it was the gut that now spoke to him and it said, 'Go on.'

CHAPTER TWENTY-ONE

A sunken kitchen garden lay fourteen feet below him. Cabbages, cauliflowers, globe artichokes and runner beans grew in well-disciplined ranks. On his right, there was a lean-to shed, then a long, low greenhouse full of tangled vines. At the far end, some forty yards away, three moss-stained steps led up to a low balustrade and open lawns.

Philip recovered his breath as he took it all in. Then he crouched down and jumped. He had let go of the top of the gate before he saw the guard. There was nothing that he could do. The man had emerged from behind the green-house. Now he walked along the lawn, just behind the balustrade. A Dobermann pinscher loped at his side.

Philip landed with a thump and a rustle of dry leaves. He pressed himself flat against the wall. The man was directly opposite him now. He strolled very slowly in the fading sunlight, kicking daisies. The dog snuffled at the turf. Either had merely to turn. Philip moved his hand very, very slowly towards his jacket pocket. They still had ten yards, nine, to go . . . From the gatehouse down to the left came the sound of men's chatter, the thudding and squeaking of a disco number from the radio.

As soon as the man and his dog passed behind the yew hedge on the left, Philip let out his breath as quietly as he could. Then he ducked down and moved, squatting, to the shelter of the lean-to shed. He squeezed in past hoes and rakes and spades to the wall at the back and knelt down on the dark sawdust between a roller and a wheelbarrow. He sighed. He was at least deep in shadow here.

The guard and his dog returned ten minutes later. They strolled at the same leisurely pace. The sounds of the radio and the voices were momentarily louder as the gatehouse door opened and shut.

Philip waited for another twenty minutes. It grew darker. The sounds from the gatehouse swelled and faded. He crept out of his shelter and stretched. He trotted up by the side of the greenhouse, glanced from side to side and vaulted the balustrade on to the lawn. A cool breeze tugged at his hair. The lawn was velvet smooth. It rolled gently down to the door at the outer apex of the horseshoe. The white gravel drive sliced diagonally across his view from the right. On the left, a dark wood curved around to the high wall which divided Sananda's domain. At least the trees offered some illusion of cover. He stooped and padded quickly over twenty yards of open turf, then scuttled along the wire around the wood.

He stopped beneath a large cedar and peered around the trunk. There were lights in the downstairs windows of the house. In the nearest, a little dark man stood with a telephone receiver tucked beneath his chin like a fiddle. He talked rapidly and rolled up his left shirt-sleeve with his right hand. Behind him, a woman with hair in a pewter-grey bun tapped Schmeisser bursts on the typewriter. The trees behind Philip now bucked and bowed in the breeze. Leaves spun past him on to the turf.

He ducked and turned to run on. Then he saw the shadow. But the shadow had a shadow of its own. Its surface glinted inky-blue and the light from the window was reflected in its eyes. And it was moving towards him fast.

His shoulders shook in a quick, convulsive shudder. He backed towards the tree. He stood sideways on, and hooked his left arm across his body.

Everything moved very slowly then. For the dog made no sound save a gurgling snarl as it hurtled towards him, kicking up little spurts of leaves. Then the flanks tautened, the thudding of the paws on the grass very suddenly stopped. And the dog leaped.

The bulging eyes glared straight at his. The teeth flashed. The breath was hot and moist on his face. When the full weight hit him, he fell backwards, hard. The wind was knocked out of him. His left forearm was sodden now. He sat forward with a grunt of pain as the dog growled and the teeth sank in smoothly and tore at the flesh again. 'Oh, Jesus!' Philip whispered and fell back again. Water filled his eyes. Ivory scraped on bone. His knee rose between the dog's legs. He kicked hard.

Its rib cage heaved. A giant wheeze like the sound of airbrakes forced its way between those teeth, but they still gripped tight. Every movement ripped raw flesh. He fumbled with the left-hand cuff of his jacket and forced his arm out of the sleeve. Somehow he twisted the jacket around and wrapped it tightly over the dog's face.

The black head shook and twitched and butted. The hind quarters bucked. Still the teeth sawed at his bone. Hot tears blurred his vision. He groped for the gun, felt the steel and the smooth butt. He brought the butt down hard on the skull. The dog only growled. Again his arm went back. He smashed the butt down. The dog's powerful hind legs kicked three times. Then the body went rigid and shuddered.

Slowly, Philip pulled his limp and dribbling arm from between the cold jaws. The wind was as piercing on the open flesh of the wound as on a nerve in a tooth. He staggered to his feet. Through the thick mist of tears and faintness he saw beneath him the dog, now on its side, legs still twitching in little running movements. A feeble whimper seeped from its open mouth. Blood gleamed there too. Then the body fell still.

'Poor bastard!' Philip whispered. He slumped down again on the grass. They would come at any moment. They must have heard. He stroked his arm, soothing it, and waited.

But nobody came. He sat there for three minutes, maybe

more, clutching his bleeding arm. The trees kept churning and hushing. The sound of the radio came to him in occasional gusts. Some small animal hopped about in the leaves behind him. The man inside slammed down the telephone, put a cigarette between his lips and paced. A light went off round the corner. No one had heard him.

He pulled himself very wearily to his feet. He grabbed the hind legs of the dog in his one good hand and dragged the corpse to the low fence around the woods. The lolling, bouncing head left a dark, oily trail on the grass. He left the corpse under a bramble bush, covered it with leaves, then quickly, almost casually, walked back over the lawn to the walls of the house.

He ducked down beneath the window and scuttled round to the very edge of the carriage sweep. He paused, pressed hard against the wall. The door stood twenty yards to his left at the apex of the horseshoe at the top of a flight of seven steps. The porch was well lit. The drive was straight. Any guard who heard a crunch of gravel would see him there, raised on a pedestal and beautifully illuminated like a plaster saint in a cathedral.

He shrugged. If they saw him, they saw him. He pulled himself upright, strolled over to the steps and trotted up them. With every step he expected to hear a yell from behind him. He turned the handle and slid in sideways. Everything seemed very silent when the wind was shut out.

The hall was circular. All around, in niches, stood marble statues. There was Hermes in his winged hat and sandals, there Persephone sowing, there Chloe, already sprouting roots. Philip tiptoed sideways to the first door on the left. From inside came a clipped Brooklyn rap. 'Yeah, yeah. OK, so what else is new for tomorrow's spiel? We got the Polynesian tidal wave, we got the murders in Oregon. That's the Sodom and Gomorrah bit an' the consequences of materialism sewn up, but we gotta have the triumph of the individual spirit, the heartwarming bit . . .'

Philip slid on round, past Poseidon and Laocoon. He turned the handle of the big white door opposite the entrance. It rattled, but the door opened.

He was in a narrow passage. There were two doors on either side. The pictures on the walls were just black oblongs in the dim light. Through the glass doors at the end he could see the swimming pool and the floodlit statues.

'Don't worry, Mrs Maystrom . . .' Something suddenly moved not ten yards away on the patio. Philip spun round and stepped back into a dark doorway. The jamb hit his arm. He winced. 'I'll do that,' said the girl's voice. 'You've had a long day.

Philip started and peered around. It was an English voice. The dumpy woman whom he had seen earlier stood on the flagstones by the pool. She carried a tray. Something steamed in a covered dish. 'Now you just stop fussing, Andy,' she scolded. 'I'm just fine. I'm used to it. You go to bed and get rid of that cold.'

The tall redhead clicked forward on high heels. 'Seems funny, having the place all to ourselves, doesn't it,' she said. 'How is she now?'

'Oh, she's fine, just fine. Much better. Still distressed, of course, still a bit tearful, but that's only natural. She's calmer. I think she's accepted it now.'

'Well, that's the main thing. She always was a bit of a passionate, hot-blooded sort anyhow. A true Latin. She really must have loved him, I suppose.'

'I suppose so, I suppose so,' the nurse trilled and moved on. She tutted. 'Funny old thing, love.'

'Isn't it just!' Andy laughed. The door handle clicked. She stepped in through the glass door. The draught caught it and slammed it against the wall. Philip ducked back into the doorway. For a moment the passage was full of wind. A single leaf skidded across the parquet at his feet. Then the door closed. He heard a little tuneless song as she walked up the passage. Something clattered on to the floor. She said, 'Damn.' Her footsteps stopped. For a second Philip saw her hair, just feet away. Then the song began again. A door on the other side opened and shut. The singing continued, very faint.

He slipped from the doorway and padded down the passage. He sidestepped in through the last door on his right and knew, at a glance, that he was in the right place.

The glow from outside was partially smothered by deep-red velvet curtains hanging on either side of the windows. Everything cast long-toothed shadows. There was a Regency sofa covered in striped brocade, a couple of deep-winged, quilted-leather armchairs, low tables crowded with bronzes, an embroidered Chinese screen — then a huge desk and a three-sided, glass-fronted bookcase.

Philip walked over to the desk. As his eyes grew accustomed to the darkness, he could make out the photographs that littered the embossed leather top: Sananda with JFK, Sananda with Nelson Rockefeller, Sananda with Timothy Leary, Sananda doing a floral dance with the Children at some commune. They were on the walls too. Countless photographs of Sananda with the famous or about his business.

There was a click outside. Philip looked up. Mrs Maystrom descended from the white hut on the other side of the swimming pool. She carried a little kidney-shaped tray on which something made of glass glinted. He ducked and started counting.

At twenty, he could feel the blood from his arm seeping through the fabric of his trousers. At sixty, he reckoned the danger was past. He took a deep breath and, still crouching, he crawled back round the desk to the door behind the sofa. A bathroom. He shut the door behind him. A ventilator purred into life. There were no windows. He switched on the light.

His face in the mirror above the basin was white under the tan. The eyes that stared at him were angry and shocked. He smiled soothingly and very slowly turned the cold tap.

He washed his hands and soaked the torn fabric of his sleeve. Already dried blood restricted his movements and scab tissue ripped as he leaned forward. The cold water touched the wound. His face muscles tautened and twitched.

Wincing, he pulled back the blood-soaked poplin that had seemed so fresh a hundred years ago this morning. He looked for antiseptic in the bathroom cabinet, but there was none, only bath oils and powders, massage oils and vaporizer bottles. He pulled out a large bottle of eau-de-Cologne, gritted his teeth and poured. The liquid bit harder than the dog, and deeper. As he pranced and scrabbled with his nails at the enamel, he looked down at the bloody flaps of skin, expecting to see them smoke.

Gulping and blinking, he grabbed a little hand towel from the towel rail and wrapped it tightly around his forearm. Thank God, it was warm. The pain subsided into a deep regular throbbing.

He was about to switch off the light when he saw the trail of blood on the tiled floor. The corner of his mouth twitched. It would probably be all over the carpet next door. He pulled some paper off the roll, squatted down and mopped up the red spots. He found it surprisingly difficult to get to his feet again. He had to lean on the basin for a full minute before at last he could turn, switch off the light and return to the drawing-room.

He stood still then, looking for a suitable hiding place in which to await Sananda's return. The plate-glass windows made life difficult. He must be invisible to anyone outside as much as to those who came in. He considered the leather armchairs, but they would have to be moved a couple of feet. The screen was in a part of the room which was too well lit. There might be shadows.

He walked over to the office section. Between the far end of the desk and the wall, there was a square of carpet that was large enough for him if he squatted. A tooled leather chest stood against the wall nearby and would hide him from view provided no one came to sit at the desk and provided . . .

His stomach muscles contracted before he knew why. He jack-knifed as though punched in the gut and dived into the shadows behind the desk. Someone was out there on the patio. He sat there, hugging his knees and panting. Sweat broke from his forehead and wriggled like a worm down his back. Someone had seen him. He had seen the glimmer of white robes, the last flap of fabric as the figure passed. And he knew that someone had been watching him ever since he had re-entered the room. He rested his forehead on his knees and tried to steady his breathing, regulate the thudding of his heart.

There were quick footsteps outside in the passage. The door opened. The lights came on. Philip blinked and sat still.

The footsteps were soft now on the thick carpet. They came close. Philip saw shiny black slippers, red socks and pale-grey trouser cuffs under the desk. He looked down at his right hand. It trembled rapidly, as a dog trembles before a thunderstorm. The man, whoever he was, was no more than six feet away. He was whistling to himself, very softly.

Above him, Philip heard a sudden thud as something was dropped on the desktop. The slippers swivelled round. The feet walked away and vanished. The lights snapped off. He was alone again.

He peered cautiously over the desktop. The man had left a sheaf of papers there. Additions, presumably, to Sananda's speech for tomorrow. So when would the guards arrive? Or had he imagined that ghostly white figure out there on the patio? No. He was sure that his brain was still working rationally and well. He was sure that that figure had been there. And whoever it was, was playing with him.

He stayed there for four hours. Twice the telephone rang. Twice cars came crunching up the drive and the light beams swung vertically across the ceiling, then horizontally over the paintings on the wall. Philip's arm now throbbed like a funeral drum. The towel was hot and slippery with blood. His eyes misted and cleared, misted and cleared, as though someone were adjusting the focus. His brain still raced, but his body seemed heavy and numb. It was no ordinary sleep that awaited him if once he closed his eyes. He shivered a lot and his teeth chattered.

The cortège of cars arrived back just before midnight. The crunching of the gravel was louder than the purring of their engines. The whole room was full of light and black shadows as doors clunked shut and voices called above the wind. 'Oh, God, is it good to be back!' A girl's voice, yawning.

'Come on. Let's get out of this wind.'

'Wasn't it fantastic? You were brilliant, Father, you really were . . .'

'Yeah, the best yet.' A man's nasal twang. 'You slayed 'em.'

'And Laura. Superb. Really.'

The light withdrew, the sound of the engines receded. Feet clicked. The voices came closer.

'I'm gonna sleep till Doomsday.'

'Me too.'

'And you, Laura.' Sananda's husky whine. 'You too must sleep . . .' The glass door opened. The wind sucked and sighed. 'You have a long day tomorrow, my love.'

The voices were suddenly very close. They echoed in the passage. Lights came on and slid under the door.

'Anyone want a quick drink? A cup of coffee or anything?' asked a girl.

'No, thanks.'

'Anything for you, Father?'

'Thank you, no.' The door handle moved. 'I too am tired and must compose myself. Thank you, my Children, thank you all . . .' The door opened inwards, pushing a guillotine blade of yellow light across the carpet. 'And you, my Divine Mother, my little mother, bless you . . .' Philip heard a kiss, a little murmur. He licked his lips. They stuck to his tongue. The lights came on again. The door clicked quietly shut.

Sananda let out a deep sigh and padded into the centre of the room. Philip caught a glimpse of the brown sandalled feet and the swinging white robe, then the curtains were drawn shut with a hiss. There were still distant voices from the other side of the house. Taps gurgled and hummed. Sananda turned down the lights and once more sighed wearily.

There was a lot of rustling then. Beneath the desk, Philip saw the sandals, now kicked off. The broad, bare feet came nearer. Then the shins descended into view, the knees, the folds of the robe. A strange crooning sound started. The man was meditating.

Philip waited for two minutes more, then the light in the passage went off. The house fell silent. There was only the sound of Sananda's breathing, his curious muttering drone, the rustle of the robe, the rushing of the wind outside.

The fingers of Philip's good hand fumbled under his shirt, grasped Kailash Baba's amulet and held it tightly. 'Give me strength,' he whispered. 'Just give me strength for a few minutes longer.' Philip stood. He had to lean against the wall.

Sananda sat cross-legged just three yards away. His face was half turned towards the far door, so that Philip could see just the line of his cheek, the dark hollow of one eye. Sananda could not have seen him, but the muttering had stopped.

Then Philip saw why. Sananda's eyes rested on a loose

chain of dark marks that twisted over the carpet before him. They led to the bathroom door.

'Who is there?' he suddenly called. 'Come on out . . .'

'I'm here, Sananda,' said Philip quietly.

Sananda's head jerked round. He looked Philip full in the face, then nodded slowly, as though he had expected this. 'You are hurt,' he said. 'You'd better sit down.'

'I'm OK.' Philip stepped forward. 'I'm fine.'

'You have lost a lot of blood.' Sananda raised a hand to smooth his brow. The gold identity bracelet clinked. 'I suppose you want money. I have two thousand dollars in the safe.' He stood with surprising agility.

'Stay still!' Philip snapped, then, 'Stay still, damn you.' He fumbled in his pocket and drew out the gun. He circled the desk. 'Stay very still. I don't want your money. I want to talk to you.'

Sananda spread out his hands like a priest. He was smaller and older than Philip had imagined. 'So talk,' he shrugged. 'What can I do for you?'

'I am a friend of Laura's,' Philip spat. He now stood a mere six feet from the smaller man.

'Oh,' Sananda sighed. 'I see. May I sit down?'

Philip waved the gun towards the armchair behind Sananda. 'All right. Sit. But I'll shoot you dead if you move. I promise you.'

'I can see that,' said Sananda. His voice trembled a little. He sat and smoothed down his robes. The scars on his cheeks were suddenly very red.

'We were close, Laura and I,' said Philip. 'Close enough to care in a way you could never understand. How could you do that to her? You've destroyed her. You've used her. You've — quite literally — corrupted her, and all so that she could be a pawn in your great charade. The Divine Mother!' he sneered.

'You do not understand.' Sananda's eyes remained on the point of the gun. 'It is not easy to explain. Not easy at all.

But the divine spirit of Devi came down and made herself manifest to me in Laura's form. She made herself incarnate . . .'

Philip waved the gun again. 'Cut it out!' he snarled. 'You don't believe that any more than I do.'

Sananda watched the gun move. 'And I love her,' he said plaintively, 'really I do. She — she will share my kingdom.'

'Love,' said Philip. 'Love. You call that love? You don't know what love is, not human love. Taking away all the spirit that might resist you, all the loves and loyalties that made her, until there's nothing left but a dry husk. Oh, sure, she's amenable then — she's unquestioning then, but *love*?'

'She has found the way. Her way. It may not be yours . . .'

'And is it love to break a hundred thousand homes?' Philip interrupted. 'Is that your idea of love? Families, friends, futures, all sacrificed in the cause of — what? We are talking about people, real people with their own dreams, their own hopes, their own feelings . . . Is that love, Sananda?'

Sananda looked up at Philip. His mouth wriggled. He looked almost sheepish, almost shy. 'So what do you want of me? That I give her up? I promise you that no one is held here against their will. We can go and talk to her. If Laura wants to leave, I will do nothing to stop her.'

'Sit down!' Philip hissed. He shook his head. 'A month ago, you know, I'd have accepted your offer gladly. Now it's too late. I've seen too much misery, too much manipulation of young ideals, too much pain, too many dashed hopes. Freeing Laura from this hell — no, this limbo — is no longer enough. Tell me why I shouldn't free them *all*, now with a bullet through your skull . . . And I'll do it, Sananda, I'll do it. There's nothing to stop me. I'm not afraid. I have nothing to lose. Just tell me.'

'I cannot tell you,' said Sananda.

'What?'

'I cannot tell you. You talk of sacrifice, of hardship, of pain. Don't ask me, then. Ask the Children themselves. Ask them whether the sacrifice is worthwhile, whether now their hearts sing, whether they have any desire to return to your so wonderful world?'

'You know very well, Sananda, they can no longer judge for themselves.' Philip blinked away the mist that now blurred the edges of his vision. 'You have used every trick in the book to brainwash them.'

'Liberate,' said Sananda, 'liberate. It is your society which has conditioned, brainwashed them from birth. Your society which has imposed its values, squashed their spirits, made them cogs in a machine. A child must be cleansed of a lifetime of prejudice, of rhetoric, of false values. Only then is he free, only then can he hear the music of the spheres.'

'They have no wills of their own now, Sananda. You call that liberation? You have betrayed their trust as you betrayed Kailash Baba's trust before.'

'Don't speak of him,' said Sananda contemptuously. 'You understand nothing.' He smiled for the first time. 'If you will listen, I will tell you. You can judge for yourself. You know, when I joined Kailash Baba, I too was young and full of ideals. I had never met anyone like him. He made me feel so humble. He had power, wisdom, and I thought he held the key to spiritual happiness. They were the most exhilarating years of my life. I felt so close to the great mysteries. Just one more turn of the key and all would be revealed to me. I woke up each day trembling with excitement, fired with purpose. And why? Because I believed in Kailash Baba and his divinity.

'I had turned my heart away from worldly ambition. When Guthro arrived at the palace and he told me that he could make me a king, that I would have thousands of followers, that he could make me rich and powerful in a great land across the waters, he did not tempt me. These things were nothing but distractions for idle minds. I could ask for no greater gift than having Kailash Baba as my guide. Or so I thought.' He sighed. 'But it was not to be. One morning I found out a secret. My faith was shattered.'

Philip waved the gun. 'Go on.'

'That morning Kailash Baba's manservant was sick. Guthro and I were tending to his needs. At first light, we collected water from the river and made ready for his shower. Master stood on a small wooden platform, and we poured water slowly through a funnel. From where we stood, we could see the birthmark at the base of his spine, the birthmark which was the sign of his divinity. Guthro pointed, then whispered to me, "It's a tattoo." I did not even know what a tattoo was, but when Guthro explained, when I looked close and saw the hundreds of little pinpricks, my head reeled. I was so confused. At first I would not believe him. I wanted only to forget. I wanted so much to believe and be part of that rich world. Yet now I felt cheated. The illusion was shattered. I left with Guthro for the States a few weeks later.

'Oh, in the months that followed I lost my bitterness towards Kailash Baba, or whoever he really was. I began to realize after all how much I owed him. My belief in him had given my life a rich purpose. It had fired my soul. I had performed the most menial task with a song in my heart simply because I believed.

'And I saw in the States the same desperate searching, the same aimlessness that I had felt before I met Master. The same desperate longing to belong, to believe. Their hearts cried out that there must be more, and I gave them more. I gave them my vision of the New Kingdom, a grand, maybe quixotic vision of a world in harmony, a world of love. I gave them the purpose that I myself had lost.' His body tensed. His head darted forward. 'Was that so evil?'

'They flocked in hundreds, then thousands to hear "The Enlightened One" from Nepal. Soon it was no longer a dream. Perhaps we could be a force in the world. Perhaps we really could bring in a New Order. We had political influence, we had money, we had people. Don't ask me why they came in thousands. Don't ask me why they wanted out of your world. To society, they are the drop-outs, the insecure, the weak, the misfits, junk people. To me, they were the unhappy, the lonely, the purposeless, the lost. They came to me as a child comes to his father, and I gave them a new home, I gave them a reason for living, I gave them self-respect. Was that so evil?

'And if you pull the trigger now, you will shatter that dream. And then what will happen? Who will take over? Guthro — yes, Guthro could have. He knew enough, he could have held it together. Now that he is dead, there is no one. The Children's lives will quite simply be shattered. All that work, all that faith, all that hope will be lost. Some might be strong enough to start life afresh. Others will drift back to what? To drugs? To crime? And there will be suicides. Oh, yes, with the death of a dream, I am afraid there will be suicides.

'If you kill me now, you will bear not just the stain of my blood but of thousands of others. If you live, it will be with the cry of anguish in your ears. If that is what you want, if that is the price of revenge, pull that trigger, my friend.'

Philip's hand started to tremble again. The dark eyes before him shifted and swam. There were four of them, bobbing, circling. He was looking at a Cubist portrait of Sananda, and the paint was running.

There was an eerie logic behind Sananda's words. The minds of the Children had been closed to all but his warped vision of bliss. Their personalities had changed, their frames of reference distorted. This man was their only reason for living.

Philip breathed in deeply through his nose and wiped his brow. 'OK,' he said. 'Take me to Laura. I want to talk to Laura.'

Sananda sighed. He nodded. He too had sweat drops trickling down his temples, and the veins in them pulsed.

'And get a bloody move on!' Philip ordered.

Sananda jumped to his feet. 'Yes,' he said. 'Yes. All right. Come on. Please be careful . . .'

'And if she wants to come with me, she comes. You understand?'

'Yes.' Sananda slid the door open. The wind picked up his robes and wrapped them tightly about him. He executed three hasty little bows. 'Yes,' he said. 'Of course.'

'You go on.' Philip nodded. 'I'll be right behind you.'

Sananda stepped out on to the flagstones. The wind buffeted Philip's face. He felt better for it. Ahead of him, Sananda scuttled towards the swimming pool, almost bent double as he held down his flapping robes. His bare feet left perfect impressions on the stone which faded as soon as they were made. The trees below the lawns were dancing frenziedly now.

Philip stayed just five yards behind Sananda. They walked round the edge of the swimming pool towards the last room on the eastern side of the horseshoe. All the curtains were drawn. All the lights were off. The stars above the building seemed to bob like gnats.

Then Sananda stopped. The figure that emerged from behind the end of the building was also in white, but the reflected light from the pool shifted on the nightdress like flecks of light in a forest, making it seem pale blue. The wild hair and the wild eyes also caught the blue light as the right arm rose.

For an instant those moonstone eyes seemed blind, like those of an old man whom Philip had once met. But then the black eyebrows snapped down and he knew. He had been here before.

Sananda turned towards Philip. His arm stretched out to him. His eyes were wide, imploring. Philip dropped the gun with a clatter and slowly, far too slowly, lunged forward, but already he could see the ice-bright blade spinning through the darkness. Suddenly Sananda's eyes shut tight. Suddenly his mouth opened in a silent scream. The belly jerked forward. The white arms flailed. And the brown fingers clutched like claws at nothing.

Philip grasped the falling body. For a moment he held it up in a clumsy one-handed embrace, but the weight was too great. Philip overbalanced, nearly toppled, and let go. Something squelched and bubbled in Sananda's throat. His lips opened and shut like those of a ventriloquist's doll just below Philip's chin. Black blood sprang from the corner of his mouth and dribbled down his jaw.

Unsupported, Sananda reeled and slid sideways. For a moment he lay half in, half out of the pool and the blood trickled down in little cloudy brown spots. Then the weight of his head pulled him sliding into the water like a seal. Face down and hideously hunched, his body slowly described a circle in the blue water. The white robes spread outwards. The black hilt of the knife bobbed above the surface. The blade was sunk deep in his spine.

Philip looked up. He and Cristiana were alone.

She stood still like a stringless puppet. Her right arm now hung loose at her side. Her left clasped a bunch of white material. The wind made the nightdress stick to the contours of her body, flicked up the hem high on her right thigh. Her face was turned downwards, but her eyes looked up at Philip from under frowning black brows. A light came on in the room to her right, then another, then another. She smiled. Her hair was swept in black streaks over her face. She licked her lips. 'He was mine, barrister-at-law,' she said. Her words were punched away by the wind. 'He was mine.'

Doors banged. A girl shrieked. Bare feet padded across the courtyard. Girls in towels and nightdresses, aides hastily tying dressing gowns, trotted or strode towards them.

'What's happening, for God's sake?'

'Jesus, who *are* you?'

'Cristiana . . .?'

Cristiana looked up at last. She seemed to stretch and to

take a deep satisfied breath of the night air, then her legs gave way and she sank to the ground.

Philip stood still, swaying. All around him people were shrieking, moaning and questioning. Lights flashed on wherever he turned. He was dazzled. Someone grabbed his right arm, then let go. He too sat, weary and confused, on the flags and bowed his head. It was time to sleep.

Then hair whispered around his cheek and his lips and warm arms curled around him. 'Philip,' a voice sobbed, 'Philip, is it really you?'

He heard his voice say, 'Laura . . .'

'It wasn't you, was it? It was her who . . . who killed him.'

'Yes,' he nodded slowly. 'Yes, it was her. I . . . I . . .' He turned his head and at last the tears flowed from his eyes and his shoulders shook as he pushed his head into the softness and the darkness of her breast and cried, 'Laura. Oh, God, Laura . . .'

The arms held him close and gently kissed the top of his head, his eyes, his cheeks, and there was a catch in her voice as she said, 'I've dreamed, you know, so often . . .'

'I know,' he sobbed, and looked up at her. 'I know.'

Her eyes too were filled with tears. She half smiled and stroked his hair. 'It's all right now,' she said in a little voice. 'I'm back. It's going to be all right. I'm so sorry, Philip.'

He laid his head on her breast again and closed his eyes. 'For God's sake, hold me,' he said. 'It's so bloody cold . . .'

EPILOGUE

'Do you realize what you would be doing to those good people out there?' Jansen hissed. The beaming face of two nights before was drawn and distorted with anger. Stage make-up clogged the stubble on his chin. 'Do you know what it means? You will destroy their lives — everything they have worked for. And you want to take it away from them just like that?' He snapped his fingers and spun round. He pointed to Laura where she sat. 'You were chosen as the Divine Mother, the progenitor of the order's new blood . . .'

'Not unless we're going to have an immaculate conception as well,' said Laura drily.

Jansen did not hear. 'You became the Divine Mother of your own free will . . .'

'Hardly *free* will, Mr Jansen.' The words were scarcely audible. The expectant hum of the crowd below and behind the curtains made the boards shake.

'So you say, so you say.' Jansen leaned forward on the table. 'But they need you, Divine Mother, they need you. Have you thought what will happen to all of them if this thing suddenly stops? It's their whole life now, their reason for living. What do you want to see? Suicides? Look, those guys out there.' He gestured at the curtains. 'So far they don't know about Father, but they've got to be told tonight. So do we go out there and say, "Sorry, friends, the party's over," or do we say, "The king is dead, but don't worry, don't jump off the building, it's OK, his soul lives on in his chosen heir . . . "?'

'Heiress,' said Philip quietly from the corner.

'What?' Jansen turned. 'Oh, yes. Right. Heiress. Sorry.' He looked back at Laura. 'Well?'

Philip strolled over to Laura. His left arm was in a

spotless sling. With his right hand, he grasped her shoulder and squeezed. She looked up at him. Her hand covered his. 'Er, would you leave us alone, please?' he said.

'Hey, now! Hold on in there if you please!' Charomski stood. 'Where do you get off telling us what to do, huh? I mean just hold it, right? We are running one big, big organization and right now it's hanging in the balance. We gotta decide how to save this goose. This little lady an' you turn up all of a sudden an' start tellin' us . . .'

'Would you leave us alone, please?' Philip interrupted amiably. 'The Divine Mother and I have things to discuss.'

'Yes,' said Laura. 'Please leave.'

Charomski turned to the other three men and shrugged. They walked sullenly towards the door. 'Oh, and by the way, Charomski . . .'

The little man turned in the doorway. 'Yeah?'

'Whatever the future of this organization, there will be no further marketing, so your expert advice is no longer needed.'

Charomski's lips twitched. 'Who says?' He thrust out his jaw.

'I say.' Laura stood. 'We want no more converts.'

'You can't do that,' Charomski stammered. 'You don't understand.' He squealed through the door. 'You — hey, you guys, you hear what this kook is saying?' There was a low murmur. A hand patted his arm. 'No, but . . .' Charomski started, and the door slammed behind him.

Philip sighed and sat down beside Laura. She took his hand. 'OK?' she asked.

'Fine. Bit tired, but we can sleep all day tomorrow.'

There was a pause then. Laura held up Philip's little finger and studied it. She chewed her lip. The rattle and rumble from the auditorium grew louder.

'What do you think, Philip?' she sighed.

Philip shook his head slowly. 'I think — oh, hell, I think they are probably right. Sananda's left them with nothing else. They are innocents now — literally children. Would they be able to survive without the family?'

She nodded. 'So we run it down slowly.'

'Yup,' he said sadly. 'I'm afraid it'll take a long, long time.'

'And you don't mind having a Divine Mother as your . . .'

'As your *what*, precisely?' Philip smiled.

'Girlfriend.' She shrugged, and scanned the walls. 'Lover . . . whatever.'

'I think,' he said softly, and his arms curled around her, 'that a divine whatever is all that I've ever really wanted in my life.'

She turned and looked at him. Her eyes moved all over his face, wondering. Then she said, 'Philip . . .' so close that he felt the sound touch his lips, and she threw her arms around him and pressed her body close. His arm tightened and suddenly the smell of her hair was in his nostrils and her cheek was damp against his.

For a second then they gazed into one another's eyes, then he saw the white glint of her teeth. Her eyes closed and her lips were soft against his and he trembled with the force of it as those lips opened and he gripped her tight. Her fingers stroked his hair, fluttered down his bandaged arm, gripping . . .

'Ow!' he growled.

She looked up. She giggled. Her blue eyes glittered. 'Don't worry, darling,' she said, 'I'll be gentle with you.'

Five minutes later, a great roar went up as Laura stepped out on to the stage. Philip watched from above as she walked briskly to the centre and screwed up her eyes against the dazzling lights. She held up her hands for silence and said, 'Brothers and sisters. Our world has changed, as all things must change . . .'

VIRGINIA ANDREWS
is a phenomenon

Flowers in the Attic

— the spellbinding story of the days four children spent imprisoned in the attic, days that stretched into years — just to gain their mother's inheritance . . .

Petals on the Wind

— continues the harrowing story of the children who escape their prison and are bent on revenge . . .

If There Be Thorns

— is the third novel in this extraordinary saga of the family who survive their loveless past and defied their black heritage . . .

Seeds of Yesterday

— completes the story of the Dollanganger family who return to the great house of their grandmother.

FONTANA PAPERBACKS

Helen MacInnes

Born in Scotland, Helen MacInnes has lived in the USA since 1937. Her first book, *Above Suspicion*, was an immediate success and launched her on a spectacular writing career that has made her an international favourite.

'She is the queen of spy-writers.' *Sunday Express*

'She can hang up her cloak and dagger right there with Eric Ambler and Graham Greene.'
Newsweek

THE SNARE OF THE HUNTER
HORIZON
ABOVE SUSPICION
MESSAGE FROM MALAGA
REST AND BE THANKFUL
PRELUDE TO TERROR
NORTH FROM ROME
THE HIDDEN TARGET
I AND MY TRUE LOVE
THE VENETIAN AFFAIR
ASSIGNMENT IN BRITTANY
DECISION AT DELPHI
NEITHER FIVE NOR THREE
THE UNCONQUERABLE
CLOAK OF DARKNESS
RIDE A PALE HORSE

FONTANA PAPERBACKS

Stephen Donaldson

The Chronicles of Thomas Covenant, the Unbeliever

'Comparable to Tolkien at his best . . . will certainly find a place on the small list of true classics.' *Washington Post*

'An irresistible epic.' *Chicago Daily News*

'The most original fantasy since *Lord of the Rings* and an outstanding novel to boot.' *Time Out*, London

'Intricate, absorbing, these volumes create a whole new world.' *Sunday Press*, Dublin

The First Chronicles of Thomas Covenant, the Unbeliever

LORD FOUL'S BANE
THE ILLEARTH WAR
THE POWER THAT PRESERVES

The Second Chronicles of Thomas Covenant

THE WOUNDED LAND
THE ONE TREE
WHITE GOLD WIELDER

FONTANA PAPERBACKS

Desmond Bagley

– a master of suspense –

'I've read all Bagley's books and he's marvellous, the best.' *Alistair MacLean*

THE ENEMY
FLYAWAY
THE FREEDOM TRAP
THE GOLDEN KEEL
LANDSLIDE
RUNNING BLIND
THE TIGHTROPE MEN
THE VIVERO LETTER
WYATT'S HURRICANE
BAHAMA CRISIS
WINDFALL
NIGHT OF ERROR
JUGGERNAUT
THE SNOW TIGER
THE SPOILERS

FONTANA PAPERBACKS

Fontana Paperbacks: Fiction

Fontana is a leading paperback publisher of both non-fiction, popular and academic, and fiction. Below are some recent fiction titles.

You can buy Fontana paperbacks at your local bookshop or newsagent. Or you can order them from Fontana Paperbacks, Cash Sales Department, Box 29, Douglas, Isle of Man. Please send a cheque, postal or money order (not currency) worth the purchase price plus 15p per book for postage (maximum postage required is £3.00 for orders within the UK).

NAME (Block letters) _____

ADDRESS _____

_____

_____